Shadowed Truth

DISCOVERY

by Catie Jax

RoseDog Books

PITTSBURGH, PENNSYLVANIA 15238

RoseDog Books
585 Alpha Drive
Suite 103
Pittsburgh, PA 15238
Visit our website at *www. rosedogbookstore. com*

ISBN: 978-1-6386-7390-3
eISBN: 978-1-6386-7491-7

Pronunciations

Htiaf . . . . Tee af
Epoh . . . . Ee po
Ari . . . . Air ee
Alik`ram . . . . A leek rum
Kaazi . . . . Kah zee
Isbeth . . . . Iz beth
Ashi`nat. . . . . A shy nah
Ayotal . . . . ye oh tal
Gyasi . . . . Gah zee
Ja'nek . . . . Jay nek
Si'kram . . . . See krum
Nadroj . . . . Nay drawj

PROLOGUE

Violently whipping in from the north, chilling winds drove leaves and debris over the barren scape. Eerily desolate, meandering through the mountains the bleak passage chilled the soul. Temperatures plummeting below zero with the disappearance of the sun; winds raging, howling and tearing at everything in its path. Light flurries glistening at twilight turning vehemently savage, slowly at first then in torrents. Visibility, virtually non-existent, compounding tension had Htiaf and Epoh teetering on the edge.

Htiaf, was chosen, chosen specifically for the task of transporting their special cargo by Ayotal; Ayotal, The Hierophant, the most revered of all their people. An extreme honor to be selected by her; Ayotal rarely engaged in selecting operatives for special missions, this was the exception. Experienced, Htiaf had excelled at numerous priority transfers, covert reconnaissance missions, and special assignments throughout the years; but this was the first time he was chosen by The Hierophant. Unnerved, Htiaf's trepidation grew.

"Precious cargo," Ayotal emphasized, *"the safe delivery of this package is our peoples only hope."* Lovingly she caressed the case, then turned to Htiaf once again, *"Keep it safe!"* she had said. Vivid images of Ayotal, the urgency and anxiety in her countenance, impressed upon him the importance of the mission. *Cargo, what was it and why was it so important? Why this mode of transportation? There were safer and faster transport methods, why by truck?*

Safely stored in the unmarked van should have eased his mind, but his uneasiness grew like darkness looming over the countryside. Danger was everywhere.

Large and brawny, with wide sweeping shoulders, he was formidable, capable of handling any trouble coming his way. Nonetheless, Htiaf was on high alert. Vigilance sharpening his emerald green eyes, flaring with intensity. Furrows digging deep into his handsome features as uneasy apprehension loomed like a deadly specter over this mission. A constant gnawing in his gut, something was wrong, a feeling he couldn't shake; as he inadvertently began tugging his golden-brown curls with frustration, his friend was nervously eying him as tensions mounted.

Epoh was Htiaf's partner on this mission. A tall man, slender with fire-red hair drawn back and secured at the neck. Richly bronzed skin accentuated his beauty. But his eyes, eyes like beacons shining brightly guiding travelers through the darkness, beaming like crystalline gemstones, sparkling aquamarine. Leaner than Htiaf, but by no means incapable of handling himself against a foe bent on mayhem. Fun-loving, nothing ever seemed to get under Epoh's skin or get him riled, but tonight was different. It was as if the ravaging storm was sending them a message, danger was lurking around every corner.

"Htiaf, I don't like the feel of this storm. We should stop at the next town and wait until the weather clears." said Epoh nervously, gritting his teeth and unconsciously tightly gripping the handle above the door.

Htiaf was silent for a moment then grunted, "I know…the storm is bad and getting worse. I can hardly see two feet ahead of me in this blinding snow, but we have a deadline to meet and you know how they get when we're late."

"Better late than not getting there at all don't you think?" said Epoh dryly, tightening his grip on the handle as Htiaf swerved the truck trying to avoid a tree. Drifting off to the side of the road, he was unable to determine where the road ended, and the embankment began.

"Whoa! That was a close one." Htiaf exclaimed. Slowing the truck, it swerved even more as he attempted to avoid a spin; the road was treacherously icy.

"My point exactly!" Epoh screeched as his left hand slammed on the dashboard to brace himself.

"Fine, look on the map and find out where the next town is and how far we have to go to get there," Htiaf ordered, never taking his eyes off the road.

Quickly Epoh began searching through the cab for the map, shuffling through piles of papers. Finally, he found the map stuffed under the seat. Pulling out a small round device from under the seat, Epoh's touch lit up the map.

Calculating their exact location, the image filled the entire cab. They had been on the road for days leaving basecamp weeks ago. Traveling every twisting, turning, winding back road imaginable, slowly traveling to their new permanent base. Traveling this way was so antiquated, it was just so slow; but the cargo couldn't be transported any other way.

The trip from Que City was wonderful; travelling along the Law River was spectacular even in winter. Each day the countryside was covered by a light dusting of crystal white snow which dazzled the eyes. As the rising sun brought forth spectacular vistas of frosted trees, sparkling rays of sunlight danced over open fields and barren woods, a far cry from the vehemently ferocious wind pelting the truck now.

Looking at the map was discouraging. There was no suitable place to stop. Epoh sighed anxiously, "We won't be able to stop for miles according to the map. The road up ahead is snaking...twisting and turning...there is no place to pull over safely."

"Well, we will just have to use extra care and cautiously keep moving... slowly." Htiaf said with added determination, as his uneasiness was continuing to increase.

The wind increased, whistling and howling eerily. Even though it was cool in the cab, sweat was pouring off the pair, stress mounting. Looking out the window was futile. All that was seen were streaks of white like a wall, blinding and impregnable. Seconds seemed like minutes, minutes seemed like hours. There were no signs or landmarks to identify where they were or how far they had travelled since the last landmark several miles back. They had no idea how far they had yet to travel to make it to the next town. The immediate danger they faced from the weather was secondary compared with safe delivery of the precious cargo tucked in the back of the truck. It was essential that they safely deliver their package at all cost, billions of lives depended on them accomplishing this task. If they failed to fulfill their mission, the *enemy* will have won and devastation of all that is good in the world would be the outcome.

Htiaf wasn't aware that as he was carefully maneuvering the truck, he was approaching an area of the road which was extremely treacherous. One side of the road snuggly hugged the side of the mountain, the other side, guarded by a single metal guide rail, had a steep drop which if breached would plunge an unsuspecting victim into the river below. It was about a

300-foot drop into frigid icy water. It had been raining earlier in the day; the river was high, raging, surging quickly downstream. When the temperature dropped, a smooth layer of ice formed a slick glaze over the road now covered by thick heavy snow.

Epoh noticed the road sign first and said with relieved excitement, "Look only a few miles to the next town, then we can stop for a while. I can even clean out the cab. It's getting awfully grubby in here."

"Good…I can't wait to get there. I need to pull over for some rest. I'm so tense my hands are becoming fused to the wheel." Pausing momentarily, he smiled, an impish glint lit his mien, "It's about time you decided to clean up this mess it's beginning to stink in here!" as he sniffed the air. Grinning he started laughing at Epoh as his face soured with indignation.

"Well you know you could have cleaned up the cab when I was driving." Epoh sputtered as Htiaf's laughter increased.

With mocking insincerity Htiaf said, "Are you kidding, that's your job."

Just then several things happened at once. A dark streak flashed in front of the truck ensued by a complete white out. Htiaf slammed on the breaks jerking the truck into a spin. Spinning out of control the truck slammed into the fallen tree spanning the width of the road. Propelling the truck into the guard rail plunging the back axle over the cliff. Teetering suspended on the rail the truck was precariously rocking in mid-air.

Like ragdolls both were tossed around in the cab, slamming into the windshield, thrown into the side doors then jolted back against their seats. Htiaf was driving, his chest was flung into the steering wheel knocking the wind out of him; both were unconscious. Epoh came to first; having smashed his head into the windshield and side window he was dazed. Several cuts on his face were bleeding but he seemed to be otherwise unharmed. Htiaf on the other hand was still unconscious. Assessing him, there was a large gash near his left temple, a large protrusion of bone that was pushing through the skin of his left arm, and with the impact of the steering wheel there were probable fractured ribs.

Epoh was trying to clear his head when he heard Htiaf moan. He whispered, "Htiaf are you alright?"

"Never mind about me, the package, what happened to the package? Is the package alright?" Htiaf groaned frantically as he desperately tried to move.

"I don't know. I haven't checked yet. Are you going to be alright if I leave you for a few minutes to find out?" Epoh asked with grave concern.

"I'll be fine...GO! See to the package...NOW!" Htiaf commanded urgently as he winched in pain.

As Epoh got out of the truck, he felt the truck rock. He wasn't sure if it was the truck or just the effect of the crash on his head. When he rounded the truck, he saw that it was teetering on the guard rail and the whole truck could plunge down the mountain at any time. He raced back to tell Htiaf and to get him out of the truck.

"Epoh you have to get the cargo out first, then me. It's too important. Now do it!" ordered Htiaf as he watched the turmoil in Epoh's face. The struggle between getting the cargo and helping his best friend was tearing him apart. Knowing that the lives of so many people depended on the cargo finally won out. Sadly, Epoh left Htiaf in the cab.

Epoh grabbing rope from the emergency equipment, tied one end to the front bumper of the truck and ran to secure the other end to a tree on the other side of the road close to the mountain. Securing another rope to an undamaged section of the guard rail, he then tied the loose end around his waist. Climbing over the guard rail, he stepped onto a few inches of solid ground before the drop. Quickly he proceeded to open the back of the truck. Carefully climbing up into the truck to ascertain whether the package had sustained any damage, the truck creaked.

The crates were all secure. The cargo fared far better than they did. Epoh approached the largest crate and opened it. Inside the crate was a large silver storm case which appeared to be undamaged. Opening the case very carefully, he made a thorough assessment. The control panel in the top of the case was still operational; it was performing and recording its vital monitoring functions. All recorded data was within normal limits, the unit was functioning normally. Epoh sighed with relief as he observed the opaque orb resting, suspended within the case, safe and secure.

As he was closing the case, he felt the truck slip. He knew he had to hurry. As he picked up the storm case to carry it out of the truck, the truck lurched, the rope was giving way. The sudden jolt knocked Epoh over into the snow; losing his grip, the case went sliding down the side of the mountain plunging into the raging river below. The rope securing the truck to the tree gave way under the strain. The weight of the truck on the guard rail collapsed the damaged section. The truck roared down the side of the mountain just missing Epoh by inches. He gasped and watched in horror as the truck plummeted down the slope of the cliff with Htiaf, broken and wounded inside unable to get out. The case gone, disappeared into the river, the hope of billions lost. Htiaf gone, sliding down the mountain to the same fate. All was lost, they had failed.

A lone figure stood at the top of the ridge smiling with satisfaction at the tragedy below.

Chapter

Finally, the day arrived. Confidently standing before the chamber door, Ari entered the room. The door immediately closing after her. Darkness, complete darkness engulfed her. Senses struggling to compensate, attempting to comprehend even the slightest stimulus, but nothing, there was absolutely nothing. Unable to see through the darkness, she reached out with her mind attempting to make a connection. She sensed nothing—no presence, no vision flash, just blackness. She felt emptiness—a complete void of thought, emotion, life. Ari made her way to the wall of the chamber and started feeling her way around. Her great-grandfather's journal spoke of a raised area in the chamber with protruding crystals to the right of the door. Making her way to the corner her grandfather described, she found nothing. A little confused Ari felt her way around the whole chamber. The walls were carved smooth—not a raised area to be found.

The journal explained that her great-grandfather experienced the same thing—nothingness, nothing occurred for a while when he entered the chamber. Ari decided to sit and meditate to clear her mind of all thought.

Tirelessly Ari sat for hours meditating. Emptying her mind of all thoughts and emotions, all except one—hope. A great stillness came upon her as if she had taken on the great void she felt when she first entered the room. Time past as she sat on the floor of the chamber, some moments as fast as a twinkling of an eye then in other instances as if in slow motion. Measuring the passage of time by her breathing, she attempted to even the pace, but it seemed like it was being controlled by the void…but how could that be?

After a while, the chamber felt warmer. Ari noticed a faint glow within the walls, floor and ceiling. Large mounds of dirt, rock, salt, and metals surrounded her. It was as if Ari was witnessing the formation of them at the beginning, the beginning of time. Periodically, heat radiated from the mounds of earth altering with episodic cooling. The cycle repeated several times. From each of the mounds, tentacles emerged. The appendages consisted of the different substances making up the mounds—each one unique. They reached for Ari to make contact. Instantly, as they touched her, Ari convulsed. Her mind exploded with sensations—brightness, hardness, softness, darkness, hotness, coldness. She was overwhelmed by the onslaught. If there was a purpose for this, she didn't understand what it was, but she was determine; determined to find it. Searching the inner most regions of her mind, body, and soul for comprehension, she found nothing. Stretching her mind, reaching outward, probing the mounds, one thought smashed into her—*'You are us.'* The pain she felt from that impression knocked her over.

'You are us'—what does that mean? Ari thought. Desperate to know, but she had no idea. It was as if a million tiny red-hot needles were probing her mind, searching. Never having thought such agony was possible, she was inundated with new hellacious sensations which enveloped her as if thousands of fire ants were dissecting every cell in her body. Distantly she heard a terrifying screech, startling her until she realized she was the one screaming. The assault of her mind and body intensified. It raged violently on like a tornado, twisting and turning her form.

Just when Ari felt she could endure no more, the mounds surrounding her began pelting her body with dirt, sand, salt and metals—the entire composition of the mound joined the assault. Ari knew she was going to die; she would never survive such an onslaught. *'Why? What did I do wrong?'* As certain death bore down, her mind floated back to the beginning, back home to a beautiful day on her mountain…

Nestled in the mountains far away from the usual hustle and bustle of modern urban life, the Lovell family was beginning their day. Life on the ranch was relaxed but very busy at times, it being a working ranch. Spring was the busiest, a wonderful time of year when life flourished. With the farm animals giving birth and the horse's foaling, the ranch hands had been working since dawn.

Ariella Lovell, Martin and Ena Lovell's daughter, stepped out onto the wraparound porch of the main house. Another beautiful spring day greeted her, the sun shining, blue skies, and a warm breeze. Ari, as most everyone called Ariella, loved the outdoors. She felt a kinship with nature unlike most people her age, those more interested in technology than nature; a warm sense of contentment surged through her as she took in the warm sweet air. It was simply gorgeous, irresistibly so. Ari was compelled to be outside; to be inside, was like being in prison, intolerable. The air was fresh, filled with the scent of spring flowers, new grass, and pine; aromas she never tired of, intensely appealing, intoxicating to her senses.

Ari was on a mission; she had to decide which university she would be attending in the fall. She had been putting it off, procrastinating; she was having a great deal of anxiety because of what it entailed. As a small child, she attended the local elementary school with the other children in the area. It quickly became apparent to Ari that she didn't fit in; she didn't look like the other children, she didn't think like them, and she didn't have the same interests as them. Dejected and alone Ari felt like an outcast. She tried everything imaginable to blend in, to belong; her efforts were fruitless, all in vain. The children made fun of her, ridiculed her for her height; she was always taller than the others and slender for her age. The other girls were jealous, pulling her long beautiful hair, calling her names like 'freak', 'red giant', and 'ugly bean pole' when she tried to play with them. If that wasn't bad enough, her intellect was far superior to theirs; praised by her teachers, she received awards for academic achievement, further alienating her from her peers. Alone and isolated; she withdrew into herself.

By the time she reached middle school, Ari feigned illness daily in hopes of avoiding her torment. Her parents decided to home school the rest of her education. Providing challenging material for her was the pretense for the change, but her parents had seen Ari's anguish increase over the years; she would come home crying day after day, it was heartbreaking.

Slowly as she began to be home schooled, her parents noticed good changes in her; not only did she excel at her studies, she relaxed and was much happier. Her friends were the animals on the ranch, especially the horses. Along with the animals, she became friends with the ranch hands, spending hours with them as they taught her everything they knew about ranching; they doted on Ari as if she were their own daughter. Even though she was accepted and loved at the ranch, Ari never quite felt like she completely belonged.

For years Ari didn't understand why the other kids hated her so, she tried very hard to be nice and friendly, going out of her way to be so, but they never would accept her which she regretted. It was also the cause of her anxiety. She was going to be attending a university filled with students. How would they treat her? Would they be mean and cruel, ridiculing her for how she looked or how tall she was? The uncertainty was distressing, causing a great deal of apprehension.

Ari was a stunningly beautiful young woman with deep rich auburn-red hair, accentuated by strands of gold when bathed in sunlight, dazzling the minds-eye. Hers was the face of an angel, perfect, delicately oval with a pert little nose, exquisitely lush lips, and the deepest cobalt blue eyes. Tall and sleek compared to most of the girls she knew, which wasn't that many at all since she stayed on the ranch most of the time. The few she did know were short, round, and plain with the exception of Jenkins daughter, the owner of the G & T store at the base of the mountain. Ari's parents were average height and round too. In fact, most of the families in the area were the same; Ari stood out among the mountain folk.

Walking lively to the barn, Ari had decided to hurry with her chores so she could concentrate on the pile of acceptance letters she had received. Just thinking about the task ahead gave her butterflies; her belly was fluttering so, she tried to focus on the task at hand.

One of Ari's jobs was to care for the family's horses; the ranch hands took care of their own. Since there was only her mother, father, and herself, she only had three horses to care for, but she did everything from feeding them to shoveling out the stalls. It was a dirty job, but she didn't mind; she loved the horses, they were her friends. As she was cleaning out the stalls and laying new straw, she realized she would be losing her friends when she went away, lone-liness slowly crept into Ari's heart consuming her with longing. A yearning for home, for security, for the familiar was gripping her tightly, squeezing her heart, distracting her from her routine and she hadn't even left yet; she felt the tears well up threatening to reveal her despair.

Shaking it off, she quickly finished with the horses, promised them she would be back later to see them and gave them each some sugar. Snowflake bobbed his head, nuzzling her as if he understood everything she said. He was Ari's horse, there when he was born, welcoming him into the world, scrawny and weak; it was love at first sight. Over the last two years, Ari had spent hours with him, training and caring for him, in a way they did have an understanding. One last stroke and Ari was out the barn door.

On her way to tackle the acceptance letters, Ari heard a low mewing sound. Looking around, she caught sight of Rufus, the old tomcat, over by the rose bushes. As she approached, his mewing became louder, more pronounced, urgent. On closer inspection she noticed he was stuck in among the briars, which were tearing at his fur. She knelt down next to him.

"Oh…you poor baby, what did you do? Got yourself all caught up in the briar. Now hold still while I get you loose," she purred to him as she removed his fur from the briar. Unfortunately for Rufus, he had a large gash oozing blood, his back was covered. As she cradled the cat, she whispered, "It's okay… we'll get that cleaned up and put some ointment on it, we don't want you to get an infection."

Ari suddenly felt warm all over, starting from her belly traveling to her hands. She didn't think much of it as she was walking to the treatment room next to the barn to get supplies to care for the wound. Her father kept an area close to the barn and corral with antiseptics, bandages, and other medical supplies for the vet when he came. She would be able to clean Rufus's injuries there.

When she put the cat on the table, she gathered what she needed; with gauze saturated with antiseptic in one hand, she attempted to find the cuts with the other. She went all the way through his fur but couldn't find the cuts; it was bazaar. The cat was injured; she was sure of it, the blood on her hands from the cuts confirmed it, but the wounds were gone. How was that possible? It was weird, wounds don't just disappear. She was confounded, but at least she wouldn't have to worry about him getting an infection. Ari hugged Rufus, put him gently on the ground and watched him scurry off around the barn.

Ari headed for the house a second time. Her father was coming out of the house as she was coming up to the porch. Martin Lovell was a very good man; he would go out of his way to help anyone in trouble. If his neighbors or even a stranger found themselves tapped-out financially or unable to obtain food, he would make sure they didn't go hungry, providing as much as he could to meet their needs. People mattered, unlike the harsh cold estrangement found in cities; he had a real sense of community. This was the way of the Lovell's from the time they came to the mountain hundreds of years past. In the old times, Martin's family had fled Europe escaping political and civil unrest. They were persecuted for their beliefs, thus the family had a strict value of tolerance, helping and assisting wherever the need maybe.

Like most of the mountain families, he was round and thick, but far from fat, standing approximately five foot four inches, on the short side for a man. A full face, almost cherubic, with the semblance of innocence which made people want to put their trust in him. Recently his wavy black hair had been sprinkled with white giving him a dignified salt and pepper look, enhancing his deep rich brown eyes, warm and tender.

He greeted Ari with a big, sunny smile that brightened his face. "Hey, honey, you all done in the barn?"

"Yeah…now I have a bigger job to tackle, sifting through all those letters," said Ari as she scrunched up her nose as if she smelled something foul. She had put it off long enough; there was no getting around it.

"Well…I'll let you get to it. I know you'll pick the right one, sweetie," said Martin as he kissed Ari on the forehead.

Just as Ari was turning to go into the house, an old rusty black truck roared up the drive honking its horn. Looking over her shoulder she saw John Lee, her father's friend from the mountain on the south side of the G & T store looking rather frantic. Ari looked at her father; raised brow, he was just as intrigued as she was wondering what John Lee was in such an all-fired hurry about.

If there was any news to be spread, John Lee usually was the one to spread it. Ari thought he had several extra pairs of ears. The juicy tidbits he picked up were mind-boggling, anything from actual news to hearsay gossip to outright fictitious storytelling, he knew it; John Lee was a regular infor-mation broker.

Stopping the truck inches from Martin, John Lee sprang out of the truck waving as he spoke, "Hey, Martin!"

"Hello, John Lee...what's got you in such an all-fired hurry today?" Martin asked as he approached the man whose pale blonde hair was wind-blown, in disarray, with several strands frizzed, pointed, and completely askew—adding a wildly crazed look to his already unique features. Large bulging eyes, the most prominent feature of his plump robust face, stared at Martin. Well it looked like he was staring, it was difficult to tell; he had lazy eyes, they appeared to move independently like a chameleon's. Ari thought it rather creepy; she always avoided direct eye contact with him even though she felt a fondness for the eccentric old man.

"I come tah warn ya right away. I was talkin' to Horace who'd jus' come from Henry's place, he run into Jed who'd been visitin' Micah day before yesterday. Well, Micah run into Danny at the Ol' Jin House havin' some brew. Ya know they hadn't seen each other for a while so they got talkin' an' carryin' on 'bout huntin' an' trappin'..."

"John Lee...slow down...stay on track here...what is it you have to warn me about?" Martin asked refocusing him. Martin knew John Lee would continue to go off on different tangents, talking about this, talking about that, everything except the reason he had come. If he didn't reel him in, he would never find out what had him in an uproar.

"Huh...oh...oh...right...well Danny said he saw that minin' comp'ny truck sniffing around yer mountain. That cidy-slicker was askin' a passel of questions, bout you, the ranch, 'nd yer family down at the G & T," John Lee spewed excitedly.

All the folks in the area knew how Martin felt about big corporations that bulldozed the little man, running over them with a heavy roller, taking every inch of what took years of hard work and sweat to eke out just to survive. He despised their heavy handedness, their trickery, their greed; he fought them tooth and nail not once giving into seductive lures.

Years ago, before his father passed, the mining company came sniffing around the ranch to exploit untouched land for mining rights. Charles Lovell, Martin's father, chased the company's man right off his property with his shotgun; he told his son in no uncertain terms that 'the land is forever—it's precious and needs to be protected.' Martin not only felt a responsibility to protect his heritage from shameless greedy carpetbaggers, but the land was in his blood, it was his life, his kin; his soul was wrapped up in his mountain and as long as he drew breath, no one would ravage *his* legacy.

"Thank you, John Lee, for letting me know. Those making inquiries might come back. If you could do me a favor, keep an ear out; if you hear anything else, let me know right away," Martin implored clapping him on the back in gratitude.

Year after year, Martin watched as his neighbors had been suckered into signing mining contracts. The contracts were extremely lucrative, but each one watched their land be desolated, stripped of natural resources, polluted by drilling, overrun by waste products until it was unusable, unable to sustain life. Several neighbors were scourged with devastating sickness, suffering, agonizing in pain from loathsome diseases, finally succumbing—to death, inevitable death. It was not going to happen on his mountain; Martin had never been more determined.

"You betcha, Martin!" John Lee said eager to be on his way now that he had a mission.

"Would you like a drink or something John Lee? We can sit and chew the fat for a while," Martin invited.

"No…no…I gotta go see Eli, he's expectin' me. I'll be keepin' me ears open…Martin," he nodded and just as fast as he arrived, he vanished down the drive in his rusty old truck.

"Dad do you think the mining company will try to get a contract from you?" Ari asked as she came up from behind her father and wrapped her arm around his waist. She had been listening and didn't like what she heard.

Martin was silent for several moments before he turned to her, "They may come…they probably will. We have the only mountain in the area that hasn't been touched. These people never stop until they get everything they want, insidious and loathsome is what they are; but whether they come or not they will never get our mountain!"

Several days had past; Ari had narrowed her choice of universities to five. Dauntingly grueling and tedious was the time spent researching programs, activities, along with other aspects of college life. She needed a break before she started pulling her hair out, frustration escalating. A reprieve to the kitchen for a snack, fortification to strengthen her was just what she needed. Raspberry ice, she thought, as her mouth began to water; it was the one treat irresistible to her. Hurrying to the kitchen, she was distracted by a commotion coming from the front yard. She heard her father calling to her mother; he was riding up to the corral with one of the workers, she couldn't make out which one. As she watched from the doorway, Martin helped the man from his horse, it looked like Connie. He was injured, assisted to the vet's room; she set out to see if she could help.

Ena, Ari's mother, took charge giving instructions. Connie was put on the table so she could get a good look at the injury. Ena like her husband had a kind and gentle heart, caring for the sick and injured, always helping the underdog despite any consequences to herself. She was a petite woman, only reaching five foot two inches in height. Long golden blonde hair, which she wore in a braid, ran down the length of her back; her fair skin had a few freckles smattered across her nose giving her a youthful mien. Sparkling pale blue eyes, appearing grey at times, were full of life, emanating love, warmth. A round woman, but not fat, having a soft cuddly aura, making people feel relaxed and comfortable.

"What happened?" Ena asked as she grabbed a cloth to put under his leg.

"His horse got spooked and threw him. His leg got caught up in the stirrup as his mount took off with him still attached. Connie said he heard a snap just as he hit the ground," said Martin, breathing heavily from struggling to get Connie up onto the table.

"He probably broke an ankle or leg," Ena said as she turned her attention to his right leg, turned and twisted, she was sure it was. Connie was moaning in pain, his head spinning. He took one look at his foot; it was facing in the wrong direction and passed out.

"Well…it's probably for the best that he's out cold," Martin said knowing how much it was going to hurt to set the bone having been the recipient of such pain several times.

Ari had reached them by then, she watched as her mother supported Connie's leg and as her father cut through his pants in an attempt to remove his boot; if it proved too difficult, he would have to cut the boot off. With teamwork, they quickly removed the boot. While assessing the skin, there was no doubt the leg just above the ankle was broken; there was a large protrusion of bone pressing against the skin, a swollen mound had formed, purplish-red.

"Martin, we have to splint the leg before we take him to the hospital. Do we have splints?" Ena asked as she rummaged through the cabinets. "We should have some in the bottom draw. Let me see," Martin said as he started pulling out drawers, both searching for them. They were a team, forming a true partnership over the years. What one lacked the other made up for, true oneness, unity of mind and spirit. Hastily, they pulled out a variety of supplies needed.

Connie started to moan, eyes fluttering trying to open, he was regaining consciousness; Ari wanted to help, she wet a cloth with cool water, placing it on his head, the cool sensation provided a small distraction. With the compress in place, she grabbed Connie's hand, holding it, offering him her strength. A powerful surge of energy was being generated inside her, she felt like her whole body was electrified; it was the second time she felt that strange potent force building in her. This time she felt more, she could feel a warm tingling move through her, traveling into her arms, her hands, then it vanished. What was that she thought?

"Here they are," Ena said as she grabbed several different sized splints taking them over to the table. "Martin…look at this!" Ena exclaimed.

"What?" Martin moved to the table next to Ena. Stunned, they both stared at Connie's leg. It looked perfectly normal, no discoloration, no swelling, no protruding bone under the skin, nothing. It was impossible, completely healed. Ena ran her hand over the area, strong and sturdy, no sign of injury. Neither of them had any idea of how this happened, how it was even possible, but the evidence was right in front of them, unable to be denied.

Ari moved closer to see what they were looking at, a perfectly normal looking leg. What was going on? First Rufus, now Connie, these things didn't just happen, open wounds don't just heal and disappear; neither do broken bones mend themselves. Something bazaar was happening, she wondered if she should tell her parents about Rufus or would they think she was crazy. Too much stress is what they would probably say, the mind playing tricks, but it still didn't explain what just happened or Rufus. She remained silent.

Ena noticed that Ari was holding Connie's hand as he fully regained consciousness. His eyes opened; looking up at Ari, he smiled. Looking around he saw Martin and Ena by his leg. Confused, he had no pain, but he should have pain. He had pain earlier. Why didn't he, he wondered? He started to sit up to ask if they had given him something when he saw his leg; it looked normal!

"What happened?" Connie asked dumbfounded. He was positive he had broken his leg.

"Uh...um...nothing?" said Martin completely lost for words. He had no idea what to tell Connie, what was there to tell him? 'Oh yeah Connie, your leg was broken, we turned our backs to gather supplies and when we turned back again your leg was healed'; he'd think we'd gone bonkers, Martin thought.

"Your leg is *not* broken," said Ena. "We thought it was, but we were wrong. How do you feel?"

"I feel great!" said Connie, "Actually, I've never felt better in my life. I should fall off my horse all the time." He chuckled to himself.

"Why don't you go to the bunk house and gets some rest for a while just to be on the safe side," said Martin. "Ari can you help Connie back to his room?"

"Sure...come on Connie...I'll help."

"I'm fine...really..." Connie insisted, but Ari took him by the arm and headed across the yard.

Ena watched as they walked away making sure they were out of hearing distance. Turning to Martin she whispered, "Martin...Ari was holding Connie's hand when we were looking for the splints. Do you think she could have something to do with his leg being healed?"

"I don't know. I suppose it's possible, but she's been around others when they have been injured before, nothing like this has ever happened. I don't know...I just don't know. Ari would tell us if something strange, out of the ordinary happened, don't you think?"

"Martin...what if she doesn't realize she is doing it? We really don't know if she has any special abilities, do we? It's all supposition. Yes, we found her under unusual circumstances, but...that's all we know, except that incident when she was small, nothing since."

"Well...if it is her doing, we have to keep this quiet. We can't let anyone know. We could lose her," Martin was terrified at the thought. He drew Ena close, deriving strength from each other as they faced an uncertain future.

Chapter

2

Chores done, ranch hands out rounding up strays, and her parents off buying supplies, Ari was alone. She was used to being alone, everyone off busy prattling about doing their jobs. This was her time to daydream, free her mind as she took in the spirit of the day. Sitting in an old rocker on the back porch, Ari closed her eyes. As her mind drifted, she began to visualize images; she could see in her mind the long winding drive lined with beautifully manicured fencing, white, standing out against a backdrop of lush green foliage. Standing at attention, the great old oaks protected what lay beyond, standing guard like centurions along the drive's edge. The ranch was large, encompassing a whole mountain; it was her sanctuary. Impressive to outsiders and ultimately intimidating when they first arrive, but it was her home, one she loved dearly.

Coming up from the narrow drive, the first site seen was the old stately manor situated in front, center of all activity. A stately bluish-grey was the main house trimmed with a white wraparound porch, well maintained with a few modern updates. Various flowers with their sweet aroma filled the air; rose bushes, colorful and enticing, skirted the porch offering an inviting scene. To the right of the house was the bunk house, more grey than bluish-grey with white trim, haven for the ranch hands.

Far to the left of the cobble-stone entry yard were several barns, the corral, and the vet's room. The barns were very large to accommodate all the livestock on the ranch; as large as they were, they became very cramped when severe weather brought the majority of the animals in. Beyond the barns, wide open spaces used as pastureland for the horses and the cattle, it opened the ranch up giving it a feeling of infinite space and peace. The pastures were bordered by forests teaming with life; Martin only cleared more space when he needed to, he wanted to maintain the natural beauty of the land.

Thinking about the ranch, pastures, and trees, a strong desire began to well up, urging her to skip and dance, ride freely on Snowflake, wind blowing through her hair. Not able to contain it any longer, she headed for the barn to saddle him up. As she rounded the corner of the house, she heard a commotion, chirping and flailing wings, over by the old oak tree. A tiny little fledgling robin squawking panicked because he was unable to flap his right wing to fly away. Rufus, the cat, slowly approached to investigate the ruckus. Crippled and trapped, the robin, was frantic at seeing the prowling cat; wildly flapping he was unable to return to his perch in the tree. Struggling to use his injured wing was causing his wound to become worse. If he only understood, old Rufus could barely see, really in capable to cause any harm.

Rufus, approaching the old oak, creeping slowly toward the injured bird crouched as Ari came near. She gently shooed him away to put the bird at ease. As soon as Rufus was away, the baby robin quieted. Ari had a way with animals; sensing that she would never hurt them, they became docile at her touch. Her calming effect seemed instinctive, as though she was able to communicate with them. As far back as she could remember, she had this special ability to soothe and calm animals, recently the skill was intensifying, with odd things occurring.

Ari knelt down to pick up the baby robin. He was fluttering so much she had to cover the bird with her left hand to hold him still. She could feel the break in the wing. He would never survive on his own.

Ari recalled Rufus and Connie, turning the incidents over and over in her mind, she wondered how they were healed; a fanciful idea came to her, she decided to try an experiment. With Rufus and Connie, she remembered wishing she could heal them, but that was nothing new; she had been around injured animals and birds in the past and they were never healed. It had to be something else. Continuing to recall events in her mind, looking for anything different she might have done; it came to her, she was touching each of them, direct physical contact. Already holding the bird, she closed her eyes and concentrated on healing the robin's wing.

A familiar warm sensation started to well up from deep within her like an electric surge building, intensifying, vibrating from her very core until it was channeled into her hands. The bird became very still, Ari became concerned but then felt the robin's wing straighten, she opened her hands and the baby robin flapped his wings, testing them. After he made sure it was functional, he flew up into the old oak.

Ari was thrilled and amazed. She couldn't help wondering how she was able to do these wonderful things. Ari was determined to know, but how? She was adopted, not something she and her parents talked about much. Maybe they knew more than they were telling her; when they got home, she would find out more details about her adoption, she thought.

The afternoon dragged on, even after a long ride on Snowflake. Riding the trails was one of Ari's favorite pastimes; but with anticipation building, she was eager to confront her parents. Galloping up to the main house she saw the truck, her parents had returned; excitement flooded through her. Taking Snowflake to the barn, she settled him quickly; she needed answers and was becoming increasingly anxious.

Martin and Ena were in the kitchen. Martin was sitting on a stool talking with Ena while she scurried around gathering foodstuff to prepare their evening meal. Laughter filled the air as Ari entered through the back door; it was, as usual, a happy place. She greeted her parents with a smile and was less than tactful as she blurted out her request.

"Who am I? Why don't we ever talk about my adoption?" Ari said more forcefully than she had meant to. Taken aback, Martin and Ena were stunned; staring at her, they were speechless.

Ena spoke first, "We haven't spoken of it, honey, because you've never asked."

"I'm sorry for just blurting that out…I didn't mean it the way it sounded… it's just that I have been waiting to talk to you all day…it just came out wrong," Ari apologized for her rudeness, she didn't usually act that way especially with her parents. "Can we talk about it now?"

"Of course, we can," said Ena, "What would you like to know?" Ena looked at Martin with trepidation, she knew this day would come, she had always been fearful of the result. What would Ari do with the information she was about to receive. .

"Everything that you know," said Ari eagerly; she felt driven to discover the truth.

"We adopted you when you were a baby…that you know…but what you don't know is it wasn't a normal adoption." Martin paused to let Ari assimilate what he said as they moved into the living room. Ari slowly lowered herself onto the couch. Not a normal adoption? What does that mean, she thought as she turned back to Martin? "Well if it wasn't a normal adoption from an adoption agency, how did you adopt me?" Ari asked after several minutes wondering if she really wanted to know. Yes, she had to know, there was something different about her; she had to discover the truth.

Martin continued, "Your mother and I went up to the Adirondack Mountains for a camping trip; New York is wonderful in the summer. We were going to meet your uncle Tony and his new girlfriend for a week of fishing, hiking, and boating. Your mom and I arrived a few days ahead of Tony; we wanted some alone time. You know how crazy your uncle can get; we knew we wouldn't get a moments peace after he arrived. After we set up camp, we decided to hike along the river scoping out the best fishing spots. As we were walking, your mother noticed something glistening in the sunlight; a large metallic box lodged in between two large rocks shimmering, fading in and out of sight. Curious, we went to investigate, one second we could see it, the next it was invisible. A real mystery was in front of us, we were intrigued. Onto the riverbank, we pulled the box to examine it; the box was heavy, it wasn't easy to get it out of the water. So excited, we opened the case. What we saw was fascinating. In the top of the case, lights were blinking; it looked like a computer control panel. Signs, symbols, and writing we couldn't read…actually, we had never seen anything like it before…were displayed on the monitor. Inside the case suspended in mid-air was a light brown egg or what looked like an egg. It was much larger than any normal egg; the shell was pliable, not hard. The outer layer or skin was fibrous, made up of what looked like thousands of tiny opaque fibers. The sphere was about the size of a large elongated beach ball; thick vein-like structures, metallic silver, appeared to be stretching throughout the orb. It looked more organic than metal or a combination of both, we just weren't sure." Martin paused. Ari was having a difficult time believing his story.

"Dad…are you telling me another one of your tall tales?" she said with a laugh as she shook her head and scanned both her parents waiting for them to confess they were just pulling her leg. The story was a little far-fetched even for her fun-loving father.

"Ariella…your father is telling you the truth…that's just the way it happened 17 years ago." Ena said as she moved over to the couch where Ari was sitting. She pulled Ari close to her, comforting her, shielding her from the disturbing circumstances surrounding her entrance into the Lovell's lives.

"Okay let's say it's true, what does this have to do with me?" Ari asked skeptically.

"Ariella….I know all of this sounds far-fetched but it is all true. Now where was I? Oh, yeah, we were so fascinated we closed the lid and carried it back to our campsite to examine it more closely. Trying to decide what to do with it, turn in to the authorities or maybe a university for further study; we spent several hours trying to decipher the signs and symbols with no success. By that time frustration was setting in, it was clear we would never be able to decipher the writing without help since neither of us were linguists. The one thing we were sure of was we wanted answers. *What was the orb? Where did it come from?* Well to make a long story short; we decided to take the box to the local police the next day to see if anyone reported it missing. About an hour before dawn Ena woke me; she said she heard something whimpering. I thought she was dreaming until I heard it too. Looking around the tent, we discovered the whimpering was coming from the box. The cover was ajar, we never closed it completely before we went to sleep; we don't know if it was leaving the top open or if we accidently hit a button on the panel, but whichever it was, we were totally amazed at what we found when we lifted the lid."

"What did you find…Dad? …Mom? …What was it?" Ari said eagerly. Intrigued at what her parents had discovered Ari's curious nature was now peeked.

"We found you!" Martin and Ena said in unison, great joy echoing in their voices.

"Me? …You mean I came from an egg?" Ari exclaimed in disbelief. She was some kind of freak, the kids at school were right, a freak who came from an egg. Confused and despondent, she had more questions now than answers. Unable to say anything at the moment, she recounted everything her father had just told her.

"Your father and I have speculated about this for years. We believe the egg sphere was some sort of suspended animation or cryogenic storage unit suspended by an energy field. The technology was way beyond anything human. Martin and I have lots of theories but very few facts. When the sphere opened, it was evident you were at least 6 months old not a newborn. The most beautiful baby I had ever seen was looking up, whimpering at me. Your skin was like a sea of crystal, translucent and sparkling. No ordinary baby ever looked like you, we knew you were special. Just look at you, even more beautiful than you were as baby; you're flawless, your skin has muted, it doesn't sparkle like it did, but it still has its translucent quality, nonetheless, it's much different than ours. It's like mother of pearl, soft and willowy, whereas mine is like pewter, dull and flat. You have never once been sick a day in your life, not even a sniffle. When you were four years old, you were running after Rufus and fell over a root sticking up from the ground. You cut your hands and knees and hit your head on a rock which left a large gash on your forehead. There was blood everywhere. By the time we got you into the house to tend to the wounds, they had healed without so much as a single scar. Ordinary people can't do that Ariella," Ena explained as she held Ari's hand.

Looking at her hands, arms, and legs, Ari was comparing hers and Ena's; feeling her skin and examining its texture, Ena was right. Ari's skin was light translucent beige, soft and pliant, whereas Ena's was pale, dull and stiff. There was a noticeable difference between her hand and Ena's. Ena's skin had multiple scars from wounds obtained over the years, years working on the ranch; it was also rough, starting to show dryness from work and age. Ari's skin on the other hand was soft, firmer, flexible, and more elastic with no scars or dryness. Pondering the differences, she thought, 'how can this be I do the same chores around the ranch as mom; actually, I do more of the rough work, my hands should be worse than hers.'

Finally, she looked up and said, "What am I? Who am I? Where did I come from?"

Martin got up and went over to the kitchen to get a drink of water. He had been anticipating Ari's next question. Having no answers, he had no idea what to tell her. Martin glanced at Ena and then to Ari and shook his head, "We don't know Ariella. We went to the local police to inquire whether or not someone had reported a missing child or even a missing box, no one had. No one around the campground knew anything about you or the box; we searched the surrounding area thoroughly and came up empty handed. We were at a loss as to what to do when the police officer suggested that we adopt you. It was something we hadn't considered right away, adoptions can take months with a lot of red tape, but the officer's brother, the judge for the county, was willing to help us speed up the process. Under the circumstances, we were very fortunate. The county didn't have the resources to take in another homeless child, thus the willingness to help us. Since, no one had claimed you, we were thrilled to keep you and love you. You have been such a blessing to us especially since we found out later that we were unable to have children."

"Was there any clue as to where I came from?" Ari asked hoping for even the tiniest bit of information as to her identity.

Ena got up from the couch, went into her bedroom. A few moments later she came back with a small box and handed it to Ari. "You had this with you when we found you. It was the only object in the case that wasn't part of the stasis unit."

Ari opened the box and lifted up a golden pendant. It was the size of a half-dollar, circular. Etched in the center of the pendant was a triangle overlaid with an inverted triangle. In the center of the triangles was an encircled symbol, At the top left corner, there was a smaller triangle; an inverted small triangle was in the top right corner. In left bottom corner, was an inverted triangle with a line through the wider aspect; the right bottom corner also had a triangle, but the line was through the tip. The etching on the pendant was very intricate, exquisitely refined; it was masterfully carved. On the back of the pendant, with similar etched intricacy foreign writing or symbols were inscribed, recognized by none.

"It's beautiful!" Ari exclaimed, so overcome with emotions she could hardly manage to speak.

"We have kept the pendant safe, saving it for this moment, the time you would start asking questions." Ena said as she wrapped her arms around Ari protectively; she wanted Ari to feel secure and supported, not alone, they would always be there for her.

"When the adoption was complete, we came back home and we have been waiting ever since." Martin frowned. The possibility that her people would come in search of her someday or that Ari would set out on her own to find answers hung over them like threatening storm clouds.

"Waiting for what dad?" Ari asked not sure of what he meant.

"Years we have been waiting for something unusual to happen or some stranger to show up here looking for you to take you away." Despair was starting to show on Martin's face as he turned to look out the window, talking about losing Ari was very upsetting to both him and Ena. No one said a thing after that; they all could feel that change was approaching like an insidious stalker looming around the corner.

Chapter

3

ire! It was raining fire from the night sky; everywhere he looked, he saw fire. Bright streaks of red and orange flashed against the blackness, pitch-black; the twinkling stars and the luminous moon absconded by clouds. Peering out the window next to his bed, the small child rubbed his eyes, sleep blurred his vision. He was alone in the small cottage on the edge of the village; his parents gone. Where would they go? Why would they leave him alone?

They should have been tucked in the little bed across the room, but it was empty. Fear gripped him as he franticly searched the one room cottage, his heart racing, and his breath ragged; looking for something, anything familiar, but found nothing. He raced to the door, threw it open hoping to see his mother, his father, anybody who might know where they were, where they could be found.

People, lots of people running through the dark smoke ridden streets, screaming in terror; struck by horror as he watched the helpless villagers dragging injured loved ones to safety, but there was no safety. Panic and chaos ensued as the fire rained from the sky bombarding the village. Buildings exploded as the sky fire hit, smashing them to rubble, sending debris high into the air, igniting the fires that followed. The whole village was being consumed by the blazing infernos; plumbs of billowing smoke rose higher and higher into the night air spreading through the village like an insidious viper choking the inhabitants, inhibiting their escape.

Never had anyone seen such destruction as this before; the villagers were terrified, screaming *'God's wrath is upon us'* as they scrambled through the desolated village, they once called home. Panicked, tears streaming down his chubby cheeks, the boy started running, he had to find them, his parents, why would they leave him; his little bare feet scrambled across the cold ground, searching, hoping, fear growing steadily.

He was almost to the old chestnut tree in the center of the village when he saw *them*. Soldiers marching into the village, the bad soldiers; the ones that hurt, the ones that brought terror, the ones his parents had warned him to hide from. The boy huddled down behind some bushes fearful of being seen. He watched; the soldiers were slashing and striking at the helpless townsfolk, killing everyone as they tried to flee the village, the innocent desperately trying to escape, their only crime being alive. In the wrong place at the wrong time, it was the fate of the innocent throughout history; occupying the village that *they*, the bad soldiers wanted.

A heavily armored soldier approached his hiding place. He held his breath, heart pounding, beating so hard he was sure it was going to explode from his chest. Terrified, wanting to escape, run to safety, to get away from the bad soldiers, longing for the comfort and security of his parents embrace, he knew he had to stay still, to move would mean certain death; the bushes would give him away if he moved, with all his might he willed himself motionless. The smoke was burning his eyes and his throat, suffocating him; he was trying to breathe while suppressing the cough building within, struggling to remain silent, he closed his mouth, covered his head with his arms and buried his face in the sweet-smelling grass.

After several long drawn out minutes, the soldier moved off in another direction. A surge of relief filled him, he began to breathe easier. Slowly he got up and turned to continue his search; but he slammed right into another soldier.

The menacing giant picked him up by the scruff of his neck and grinned, "Well...what do we have here..."

Jace sprang up quickly, wide eyed, panting, his heart racing, droplets of moisture glazed his brow; frantic, he swiftly glanced around the hazy, dimly lit room. *'Ugh'* he moaned as he flopped back onto the bed, a dream, no…a nightmare, a horrible nightmare; one he wished he could erase from his memory. Reliving that horrid night over and over in his dreams was becoming tedious; every time he searched for something, the memory relived, it was maddening. He could still smell the smoke choking him, burning and stinging his eyes; the fear and panic of being alone, abandoned by his parents. The memory tortured him, haunting him like a malevolent specter in the night.

Jace and his parents had been traveling to the location of their new city in the secluded wilderness just north of Pudoze in northern region; not the normal way of traveling for Jace and his people. It was supposed to be a leisurely jaunt through what was thought to be safe territory; it was anything but safe, scarring him permanently, not on the outside but deep within. He wiped the perspiration from his forehead and covered his eyes trying to shake the horror from his mind, but visions of death flooded through him turning him cold, paralyzed by the dead faces peering up at him.

He was saved that night, by a fluke of nature, or so he thought. As he was dangling in mid-air, struggling to get away from the giant, the soldier pulled out a large blade, shiny metal with serrated teeth, reflecting the light of the blazing fires. His smile, a wide evil malicious grin; his eyes narrowed, dark menacing evil reflected in those eyes, eyes Jace would never forget, virulent and venomous, but something more. Pleasure, sinister pleasure, the thrill and excited anticipation of extinguishing another's life reflected in those eyes. A terrifying chill ran up Jace's spine at the thought.

Slashing the air with one stroke, the soldier focused on Jace anticipating the next swing. Jace squeezed his eyes shut, he knew what was coming. Thud! Not what he was expecting. He made a loud thump as he hit the ground. Stunned his eyes snapped open, he was on the ground with the soldier next to him. What had happened? Why was he still alive?

The blade was firmly implanted in the man's chest, but how? No one was around, no one who could have helped. Jace wasn't going to wait around to find out, his heart was pounding like stampeding elephants trying to escape a predator; he ran as fast as he could back in the direction of the cottage, ducking behind trees and bushes to avoid detection. He saw nothing but smoke, fire, and dead bodies which lined the streets. The soldiers had marched from one end of the village to the other end killing everyone; then they left, they didn't make camp, they didn't leave sentries, nothing—they just left. It made no sense, why would they do that? Life was precious, too precious to waste on a whim, but they slaughtered the innocent, why?

Just one of so many memories, the soldiers were relentless, constantly pursuing his people, bent on genocide. If a solution wasn't found soon, his people would be annihilated. The assignment was simple, find the girl, somehow, she was key; the key to end the illimitable enmity between two races. Jace had his doubts; after all, what could one girl do against an evil malicious army of soldiers? For two weeks he had been searching peaks and valleys of the mountain region, the area where the signal had originated, but it was intermittent at best. The mountains were interfering with the locator beacon.

Taking rural roads and staying off the main highways offered beautiful scenic vistas, plus an opportunity to hobnob with the locals. Information was key; a smiling face and friendly chit chat was all it took for most locals to spew precious little tidbits. He had been staying in every sleazy, moth ridden, flea infested roadhouse along the way, picking up bits and pieces of gossip here and there. Staying out of sight, not drawing attention to his presence and blending in with the natives, it wasn't easy with his six-foot stature; he stuck out like a sore thumb. His people were tall and slender, completely different from the more rounded features of the local inhabitants. Stealth had been his people's most effective defense for millenniums from the Emigee soldiers, the soldiers of his nightmares; but it was proving difficult to be covert in this locale.

Yesterday, one particularly long day of searching, he was relieved to have spotted an inn situated near a stream. Exhausted he took a room. To his sheer delight, he discovered the inn had a garden overlooking a rolling brook. A passion for nature was inherent to all his people but he obtained his love for gardens from his mother; hours upon hours they had spent in their garden together enjoying the gifts that grew. Jace stepped into the garden area, grinning instantly at the sight and smell of fresh lilacs blooming, inhaling deeply, taking in the delicious heady aromas, he was immediately exhilarated.

To the left, he saw a three-tiered wall, each tier displaying lavish varieties of exotic grasses, flowing vines, and blooming flowers; it was exquisite. To the right, was a large antique white gazebo surrounded by flowing shrubs. Flagstone stabs marked the walkways bordered on both sides by red creeping thyme. Four large boulders lined the bank of the stream offering a perch to enjoy the relaxing cascading ripples of swooshing water flowing over rocks. It was just what he needed to relax his mind after a very unproductive day.

Perched on a large rock by the stream, eyes closed, he took several deep breaths; with each breath he let his body relax, replacing the tension with the symphony surrounding him, natures song, singing birds, a babbling brook, scurrying creatures, foliage rustling—it was beautifully refreshing. As Jace was enjoying the garden, he noticed a new sound, a sound that didn't belong in the garden—*cleek…crunch…cleek…crunch.*

"Hey mister, whacha doin'?" a little voice squeaked.

Jace turned to see a little blonde boy with big brown puppy dog eyes peering up at him curiously. He was dressed in little denim overalls with a blue gingham shirt. Strapped to both legs were braces meant to straighten and support; saddened at seeing the braces Jace frowned slightly, children should be able to run, jump, and play uninhibited, but the cumbersome braces didn't seem to slow this precocious little guy.

"Well hey there little man…I'm just listening to the music."

"There ain't no music mister," the boy said as he peered at Jace, confusion spread over his angelic face.

"What's your name son?"

"Ollie, what's yours?" Jace snickered at his response, precocious indeed.

"I'm Jace, Ollie…nice to meet you," Jace stretched out his hand to shake Ollie's. Grinning from ear to ear, Ollie's tiny little hand was lost in Jace's. "Well…Ollie if you listen carefully you can hear a symphony of nature's music."

"Nature's music, what's that?"

"Come on up here and sit a while and I'll tell you," Jace said as he helped Ollie up onto one of the boulders next to him. He situated himself next to Jace then eagerly waited for an explanation. "Listen carefully…what do you hear?"

Ollie scrunched up his face and bowed his head slightly listening intently for the music, "I hear water…leaves crunching…birds…"

"Good…I hear those things too, but I also hear the leaves rustling in the wind, the squirrels, chipmunks, and other creatures chattering and moving through the brush, and twigs snapping; when you listen to all those things together a symphony of music forms. It is soothing and pleasant to listen to… can you hear it?"

Silent for a few minutes, Ollie listened; he sucked in a deep breath and his eyes snapped open. Wide-eyed with excitement, he blurted, "I can hear it Jace…I can hear the nature's music!"

The excitement of discovery; watching a child explore and recognize the beauty of nature filled Jace with warmth and contentment. He had no children of his own nor did he have any future plans of having any; not with the Emigee problem looming over his people. It was doubtful he would ever experience the joy of fatherhood since he had no mate. Jace avoided close ties, the ties that bind, the ones that anchor one's soul; he endured a tragic loss, a loss that marred him to the very core of his being, a loss he never wanted to know again.

Jace grinned with delight at Ollie's enthusiasm, "Good Ollie…very good. It's beautiful isn't it?"

Ollie nodded his head as he listened. They spent some time together talking about fishing, helping his mom in the garden, and other things he liked to do; then about things he didn't like so much, like doctors and operations, needles and bad tasting medicine. Ollie had been through many bad times for being so young; a degenerative bone disease with crippling effects is what he had to look forward to according to doctors.

"Ollie…" echoed from a distance, somewhere within the inn.

"My mom's callin' me. I have to go Jace."

Jace reached out his hand to shake Ollie's. The familiar warmth growing deep within his core, building, intensifying into a tingling current flowing through his arm and hand, the same hand which held Ollie's; a gift for a precocious little boy for a better future.

"It was very nice meeting you Ollie…live well," Jace said in parting. His people had the gift of healing; for millennium before the destruction it was openly practiced but now it was used only to preserve life. Jace made an exception for the little man he found fascinating, having a captivatingly elfin appeal. He felt joy that Ollie *would* live better; joy was good, especially after a long and unproductive day.

On the road again heading north, the direction the locator beacon signaled; it was coming in strong today. Jace was going to take full advantage while he had the beacons help. He sped closer and closer to the signal's destination, anticipation growing. How would he approach the girl? What would he say? Should he just tell her everything all at once or should he take time and ease into it? Time is something they had little of, too much was at stake. The Emigee could find them, capture or even kill them; they weren't going to be safe until they were home, back with their people. Riding all day and into the evening, Jace had covered a great distance. The signal was strong, he was closing in, but he was running out of daylight.

The sky was clear, moon full, and stars twinkling on a velvety black canvas high in the heavens, a beautiful night to be out, not to hot, not to cold, perfect; Jace decided to stop by a stream and camp for the night. He was drawn to nature as the rest of his people had been for millenniums; he looked forward to a restful sleep under the stars. Reaching into a bag on his bike, he retrieved a pouch and sprinkled a very fine powder on the ground under a very large hickory tree. Within minutes, the area was covered with what looked like fresh new cushiony moss; the powder combined with the natural elements of the earth formed a bio-bed, a genetically compatible homeostasis mat, a comfort mat to maintain optimal body temperature and function.

Jace spread out, arms and legs outstretched, releasing the tension of the day, gazing at the sky; his mind drifted, drifted to the past, the distant past when peace abounded and no one knew about the Emigee, the destruction, or the never ending fear. The time of the ancient ones, great cities, timeless music and art; a time when the earth was whole, lush and fruitful, unmarred by the destruction, when happiness flourished. A time when Te'rellean civilization had prospered for millenniums before the destruction; when science and advances in technology enhanced life, worked in harmony with our mother earth, the provider of all that is good. Far different than the advances made today which destroy, mangle, and decimate the earth, she will die if something was not done soon; the Emigee have no regard for the natural order of things and the humans follow in their wake. With heavy eyelids, he wondered, *'What can be done? What can be…'*

◆◆◆

Running… he was running as fast as his little legs could carry him back to the cottage. Closer he was getting when he saw a shadow, a shadow forming out of the dark smoke suspended through the village. Eerily floating toward him;

Jace stopped in his tracks, a chill ran through him fearful another soldier was approaching. He rubbed his eyes trying to clear the tears clouding his vision; it was no soldier approaching, a familiar figure—his mother. His mother was approaching as she was frantically searching the village for him.

"Mother…I'm here…" he cried out gleefully. Tears of fear and anguish instantly turned to tears of joy, relief, and exultation. His mother swept him up in her arms and exclaimed, "Where have you been, we have been looking for you everywhere!" Squeezing him, relief flooded through the beautiful dark-haired woman. "We must go! We must find your father; he is searching for you outside the village."

Carefully they made their way to the edge of the village when out of the smoke appeared a soldier, an Emigee soldier. Jace was shoved behind his mother protectively; doing anything to protect her son, she readied herself. The soldier grinned fiendishly as he saw the determination on the woman's face, excitement surged through him. He had a pistol in hand but put it away. Reaching for his blade, his bloodthirsty grin widened. Keeping Jace securely behind her, she kicked off her shoes. Manipulating the earth was her ability, but she had to have contact with the ground. Planting her feet firmly in the soil, tendrils of dirt wrapped around the Emigee's feet immobilizing him.

Struggling to free himself from the soil, he reached for his laser pistol, but the slithering tentacles from the earth meandered up the length of his body to secure his extremities. Jace peeked out from behind his mother to see the soldier firmly encased like a statue molded from a sculptor's clay.

Grabbing Jace's hand and pulling him to her front, she whispered, "We must find your father…*Run!*"

Running as fast as he could Jace and his mother were approaching the edge of the village; his father waiting. Joy flooded through him as each step brought him closer to the man he had been urgently searching for, the man who always chased away his fears. Within a beat of his heart, he watched his father's happy relieved face turn to horrified terror, anguish, and despair. As if he was moving in slow motion, Jace turned to discover what his father had seen. Disbelief in his eyes, he saw another Emigee soldier, viciously, sadistically, yank his mother to the ground and plunge his blade into her heart twisting and turning as he glared savagely, vindictively in their direction.

Two as one screamed in anguish, "*Nooooooooo!*"

Chapter

Discovery was enlightening but extremely frustrating. A few weeks passed since the revelation of her adoption. Ari was glad to know the circumstances of how the Lovell's had come to welcome her into their family; she couldn't have asked for better parents. The quandary she faced was daunting; how was she ever going to find out who she really was, where she came from? All she had was a pendant with writing no one could translate. Frustration, growing daily, was starting to affect her; snapping at her parents and friends increased in frequency.

After Ari had completed her chores, she decided to take Snowflake out for some exercise. Of course, that was just an excuse, Ari needed to clear her head, decide what to do, and figure out the best course of action to take to discover her true origins. Riding the trails gave Ari a sense of belonging, a fellowship with nature she felt nowhere else. A deep-seated serenity and contentment she found with all living creatures flowed through her when she was meandering the trails. It was as though when she was amidst the giant towering trees, the forest's canopy, she was an integral part of them, sharing the peaceful tranquility in which they thrived.

Urgently she felt the need for some sort of serenity, peace; peace to ease a troubled mind was exactly what she needed. Snowflake was happily trotting along the long winding trail leading higher into the mountains. The gentle rocking on Snowflake relaxed Ari enough for her mind to stretch out like tendrils into the surrounding forest. Squirrels gathering their nuts, deer drinking from the stream, a bobcat prowling a rock cliff, and a bear foraging for berries she watched.

Ari blinked, then, quickly surveyed the immediate area anxiously; alarmed by what she had seen, relief surged. She was alone and safe, the only animals around at the moment were a few chipmunks and birds singing in the trees. Ari was amazed; she had seen all of the other animals with her mind as it pushed out from her core into the surrounding forest. In the past, she was able to recall images clearly in her mind; familiar surroundings, but she didn't know if peering into the forest seeing unfamiliar surroundings was a new ability. Ari found herself questioning everything she did, not knowing if it was something she was always able to do or not. With her new healing ability, she wondered what other abilities she had or would develop.

She continued on her way up the mountain path enjoying the sights, sounds, and aromas of the forest. Losing herself in the fragrances of the musky earth, the pine trees, and the wildflowers, she allowed her mind to stretch out into the forest again. She came upon the creek but this time an unexpected sight was seen. A young man was crouching at the creek bank to fill a bottle. He was dressed in blue jeans which hugged his lean muscular frame like a second skin. His tee-shirt similarly hugged his broad back and shoulders outlining tightly sculptured muscles rising from his waist up his back to broad shoulders then down the length of his bronzed colored arms. What a sight to behold Ari thought, she had never seen anyone more magnificent in form in her life. If he would just turn around so she could see his face, she felt an intense need to see this man which surprised her. After a few minutes, Ari's hope was fulfilled. The young man turned. Ari gasped when she saw his face, an incredibly beautiful face. He was something out of mythology, a god, to perfect for this world.

Ari drew breath again, she hadn't realized she was holding it, forgetting to breathe; she was enthralled. She had seen handsome men before but never had she seen a man who was perfectly flawless. Deep ebony hair with wavy curls reaching to just below his ears enticed her, she had an urge to run her fingers through the soft curls. His face was square, manly and rugged, not a hint of facial hair; his skin looked as smooth as baby's skin, like silk. It was a contradiction from what she knew men to be, but nonetheless there he was, unique. His eyes were the most exquisite emerald green, vibrant and captivating. Ari was caught by his eyes, pressure rising from her core, warm and tingly; never experiencing such sensations she was disturbed by the feelings stirring within her. She broke off from admiring his eyes, to assimilate all. His nose was slender and straight, his lips were thick. Ari wondered what it would be like to kiss those thick lush lips.

It was getting extremely warm, her face blushed rose; it felt like she had worn too many clothes for her ride. If the creek wasn't occupied, she would have ridden to it, plunged into the cool water for the relief it offered. Never had she experienced such feelings for any boy or young man before, it was quite a surprise.

There had been boys and even men who had shown an interest in her but none of them stirred in her the feelings this man did. Suddenly, as she was watching him, she noticed movement in the background. Ari scanned the area, moving slowly along the tree line was a bear. The bear she had seen earlier was coming up from behind the man; he hadn't noticed. Ari gasped and immediately set Snowflake off galloping toward the creek. The young man was going to be mauled to death and he would never see it coming from behind him. As she was twisting and turning through the forest, Ari's biggest fear emerged, 'what was she going to be able to do about the bear'?

Ari was terrified for the man, he didn't see the danger he was in from the deadly animal. He was to perfect to be torn apart, shred into pieces. She had to do something, but what? What could she do against a bear? As she was racing to the creek, she could see the bear rear up on his back legs and let out a loud growl. The man jumped but didn't panic which was good. The last thing a person should do when confronted with a bear is run. He was standing his ground but so was the bear. The man was slowly backing away when suddenly he jumped and turned in the other direction, the direction Ari was coming from which left his back toward the bear. The bear started running toward the man. Ari panicked, instinct took over instantly; she saw a log about the size of a fence post, probably felled by a beaver, lying on the ground. Without thinking about what she was doing, she motioned with her right arm. The movement she made was as if she was picking up the log to swing it at the bear, all the while she was maneuvering Snowflake between the bear and the man. The log went flying at the bear hitting him in the head which made him run off in the other direction. Ari and the man watched as the bear ran off into the forest.

Turning her attention to the man Ari exclaimed, "Are you alright?" Heart racing, pounding rapidly, she struggled to rein in her fear.

He just stared at her in amazement. So stunned at what he had just witnessed, all he could do was shake his head yes. Ari dismounted from Snowflake and led him over to the stream for a drink, giving her a chance to compose her feelings; she found herself weak kneed and trembling, not the first impression she wanted to make.

Ari turned to the young man and said abruptly, "Who are you and why are you here?"

That question brought the man back to his senses. Enthralled and amazed at what happened and so awed by the beauty of this young woman he was speechless. As he gathered his thoughts, he displayed a dazzling smile and replied, "My name is Jace. I was heading toward the Lovell Ranch, but I think I got turned around somehow."

He took her breath away, no one should look so magnificent, even more so when he smiled. "You didn't get turned around too much, you passed the road to the main house a few miles back. This is the Lovell ranch. My father owns the ranch and the mountain," said Ari fighting for some semblance of calm.

"Great...would you point me in the direction of the main house, Miss Lovell? I would like to talk to your father." Jace asked as he smiled at Ari again; a smile that lit up his whole face making Ari's heart flutter. He was perfect before, as she watched him with her mind, but now up close, he was beyond perfect, an Adonis. Ari was breathless.

Hesitantly, because she couldn't think straight with him so close, she gathered her composure and replied, "My name is Ariella, but my friends call me Ari." For some odd reason, she felt herself getting warm again as the blush rose through her cheeks. Never had she had this reaction when speaking with others, he was different, something more than his obvious beauty, but she couldn't put her finger on it; she wanted to know why. Continuing Ari said, "I can point you in the right direction, but my father won't be home until later this afternoon. He went to town for supplies."

"Oh...do you mind if I wait on the ranch Ari?" Jace asked. At hearing him say her name, Ari became a little flustered, again. All she could do was nod her head to answer, no she didn't mind at all. She was not herself, she was acting like her neighbor down the mountain and didn't like it one bit. Jace was for some unknown reason making her senses go askew. Bringing her attention back to him, Jace asked cautiously, "In that case...can I ask you a question?"

"Sure...you can ask but it doesn't mean I'll answer," Ari replied with a little laugh, regaining some of her composure. They both chuckled.

"Fair enough...what just happened here? Did you make that log hit the bear?" Jace was watching Ari with a discerning eye. All the color drained from her face, he could see she was getting nervous, grabbing for the reins of her horse and fidgeting.

How should she respond, she certainly wasn't expecting that question? A stranger, she didn't know this person, but even so, somehow, she felt as if she could trust him. Deciding to answer cautiously, she averted the question.

"Now how could I possibly be responsible for moving the log without touching it? It must have been the wind." She shrugged and turned away from Jace.

It was no answer and she knew it, but she suspected she was the one who caused the log to fly at the bear. Ari had no answers as to how it happened, besides who would believe her except her parents. How did she pick up the log, let alone swing it at the bear? So many unanswered questions, how was she ever going to find out?

"The wind?" Jace said, watching Ari skeptically. Who was this beautiful young woman? From the moment she came galloping out of the forest with her glorious red hair blowing in the wind, something about her intrigued him. He was never attracted to humans before, but she was exquisite, stirring feelings in him he never experienced before. Was she human? If she was, how did she throw the log? Or was she something more? As he was assessing her, his eyes came to rest on the pendant around Ari's neck and his eyes grew wide with excitement, things were starting to make sense. Carefully he changed the subject. "That's a beautiful pendant...did you buy it or was it given to you?"

Relieved by the new topic Ari responded cheerfully, "I've had it since I was a baby, but my parents just recently allowed me to wear it."

Jace nodded, she was one of his people, the one whom he had come to find. The more he spoke with her the clearer the mystery became, it made sense now; he couldn't figure out how after seventeen years the signal would all of a sudden be initiated. The pendant and the contents of the case had vanished in a freak accident. The leader of his people had ordered the Adirondacks searched three times with no success. All hope had vanished for the Te'rell and billions of humans, even though the humans had no clue that one freak accident had doomed them to a life without hope.

Out of nowhere, two weeks ago a signal was received at the tracking center, a signal from the pendant. The child, thought to be dead, was alive, reviving hope in her people for a bright future. The excitement that ensued bought new life to the Te'rell. The child, Ari Lovell, had so much to learn about herself, her people, and her abilities. Jace knew he would have to gain her trust before she would accept what he had to say. He just hoped the Emigee didn't find her before they were ready.

After several minutes of silence, Jace asked Ari about the ranch, "I was told by the owner of the G & T, the store at the base of the mountain, that your father is looking for workers. Is that true Ari?"

Ari was very surprised but said, "Yes…he hires a few seasonal workers each year mostly in the spring, some in the summer, and a few in the fall. He has to let them go for the winter months there just isn't enough work for them to do when the weather is bad. Is that why you want to talk to my father?"

"Yes…I need the work. What type of ranch do you have?" Jace asked.

"We have a little bit of everything, cattle, chickens, pigs, and goats, but mostly we have mustangs," said Ari with a grin.

"Like the one you're riding?" he said admiring the horse reaching out to pat him down. Jace loved horses and Ari's horse was a beauty.

Ari noticed that Jace wasn't afraid of horses which endured him even more to her. Less nervous the more she spoke; she was relaxing, behaving more like herself with Jace. "Yes…Snowflake was born on the ranch two years ago. He's my baby; I was there when he was born, and we've been together ever since. We have the best mustangs on the east coast," Ari said.

Looking around at the idyllic setting before him, Jace admitted, "I don't know how I missed the road to the main house, I guess I got caught up by the beauty of the forest."

"You appreciate nature, many people are oblivious. Most people are too busy to notice the abundance of life so prevalent around us." Appreciatively, Ari looked around from the creek to the trees inspired by the beauty around her. She couldn't believe she had so much in common with a man she had just met.

Jace couldn't have been more pleased; she had a deep love for the earth and nature. Jace confessed, "When I'm out here in the forest or anywhere alone away from the modern world, the earth sings to me. Listen, can you here it?"

Ari closed her eyes after she sat down on a large boulder at the creek bank. She heard the water flowing down stream, the leaves rustling in the wind, the birds singing, the squirrels chattering, and the foliage rustling; then as she focused, the random sounds developed into a symphony unlike anything she had experienced. It was whispering her name '*Ari…ella…Ari…ella…*' "It's calling my name…Jace…I can hear it calling my name." Ari was thrilled. Her abilities were becoming more defined and easier to access.

After some time listening to the euphony of their surroundings together, Snowflake wandered over to Ari and nudged her. Bringing her attention to Snowflake, she realized she had been gone from home to long. It was amazing how quickly time flew by with someone who appreciated the same things. Talking and laughing as if she had known Jace her entire life even though she had just met him; Ari felt a kinship she never felt before, not even with her parents. Ari glanced up at the sky. The sun was starting its decent in the west, late afternoon by her estimation, supper would be ready soon. Ari turned to Jace and said, "It's getting late. I have to get back. If you want to follow me, I'll show you where the main house is located. My father should be home by now."

Jace agreed, concerned he asked, "My bike isn't going to upset your horse is it?" He pointed over to the edge of the forest where his sports rider was parked. The motorcycle was big black and sleek. Streamlined for speed, the bike looked menacing but excitingly thrilling.

Ari was thinking how much she'd like to ride on the back of the bike with Jace so she could wrap her arms around him. Snapping back to reality, she started to scold herself. 'You just met this guy, first you want to kiss him, now you want to go off riding a motorcycle with him. What's wrong with you today, you never act this way?'

Annoyed by her thoughts and the feelings Jace evoked, she continued to chastise herself. She was attracted to him for sure, but it was more than that, it felt like they were kindred spirits, her yin to his yang, two halves of a whole, like they had known each other for centuries; but they had just met. Ari knew she needed to exercise a little caution, after all she knew nothing about him.

"Snowflake is very calm and gentle he won't be upset by the motorcycle." Ari assured Jace as she mounted Snowflake. Ari settled in the saddle and watched Jace as he sauntered over to the bike; even his walk is perfect Ari thought.

Jace mounted the bike then turned to Ari and nodded for her to lead the way. Ari headed for the trees, she navigated masterfully through the forest to the trail. They were about fifteen minutes from the main house.

"Martin she has been gone all afternoon. I know she knows the trails like the back of her hand, but I have an uneasy feeling," Ena said as she was helping to unload the supplies from the truck. Ever since the adoption talk, she had an uneasy feeling, a feeling that she would lose Ari.

Martin stopped what he was doing, took Ena in his arms to comfort her and said, "If she's not back by the time we're finished unloading the supplies, Hank and I will go out and look for her. Stop worrying, we'll find her."

No more than two minutes later, Martin, Ena, and Hank looked up and saw Ari riding up the driveway on Snowflake followed by a young man on a motorcycle. The two men looked at each other with that all knowing look men have when 'girl meets boy' is the scenario. Ena was just relieved.

"Well looks like she brought home another stray," said Hank with his crooked grin. Martin just rolled his eyes. Hank was a permanent ranch hand and had been with the Lovell family for over twenty-five years. He was hired by Martin's father before the ranch passed to Martin. A cantankerous old fella, Hank was gruff but had a heart of gold. He would do anything to help a person out but he'd blister an ear first with his ranting and raving, it was his way. Hank had the characteristic mountain folk look, average height and stout. About fifteen years Martin's senior, Hank had a seasoned look, salt and pepper hair—more salt than pepper, weather beaten skin that looked like old leather and a scruffy-looking beard with streaks of grey. The most incredibly appealing thing about Hank was the impish sparkle in his dark brown eyes that didn't make him as threatening as he would have liked. Hank was like a member of the family and teased Ari like an uncle, she just adored him.

Ari rode up to the truck where her parents and Hank were unloading supplies. Jace pulled alongside her and turned off the motorcycle. When he removed his helmet, everyone went still. The similarity to Ari was incredible, the flawless beauty, the same sleekness and height, and his skin even though it was bronze was identical to Ari's in texture, firm but silky smooth with not a single scar noted.

Ari said, "Mom, Dad, Hank this is Jace. Jenkins from the G & T told him about the seasonal work we have up here. We met in the forest by the creek. He missed the road to the main house."

"Nice to meet you Jace," said Ena with a welcoming smile and all the warmth of a loving mother.

"Jace," Martin nodded and added, "So you're looking for work?" Martin with his eagle eye was cautious but polite. He couldn't help but wonder about the similarity between Ari and him.

Jace acknowledged each one politely but focused his attention on Martin. "Yes sir, I hope you haven't filled all the positions Mr. Lovell."

"No…I haven't yet…Jace…do you have any experience working on a ranch?" Martin asked listening intently to every inflection, carefully scrutinizing Jace's every mannerism, wondering. Wondering why Jace was here, now, what his motives were, and why he was in the forest.

"Yes sir…I grew up on a ranch in Colorado. I've done everything from round-up to cleaning out stalls in the barn. I work hard and do what I'm told." Jace assured Martin who raised a brow and glanced at Hank.

"Do you have references?" Martin asked. Ena elbowed Martin in the side, then with a nod motioned for them to go into the house to talk about things in more detail.

Hank wasn't going to wait to get an answer to the question, he wanted answers, so he asked boldly, "What made you leave Colorado young gun?"

Jace turned to Hank, "Well…I wanted to see the rest of the country. So I travel from ranch to ranch in different states looking for seasonal work. I make enough money to support myself and I meet a lot of nice people. I see the sights then move on to the next locale." Jace turned to Martin and replied, "To answer your question Mr. Lovell, I have several letters of recommendation."

Martin was starting to relax a bit then added, "You won't mind then if I check your references will you Jace?"

Jace smiled warmly, "Not at all Mr. Lovell, I hope you do."

"Good…now that the background info is taken care of, Jace we would like you to join us for supper wouldn't we Martin?" Ena said cheerfully as she glanced at Martin for affirmation.

"Yes…Jace we would like for you to join us for supper." Martin added as he gazed affectionately at his wife. Ena would never let anyone leave the ranch hungry if she had anything to do with it. Hospitality was very important to Ena for which Martin was thankful; it would give him an opportunity to converse with Jace, to get a better sense of the young man who so remarkably resembles his daughter. Having similar features to Ari can't be just a coincidence.

The evening was pleasant, the family warm and welcoming. Ari was an intelligent girl considering that her education was limited by the standards of their people. Jace had to report to the leader that contact had been made and everything was proceeding as planned.

In the meantime, Jace knew he had to take every opportunity to gain Ari's trust. He just hoped he could keep his mission and his feelings separate. When he had first seen Ari ride out of the forest on her snow-white steed, he thought he was dreaming. Her glorious red hair billowing like flames in the wind around that angelic face so radiantly brilliant; he was momentarily suspended in time, unable to catch a breath. Stirring something deep within, almost primal; a need, a deep-seated desire, feelings etched in the inner recess of his very essence, she pierced a part of him long hidden. The part of him he kept well-guarded; encased and sealed. No one had breached his barrier, she was dangerous but oh so beautiful. Not only was she beautiful, she had an innocence that he hadn't expected or seen for such a longtime, unfortunately, he knew he was going to have to teach her the harsh realities of their existence.

The following day after Martin had the assurance he needed from the reference checks, Jace was shown to his room in the bunkhouse by Hank. A surly old coot, Jace knew Hank didn't trust him and suspected he would cause some trouble, nothing Jace couldn't handle. Lost in his thoughts, Jace was settling into the workers quarters which were by far better than some of the places he had stayed at recently in his search for Ari. All the quarters were private even if they were small. To have a measure of privacy was an unexpected benefit. Each room had a single bed, a small table, and a wardrobe to store belongs.

Jace traveled light; just a couple of changes of clothes and his communication device was all he carried with him.

He would have to find a safe hiding place to store the communication device since he didn't want to have to explain it to anyone who might come across it by accident or by snooping. Hank was very protective of the family, he could tell, and might take it upon himself to look around a bit. Jace went from one end of the room to the other looking for a suitable hiding spot. Moving each piece of furniture, he checked the planking and floorboards. Wiggling the boards, he found a loose plank in the corner wall to which the bed was adjacent and was close enough to the floor that the bed covered any irregularities in the planking itself. Prying the plank out just enough, he slipped the com in behind it. Just as he secured the plank, he heard a light knock on his door.

Opening the door, he found Ari standing there; Jace smiled as his heart fluttered. "Ari is something wrong?" he asked. The attraction he felt was unsettling.

"No…I just wanted to see if you had everything you needed and to thank you," Ari said quietly, not wanting to tell him the other reason she had come. Ari felt a connection to him that she just didn't understand or want to let go of, she wanted to be close to him.

"Thank me? Thank me for what? I didn't do anything," said Jace as his interest mounted. His curiosity and the excitement she made him feel, was drawing him somehow. Even though he knew he shouldn't, he was more than willing to be captured by her allure.

"Yes, you did. You didn't tell my parents the circumstances of how we met and I appreciate it; they already worry too much. Since everything turned out fine, can we just keep the bear incident to ourselves?" Ari pleaded with her eyes. Ensnared, by a pair of captivatingly blue eyes, deep pools, ravishing Jace to the core, he dissolved like sweet warm butter on blistering hot day.

"Ari I'm not going to say anything to your parents, but you have to tell me, did you throw the log at the bear?" Jace asked gently as he assured her of his confidence. Trust was essential to their relationship; lives depended on it. She had to start trusting him, now was a good time to take the first step. What he had to teach her was going to take a leap of faith and trust would solidify understanding.

Ari didn't say anything for quite a while, and then she turned to look at Jace and was pulled by an invisible force, embraced by emerald green eyes, coaxing and pleading with her to tell him the truth. How could she resist? Resisting was futile, she could only hold out so long. She acquiesced and acknowledged, "Yes...I did it." Quickly she turned and ran out of the quarters. Jace was elated, it was just the second day and she had trusted him enough to acknowledge her ability to him.

Chapter

Jace didn't know when he had crossed the line from friend to something more, but he felt the dramatic, disturbing change. Ever vigilant, he was becoming obsessively protective of Ari; possessive, as if his life were dependent on his responsiveness, *no* harm could come to her. Jace and Ari were becoming close friends which was the plan; the problem was Jace was losing site of the boundaries between friendship and something more.

The something more he couldn't even think about; over the years, he had built a protective wall around his heart to keep out love, pain, virtually everything. It was crumbling; somehow Ari was breaking through his barriers and he was confounded as to how he let it happen. No one had ever penetrated his defenses but being with her was easy; she was funny, smart, and made him feel again, something he didn't think possible. He was determined to protect her, no matter the cost.

Last week when Ari's favorite mare was giving birth; she, as he was learning, was right in the thick of things, jumping in, getting her hands dirty helping Stardust to deliver. The mare, in the middle of a contraction, jerked and would have kicked Ari's head if he hadn't noticed and used his telekinetic ability to hold the mare's legs until she relaxed. It was a close call.

Just yesterday Ari was in the corral where Goliath, the prize bull, exercised. One of the workers was distracted, let Goliath into the corral to exercise and mate, but didn't notice Ari was in the corral. With no cows in the pen at the time, Goliath focused his attention on Ari and charged her. Again, Jace used his abilities to protect Ari just in time to prevent serious injury. It was becoming a habit, one he was becoming accustomed to; her need to be at the center of activity was going to make it difficult to protect her. How did she ever survive this long, he wondered?

Sunday was a day of relaxation on the ranch, customarily a day for cookouts and friendly competition between the men on the ranch. Ari had asked Jace if he would like to go riding with her. Of course, Jace jumped at the chance to be alone with her. It would be a perfect opportunity to reveal his secret. Jace was in the barnyard making ready his horse, Star, a high-spirited black mustang, when Ari walked out of the barn with Snowflake.

"Are you ready?" she asked as she flashed her sparking deep blue eyes and impish grin at Jace.

Stirring something deep within Jace, an intrinsic desire longing to be with her, touch her, hold her in his arms, he quivered. What was wrong with him, for years he had kept himself away from the entanglements of emotional sentiment, but he was letting this girl get under his skin, but the way she did, he wondered if he could escape it; no girl had ever affected him this way before. Focus, he lost his objective, he needed to focus his attention on his assignment not his feelings, but it appeared he was going to have to do both.

He turned to Ari, "I'm ready whenever you are." Holding Snowflake as Ari mounted and settled into the saddle, he handed her the reins, then, he mounted Star. Together they headed up the trail.

"So where would you like to go?" Ari asked with great anticipation. The mountain had many trails, each one with intoxicating vistas.

"Surprise me," Jace replied with a grin. He was trying to imagine a place he wouldn't like. As long as Ari was with him, he was content with everything; she had a way of bringing out his better nature.

Ari thought about it for a moment then said, "I have just the place. Follow me."

As she coaxed Snowflake into an easy trot, the two ascended higher into the mountains as they followed a meandering trail through the forest. The trees were thick as they lined the narrow trail; large, majestic old pines, hundreds of years old, guarded the way as if they were protecting the unscathed mountain beyond. The area was teaming with life, birds singing in the trees, smaller animals scurried away from foraging food after hearing the horses; it was a bustling community of wild creatures. After some time, they reached a plateau clearing. Dismounting, Ari tied Snowflake to a bush so he could graze. Jace did the same with Star.

Heading toward a large rock formation jutting out from the mountain, Ari took her favorite perch. "This is one of my favorite places to come when I feel the need for reflection. I throw my worries out over the mountains then wait. As I wait, resolution often comes to me. This is the perfect place, the picturesque beauty sets the mood, it's rivetingly breathtaking," Ari told Jace as she gazed out over the mountain's vista. Breathtaking beauty indeed, as far as the eye could see, glorious forms of rolling peaks and valleys, creation accentuated in dramatic array of colors.

Jace joined Ari admiring the spectacular view. A light hazy mist hung over the mountain tops blending the distinctive lines into subtle waves stretching to the horizon, ripples continually flowing like gentle waves over the ocean. A peaceful tranquility engulfed each of them as they admired the panorama.

"This is incredible." Jace said in amazement. He felt a peace he had not known for some time. He longed for peace, serenity, a private place to enjoy what the earth provided.

"How's that for a surprise?" Ari asked with a giggle as she watched Jace's face brighten with delight.

"It's an incredible surprise, one very much appreciated." Jace said still admiring the scenery, "But now I have one for you."

"A surprise—for me? What kind of surprise?" Ari asked curiously. Intrigued, she couldn't imagine what kind of surprise Jace had for her.

"I have something to show you." Jace said as he reached under his shirt and pulled out the pendant he wore around his neck. He slipped the pendant over his head and handed it to Ari.

Ari was stunned as she took the pendant in her hand and examined the markings. It was just like hers. Triangles etched on the front and on the back inscribed with the same masterful craftsmanship; different than hers but similar all the same.

"Where did you get this?" Ari demanded. The only link she had to her true identity and now another person had a pendant similar to hers.

"It was given to me when I was born." Jace explained slowly, "Everyone who is born to our people is given one of these pendants."

"What do you mean born to our people? Who are you?' Ari asked with excitement. She couldn't believe that she was talking to someone who would be able to answer her questions about where she came from, possibly knowing her true identity.

"Our people are called the Te'rell. I will tell you everything you want to know but I don't want to overwhelm you." Jace assured her. "The pendants are made for our people, each one is unique. The DNA from the person to whom the pendant will be given is embedded into the metal at the molecular level. It ties the individual to our people; it can only be activated by the person to whom it belongs and if they die it deactivates. All the pendants send out a unique signal detectable only to the Te'rell so our tracking center can identify and locate our people living in different parts of the world."

"So what you're saying is my pendant has my DNA in it...when my mother gave me the pendant, I activated it...when I touched the metal, it sent out a signal? That's how you found me?" Ari stated as she eagerly awaited Jace's affirmation. She was right on track but was completely overcome by the enormity of these revelations.

"Exactly," Jace confirmed, delighted that Ari was eager to learn more about their people.

"Why is it necessary for the Te'rell to keep track of its people so closely?" Ari inquired, she didn't like the idea of being tracked, monitored wherever she went; it was a new notion for her.

"We are at war with a group of people, outsiders, called the Emigee," Jace explained, careful not to give her too much information all at once, "we have been at war for thousands of years."

"Thousands of years at war is a long time to be in conflict. Why has the war lasted so long?" Ari asked; she was immensely curious but beginning to get concerned. At war she thought, what would this mean for her? Ari didn't like fighting, even when she studied the subject in schoolbooks, she discovered she had an aversion to the very idea of groups of people resorting to violence to solve their problems. She had never been at war with anyone. How would she deal with it now?

"This might be a little difficult to wrap yourself around at first, but I assure you it's true. Everything you have been taught about the history of the earth is false. It's not true, it is just propaganda set in motion to mislead the humans regarding their origin. The Emigee fashioned the humans to be a slave race, easily controlled and manipulated. No Te'rellean agrees with this philosophy. There are other reasons too but I don't want to scare you away already," Jace laughed. He didn't want to focus on the negative aspects of their history. He wanted to give her hope and encouragement, the negative would inevitably descend upon them soon enough.

"Humans were fashioned by the Emigee? We aren't human?" Ari mumbled—she was completely taken aback. "If we aren't human, what are we?"

"We are similar to humans obviously otherwise we wouldn't be able to blend in with them. We have superior intellect using a far larger portion of our brain's capacity than humans. We can be killed if a wound is severe enough, but many of our people are thousands of years old. We don't grow old and die; we also have self-healing abilities, minor wounds can be healed without difficulty with little to no intervention," Jace paused to let Ari recover from the shock she was experiencing. To suddenly be told that everything you have been taught was wrong, definitely takes time to assimilate. A strange expression came across Ari's face suddenly, almost comical.

"Are you messing with me? You think I'm a gullible seventeen-year-old country girl who is going to believe some far-fetched story just because you know I'm adopted and I don't know my real parents. Well, I'm not that naïve," Ari said defiantly as she shook her head in disbelief.

"You want proof?" Jace raised his brow and said, "Okay, I'll show you a few things." Jace took out his knife and sliced through his left palm; he cut deeply to emphasize the point and lifted it to show Ari.

Horrified that he cut himself; she ran to the saddle bag on Snowflake and grabbed a cloth. By the time she got back to Jace, his hand had stopped bleeding and was visibly healing on its own. Ari slowly sat back down on the rock next to him. She took his hand into hers and watched as the edges of the lacerated skin closed, new intact flesh appeared, perfect, no scar was left where the open wound had been moments earlier. Ari was speechless; astonishment wasn't even close to describing how she felt.

Jace pointed to three stones the size of baseballs and told Ari, "Watch the stones." The stones levitated about ten feet off the ground. They started to move in a circle like someone was juggling them. Ari's jaw dropped again, she was astounded. Losing count of the times she went slack-jawed; she wondered how many flies she had swallowed while learning about her people. She really did have to remind herself to keep her mouth closed.

"Some of us have telekinetic abilities which you already know about." Jace said as he smiled at Ari.

"Yeah but the only reason that log hit the bear was because I was terrified the bear would kill you. It was a fluke." Ari said dryly discounting her own abilities.

Jace tried to reassure her, *"I have known about and been using my abilities for years, since I was a baby. It takes practice to master the skills. You are only now discovering yours. Be patient and practice whenever you can, but don't let anyone see you or you could put yourself in danger."*

"How are we able to move things with our mind?" Ari asked as she was watching the stones.

"The same way you can hear what I say even though I haven't opened my mouth to speak," said Jace using his telepathic ability.

Ari snapped her head around to look at Jace. Slack jawed again, Ari thought to herself. Jace laughed.

"Can you read my mind all the time?" Ari asked horrified at the thought. She had been thinking some very private feelings about Jace that she didn't want disclosed to him.

"I can but I don't. Our people respect individual privacy and we are taught from infancy that it is wrong to invade another's thoughts deeper than random surface thoughts. Not all of our people have telepathic abilities, just like only some of our people have telekinetic abilities. Our society is built on mutual respect; we would never infringe upon the rights of others or use our abilities to harm others. Being raised around telepaths you learn at an early age to put up walls to block your most private thoughts, its like having several levels of interaction from casual to very intimate. You'll learn how to control this ability also. Have you ever been able to pick up someone's stray thoughts?" Jace asked.

Ari thought about it, going as far back in her memory as she could, she recalled a period of time when she heard voices in her head and explained to Jace, "When I was about three years old, I remember always hearing voices in my head. I didn't like it because it made my head hurt, so I pretended I was in a bubble and the voices eventually faded."

Jace smiled at Ari and nodded his head. *"You built your own barrier without knowing what it was you were doing. Now you have to let down your barrier to practice using your ability. Practicing this ability will strengthen the skill, it's like a muscle that has to be exercised; we will only communicate telepathically when we are alone until you master the skill. I want you to say something to me using only your mind."* Jace said as he coaxed Ari.

Ari was hesitant about lowering her barrier but decided to try; after a few minutes, she felt something, she likened it to pushing her hand through a piece of elastic or plastic wrap, it would only stretch so far before the barrier broke. In her mind Ari pushed her thoughts outward, if she pushed hard enough, they would penetrate her bubble.

Jace started laughing because Ari was physically trying to push her thoughts out of her mind. Her face was scrunched up and distorted from concentrating so hard. She did manage to get a few words to come through. Jace received, *'can…hear…saying.'*

"What are you laughing at?" Ari demanded as she twisted her face in frustration.

Jace laughed even more. "You of course, you are working way too hard. The key is to relax and let your thoughts flow from you. Put out your hands palms facing me and relax your mind and body. This is an exercise we did in school." Jace pressed his palms into Ari's palms to make a connection. Skin to skin, the world around them seemed to stop; the contact between them was electrifying. Excitement surged through Ari; she felt as if she could soar, lighter than air. The exhilaration encompassing Jace was like free falling from a plane, extremely unnerving; both were stunned at the intensity. Magnetism, a potent force of nature, had nothing on the compelling lure as they gazed into each other's eyes. "Physical contact enhances telepathic ability. It will also allow you to feel how I use the ability so you can do the same. Are you ready?" Both trembling slightly as he began.

Ari nodded. Jace started talking to Ari with his mind, *"Relax Ari, feel my words. I'm going to tell you a little bit about our history. As I do, feel the flow of words and if you have questions ask with your mind. Okay?"* Ari nodded 'yes' again.

"Many millennium ago the Te'rell developed naturally from the earth. We are the original inhabitants of the planet. We are one with the earth, our strength comes

from her. Our bodies have developed a specialized organ which allows us to interact with her, use her electrical and magnetic fields along with her elemental energy, and is also the reason we have our abilities. For thousands of years, we lived in peace and unity with the earth and each other. Our civilization was highly advanced and encompassed the whole planet. Our technology is still far more advanced than anything the humans have developed. After a time, several groups curious as to the nature of the universe and what lay beyond our planet formed expeditions which were launched into space to explore and colonize the galaxy, ten in all. Thousands of years passed from the time the colonists left until the Emigee returned," said Jace.

Ari broke into his thoughts, *"You…the Emigee were…Te'rell?"*

Jace continued, *"Yes, they were once like us but after so long a time away from our earth they changed. They lost some of their abilities and because they encountered many hardships, they became militant. When they returned, we welcomed them back with open arms. We would have integrated them back into our society and eventually we would have been able to heal the mental and emotional wounds they endured while away from home, but they had changed too much. They had other ideas; they were bent on the complete annihilation of our people."*

"Why would…want to hurt their own forefathers?" Ari thought trying to conceive a reason to explain such behavior, but for Ari there was no reason good enough to justify genocide.

"You are doing very good projecting your thoughts to me. You learn quickly, the more you practice the better you will get," Jace said as he smiled encouragingly.

Ari blushed and said, *"You're a good teacher. It really helped to be able to feel the way you feel when you project your thoughts to me. Relaxing, not forcing helps."*

"Are you ready to try it without the physical connection?" Jace asked even though he really didn't want to lose the physical contact with Ari. A growing need imbedded deep within was urging him to keep the connection, never letting it go, but in order for her to reach her full potential he had to challenge her.

Ari frowned, she liked the warmth from his touch; being close to Jace gave her strength, but he was right to encourage her, to do better, to refine her skills. Ari looked at Jace and said, *"Let's do this."* She slowly lowered her hands into her lap and closed her eyes. Taking a deep breath, she tried to relax. To

Jace she thought, *"How…I doing. Is anything I'm thinking getting through…you?"*

Jace laughed with delight. *"You are awesome! I received almost everything you thought. For someone who has suppressed her ability all these years, you really are extraordinary."*

Ari blushed again. *"Why thank you sir. I do try,"* she said as she laughed along with Jace. *"So, when we are alone or when we are with others and we want to speak privately we are going to use telepathy right?"*

"Yes, because the more you practice the better you will become. Are you up to practicing your telekinetic skills?" Jace asked.

Ari hesitated before asking, *"I'm not frightened or scared…but…how's that going to work?"* She thought how easy it looked for Jace when he levitated the rocks, but if it was that easy, why hasn't she been able to do it before now?

Jace saw her apprehension and thought to her, *"Your abilities all come from the same source from deep within you. Don't force it, let it flow from you. Try something simple first, take one of the rocks I used and pick it up with your mind."*

Ari focused on one of the rocks, took a deep breath to relax and tried to pick up the rock. Nothing happened at first. She took another breath and the rock moved an inch. Before long, she had the rock levitating a foot in the air then two…three feet in the air.

Jace grinned and praised her efforts, *"Excellent, now try to move it over to the tree line by the horses."*

Slowly Ari managed to move the rock an inch then two but was unable to move it to the tree line then back again.

"Very good," Jace said, *"You are definitely a natural; that was an advanced exercise. With your natural ability, it's amazing that you haven't used your talents before this. Or maybe you have and just didn't realize you were doing something amazing. Have any unexplained occurrences happened on the ranch when you were around, things moving that couldn't be explained?"*

"Well now that you mentioned it, there were a couple of incidents. Once Jasper, our dog, got too close to a rattle snake, a branch from a tree fell between the two before the snake could strike; it saved his life. Another time, my father and I went to the G & T store. Jenkins was on his ladder reaching for a case of solid rock salt; it was on the top shelf. He lost his balance, started to fall, and landed in a large container of

bedding that wasn't there a few minutes earlier. Do you think that was me?" Ari asked surprised at the implications. She had used her abilities and didn't even know she had.

Jace confirmed what she surmised herself, *"More than likely you used your abilities to save Jasper and Jenkins. Ari you have made great progress today, keep practicing when no one is around, you will gain control rapidly. That's enough for today."*

"Jace will I be able to meet more of our people?" Ari asked hopefully. "I have so many questions that I need answered."

"Yes…our people are very eager to meet you. I promise all your questions will be answered in time. You have so much to learn and I'm here to teach you the things you need to know. Be patient and learn well."

Chapter

"Big day today Miss Benjamin, is everything set for the meeting?" asked Stewart Braun.

Stewart Braun, not a handsome man, stout, a bit on the beefy side with a round face who had plump lips which always looked like he had just received a collagen treatment and a receding hairline with a tuft of wiry hair protruding from the center of his head, was his usual curt self. Tugging on his collar, a tell-tale sign of his anxiety, he approached the desk. It was difficult to ascertain a neck since a double chin occupied that usual space. His torso was compact, thick, which carried a rather large head and with his short stubby legs, he resembled a razorback. Stewart did have lovely deep rich chocolate brown eyes, but since they were masked by very large thick round glasses their beauty was concealed. In fact, his coke-bottle spectacles made his eyes appear squinty, even beady.

On days when important meetings were scheduled, everyone in the office was on edge; an extreme feeling of nervosity permeated the office due to his uncontrolled anxiety. Pacing back and forth in front of his executive assistant, Miss Benjamin, he continuously tapped on her desk with his sausage-like fingers. When others in the office observed this habitual peculiarity, they scattered, fearful they would be the next recipient of an explosive tirade which had occurred on numerous occasions. Obsessed, there was nothing more important to Stewart than to be successful; achieving an elite status devoured all sense.

The acquisition of money and power had consumed Stewart for more years than he could remember. It was a fluke that he was successful at all. Nearly abandoned as a child, his mother dead, his father a good-for-nothing drunk bent on brutal, merciless beatings; he was destitute, left to roam back allies, to fend for himself. Sleeping in any nook and cranny barely safe from predators, a far better alternative than living with a cruel drunk; he learned to survive.

Scrounging for food one night, he met Two Toe Joe. A drifter by circumstance Joe had been roving about for years and was making his way back to his hometown when he met Stewart. Something about Stewart reminded Joe of himself at that age with his big puppy-dog eyes; scrawny and disheveled, an imp frail and alone. An instant affinity formed with Stewart which surprised Joe who thought himself devoid of all feeling. He didn't have the heart to leave the boy without helping him, so he taught Stewart his tricks, trade secrets to survive on the street, to be invisible, especially to avoid the authorities. Learning quickly, Stewart was well on his way to becoming a first class thief in the South Bronx. There wasn't a lock made that could keep him out. His skill as a pick-pocket was masterful, all this by the age of ten. Stewart was so happy to have a friend. Joe was like the father he should have had, keeping him safe, talking with him, teaching him; but his happiness was short lived.

Coughing up blood and not eating, this once burly man was losing weight, becoming thinner and thinner; he was wasting away. Two Toe Joe was ill, severely diseased from a degenerate existence. Knowing he wasn't going to complete his journey home, Joe needed to assure his last task would be a godsend. Before he died, Joe worked tirelessly to insure Stewart's survival; one good deed for a lifetime of decadence.

Stewart woke one morning to find Joe blue, stiff as a board and not breathing, staring blankly into the air with an odd look of contentment on his face. Overcome by shock and sorrow, Stewart sobbed, heart-broken. The only friend he had was gone, left by himself, he was alone again. Stewart, hurt and angry, anguishing over his lose withdrew into the recesses of his mind.

Having no other choices, his talents provided a means to eat. Scrawny for his age, Stewart was a favorite target for bullies in the neighborhood. They delighted in using him as their personal punching bag whenever he defied them and didn't hand over his stash. Battered and bleeding after a particularly brutal beating, he was discovered by a giant. At least he was a giant to Stewart. Taken to the giant's lair, he was nursed back to health. At first Stewart thought he had gone to heaven. To be off the street, to have a bed to sleep in, food to eat, a kind word, but the generosity came at a price. A price he was still paying to this day—no way to escape.

Vorax, the giant, was massively large in both height and form with hard broad muscular shoulders and arms. Thick bulging bulbous flesh rippled under his skin, swelling like balloons, taut, ready to burst. Intimidating by any means, an asset he used effectively as a headhunter. Scouring the streets for orphaned and abandoned children, frail and helpless, the ones who were at the mercy of brutish bullies; Vorax recruited them for the Umbra. The Umbra a secret faction designed for a purpose. Once inducted into the Umbra it was for life; a life sentence, a member was released only by death, an unpleasant death at that.

At the time Stewart was game, he felt he had nothing to lose and everything to gain, especially after being seduced with promises of great wealth and power; it was better than living on the streets, at the mercy of thuggish brutes or living with a half-wit drunk. Some things come at too high a price; he didn't know that at the time. The consequences could hardly be imagined, the pain, the brutality, the barbarism; things he refused to recall. Suppressing memories of his childhood, focusing completely on acquiring power and wealth; Stewart survived as he unwittingly carried out the insidious plans of the Umbra.

An elite education is what the Umbra provided, an education of strategies designed for conquest, the acquisition of money, and power. Stewart was the youngest, also, the weakest link in the chain acquired, a chain of clone-like minions, thus, he was a target, forced to endure unrestrained harassment and ridicule. Different from the bullies on the street; his torment reached deep into the soul, tearing and ripping every moral fiber still alive within him. Any flaw in character punished, 'elite status' was perfection, cloned perfection, individuality erased, to conform to Umbra standards, the goal. Compassion and goodness had no place in the Umbra; hardcore ruthless minions, the desired result, kill or be killed, the mindset of each graduate. Somehow Stewart did graduate, but he still retained a conscience; a conscience besmirched by years of poisonous seditious ideology, but a conscience, nonetheless. He was flawed, not perfect, not a ruthless minion, he concealed this flaw with heightened anxiety the result.

The collusive nature of the Umbra required Stewart to bury the conscience that remained; drinking was his only solace, but even that was paltry. He had little relief except for the emptiness of greed and power; he immersed himself in the duplicity, the conspiracies, and the intrigues of the surreptitious Umbra. Bleak years followed; yes he obtained wealth and power, but no peace, no joy, no happiness. After three failed marriages, Stewart lived and breathed work, money, power; to his detriment stress, anxiety, and obsessive tics followed.

To effectuate complete power and control over the world's oil and mining system as the ultimate goal, he became CEO of Zenot, the world's largest oil and mining conglomerate. Today's meeting with the world's two largest financial institutions, C. J. Gashpo-Reman and Co. and Stagdon-Maschl, controlled by the Umbra, would solidify his position within the ranks of the elite or so he hoped. According to preliminary geological reports, a potential source of untouched natural resources had been located, a win fall. More extensive studies would have to be done but it was very promising. Stewart was very excited and could hardly contain his exuberance.

"Everything is ready for the meeting Mr. Braun." Isbeth Benjamin replied in her usual businesslike manner. Isbeth Benjamin was a very stiff no-nonsense type of woman who would crack a whip like a drill sergeant if you got in her way, most people stayed clear of her. Those unfortunate enough to slack off or not perform to her stringent standards paid the price. They were met with fierce censure, expecting the same quality standard from others as she, herself, gave to the company was essential. She was in control; no one in the office disputed that fact. Even Stewart conformed to her iron will most of the time; her rigorous organizational routine helped him attain success. She was so stringent and meticulous even her shoulder length raven-black hair which she wore pulled back in a twist was tight and rigid. Her eyes appeared to be cold and stern, crystal blue like slick ice, chilling anyone bold enough to make direct eye contact. The attempt to camouflage her icy eyes with rather oversized dark-rimmed glasses only intensified her intimidating appearance. The consensus among her co-workers was to obey and avoid.

Isbeth was the most efficient executive assistant Stewart had ever had and was invaluable to him. At times, it was as if Isbeth could read his mind he thought. He just wished she could speed up time to get this meeting over with, the anxiety was killing him.

"Is there anything I can do for you, Mr. Braun, before the meeting starts?" Isbeth asked as she watched Stewart pace back and forth several more times before stopping in front of her.

"No, I'll be in my office reviewing the survey. Thank you, Miss Benjamin," replied Stewart as he turned, walked to his office and closed the door.

What a creepy obnoxious little man Isbeth thought. As she watched him pace in his office, she rolled her eyes and shook her head; there was about an hour before the meeting, her boss would not relax the tiniest bit until the meeting was over. He would be back every five minutes until the meeting started asking if everything was ready. Just something more to be endured, the torturous pestering from Stewart, until it was over.

Clearing her desk, getting ready to leave for the day, Isbeth turned to check on Stewart. After the meeting several days ago, he turned from nervous wreck to happy camper in the blink of an eye. His mood-swings were worse than a hormonal woman with PMS teetering on the edge.

"Mr. Braun is there anything I can do for you before I leave for the night?" Isbeth inquired of her employer as he was sitting behind his unusually large mahogany desk drinking his nightly shot of 40-year-old Flengiddach Scotch rustling through a stack of papers in front of him.

Looking up at Isbeth from behind his coke-bottled glasses, he asked, "Miss Benjamin have you seen the new detailed geological report that was done of site 9801? I can't seem to find it in these reports."

"The original report has gone to the board for their quarterly meeting, but a copy should be in the geographical studies file in the cabinet. Let me get it for you." Isbeth said as she moved to the file cabinet. The man couldn't find his nose if it weren't attached, she thought. "Here it is. Do you need anything else before I leave?"

As she was heading toward the door, Stewart replied, "Thank you, Miss Benjamin, that's all I need for now, have a good evening."

After she left, Stewart thought he really didn't know what he would do without her. She was like a rare precious stone, priceless; irreplaceable. Picking up the report, he began to smile; caressing the paper like a lover, he swooned. Longingly he gazed at the report; he had the most lucrative venture of his career in his hands. When he met with the investors three days ago, all he had was the preliminary report which looked promising but still uncertain. Now he had confirmation of his suspicions. Site 9801 had the largest deposits of gold and silver he had ever seen in his life not to mention vast deposits of oil and natural gas. It was incredible to have discovered the site since most of the surrounding area's resources had been depleted for years. Completely enthralled, he wasn't going to look a gift horse in the mouth.

Expectation gripped him; he couldn't wait to let the investors know especially since they made him practically get down on his hands and knees to grovel for their financial backing. All of them, sitting back in their chairs smugly looking down their collective noses at him as if he was some kind of worthless animal to make sport with or even worse to blatantly humiliate; he felt like he was back in training again, reliving tortuous memories, memories he had suppressed. It sent a shiver down his back. The tension in the room was so thick Stewart could hardly put together a coherent thought. After what seemed like hours of deliberation and negotiations, they finally agreed to terms and signed a contract contingent on the detailed geological survey. Only one obstacle stood between ultimate success or unmitigated failure, the property owner.

What if he is not willing to allow drilling on his land, Stewart thought. The anxiety started to escalate as his heart raced. Unwittingly he started pacing back and forth frantically trying to analyze all possible outcomes and counter actions. Picking up his glass, he took a gulp as if it would help him come up with a solution. Then he stopped what he was doing as he came to the realization; the owner would have to be insane not to agree to such an extremely lucrative contract in which a percentage of the profits would be his for the use of his land. The owner would be a very rich man by the end of the venture. Stewart started to relax. One way or another he would know in a few days.

Chapter

7

Sunshine far and wide, not a cloud in the sky; it was an exceptionally warm and temperate spring, one beautiful day after another on the Lovell ranch. The men were rounding up a few stray mustangs that wandered to far from the north pasture. Ari's anniversary party was fast approaching, an event the whole ranch looked forward to; Martin had taken Ena into town for supplies. The party, something they did each year to celebrate Ari's arrival into the family, was no small event. Friends and neighbors gathered far and wide to kick back and have fun. For Martin and Ena, it was an expression of love; so grateful they were for Ari's miraculous survival and adoption into their family, celebration was inevitable. With everyone occupied, the main house and barracks were deserted except for Hank.

Suspicious and territorial by nature, Hank had unanswered questions, questions he was bound and determined to get answers to whether they came readily, or he had to dig for them. It was the perfect time to play detective, the ranch was void of activity. When Hank got a notion in his head, he just couldn't let it go, he had to act. Since Jace arrived, this nagging feeling that he was hiding something was pestering him. He didn't know what it was, but he was going to find out. Jace was an excellent worker, he never caused any ruckus, but there was just something about him. Flummoxed, he couldn't put his finger on it, maybe it was the fact that Ari and Jace were becoming close friends or that they were so similar in appearance or even that he never seemed to do anything wrong, which was odd in its self. It irked him; he didn't really know anything about Jace except for what Jace had told them. Very protective of Ari, she was the daughter he never had, and no one was going to meddle with her feelings. He was going to make sure that young fella didn't have any secrets that would hurt Ari.

Wide-eyed and on high alert, Hank took one last look around, looking to his right then to his left, to make sure no one was in the vicinity then he stealthily headed toward the men's barracks. Tip-toeing inside, he stopped to listen; then looked around again. Getting caught snooping was not on his list of things to do. Not a sound except for the slight breeze outside, nothing, not a peep, it was quite eerie—complete silence. The hair on the back of Hank's neck was bristling as he moved forward to Jace's room. One last time he looked up and down the hall, then, reached for the door handle. Hank slowly, quietly unlatched the handle and hesitantly pushed the door open.

BANG! A book fell to the floor. Hank jumped as a huge black blur swooped past his head screeching, *"Caaaw caaaw."* Wings flapping and talons outstretched, the formidable creature took another pass at Hank. So startled he hit the floor, heart racing in terrified horror. While covering his head and face to avoid the bird's razor-sharp claws, the raven attacked the intruder. On hands and knees, he tried to scramble out the door. Protecting her space, the bird continued to dive bomb Hank tearing at his shirt. It was all he could do to get out of the room in one piece and close the door. Out in the hallway Hank scooted up against the opposite wall panting to catch his breath.

Gathering his wits, he scanned the hallway looking for anything to defend himself against that crazed raven. Muttering under his breath, he started cussing. Showing that bird who was the boss around there just made the jump to number one on his 'to do' list. In the far corner at the end of the hall, he noticed a broom. Getting up, shaking himself off, he started toward the broom when he heard a noise out in the barnyard. Stopping to listen, he heard voices moving closer to the barracks.

He hurried to grab the broom. As nonchalant as possible, he tried to appear as if nothing was amiss, pretending to sweep the floor he began whistling an offbeat tune. Jace and the new man Andy walked into the room chatting and laughing. When they spotted Hank, they stopped dead in their tracks;

slack-mouthed they gawked. What a sight to behold, Hank in the hallway sweeping the floor looking disheveled and guilty. They glanced at each other in amazement struggling to contain their snickers. He was a sight to see, hair messed up with black feathers sticking out. His shirt sleeves were torn in strips hanging from his arms.

"Uh…Hank, are you okay?" Andy asked dumbfounded not knowing what to make of the situation.

"Course, I'm alright! Why wouldn't I be?" Hank snapped indignantly as he continued to sweep the floor, red-cheeked.

"Um…Hank, you have feathers in your hair and your sleeves are ripped to shreds," Jace replied trying to restrain a laugh after picking up Hank's random thoughts about the raven attack.

Hank glanced down at his sleeves and said, "Uh…oh that…got tangled in some wire this morning, just haven't changed yet." He couldn't think of an excuse for the feathers, so he just changed the subject completely, "What are you two doing here? Thought you were rounding up horses."

"We found them. They didn't wander too far from the pasture. We came back because we needed an extra bridle and rope. We'll be heading back out in a few minutes. I need to grab my extra gloves from my room first." Jace said as he started walking toward his room. Jace grabbed the door handle and swung the door open.

"No!" Hank yelled and hit the deck covering his head with his arms.

Andy glanced at Jace with a startled and bewildered look. Jace smiled, Andy went over to Hank and asked, "What's wrong Hank?"

Hank looked up, saw the two men gawking at him then peered into Jace's room. No raven—I'm on the floor like a damned fool and there's no raven he thought. Hank felt completely humiliated.

"There ain't nothing wrong!" Hank said as he got to his feet and stomped off to his room. Andy looked completely befuddled while Jace was laughing hysterically to himself. Jace thought, it served Hank right for sneaking into his room.

Entering his room, Jace closed the door. He looked around to see where Teta had gone. Two years before, Jace found Teta when she was a fledgling just out of the nest. Tangled in plastic string, struggling to get free, she was hurt and bleeding; she struggled so frantically the string had cut into her bone.

Jace detangled, healed, and fed her. Ever since then, she followed Jace wherever he went, even when he traveled.

Jace moved over to the window, a very large black streak flew past. On her second fly-by, she landed on the windowsill. Jace held out his hand and she took the sunflower seed he offered her.

"You've had a busy morning, haven't you? Were you protecting me Teta?" Jace asked as he cooed at her, "Well that's a good girl. You keep an eye on Hank." Teta blinked her eyes and picked up another seed.

Jace turned his head when he heard a knock on the door and Andy calling out, "Are you ready?"

"Yeah I'm ready; I'll be there in a sec." Jace replied as he grabbed a handful of seeds and laid them out for Teta. He grabbed his gloves and departed.

Listening…waiting for Jace and Andy to leave, Hank pressed his ear to the door. Hoping to get a second chance to search through Jace's room, Hank paced back and forth between the door and the window; he had to make sure the coast was clear. Determined, he would go prepared this time, he thought as he gripped the broom firmly in his hand. Hank peered out the window and watched as Jace and Andy rode off toward the north pasture.

Broom in hand, Hank stepped out of his room into the hallway, scanned for intruders then headed for Jace's room. Cautiously he opened the door, peeked his head in just enough to see if that devil bird was in the room. Sure enough the bird was perched on the windowsill eating. Hank shook his head as he marveled, eating seeds of all things as if it belonged there. Repositioning the broom in his hands, Hank slowly moved toward Teta. She blinked her eyes as she watched him come closer, not deterred she continued to eat. As soon as Hank was in striking distance, Teta screeched and spread her wings. Instantly, Hank ducked never taking his eyes off her. She took one swoop over his head and flew out the window. Hank quickly shut it before Teta could come back. Alright now, I showed that black devil whose boss, now I can get down to business, he thought.

Having no idea what he was looking for, he started with the wardrobe. On the top shelf, he found a leather duffle bag. Grabbing the bag first, he rifled through each pocket—nothing. Moving to the bookshelf, he examined each book—nothing. Foraging through Jace's clothes—nothing. Checking the bed thoroughly, he found nothing—absolutely nothing. Frustrated and about to admit defeat, he heard a faint clicking sound.

Click…click…click. Where was it coming from? Standing very still, he continuously surveyed the room to determine the direction of the sound; his attention was drawn to the bed. The bed…he had just checked the bed. No…it was coming from under the bed. Slowly Hank moved the bed away from the wall but still found nothing. About to straighten it, to put it back into place, he caught sight of the slightly raised plank in the corner. Ah ha… he thought; I've got him now.

He moved the plank with little difficulty and peered inside the wall to discover something metal reflecting the light. Reaching into its hiding place, Hank retrieved the communication device; a palm sized silver disk shaped like a hexagon with several dimples and peaks. As he was examining it, a slight vibration began to emanate from the disk; increasing in strength, it blasted Hank with an electric surge flinging him across the room like a rag doll. Crashing into the wall with a thud, he slide down to the floor. Dazed with his head whirling, he tried to focus as the room spun out of control. Completely sprawled out and motionless, he was on the floor for several minutes paralyzed and moaning. Gradually with persistent pins and needles painfully permeating his body, feeling returned.

Shell-shocked and hurting Hank regained enough control to push the bed back and drag himself to his room. Taking every ounce of energy he had to pull himself onto his bed to rest, he collapsed. Dammed fool he thought, couldn't leave it alone, always having suspicions about this or that; you're going to get yourself killed one of these days.

"Hank," Ari called out as she entered the barracks, "Hank, are you in here?" Ari looked around but no one was in sight. Looking for Hank everywhere, this was the only place she hadn't been. Promising to help her with the new colts, he never showed up which wasn't like him. Worried she started searching; if he told her he was going to do something, he would move heaven and earth to deliver. Ari knocked on Hank's door, "Hank, are you in there?" Silence, not a peep, it was almost eerie. Ari was about to leave when she heard a groan. Slowly she opened the door to peek inside; sprawled out on his bed, Hank looked half dead. She went over to him and asked, "Hank, are you alright? What's wrong?"

Looking up at her, eyes glazed-over, he was staring off into space, seeing her but with no recognition. Pale, a chalky grey hue, his skin glistened with moisture which terrified Ari. Grabbing his wrist, her hand was trembling, she gasped and felt his forehead with her other hand; diaphoretic and cold. Dying, he's dying, she thought as tears rolled down her cheeks fearful she would lose him; she started to go for help, then she stopped, turning back to him she decided to try using her healing powers instead.

Taking both of his hands in hers, she attempted to heal Hank. She could feel the energy forming around her, the power converging deep within her, flowing through her body moving into her finger tips as she held his hands. Healing energy slowly moved away from her into Hank. When she opened her eyes and focused on Hank expecting to see him completely healed, she was stunned and dismayed—it didn't work.

Running from the room, tears streaming down her face her heart was racing, she had to find help, but everyone was gone. Urgently she scanned the barracks as she sought to get help for Hank. What if he dies because I didn't get him help right away? It will be my fault, she thought. Consumed with guilt, eyes blurred with tears, she ran straight into Jace.

"*Ari what's wrong?*" Jace thought to her using his telepathy. What he got back through the sobbing was: "*Hank...dying....didn't work.*"

Jace darted to his room to drop off the package he was carrying. Straight off he saw the communication device on the floor and his window closed, Hank had been successful with his snooping. He was in trouble, serious trouble. The com's defense system scrambled neuropathways; anyone foolish enough to use his com could be dead within hours. Human physiology was fragile unlike the Te'rellean or Emigee's; deadly consequences were always the result unless treated promptly. Jace threw the package on the bed and hurried with Ari to Hanks room. One look at Hank confirmed his suspicions. Jace had seen symptoms like this before; Hank had received the full impact of his com's defenses.

Comforting Ari, holding her tight, he began to explain what had happened to Hank. "*Ari hear me. I know what's wrong with Hank.*" Jace began as he gently lifted her chin and wiped the tears from her cheeks tenderly. His heart swelled by the love and compassion she felt for that crazy old man. He was utterly and completely mesmerized by her inner beauty.

Ari stopped crying, looked at Jace urgently and asked, "*You...you know what's wrong with Hank? What? What happened to him?*" Before Jace had a chance to answer she added, *"Jace, I couldn't heal him, my healing skills didn't work even after I felt the power flowing from me!"*

"Ari…Hank was hit with a powerful electric surge from my communication device. I'll explain everything latter. We have to hurry if we are going to save him. I need to garb something in my room first," said Jace urgently as he raced to his room, grabbed a rock then quickly returned to Ari and Hank.

Ari was puzzled, *"A rock, what is that going to do?"*

Jace took her hand and walked her over to Hank's bed and said, *"This is not an ordinary rock. Remember where we come from. The earth is our mother; we have a special connection to her. This is a healing mooka. It channels the healing powers of two or more of our people through it to provide an increased concentration or focused regeneration energy. This will take all of your concentration. We will levitate the rock over Hank and focus our combined healing energy through the mooka to Hank. Are you ready?"*

Ari nodded as Jace moved around to the opposite side of the bed. Hank moaned as the rock levitated above his heart. Focused on the mooka, Jace and Ari's arms were outstretched, their wrist were bent with palms facing the mooka like they were pushing against it without touching the stone. Gradually a faint shimmer of energy began to flow down from the mooka into Hank. After several long minutes, Hank started to breathe easier and the color came back into his face. When the healing was complete, Ari sat next to Hank and caressed his head tenderly. He was not diaphoretic anymore—he was just sleeping peacefully.

"Ari let him sleep…he's going to need it." Jace encouraged as he walked around the bed and took her hand. They quietly left Hank and went to Jace's room.

Once there, Ari said, *"Jace is he going to be alright?"*

Jace nodded to reassure her that he would be just fine and replied, *"We got to him in time. He's very fortunate we came when we did. He could have very easily died."*

"What happened? How did Hank get your communication device?" Ari asked as she paced around Jace's room. She had to know how this happened and why.

"Well this is what I know…what I picked up from Hank's stray thoughts earlier today. Hank doesn't trust me. He thinks I'm hiding something, and he especially

doesn't like our friendship. He's afraid you're going to get hurt...become too attached when I leave."

"Oh, for goodness sake, the crazy old coot is trying to protect me!" Ari exclaimed as she shook her head in disbelief.

"He loves you, I can hardly blame him for having feelings for you, you're like the daughter he never had. When Andy and I came back to the barracks to get an extra bridle and rope, Hank was in here sweeping the floor. I should say pretending to sweep the floor."

"What? That's crazy...why was he doing that?" said Ari, stunned by the revelation. Hank never swept the barracks. It was one of those jobs he delegated to newbie's.

"The only thing I can think of was that he needed an excuse as to why he was in the barracks in the first place. Not only was Hank sweeping, his shirt sleeves were torn to shreds and he had feathers in his hair." Jace explained as he started to chuckle, recalling the site.

"Feathers? Why did he have feathers in his hair?" Ari asked curiously. He must have been quite the site to see, she thought.

"Well I have a friend who has been following me everywhere I go for the last two years since I rescued her. Her name is Teta, she's a raven. I leave seeds out for her during the day; with my window open, she can come and go as she pleases. When we asked Hank about the feathers in his hair, his mind was flooded with thoughts about the black devil in my room. Apparently, he startled Teta and she attacked him. Teta stopped Hank from searching my room this morning." Jace laughed and added, *"You should have seen Hank he was a sight to behold."*

Ari was shocked and a bit outraged, *"I can't believe he would invade your privacy like that even if it was to protect me."*

"He loves you." Jace said as he shrugged his shoulders. *"A person can do crazy things to protect those he loves."*

"Still it doesn't make it right. I'm going to talk to him about it in the morning!" Ari stated with that determined look she gets when her mind was made up. She was a little more than annoyed with her favorite old coot.

"Let it go Ari, I think he's learned his lesson," urged Jace. Understanding Hank's need to protect Ari, he didn't want to cause him anymore discomfort.

"Jace, if Teta stopped Hank how did he get the communication device?"

"When I went into my room to drop off the package, I noticed that my window was closed, and my com was on the floor. Hank must have tried again after Andy and I left; he closed the window to keep Teta out. He searched my room thoroughly because I had my com hidden behind a loose plank in the wall under the bed. In order to find it, you'd have to be looking extremely hard." Jace explained as he moved the bed out to show Ari where he had hidden the com.

Thorough search was an understatement. Hank must have gone over the room with a fine-tooth comb to have found where Jace had hidden the com, Ari thought. Nodding to Jace she asked, *"Why does your com have a defense mechanism?"*

"Our lives depend on us having the most up to date info; so being in communication with our people is essential. If the com fell into the wrong hands, it could be disastrous. Each com is keyed to the owner's personal DNA profile; genetically the com is an extension of the owner. If anyone other than the person the com belongs to attempts to use it, the defense system is activated. Because it delivers such a powerful surge, the healing power of just one of us is not enough to overcome the trauma to the cells." Jace said as he picked up the communication device to inspect it for damage.

"So, if I picked up your com, I would be zapped with the power surge too?" Ari asked with great interest. Curious, she wanted to see the com, hold it, touch it; this was something tangible from her people. She longed to know more.

Jace grinned at her. He could see the eager anticipation growing in her and said, *"You want to hold it don't you?"*

"Of course I do, it's the first object I have seen from our people. I want to know everything about it and how to use it." Ari said enthusiastically. Hoping there was some way to turn off the defense mechanism so she could inspect the device.

Jace handed Ari the com. Her eyes grew big with excitement. *"I turned off the defenses so you can examine it without any harm coming to you. When I turn off the defensive feature, any of our people can handle it, but the Emigee or humans will still be repelled by the power surge."*

"So how do you make it work?" Ari asked. Like a kid in a candy store eagerly awaiting her goodies, she wanted to know every detail of its function.

"As you can see, the com has no buttons. All the controls are internal. Because it is keyed to individual DNA, each person has control over who can and cannot use his

or her com. For those of us with telepathy, the controls are activated telepathically. Just as our DNA is unique, so are our thought waves and patterns. Even though the com is small, it is very complex. I have given you access to use the com. You can access my messages for me, if you would like," said Jace encouragingly as he watched Ari's excitement over such a little thing.

If he wasn't careful, he was going to be hopelessly in love with her. He laughed to himself, who was he kidding, he was already hopelessly in love with her. How did that happen? He had to forget those feelings, push them out of the way; danger lurked everywhere, he was here to protect and teach her not fall in love with her, he needed to get a grip. She had no idea the extent of the danger she was in, if the Emigee knew who she was, they would stop at nothing to capture her, even kill her. Preparation was vital; she needed to be prepared for what she was going to face in the future. But he was helpless, falling deeper under her control; this beautiful spirited sprite had captured the heart of the lone wolf with her enchanting aura. With each passing day, the empty chasm of his heart, once filled with loneliness, was filling with joy, happiness, love; he was irrecoverably under her spell.

"Really!" Ari squealed with excitement breaking into Jace's thoughts.

He grinned and said, *"Really…It's very easy, just think 'play messages'. It's that simple."*

Ari took a deep breath, thought *'play messages,'* and a beautifully serene voice spoke stating: "Jace you have one message—The Emigee have found a new source of raw materials. Be watchful, will continue to update. End of message"

"Well that was short and sweet," Jace remarked as a frown came over his normally flawless face.

"Does everyone get messages about the movements of the Emigee?" Ari asked as she handed the com to Jace reluctantly.

"Yes…we are *all* in constant danger. The more informed our people are about Emigee activities, the better the chances are our operatives will be safe. Staying alert and forewarned regarding their movements and plans, keeps us alive," said Jace with concern. Ari became uneasy. Jace felt the change in her; sensing her feelings, he was becoming increasingly sensitive to her responses, instinctively he moved closer to her. Gently pulling her into the circle of his arms, he held her close.

Instinctively wrapping her arms around his smooth muscular back, she reciprocated. Feeling him...smelling his earthy scent stirred a smoldering fire within her that was threatening to engulf her in flames. How she loved his touch, the silky smoothness of his fingers sliding over her cheeks when he wiped away her tears for Hank. The confidence and assurance he evoked when he was near was enthralling. She had never felt so many sensations all at once.

Jace lifted her face to his and peered into her eyes fanning the flames building inside her. His eyes reflected the same fire. He lowered his head slowly as he raised her chin to capture her lips when suddenly there was a bang and clawing at the window. Jace and Ari both jumped simultaneously and looked to the window. Teta was trying to get in; at the same time they heard a car pull up the driveway.

Ari looked at Jace and sighed. "You better take care of Teta and I'll go help my parents."

Jace gave her a little smile, hugged her, and kissed her on the forehead, "I'll see you later; I'll go check on Hank." The intensity of his eyes screamed, 'don't go...don't ever leave me!' which gave Ari pause; she felt the same, but she had obligations, so she turned and walked out the door. Whatever was developing between her and Jace was private. She didn't want to explain her feelings for Jace to her parents just yet. So, she would continue as before, suppressing her need to be with Jace as she walked out into the yard. Greeting her parents with open arms, Jace ardently watched from the window.

Chapter

Buzzing with excitement, the ranch was in a whirl; men energetically darting here and there like bees dancing on flowers. Their vigor had paid off with the party preparations almost complete. For over a week, they were preoccupied setting up areas for different activities and games. The 'good ol' country shindig' as Hank called Ari's party finally arrived. The anticipation and excitement wasn't limited to the ranch, friends and neighbors had been talking about nothing else for weeks. It was the highlight of the summer with everyone expecting a rip-roaring good time. Within hours, friends and family would be gathering for the festivities.

Over at the roasting pit, Hank and Martin were dutifully tending the roast. Blurry-eyed they had gotten up early, before dawn, around three in the morning. Roasting the hundred-pound pig took time. Hank was fussing that the fire was too hot, and it was going to burn the outside which had Martin was spreading the fire.

Glancing at the pair from the window Ena chuckled, "Your father and Hank are fussing again," she called out to Ari.

Moving to the window Ari snickered, "You know they're not happy unless they're fussing about something." Shaking her head and laughing she hugged Ena, "You better go out there and referee."

The men were busy putting the final touches on the activity stations. The Lovell's always had several contests for the young ones like, bobbing for apples and the greased pig contest; for the teens there was the three-legged race, the human wheelbarrow race, and the archery contest, complete with prizes. Everyone went away with something. The children also played baseball, volleyball, and everyone's favorite football. There was no shortage of activities for the adults either. Martin always had several mustangs that needed to be broke; this was a favorite among the young men. Target shooting, roping, and axe throwing, stirred-up friendly competition. Young bucks always showing off for the young ladies. The women participated in the contests if they wished, but usually they enjoyed each other's company, played cards or board games, and watched the men be ravaged by untamed animals.

Once the guests started to arrive, they came in droves, almost all at once. No one wanted to be late and miss out; the first guests started arriving around one. Greeting the guests as they arrived was very important to Ari; it was tradition, but more important, she wanted everyone to feel welcome and comfortable.

As Jace came out of the barracks waving a rope he had been working on, he stopped dead in his tracks. Catching a glimpse of Ari, he gasped; she took his breath away which left him tripping over his heart-strings. In all his years, no one ever made his heart race with excitement like Ari; she was a vision. She couldn't get any more beautiful, he was sure, but he was wrong. Ari was radiant, bathed in brilliance; as the sun caught the deep red highlights of her hair, it was as if she was ablaze, as bright and luminous as the sun itself—she was intoxicating. Accentuating her eyes, she wore deep rich blue Capri pants, a sleeveless white tank, and a sheer blouse with glittering butterflies, cobalt blue, worn loosely which was fluttering in the wind. Everything about her, her very essence was captivating.

Ari caught a glimpse of Jace from the corner of her eye standing like a statue staring. She smiled, intending to make an impression, she was delighted by his reaction; a moment's recognition was all that was needed to capture Jace's attention. Thus Ari turned to Jace from across the barnyard and thought, *"Jace... are you alright? You're just standing there like a statue...Are you coming over to join the party?"*

Jace snapped out of his daze and as he walked toward Ari smiling, suddenly he felt uncomfortably warm. She noticed a slight blush on his perfectly masculine face as he approached.

"Ari you take my breath away. You will have to fight off all the young men here once they get a look at you."

It was Ari's turn to blush. Attention from young men, she never wanted it until now; the only man's attention she wanted was Jace's. Giving Jace a warm loving smile she turned to greet the guest who had just said hello.

As Jace was meandering through the crowd, a group of single young women approached him vying for his attention. Charming as usual, he was friendly and polite, not at all what the women wanted; some were downright aggressively flaunting themselves to no avail. Having eyes for one person, one person only; vigilantly he kept his eyes on Ari. Unable to help himself; she drew him like a magnet. Caught by the kindness that emanated from her, a unique quality in the world they lived in; she truly cared about each and every one of her guests. Jace watched, amazed.

Twyla, Jenkins's daughter, was surprisingly persistent in her flirting to gain Jace's undivided attention. Twyla was a beautiful young woman with sensual allure which she flaunted at every opportunity. Long silky blonde hair, big brown eyes set nicely above a pert little nose, appealing to most men, but not Jace. The problem with Twyla was she was a spoiled brat, a shrew. Given everything she ever wanted from the time she was an infant; Twyla had never worked for or taken responsibility for anything. When an object of her affections proved difficult to obtain, she would manage to cause such a scandalous display it was just easier for her father to give in, to get it for her regardless of the cost. Never lacking for male companionship, she was a vixen, in fact, many young men in the area claimed to be courting Twyla, it was all part of her game. She had to be the center of attention or she made everyone miserable, especially her poor father.

After several attempts at throwing herself at Jace, Twyla had become very frustrated, she was getting nowhere fast. All her attempts at seduction were ignored. No one ignored Twyla; it was unheard of, most men tripped over themselves to be noticed by her. Refusing to admit defeat, Twyla sat stewing, plotting her next move. Vigilantly Ari scanned her guests to make sure they were having a good time; several times she noticed Twyla's frustrated demeanor and decided to see what she could do to help.

"What's wrong Twyla, aren't you having a good time?" Ari asked genuinely concerned. Usually, Twyla was lively and trying to be the center of attention with all the men, but not today. Today she was sulking off in a corner trying to devise a scheme to attract Jace's attention.

"Oh, that ranch hand of yours, that Jace, isn't cooperating with me." Twyla snapped in exasperation stomping her foot as she spoke. She felt slighted which was a new feeling for her. Indignant, she was having one of her temper tantrums.

"What do you mean not cooperating?" Surprised, Ari said, "Has he been rude to you?"

"Yes…yes he has, I've used every seductive innuendo I know and he continues to ignore me like I'm not there," whined Twyla in disbelief.

"Well maybe he isn't interested," Ari said hoping to divert her attention. "Maybe he is more interested in the festivities."

Twyla looked at Ari as if she had two heads and said, "What…not interested in me? Impossible…everyone wants me! Besides I'm not talking about a lifetime commitment, I'm talking about having a good time…playing around…sex."

Ari's mouth dropped to the floor as she stood up. "That is a horrible attitude Twyla! Haven't you ever heard of love, loyalty, fidelity? If playing and sex are all you want, go do it somewhere else. This is a family gathering; that kind of behavior is not wanted or appreciated!" Fuming Ari left before she did something she would regret like use her telekinetic ability to throw Twyla into the pig pen. Envisioning Twyla flying through the air, landing in the mud with the pigs brought a devilish grin to her face. The more she thought about it, the more she liked the idea. It would serve her right.

Across the yard, the bronco busting was about to begin. Ari came up alongside Jace to watch. Brutus was the first horse up to break. A beautiful honey-brown three-year-old; he was very spirited and feisty. As Brutus was being lead into the stall, he started bucking and pounding the ground with his hooves, putting on quite the display. It was as if he knew what was coming, thus, telling the contenders to beware. The crowd gasped, the competitors held their breath as Martin pulled the name of the first contestant out of a bag. Whoever was going to ride Brutus first was going to get the full brunt of his spirit, the crowd paused as Martin unfolded the paper.

Martin called out, "Joe Morley will be our first contestant. He will attempt to tame Brutus. Hope you made out your will Joe." The crowd roared with laughter and started calling out jibes to Joe as well.

Joe suddenly turned pale and broke out in a cold sweat. Being the good sport that he was, he hesitantly wandered over to mount Brutus all the while saying his prayers. As soon as Joe was out of the mounting stall with Brutus, he was lying flat on his back in the dirt. Brutus tossed Joe off his back faster than a darting hummingbird. The crowd gasped and fell silent while they waited in anticipation for Joe to get up. When he did, the crowd cheered with relief. After Joe was helped out of the corral, the anticipation for the next contestant began to build.

Martin went through several contestants who all ended flat on their back in the dirt seconds after Brutus came out of the stall; Brutus was winning the day.

Ari thought to Jace, *"I don't think anyone is going to be able to break Brutus from this unlikely group of contestants."*

Jace smiled and replied, *"Well your dad hasn't called me now has he."*

Ari smiled and said, *"Is your name in the bag?"*

Before Jace could answer, Martin called his name as the next contestant. Ari drew in a deep breath. As she watched Jace walk over to Martin, panic set in. Jace said optimistically, *"Don't worry, it's alright. Horses like me."* Like Ari, Jace had a special instinctive relationship with animals, calming, soothing.

Brutus was waiting in the stall, pounding the ground, waiting for his next victim when Jace came up to him. Jace placed his hand on Brutus' head and slowly slide it down to his nose, then whispered something to Brutus. He then moved to the side to mount. When Jace was fully seated, the stall door was opened. Instead of seeing Brutus dump his rider as he had done previously, Brutus bucked once then let Jace trot him around the corral. The crowd roared. Ari started laughing at all the amazed faces in the crowd. She felt a great sense of pride in Jace. As he rode past her, she grinned at him as her heart swelled with joy.

Jace felt an overwhelming connection to this beautiful young woman as he passed by her. Stunned by the depth of his feelings, this revelation thrilled him all the same; he looked at Ari with more love than he had ever felt in his life. His life would never be the same without Ari in it, she made it worth living. Jace led Brutus over to the far side of the corral and dismounted. Whispering to Brutus again, the horse nodded his head like he understood.

Martin approached Jace and said, "Nicely done, you have a gift with horses," as he patted him on the back.

"We understand each other." Jace laughed as he watched the crowd, "I've always had a way with animals. They like me."

Martin laughed as he guided Jace with the arm already on his back, "I think we are done with the horse breaking. We ran out of contenders."

Ari met the two as they were walking back to the main party. "That was awesome Jace, what did you whisper to Brutus?" she asked as she smiled happily at her father and Jace.

Jace looked abashed and said, "I just told Brutus that he was beautiful, thus appealing to his better nature."

Ari and Martin laughed heartily. Martin said, "Well it certainly worked for you."

They wandered over to the roasting pit and met up with Ena and Hank. Hank gave Jace a wary glance. Avoiding Jace for the past week, Hank couldn't get his poise back, his confidence was gone. The day after the incident with the com, Hank woke up a little befuddled and couldn't remember anything, nothing from the past two days.

Intuition, his intuition never failed him; it was like having hundreds of creepy crawling bugs run across bare skin. A bazaar feeling to say the least, but one that never ever failed him; something strange had occurred and Jace was somehow involved. If only he could remember, he was racking his brains to no avail. Futile, no matter how hard he tried his memory eluded him. That feeling, that nagging feeling about Jace just wouldn't go away; something was off about him. Having no idea why he felt Jace was suspect, he determined to find out what it was and whether he was a threat to the Lovell family. Until Hank was assured of no threat, he was going to keep an eye on him.

"How's the roast coming along?" Martin asked.

"It's ready." Hank said gruffly as he motioned to Martin to pick up the other side of the spit. Carrying it over to the carving station alongside the rest of the food, they laid the pig on the foil. Taking the wire off the pig; the meat slid easily from the spit. With the spit removed, Ena started carving the succulent roasted pork. Ringing the bell, Martin signaled the food was ready to eat. Ravenous crowds flocked around the three tables. Each set up buffet style with mounds of food. Like locust swarming to devour the surrounding landscape, desolating every piece of vegetation. Beans, potatoes, salads, sweet potatoes, vegetables—all kinds, pies, cakes, cookies, the list went on and on; piles of food gone in minutes. It was amazing.

After everyone ate their fill, the games continued. Toward evening the older folks broke out their musical instruments and started playing and singing old mountain folk songs. It was a favorite part of the party for Ari. It made her feel wonderfully peaceful and serene.

Jace saw Ari coming out of the house and thought to her, *"Ari I have something for you… let's go for a walk."*

She strolled over to Jace and they headed in the direction of the west pasture, her favorite, where all the mares with their new colts were kept. As they strolled along the fence line to the west pasture, Jace began, "I have a gift for you, I did some checking with our people and I found out when you were born. That's part of my gift to you. It can't be easy for you not knowing the date you were born when everyone around you does."

Ari stopped and turned to Jace, tears in her eyes. She couldn't believe she would finally know the day she was born. How did he know it was something she longed for? He was amazing, she thought. "Really," she said excitedly, "….when?"

"This might be a little bit of a shock for you, but you have to remember that you were in stasis for a while before the Lovell's found you," said Jace cautiously as he continued. "Remember our life span is infinite unless we are mortally wounded."

Briefly Ari contemplated what Jace was saying scrunching her nose with inpatient anticipation. It didn't matter if she was shocked; she was too excited to finally, after all these years of not knowing, learn the date. She realized it didn't matter, she just needed to know and assured him, "It's okay Jace just tell me. I'd rather know the truth about everything."

Hesitantly, Jace whispered, "You were born January 6 in the year 1894."

"What?" Ari exclaimed, absolutely sure she had heard him incorrectly.

"January 6, 1894." Jace said slightly louder with no hesitation this time. He knew it would take some time to adjust. Finding out she was over a hundred when she had been raised human, was a huge shock; especially, when most humans never reached that age.

"Jace, that would make me 126 and a half," Ari said shaking her head laughing in disbelief and amazement.

"I always knew I had a thing for older women." Jace teased. He was actually older than Ari, but he wasn't going to broach that subject yet.

Ari gave him a playful swat with her hand and asked, "Why was I put into stasis Jace?"

Jace sobered, "I wasn't given that information, but when we go to our people, you can ask them. Age doesn't really matter to our people because we don't grow older like humans do; we all look like we're twenty in human terms."

Teasingly Ari asked, "Well how old are you then Jace?"

"I'll never tell," he said playfully. Ari went to swat him again, but he caught her hand in his and gently pulled her over to the old oak tree. Leaning on the tree, they gazed at the beauty surrounding them. The horizon was aglow with vibrant hues, reds, yellows, and oranges dancing across the sky as the sun slowly made its decent. The dazzling sparkle of light on Ari's face gave her the appearance of an angel, glorious—far too beautiful to be thrown into the conflict that would inevitably come her way.

Jace drew her hands to his lips, tenderly kissing her palms, fingers, and wrist. Heat seared senses, a tender kiss kindled such ardent fervid. Ari pressed her body into Jace and wrapped her arms lovingly around his back. Tenderly he cupped her face in his hands and gently tilted her head to capture her sweet tender mouth. Lips to lips, sweet, luscious, merging, his to hers, each stroke, each caress ignited a whirlpool of sensation, exquisite, luxurious heat, flowing wildly between them, in seconds they were sinking, deeper and deeper, sucked into a vortex, swallowed in passions fury. Suspended, breathless, Jace could feel Ari's mind breeching the first level of bonding, breaking down all mental defenses between life partners. He felt the need to do the same—he wanted her more than he thought possible. To be mentally connected with Ari, would be like forging a connection with the earth, becoming one with all life, the ultimate achievement few attain—the desire of every Te'rellean, fulfillment of spirit.

A spark of reason penetrated Jace's mind and slowly, unwillingly he pulled away from Ari. Gently caressing her with kisses he held her tight until the fire receded. It was agonizingly painful to stop in the throngs of such passion but Jace knew that because he loved her so much, he could not be selfish, he had to be fair, to protect her for her own good.

Ari did not want to stop, she wanted his touch, to take in the enticing scent of his presence; she wanted this intimacy, but she didn't have the understanding Jace did.

"Ari we can't," Jace said with a groan. Mustering all the control he had to be firm.

She looked at Jace, longingly. Pleading with her beautifully sensual blue eyes, deep in the throngs of passion seeking an explanation, she asked, "Why?"

"Because it wouldn't be fair to you, out of all our people you have only had contact with me. We are not like humans who casually have sex for recreation. Our mating process is different, it's permanent, for life which could be a very long time. When we find the one person we are meant to be with, we transcend through several levels of intimacy until we are irrevocably bonded mentally, emotionally, and physically. The bond is eternal."

Ari didn't know how to respond to that, she was still used to thinking in human terms. It made sense though, of all the boys that have vied for her attention, not one even came close to sparking her interest. Jace was different; before she even knew who he was she was attracted to him, drawn by some mysterious force. She knew in her heart Jace was her love, her life, the very essence of her soul, but if it made him feel better, she would meet more of their people.

"Jace I know what is in my heart, but I will not push the issue because what I feel for you is not transient." Ari whispered.

"Love is eternal Ari, it is strong, enduring, and worth waiting for, nothing can prevent amore," Jace said as he held her close, knowing full well his feelings for her would never change but he was the only Te`rellean she had ever seen. Her feelings could change.

"So, when do I met our people?" Ari asked as she settled comfortably into Jace's arms.

"The plan was to teach you gradually and let you hone your skills before you get thrust into the middle of our conflict with the Emigee. Then, there are your parents to consider. What will you tell them?" A long silence ensued as Ari struggled with the idea of telling her parents everything that has happened.

"I told you the date of your birth but that was only part of the gift I had for you. The second part is your parents are eagerly anticipating your arrival at our base," Jace revealed. He heard Ari gasp as she stiffened.

She pushed away from Jace slightly to look at him and asked, "My real parents are alive? I had just assumed they had died, I never really thought about actually meeting them. Oh… my goodness Jace… what if they don't like me? What if I don't like them? What am I going to tell my parents? Uh…I mean Martin and Ena?" Ari was suddenly a bundle of nerves with this newest revelation. Her real parents; what an incredible thought.

"Ari relax, you're getting worked up for nothing. Anyone who meets you will love you. I'm sure your biological parents are asking the same questions about you, worried that you won't like them. They have been waiting for years to have you back with them. They never gave up hope of finding you even when everyone else assumed you were dead. Martin and Ena are going to be the real challenge. Since they know you are unique, you can tell them everything, being found in a stasis unit and being a member of an advanced race didn't seem to unsettle them. I'm sure they can handle the truth which is probably the best solution. Trust them, they love you and will understand." Ari's expression of panic changed Jace's direction. "Or you can devise a plan where you will be away from the ranch, so you won't have to explain anything," Jace said consolingly, "You don't have to make up your mind right now. Think about it for a few days. Just know this—the truth always comes out eventually."

Ari retreated back into Jace's comforting embrace as if she was drawing strength from his presence. They held each other in silence, absorbing the beauty and serenity of the west pasture as the last speck of orange slide down below the horizon, taking comfort in the arms of one another.

From the tree-line of the forest, Twyla stood glaring at the pair embraced under the old oak. She had just experienced the most unsatisfying encounter with Andy, the Lovell's newest ranch hand. Then to be confronted with Ari wrapped in Jace's arms, it was more than she could tolerate. She was fuming; escalating jealousy was fanning the flames of revenge. She would have her revenge, especially after Ari's little tirade earlier, how dare she scold me when she is in Jace's arms. She didn't know when or how but that little bitch would pay and pay dearly.

Chapter

Life on the ranch was sedate after the party; everyday run-of-the-mill chores resumed. With the cleanup finished, normalcy returned. Martin was conducting routine business; Hank was wrangling with the ranch hands about the right and wrong way to handle the yearlings in the east pasture. Ena and Ari were taking inventory; storehouse supplies were depleted and needed to be restocked. Heading around the corner of the storehouse, Martin felt uneasy. He didn't want to alarm Ena, but he sensed a threat looming over them. Quietly peeking his head around the corner, Martin scanned the room but didn't see the girls. As his eyes adjusted to the dimness of the room, his vision became clearer. Exploring the room with his eyes, he spotted movement in the back corner.

"Ena," he called out. "I'm expecting a man from Zenot to come by around one. I might be out with Hank if he comes early. Just give me a call on the cell if I'm not here." He hated businessmen and their smooth double talk with twisted meanings; manipulating, maneuvering, exploiting the innocent, it was just downright dishonest. Martin dreaded the meeting.

Surprised that Martin had an appointment with Zenot, Ena dropped what she was doing and hustled over to him, "What's going on? What's Zenot want with you Martin?"

"I really couldn't say for sure, but it probably has something to do with drilling on the mountain. John Lee said they were sniffing around asking questions. They milked the surrounding area dry. So they are searching for new drill sites. Since they made deals with every property owner around us which I have no doubt made them a pretty penny, they just don't want to leave us out," Martin chuckled warily. Walking over to Ena and grabbing her playfully, giving her a big bear hug and smooches, he tried to reassure her.

"Alight you two, we have work to do," Ari grinned as she teased her parents; they were forever playful.

"You're not expecting trouble, are you? I don't like those big corporations. They take and destroy, ruining everything they touch. Remember what they did over on Mc Phearson's ranch. By the time they were finished, poor Eli and Rebecca had no usable water. I was flabbergasted when Rebecca brought me into her kitchen; you could set fire to their water with a match, flames shot right out of the facet!" said Ena with disgusted horror.

"Don't worry honey, nothing like that is going to happen here. I won't let it. It'll be okay. I have to meet Hank, but I'll be back. Love you both," Martin said on his way out the door.

"Ari lets finish up here. I want to make sure everything is in order in your dad's office before the meeting. You know how he gets when he's working—papers everywhere," Ena said with a forced chuckled. She knew exactly what she was going to find in the office—a disheveled mess.

Later as Hank and Martin were walking to the house, a very large shiny black sedan pulled into the driveway and up to the house. Martin elbowed Hank to draw his attention to the opulence. The driver, an extremely large man dressed in the usual city-slicker attire complete with designer shades, got out of the car. Having massively wide shoulders resembling a brick wall, he was stiff, barely able to negotiate his body; very awkward. Glaring at Martin and Hank for several tense moments, apparently an intimidation ploy, he turned to open the door for his passenger.

Hank whispered to Martin out of the corner of his mouth, "What do you think, steroids?"

Martin shrugged and whispered, "I didn't know a body could get that huge, he's a gargantuan. Even those body builders you see on TV aren't that big, this guy is enormous."

Another large man in a grey pin-striped suit maneuvered his way over to the two men. Rigid like a Spartan with golden blond hair and dark glasses, he presented himself as a no-nonsense kind of fellow, Hank thought. Square faced and firm jawed with a most unique feature, a crooked nose which appeared to have been flattened. To cause that kind of permanent disfiguration, he looked like he'd been on the losing side of several severe bar-room brawls. Too sophisticated by far, Martin thought, he didn't look like the type that went to bars; which explains the brick wall he had as a driver.

"Mr. Lovell, I'm George Powers. It's good of you to meet with me today."

Offering Martin his hand he displayed a forced grin. As Martin assessed the man, he took the offered hand hesitantly. Then Martin said, "This is my ranch manager Hank Broderick." Gesturing to the house, he continued, "Please come into my office Mr. Powers and tell me why Zenot wanted this meeting." The three men entered Martin's office and Martin pointed to the chair next to his desk, "Please have a seat Mr. Powers. Would you care for a drink, coffee, tea, water?"

"Thank you, Mr. Lovell, but I'm fine," said Mr. Powers politely.

"Alright then let's get down to business. Why does Zenot want a meeting?" Martin said plain and straight as he glanced at Hank quickly. Hank was giving Mr. Powers his usual stone-cold glare; the same one he gave to anyone he didn't trust. Martin had to chuckle to himself. Hank was true to form, always protective.

Mr. Powers reached for his briefcase and retrieved a file folder and presentation portfolio. Typical corporate crony with his formal business-like demeanor, Mr. Powers spoke with a solemn condescending executive tone, "Mr. Lovell, Zenot is the world's largest Mining and Oil Corporation. We have done extensive development in the surrounding area and have established business contracts with many of your neighbors for very lucrative financial ventures. A geographical survey has been completed; a copy is in this proposal." Handing Martin the portfolio he continued, "You have the area's largest gold and silver deposits we have ever seen in this area within your mountain, not to mention an extremely vast untapped oil bed with pockets of natural gas. We have put together a proposed contract that will allow us drilling and mining rights. In return, you will receive 25% of the profits. We estimate the gross return to be approximately 2.5 billion dollars. Thus, 25% of the venture is worth approximately $625,000,000. You and your family would be exceedingly wealthy."

Both Martin and Hank were silent for several minutes, stunned by the outrageous estimated profit margin. Martin's head was whirling. For a split second, he actually considered the possibilities. Thinking of his father brought him back to reality.

"Well that is an interesting offer Mr. Power. I can see why my neighbors jumped at the chance to do business with you. Your company is very generous, but I have a few questions, if you don't mind?" Martin said cordially.

"By all means Mr. Lovell, what would you like to know?" Mr. Powers said confidently as if he had already caught his prey—completely arrogant.

"What kind of drilling will you want to use, and can you explain the process?" Martin asked.

"The drilling will be done by a process called hydraulic fracture. A hole or wellbore is initiated. To create a hydraulic fracture, sufficient pressure from fracturing fluids, mostly water, is pumped down the hole. This increase in pressure exceeds the fracture gradient of the rock which causes cracks. The fracturing fluid enters the fissures and with the added pressure the breach is enlarged. To keep the fractures open, sand is added to the fracturing fluid causing permeability. Pumps extract the oil and natural gas," Mr. Powers stated as a matter of fact.

Martin was silent for a few moments contemplating his response then said, "Is this the same hydraulic fracture process more commonly referred to as 'fracking'?"

Mr. Powers confirmed Martin's assumption and added, "You are familiar with fracking Mr. Lovell?"

"Let me tell you what I know about fracking Mr. Powers. You gave a nice overview of the fracking process, but you did not mention the type of fluids used in the process. While it is true the major component of the fluid is water other chemicals are added to ease the fracking process."

Martin went through some papers on his desk, found the one he was looking for then added, "For example: Hydrochloric acid is used to facilitate entry into the rock, it is an acid; glutaraldehyde and 2.2 Dibromo-3-nitrilopropionamide are used for killing bacteria, they are a biocide; peroxodisulfate is used to facilitate proppant entry, it is a breaker; tetramethylammonium chloride is used for clay stabilization; methanol is used for well maintenance, it is a corrosion inhibitor; potassium hydroxide is used as another agent to facilitate proppant entry, it is a crosslinker; sodium acrylate and polyacrylamide are used to improve surface pressure, they are friction reducers; guar gum is used for proppant placement, it is a gelling agent. This is just a partial list of chemical additives. Some of these chemicals are known carcinogens while others are endocrine disruptors, this type of chemical interrupts glands and hormones in the body that control reproduction, development, and growth. Tell me Mr. Powers if these chemicals get in to our ground water, rivers and watersheds, what is going to happen to our drinking water, our health, and our quality of life not to mention the wild life?" Martin asked.

Very nonchalantly Mr. Powers stated, "I assure you Mr. Lovell, Zenot follows all governmental regulations regarding environmental safety procedures. You will not find another corporation as safety conscience as Zenot."

"Really...I see." Martin fumbled through more papers until he found the right one, "What about the 100 cases of benzene contaminations in Colorado and Wyoming? If I'm not mistaken and I'm sure I'm not, Zenot was the company on record responsible for the fracking. A congressional study found that Zenot among other oil and gas companies injected millions of gallons of hazardous and carcinogenic chemicals into wells in more than 13 states between 2005 and 2009. Then there is an independent report by the Times based on various leaked government environmental documents which found that fracking resulted in significant increases in radioactive material such as radium being released into rivers and watersheds. From the same report, it was noted that at one site from the Allegheny River the levels of benzene were 28 times higher than acceptable levels for drinking water. The area was surrounded by numerous Zenot drilling sites. In New York and Pennsylvania, an examination of 78 private water wells showed levels of methane 64 times higher than what is normal for drinking water. In that same area, a couple and their 16-month-old granddaughter were killed as a result of a methane leak which caused their well to explode. If that's not enough Mr. Powers, it has been reported that even some of your drilling sites have had blowouts in Pennsylvania sending more than 38,000 gallons of fracking fluid into the air and surrounding area contaminating campsites and habitats for thousands of animals and birds. In addition to blowouts, it is a common practice to vent. When this occurs, a fine cloud of silica particulate is released into the atmosphere which has the potential to travel many miles on the wind and into populated areas. The chemicals released, such as: sulfuric oxide, nitrous oxide, benzene, toluene, hydrogen sulfide, and diesel fuel can have serious health implications. While your employees I'm sure have their personal protective equipment, individuals away from the site do not and are usually not aware they are being exposed to hazardous material. If that is not enough Mr. Powers, fracking has been known to destabilize geological structures which increase seismic activity in the vicinity of the drill sites. So Mr. Powers, I will review your proposal but in light of what I know about Zenot's history and fracking procedures, I will not consent to any type of drilling on my property now or ever. Knowing the health risks, environmental damage incurred, and the overall decrease in the quality of life that would occur on this ranch because of the fracking drilling process, no amount of money is worth those consequences," Martin stated.

Mr. Powers, who continued to appear unaffected by the dissertation he had just been privy to, replied, "Mr. Lovell please review the contract proposal. Here is my card if you have questions or change your mind. Thank you for meeting with me today." He turned and headed for the exit to the office. Hank and Martin followed him out then watched the black sedan roll out of the driveway.

"Well that was quite a win fall!" Hank said to Martin who was taking a seat on the porch step.

"Yeah I'll say. I almost fell out of my chair when he came up with that estimate. I'm worried Hank. With 2.5 billion dollars in potential profits, they aren't going to go away so easily," Martin said apprehensively.

"What are you going to tell Ena and Ari?" asked Hank. On high alert, very edgy, he felt very protective. "You want me to alert the ranch hands to possible trouble?"

Martin shook his head, "No not yet, let's first see if anything develops."

"Good morning ladies," Martin said cheerfully as he walked into the room. He gave Ari and Ena a kiss on the cheek and sat down at the table for breakfast. "And what are you lovely ladies up to today?"

Barely hearing the chatter at the table, Martin was lost in thought. It had been several weeks since the meeting with Powers. Everything seemed to be routine on the ranch, a few mishaps; small ordinary setbacks, equipment needing repair, human error. A few worn ropes, a broken latch on the chicken coup, a mix up in the feed, those things happen all the time. Playing with his spoon he thought, I'm being too paranoid, then he asked himself, 'Am I being to suspicious?' With a profit margin of 2.5 billion dollars, a company like Zenot isn't going to just let that go, yet nothing out of the ordinary has occurred. I should probably just forget about the meeting with Powers and concentrate on more important things; trying to reassure himself nothing had happened to cause alarm. I need to take my own advice and relax, he thought.

"Dad, are you alright?" Ari said breaking into Martin's thoughts.

"Martin, what's wrong?" Ena added as she focused her attention on Martin raising that all knowing left brow. Something was bothering him, she could feel it, he would always get that far away look when he was worried about something. "Huh…oh… I'm okay. I was just lost in thought," said Martin as he turned his attention to the ladies; trying very hard to concentrate on what they were saying. The last thing he wanted was to worry Ena. "Did you hear anything we said?" Ena asked giving Martin that disapproving you're in trouble look. Martin smiled sheepishly at Ena and said, "No, I'm sorry honey, what were you saying?"

"Actually, daddy we were discussing colleges. It's only a couple of months before college starts and I still haven't decided on which one I will be going to yet, but I have narrowed it down to two," Ari said reluctantly.

"Why the long face?" said Martin as he picked up his coffee mug. "I would really like to go to Drice, but the annual tuition is about $35,000.00, whereas tuition at Anstford for the same program is about $32,500.00," said Ari. "I know you and mom want me to go to college, but it's a lot of money and that's only for one year!"

"Listen here young lady; if you want to go to Drice, then you go to Drice. Your mother and I have the money for your education set aside. Don't you worry about how much it is going to cost." Martin went over to Ari; putting his arms around her, he lovingly embraced her. She was comforted as always in those strong muscular arms. How she love this wonderfully kind man who had cared for her since she was found. The thought of not telling her parents about the Te'rell and the Emigee or that her biological parents wanted to see her was troubling. Sparing them worry was her main focus; she didn't want them to think they would be losing her—that would never happen. Besides Ari felt that this was something she had to do without them. Going to Drice would put her close to her people and her real parents. After breakfast, she would have to find Jace and tell him it was set; she would be going to Drice in the fall. They would have to make plans. In the meantime, she would have to spend as much time with her parents as possible before she leaves.

Martin broke into her thoughts, "Now young lady you better be sending out that acceptance letter before they rescind the offer."

Ari laughed, gave him and Ena a kiss and said, "I'm going to do it right now," and left the room.

Chapter

Vacation over, the dreaded return, Isbeth Benjamin made her routine climb up twenty flights of stairs. With each ascending step, she could feel the heaviness of her assignment, the burden of her people, the stress of Stewart's anxiety, all building intensely, building to a climax. Climbing helped, the stairs her only refuge, refuge she desperately needed to reduce the tension escalating within; it was her salvation. The relief it afforded was all she had.

Working for Stewart Braun was extremely intense at times, with his incessant pacing and anxiety. The man was going to have a heart attack if he didn't learn to relax. Just being around Stewart made a person jumpy, habitual tics, anxious demeanor, definitely not conducive to a pleasant, stress-free workplace. Concerned for her own mental calm, Isbeth knew if she didn't take action, like climbing up and down the stairs at least three times a day to release her pent-up tension, she would eventually strangle Stewart.

Gyasi, her mentor and superior, would chew her out, lambasted without remorse, if she did something to compromise her assignment. A significant amount of tactical intel had been attained over the years from Stewart and his dealings with his investors. Infiltration at Zenot was the closest contact any of her people had been able attain within the Emigee's sphere of activity without being discovered. Her position was vital. Surveillance revealed to her people that the investors had direct contact with the Emigee. Stewart's ambition to be part of this so-called elite group put her in the perfect position as executive assistant to observe; all at the expense of her mental stability.

Finally, she reached the twentieth floor, but it was far too soon. Feeling the need to climb another twenty floors to completely relieve her tension, she inhaled deeply. Pausing on the landing, she straightened her clothes and smoothed her hair. Sighing several times, she closed her eyes for a moment to steel herself for what she would soon be facing.

As soon as she opened the door, Ellie, one of the secretaries, pounced on her frantically and said, "Mr. Braun has been here all night and he's pacing again."

Just what Isbeth needed to hear, she sighed again. Isbeth looked over her shoulder longingly at the door, thought about running down the stairs to escape, but instead she asked Ellie, "Where is he?"

"He's in his office, about every five minutes or so he comes out, looks toward the elevators then returns to his office to continue pacing," Ellie said nervously looking around to find her escape.

"Alright, I'll take care of him," Isbeth said. I wonder what's got him so riled up today she thought. As she approached her desk, she caught a glimpse of Stewart in his office reaching for his Scotch. This was new even for Stewart, drinking before eight in the morning.

Isbeth put away her jacket and bag and proceeded to knock on Stewart's door. Stewart was so startled he cried out, "Ahhhhh....." in a high pitched voice resembling that of a frightened woman. It was bone piercing. Scotch splashed everywhere, down the front of his shirt, over the left side of his desk, down to the floor. Stewart looked terrified. Isbeth had never seen him in such a state; she was starting to become concerned. Something had happened when she was gone, but what?

"Mr. Braun, are you alright?" she asked as she moved to the desk to clean up the spill.

"Oh my...oh...Miss Benjamin you startled me," said Stewart when he turned toward Isbeth. Shocked, she was stunned at his appearance. A face, nicely round and plump like a membrane pulled taut on a kettle drum, was expected. Not this face, foreign, weak, drawn, and drooping; it was astonishing. Stewart had changed drastically! To dramatize the effect, his eyes were blood shot and blurred with deep dark cavernous lines beneath his swollen orbs. It appeared as if he had been sobbing through the night. Nothing but a shell of his former self was this man before her.

"What's wrong Mr. Braun? What can I do for you?" Isbeth said with sincere concern for him, almost feeling guilty for what she thought a few minutes before. After she cleaned up the spill, she closed the office door and went to his closet to retrieve a clean shirt and tie for him. Isbeth pointed Stewart to his lavatory to wash up and don the clean articles of clothing she had selected for him. Like a lost little boy, Stewart obediently surrendered to her direction. He was actually relieved that he didn't have to think for the moment. Having done too much thinking over the past three weeks, it was nice to relinquish the burden.

"Thank you, Miss Benjamin, I'm very happy you're back from vacation. It has been a long three weeks for me without you here," Stewart was so distraught he was only able to muster a faint whisper.

"I'm here now, Mr. Braun, why don't you lay on the chaise and rest. You don't look like you have slept since I left," Isbeth said in a gentle but commanding tone. She was hoping that he would relax enough for her to sort through his jumbled thoughts. To find out what the problem was, and possibly help him find a solution. Isbeth took Stewart by the arm and lead him to the chaise where he reclined and closed his eyes.

Before she left, he called out to her, "Miss Benjamin, would you do me a favor and work in here while I rest. I would feel better knowing you're here, it's comforting to know you're close."

His plea was so hopelessly pathetic she couldn't refuse him, "Yes, Mr. Braun, I'll work in here for a while." Isbeth was at a loss as to why Stewart was so traumatized. Relieved, she now had an excuse to be in close proximity to Stewart; it would be easier for her to read his thoughts from inside his office than from hers.

Stewart started to drift in and out of consciousness. As he slid into a deeper sleep, he began reliving the last three weeks as he dreamed. It started with a visit from George Powers who was a field representative from Zenot. Isbeth had seen him occasionally when Stewart discovered new drilling sites. As she was probing his mind, Isbeth could sense Stewart was feeling panicked disappointment. The memories were gradually becoming clearer. Powers was reporting on site 9801, the new site Stewart was excited about before she went back to base. The scene was being played like a movie in her head now that Stewart had relaxed.

"Mr. Powers how did your meeting go with the owner of site 9801?" Stewart asked cheerfully. *He signaled for Powers to have a seat.*

"I met with the owner, Mr. Braun, but unfortunately the meeting did not go as you had hoped. This was no ordinary country bumpkin who would sell his mother for a few dollars. This man knew why I had come, and he was prepared. A dangerous man Mr. Braun; he is educated, passionate, and principled. Armed with documented cases of environmental damage, health hazards from chemical contaminants, and geographical instability, he flatly and in no uncertain terms stated he would never contract with us for any amount of money," Powers relayed in his usual unfettered businesslike manner.

Stewart was stone-cold panicked by the time Powers had finished the report and left. Over on the chaise, Stewart started tossing and turning. He was highly agitated.

Isbeth tried to calm him by singing to him with whispers in his mind. Her mother had done the same, singing to her in whispers when she was afraid as a child, curled up in her arms, waiting for the Emigee invaders to retreat. She felt such comfort and love when she was caressed with whisper songs, like being swaddled in a soft comfy blanket until securely settled.

Isbeth could feel Stewart nestle back into a relaxed peaceful sleep. His memories started to flow again, gradually becoming clearer with each passing moment.

Stewart was pacing again in his office trying to muster up the courage to notify the investors of his failure to obtain a signed contract to drill at site 9801. Fear—Stewart was terrified of them.

But why, Isbeth thought. He has been doing business with them for years. She focused more intensely to see Stewart's memories.

Stewart was on the phone. *"Mr. Farsa, I regret to inform you that we were unable to get a signed contract for site 9801,"* he said.

After he hung up the phone, Stewart was pacing again.

His mind jumped to another memory.

Alone in his office at night, dark, office lights dimmed, a large man in a dark overcoat entered Stewart's office followed by the four investors, Mr. Farsa, Mr. Thir-

doch, Mr. Saiker, and Mr. Felckroll. The men seated themselves in various locations around the room positioning themselves so as to surround Stewart, a definite intimidation tactic.

"*Umbra is very disappointed, Mr. Braun. When we do business with individuals of you stature, we expect results. You assured us the contract would be signed and delivered by the end of the month. You have always been a man of your word Mr. Braun which is why we continue to do business with you. Now it seems that we can't trust you to keep your word. How unfortunate for you,*" Mr. Farsa growled maliciously.

Stewart, terrified and trembling, replied, "*Mr. Powers, is our best field representative, he was the one who attempted to acquire the contract. He insisted the man was very determined from the beginning to refuse our offer. The owner had documented evidences of contamination and safety infractions. Powers also stated that in his opinion, the owner was dangerous due to the fact he is educated, passionate, and principled. He would never sign a drilling contract no matter what the profits.*"

"*He doesn't sound that intelligent if he doesn't care about profits,*" snarled Thirdoch. His partners joined in the snide laughter.

"*It sounds like you are making excuses Mr. Braun, blaming poor Mr. Powers for your inept business dealings. What should we do with you Mr. Braun?*" Farsa said narrowing his brow contemplating his options.

Saiker cut in with his sadistic remarks, "*We could always take him hunting and shoot him, accidently of course. Hunting accidents happen all the time, even to the best hunters.*" Stewart suddenly became ashen and diaphoretic.

Thirdoch said fiendishly, "*We could take him sailing with us on Saturday. We wouldn't have to buy fish bait. We could just chop him up and have pieces of Stewart as our bait. We wouldn't have to buy bait for a year.*" Even though the investors were laughing and joking, something in their eyes, malice, evil, said they would eliminate Stewart in a heartbeat if he was no longer useful. Stewart had no idea how he was going to get out of this alive.

"*You two are being to kind. We should bankrupt him,*" said Felckroll as he grinned at his partners viciously. The men nodded with delighted satisfaction at the prospect, a destitute Stewart.

Stewart gasped, became weak in the knees, and pasted out. The thought of such a horrible future, no money, destitute, living on the streets like a vagabond, was too much to bear. When Stewart revived awhile later, a very large, extremely tall and muscular man was hovering above his face slapping him. A pair of lusterless pitch-black eyes; staring down at him, ruthless and oppressive, were the first things he saw. The left side of the man's face was branded with an unusual tattoo. Starting at the forehead with an almond shaped figure with a dark circle in the center; it resembled an eye. Three thick black horizontal lines below the man's left eye, one directly under the eye, the second mid-cheek, and the third at the jaw line covered the left half of his face. One thick black line ran vertical from the eye-shaped figure to the three lines below connecting them. Unsettling, Stewart's heart raced at seeing this man with the strange tattoo glaring at him.

Isbeth gasped as she saw the full view of the tattoo. She recognized it, an Emigee military insignia. Worse yet, the face it was attached to, a face she would never forget—*Hamer!* He was responsible for the slaughter of two hundred and fifty women and children in Nepal sixty years prior. The terror and mayhem this man was responsible for was unprecedented. With his team, they had become notorious in their lust for carnage.

"*He's awake,*" the man said.

"*Glad you could join us again Mr. Braun. My companions and I have been discussing the situation. We have decided that since this is the first time you have disappointed us, we will be lenient with you and use this as a learning experience. Your education will be a slight chastisement, so to speak. Once you have recovered, your understanding will be complete; the Umbra is quite serious about failure and especially in the way it handles the acquisition of drilling contracts. You WILL learn no matter what obstacles you must overcome, you must NEVER disappoint us again,*" said Farsa with a commanding voice. "*Let me introduce you to your teacher. Mr. Hamer, Mr. Braun is awaiting his instructions. We will be in touch Mr. Braun.*" The four men left the room which left Stewart and Hamer alone in his office. Since it was nine pm and everyone had left hours ago for the night, Stewart knew nothing could save him from the inevitable.

Hamer looked at Stewart and smiled vindictively, in a deep menacing voice which lingered in the air, he said, "*Let the lessons begin.*"

Stewart stiffened, knees trembling, heart racing like stampeding cattle; his head was spinning, he was going to pass out from fright as he gawked at Hamer. Stupefied, the revealing of Hamer's true form under his trench coat had Stewart holding his breath. He was massive, big bulky shoulders larger than the entrance to his office. His forearms and fists were herculean, larger than sledgehammers. Stewart was paralyzed; he knew he was going to die.

In a split second, Hamer landed one punch to Stewart's abdomen and he was flat on the floor unconscious. When Stewart woke, it was the next morning. He could hardly breathe. When he tried to get up from the floor, he felt the most excruciating pain he had ever felt in his life. Slowly, agonizingly Stewart crawled to the lavatory to assess the damage to his body. Pulling himself up inch by inch, he managed to stumble to his feet. Looking in the mirror, he was appalled; he counted five separate Hamer size bruises, two on the ribs and three on the abdomen. It was no wonder he couldn't breathe.

Stewart started gasping for breath on the chaise. The memories were exceedingly traumatic. For him to continually relive them was unbearably cruel. Isbeth decided to attempt a thought implant to ease his pain. An image of a sun-drenched meadow blanketed with fragrant wildflowers dancing in the warm breeze is what she decided to give him. Bright vivid blues and reds, dynamic yellows and oranges, and subtle pinks and whites all blending together; a vision of peace for a tortured mind, bountiful wild flowers swaying over the hills into the meadow to soothe his frayed nerves, making his spirit soar, providing a measure of relief for his troubled soul. The sparkling blue skies with fluffy white clouds that looked like soft cuddly animals were calming his mind. Fluttering butterflies filling the air and singing birds heard from adjacent trees were easing his troubled spirit. The image, a memory, one of Isbeth's favorite places, was a meadow not far from the base her people had set up in Nepal. It was the most peaceful serene place she had seen in a hundred years.

As Stewart settled into this new image, he started to relax and breathe easier. Then a new memory entered his mind.

It was of Hamer reviewing the file on site 9801. Hamer looked at Stewart and said, "Mr. Braun, now you will see how to successfully attain a signed contract from the owner of 9801, this Mr. Lovell. Principled men are more concerned and care about those around them than they care about themselves. Apparently, this Mr. Lovell has a wife, a daughter, and many friends. When unforeseen incidents start happening to those he cares about, he will change his mind."

"You aren't going to kill them, are you?" Stewart said horrified.

"I don't think it will come to that Mr. Braun. If Martin Lovell is as principled as you say, the safety of his wife Ena and his daughter Ariella will matter more than a few drill sites," said Hamer arrogantly.

Isbeth gasped at the name Ariella. The Emigee were after Ariella Lovell and her human family! She had to contact Gyasi immediately.

Chapter

Waiting, always waiting for someone or something to happen; it was maddening. As the rain poured down the window of the small café, memories of a more antiquated times flood through his mind…

Rain pounding on the roof continued, for days it had been pouring, it was irksome. His only solace in the dark dank tavern was the food; piled high on the plate, the food was very tasty but undistinguishable. A good meal, something he was extremely grateful for; the last few places he had stopped to sup were disgusting. Food with maggots squirming in it, hardly appetizing, made him want to vomit. Finally finding an acceptable tavern, secluded, near Guinegate, a small village in rural France; he savored the meal and drink while keeping warm by the fire—waiting. Henry was late, probably held up by the rain. Time was running out, if only these primitives could travel the way he did, it was faster and less time consuming unfortunately it was too conspicuous. Stealth was the key to success, so horses had to do. Horses…a slow way to travel especially in the rain; they were always getting bogged down with mud.

Waiting, hours spent waiting, he was about to go in search of Henry when the door of the tavern swung open with a bang and a cloaked man stood in the doorway. Rain drenched, the man stood surveying the room until his eyes espied the man by the fire. Moving regally, splashing water on patrons who grumbled as he passed, he threw off his cloak by the fire.

"You're late!"

Henry furrowed his brow, "The roads were treacherous; several were completely washed out."

"Sit down and dry off, Max hasn't shown up yet either." Hamer waved to the tavern wench to bring more drinks. Before she had brought the refreshments, the tavern door swung open again. Both men looked up, Hamer nodded; the tall figure standing in the doorway sauntered over to the fire dripping water with each step.

"Max, are your forces set?" Henry asked eagerly. Max nodded his affirmation then focused his attention on Hamer.

"You're late!" Hamer barked, stern and unrelenting.

"I beg your pardon, my lord. The weather was not conducive to swift and speedy travel," said Max curtly. Hating condemnation from an outsider, Max had to restrain his temper; he needed Hamer to achieve his goals. Miraculously, Hamer had pulled off some amazing victories in the past. Commanding lightening on demand in Venice, ordering fire from the sky in Florence; anyone with that kind of power needed to be an ally not a foe.

"Sit down; now that the two of you are here, I have information that will solidify your hold on French territory, thus weakening the French contingent. Louis de Longueville is marching to Guinegate in two days, take him there, you will cut the French forces by a third and sack their supply line," Hamer revealed. The two men sat back and glared at Hamer in disbelief.

"How do you come by this information?" Henry queried hoping Hamer would reveal his source.

"Has my information ever been wrong? Why do you question me now? All you need to know is that my masters have informants everywhere setting the stage to assist you in securing your prize, the targeted French territory you covet so much." Hamer's indignant reply silenced the upstart king.

"My lord, may I ask, of what benefit is our securing the French territory for your masters?" the older more refined king asked.

"My masters do not always divulge details; be assured they always have a purpose, some objective I might not be privy too, but in this instance, I am aware of a rare mineral that is sought. If my masters desire it, they will acquire it. Our alliance assures easy access." Hamer was not about to inform his allied kings that the Emigee use any and all means to achieve their goals, whether it is exerting influence on one individual, groups of people, or manipulating entire governments to suit their needs. No, these greedy men would be satisfied with their token victory.

"You help us for minerals?" said Maximilian I of Austria. "Is it gold... silver?"

"No," said Hamer and refused to say another word about the masters.

Pulling out a map of the area, he changed the subject; the three men discussed tactics, positioning of forces, and attack strategies. After several hours, the two kings departed leaving Hamer by the fire eager for another fine tasty meal.

Waiting was not his strong suit, for hundreds of years it seemed punctuality still eluded most people even his own, he was always waiting for someone to show up. Thankfully, the little dive he was in had decent food. There was nothing he hated more than a lousy meal. Why was it, the tastiest food came from the smallest out of the way greasy spoon restaurants, Hamer wondered as he finished his plate. The house special, not sure of the contents, but it tasted great; and he really wasn't sure he wanted to know what was in the tasty combination he had just finished, no probably not, he thought. If he was going to be in the area for an extended visit, he would have to remember this place—Man Lee's Café. Not knowing how long it would take to get the contract signed or how long he'd be in the area, a good place to eat was essential information. As long as he was in this backwater town, he would make sure he ate well. Looking at his watch, he became agitated, they're late. Why can't anyone be punctual?

The French garrison was eagerly awaiting the supply column; the men on the watchtowers had been keeping watch for several hours. Supplies had been severely depleted; the men close to starvation, provisions were sorely needed. At the top of a knoll just behind the tree line, Hamer, Max and Henry kept the vigil. The combined forces positioned, anticipation heightened waiting for the signal. After several hours, the French cavalry with the relief supplies marched toward the village.

"Send Percy the signal," Henry commanded his steward.

Henry Algernon Percy, the fifth Earl of Northumberland, commanded 500 cavalry men. Surprising the French, Percy appeared in front of the French column blocking access to the village.

Excitedly Henry shouted, "Flank them with our archers on the left."

Max sent his steward off running with a commanding bark, "Ready the artillery on the right, encircle them."

Suddenly the French realized they were outwitted; the English had their cavalry in front of them, with archers on the left and Austrian artillery on the right. In a panicked frenzy, the French dropped their weapons and armor, spurred their horses mercilessly to facilitate their escape, desperately fleeing the combined forces of the English and Austrian kings. Bolting to the east, a few men made a stand so that others could escape, but it was futile. Several key military leaders were captured, and the territory was now controlled by the English.

Young Henry secured his prize giving him a triumphant military victory over the French. Max was delighted to curb the French drive for conquest into territories conflicting with his own interests, especially Milan. Roetan, we got the roetan, Hamer thought; that precious rare roetan. Plentiful on their devastated home world, but so very rare here on earth, his people search extensively to obtain even the smallest quantities of the coveted mineral; their existence depended on it.

Contemplating what a win fall the roetan would be for his people, Hamer heard the cling clang of the bell above the door, bringing him back to the present. The whole café became silent. Turning to see who had walked in, his anger blazed. Standing at the door were three men as tall and muscular as him. Two of the men had distinctive tattoos on their faces indicating their status while the other man had none.

The first man wore black leather pants with cut-outs on the side which laced from top to bottom, biker boots, chains looped around his waist and a black leather vest accentuating his resoundingly bulbous arms. The second man wore tight black leather pants with chainmail overlays which defined his large sinewy thighs, steel toed boots with spikes on the heels and toes, a chainmail vest, and spiked forearm bands.

The customers, stupefied, all sat gawking at the men as if they had just been invaded by zombies. One man spilled his drink, a young woman with two small children gathered them close, others became unusually attentive to their meals, hurrying to finish. A usual response from humans when his companions arrived together, their appearance and stature was uniquely unsettling to say the least.

They noticed Hamer at the far end of the café and marched over to his table knocking over chairs as their massively huge bodies meandered between tables. Hamer acknowledged their presence and motioned for them to sit down. The waitress nervously inquired if they would like to eat and was extremely relieved when they declined.

Hamer barked, "You're late!"

"This place is such a hole in the wall it was hard to find," said the man with no markings. He was a large man like the others but not as intimidating in appearance; dressed casually in jeans and a tee shirt, he was quite handsome.

"Has Si`kram informed you of our assignment?"

"Our orders were to meet you here and that you would explain the details," said Camden. Camden's appearance was designed for a purpose, different from the other three; he was pleasing to humans, someone to trust. No tattoo on his face, his countenance appeared softer and more inviting which made him more dangerous for covet operations. He could interact with the intended targets while not revealing his identity. Camden was ruggedly handsome with blond hair, high-cheekbones, and a strong chin. His eyes were not the usual pitch-black that identified his people but a softer silver-gray which added to his appeal with humans and had proven to be lethally deceptive in the past. His inviting appearance was like a decoy to lure his prey. It was extremely effective.

The other two men were members of the special ops unit under their military leader Si`kram. Hamer was a member of that same unit. The tattoos represented their rank which was similar to that of the human military designations. Si`kram was a lare, their leader. The three lines on Hamer's cheek identified his designation as a leno, leader of a covert field team.

Ja`nek was a lower rank than Hamer designated by his tattoo. Similar to Hamer's with the exception he had two lines across the cheek instead of three. This designation was roj. Stoic and resigned, Ja`nek was completely unaffected by his surroundings or the effect he had on others. Eyes, pitch-black, cold and empty, a face battle worn with multiple scars cris-crossing; forming what appeared to be a lopsided checkerboard. Yet Ja`nek was not the most intimidating of the four.

Ki had an aura about him that made most men quiver with fear. Personifying danger, not one customer in the café dared glance at him twice. In fact, as Ki glanced around the room, most of the customers found their meal extremely fascinating avoiding any kind of eye contact; patrons finished quickly and left. Having a slightly diabolical slant, his pitch-black eyes had a deadly connotation. Ki held the rank niat. Just one line across the cheek, one line more malevolent, more vindictively evil than Hamer's three; he was nefariously depraved. Unlike the others, Ki chose to shave his head. *'To let the blood flow unencumbered, my enemies' life force must be freely absorbed,'* was his response when asked why he preferred a bald head. Hanging his enemies by their feet, slitting their throats, and letting the blood flow over him to absorb their power was his custom. His thirst for blood was unprecedented among the Emigee.

Hamer began to explain the plan, "Camden will go in first to obtain intel from the locals. Ja`nek, Ki and I will implement surveillance of Lovell's property. It is quite extensive. We will need to know the lay-out of the land and any tactical advantages. Si`kram's orders are explicit; no one is to be injured at this time. Do you understand?"

Hamer was looking directly at Ki, he wanted no trouble from Si`kram. Disobeying direct orders was severely punished. Everyone, including Ki, acknowledged the direct order. Hamer continued, "There is a store at the base of the mountain. Camden, you may find friends of the Lovell's at the store. We will rendezvous here in two days to coordinate the next stage of this operation."

With their instructions given, Camden left the others and headed for the store at the base of the mountain. Hamer, Ja`nek, and Ki divided the mountain into sections with each one taking a third. Hamer took the area around the ranch house and main complex. Sending Ki to the most remote section to explore; he was less likely to come in contact with humans from the ranch, thus, his thirst for blood would not be tempted.

Twyla was holding court at the G & T, the storefront was center stage. Several young men were vying for Twyla's attention. As usual she gave each one just enough attention, titillating their already overactive hormones—dangling the carrot so to speak. Keeping her would be suitors coming back was the game. Many had hopes of procuring favors from Twyla, a highly sensual game on which she thrived.

The day was sultry, steaming hot which she used to her advantage tantalizing the men folk who frequented the establishment. An orange string bikini with a sheer lace cover-up was her weapon of choice which obtained the desired responses from her suitors, pacifying her insatiable need for attention. Needless to say, any man unfortunate enough to visit the G & T unwittingly fell under her spell, thus the ogling gratified her ego.

Quite content, until a new bright red sports coupe roared into the parking lot. Lean and sleek, meant for speed, the roadster elicited the desired response as it sparkled in the sunshine. What Twyla saw next had her all but drooling, tall, muscular, and gorgeous. As if in slow motion, Camden got out of the car and sauntered to the entrance of the G & T, Twyla was bursting into flames; desire exploding, she dismissed her suitors.

Putting herself on display, to entice, to draw Camden's attention was her new challenge. Wanting to roll his eyes and laugh at her pathetic display, so common among humans, he would, instead, grasp the occasion to use the chit. He had no interest in humans, never giving them a second thought. As far as his people were concerned, humans were pawns, a means to accomplish their plans, nothing more. This chit was an opportunity, an easy mark, to obtain intel on the Lovell's, so he played along.

"Hi there handsome…nice car…very nice car," she purred. "What kind is it?" Twyla cooed in her most flirtatious manner, thrusting her chest out as she seductively traversed the walkway.

"Well hello there," Camden said in his most charismatic churr, "do you like sports cars sweetling?"

One little query and Camden had Twyla gushing like a newly opened soda can, hot and shaken.

"I adore sports cars, but you haven't told me what kind it is." Moving closer to Camden, purposely brushing her body against his, she maneuvered around him to get a better look.

"She's a Chepors Bumballa Mirage GT, 0-62 in 3.7 seconds," said Camden hooking his fish.

"Nice…are you as fast as your car?" Twyla whispered seductively as she circled Camden dragging her finger around his back and chest as she came.

"Want to go for a ride…see for yourself?" Camden whispered alluringly.

Twyla lit up with excitement, "Sure, let's go!" She grabbed Camden's hand dragging him to the car as her would be hopefuls watched from the storefront bemoaning their loss. As Camden started the car, Jenkins appeared at the door with one of the boys and called out, "Twyla, get out of that man's car now!"

Camden glanced at Twyla, she exclaimed, "Go!" The car spun out of the parking lot and flew down the road toward the mountain.

"Whoooo!" Twyla squealed as they raced down the road at 120 mph. Half-way up the mountain Camden noticed a secluded lookout area tourist used to enjoy the view. He screeched the car to a halt and got out of the car. Twyla followed, like a puppy wagging her tail she went.

"Is this fast enough for you?" Camden said as he pulled Twyla into his arms. He grabbed the back of her hair and kissed her hard. As he kissed her, he reached into his pocket for the SIRD, a sub-conscience information retrieval device, and attached it to the base of her neck. Once attached to Twyla's neck, Camden immediately released her and wiped his mouth in disgust. She stood in front of Camden with a blank expression, completely subservient, ready for information retrieval.

Camden began the questioning, "What can you tell me about the Lovell's?"

"I'm going to get even with that bitch Ari!" Twyla said as the SIRD reached into her sub-conscience.

"Who is Ari?" "Martin Lovell's daughter." Expressionless, she answered.
"Why are you going to get even with the daughter, Ari?" Camden probed.

"That bitch took Jace away from me. I'm going to get even with her," Twyla snarled. For her to even show the slightest emotion when the SIRD was attached, she had to have very vicious and hostile intentions toward the girl. Camden didn't know if he would be able to use that piece of information to his advantage or not. He kept digging.

"Who is Jace?" Camden probed, wanting to know if there was going to be trouble from a boyfriend.

"One of the Lovell's ranch hands," Twyla said, "Martin hires temporary ranch hands every year during spring, then let's them go during the winter." Intrigued, by the notion of infiltrating as a worker he continued.

"Do you know if he needs anymore workers?" Camden said. This would be a great way to get close to the people who worked on the ranch and discover the best way to achieve the objective.

"Martin has only hired three this year he usually hires six," she said mechanically as if she was an automaton.

"Who else lives on the ranch?" Camden asked.

"Martin's wife Ena, Hank the ranch manager, that bitch Ari, and the ranch hands." Twyla said, dryly and emotionless.

Camden was satisfied with the information that he obtained. Helping Twyla get revenge on Lovell's daughter was disturbing, probably because she repulsed him immensely, by the time his team finished with Lovell and his family, the revenge would be complete; until then he would seek employment on the ranch. It was perfect.

Camden placed Twyla in the car and started down the road to the G & T. Pulling into the parking lot, he stopped the car by a large tree. Kissing Twyla again he removed the SIRD. Still dazed he told her, "You will remember nothing except racing down the road in the Chepors and sensual kisses. Now get out of the car and go to your room."

As soon as Twyla got out of the car, Camden left to search for a beaten-up old car suitable for an out of work ranch hand, he had to play his part. If he showed up in his Chepors, they would never hire him. Heading back to the town to search, he remembered seeing a car dealership on the edge of the village.

◆◆◆

Reviewing the monthly accounts, Martin was in his office when he heard a knock on the door. "Come in," he called out.

Ena opened the door, "Martin you have a young man out here who is looking for work."

"Send him in honey," Martin said with a smile. Shuffling the papers into a stack and putting them to the side, Martin stood up to greet the young man standing before him.

"Mr. Lovell, my name is Camden De`Adly. I heard you're looking for ranch hands. I'd like to apply for a job," Camden said with all the charm he could muster.

"Who told you about the work here?" Martin asked as he motioned for Camden to have a seat. Camden sat in the chair in front of Martin's desk while Martin reached for refreshments.

"Twyla down at the G & T mentioned that you might need help." Camden replied. Lovell wasn't what Camden was expecting, he really didn't know what to expect. Something about this man, something different, made you want to trust him; he never had that reaction to a human before.

"Have you ever worked on a ranch before Camden?" Martin asked, surmising he hadn't. Lack of experience never stopped him from hiring anyone in the past. Martin trusted his feelings, they never steered him wrong. Sensing the young man was searching, searching for something that somehow eluded him. Martin remembered being young and searching for that undetermined thing, purpose, path; not knowing exactly what he was searching for but he continued to search nonetheless.

"Well, no but I'm a hard worker and I learn quickly. I have other work experience and references," Camden said with great passion hoping that Martin would validate his eagerness.

"Give me your references, I'll check them out. You're hired contingent on your references. You won't start until I have checked them; if they are good you can start in the morning. You can go over to the workers barracks and see Hank. He's my ranch manager; he will show you to your room. Glad to have you on board Camden," Martin said with all sincerity.

Hamer was watching several ranch hands herding about twenty head of cattle into a corral. He noticed four men, three young men and an older man who was giving the orders. As he was watching, one of the men caught his attention, something familiar about him. Unusually tall and muscular for a human, he resembled his enemies… Suspended in mid-thought, he caught the man's scent on the wind. Heightened senses and self-healing were the only abilities most of the Emigee retained from their original ancestors. After they left earth, the abilities of telekinesis, telepathy, and power sensing were lost to them. Gradually, the Emigee developed an increase physical musculature and increased strength. They retained the self-healing ability with the exception of an Achilles heel; a vulnerability. A weakness, one area of their bodies was susceptible, a frailty, a shameful thing to the Emigee. If the Emigee were wounded in the left ear, they would die. For that reason, the designation of rank was on the left side of the face. It was a symbol of strength in their culture, to cover weakness.

The man's scent was strong and unmistakably Te`rellean. Why is a Te`rellean here on this ranch, Hamer wondered. This changed the circumstances of the assignment, their previous orders no longer applied. Dealing with Te`relleans took priority over human endeavors. Te`relleans always have a reason for their actions and he would have to find out why this one was here. Si`kram was not going to be happy; the supply of roetan was diminished. Getting the signed contract was imperative to replenish their cache, but now Te`relleans were here. Urgently he left to meet up with Ja`nek and Ki then head back to town to meet with Camden.

Camden was the first one to show up at Man Lee's Café, he was rather pleased with himself. Securing a job on the ranch was an added bonus, one he had not expected when he obtained valuable information from that human. The front door to the café opened, Hamer, Ja`nek, and Ki appeared. They surveyed the café and spotted Camden at the far end of the room at a table in the corner. Quickly the three crossed the room.

"How much intel did you obtain?" Hamer asked Camden as the three men sat down.

"I discovered that Lovell hires temporary help and hadn't reached his quota. So I applied for work as a ranch hand and was hired," Camden replied.

"Really, you met Lovell? Did you meet anyone else?" Hamer asked, eager for any information he could get on the Te'rellean who's working on the ranch.

"Just his wife who let me in…oh…and the ranch manager…why?" Camden asked curiously. He knew that look on Hamer's face, something was wrong, when his right eye started to twitch trouble usually followed.

"During my surveillance, I discovered a Te`rellean working on the ranch," said Hamer.

"What?" said Ki, excitement engulfed him. "I have first dibs on him, filet Te`rellean, my favorite."

The four men laughed, each recalling previous missions where Ki was engrossed in the throngs of blood-lust. Ja`nek asked, "Why would a Te`rellean be on this ranch?"

"That would be the question. Si`kram wants to know that as well. Our primary objective now is to discover what this Te`rellean's interest is in the Lovell ranch. Obtaining the contract is no longer a priority," Hamer ordered. "We will have to go to ground. Ja`nek, Ki did either of you find a secluded, concealed area where we can set up a base?"

"I found a cave on the west side of the mountain, off the main trails. It will suffice for base camp. There is a spring coming off the mountain, a good source of water. We'll be well concealed there," Ja`nek informed the group.

"Good then we will use the cave. Caution is needed Camden; the Te`rellean will know who you are immediately, but it's doubtful he'll act against you with the humans around," Hamer warned. "

Are you sure I can't just filet him" Ki whined. Maintaining control when there was a Te`rellean in the area was impossible for Ki, his need to kill was intractable.

"These orders are from Si`kram. If you want to defy him, that's your choice," Hamer said with annoyance. "Camden, come to the cave when you have a chance. We will stay hidden for the time to let you do your work. See you in a week," Hamer said as he, Ja`nek and Ki left the table.

Chapter

Racking his brains, Hank scratched his head, trying to figure out who to buddy Camden with since he had never worked on a ranch before, a greenback, another blasted newbie. Greenbacks were more trouble than their worth, usually weren't suitable for ranch work for at least three months after being hired, but Martin was a good man, rarely turned away a body willing to work.

Only two choices, Connie had been on the ranch the longest but Jace was by far the best worker. The problem was Jace took Andy under his wing. Did a damn good job of showing Andy the ropes too, but I'll never admit that to him, Hank thought. Still it's not right to give him two newbie's.

"Connie," Hank barked gruffly. "Come over here." Connie grinned and meandered his way over to Hank who was sitting on the lounge chair in the common room. An easy going sort, Connie, loved ranch work. In fact, this was his fifth year working for Martin and Hank. Working spring through fall, saving as much money as he could to live through the winter, usually vacationing somewhere warm, he would come back the next spring to hire up again. Sandy brown hair, hazel eyes, with an oval face, Connie was a good-looking guy except for his most prominent feature. His nose was slightly off-center and crooked, an incident with the back end of a horse.

"What's up Hank?" Connie asked in his usual carefree fashion.

"We got a new guy starting today. I want you to show him the ropes," Hank blurted out in his thick country drawl. "Oh, by the way, he has never worked on a ranch before."

"Awe Hank, you're giving me a cherry!" Connie moaned as he kicked at the floor. Connie loved ranch work, he hated teaching greenbacks; they slowed him down.

"I wouldn't call him that if I were you. He's a big fella. Ya might find yourself on the ground," Hank chuckled at the thought. Knowing Connie would grouch and moan a lot before he eventually conceded, he sternly waited it out.

Just as Hank had finished speaking, Camden walked in the room. Hank stood up and started making introductions.

"Camden, this is Connie you'll be working with him, he'll show you the ropes around here. Over there by the sink is Andy... and...uh...where's Jace?" Hank asked as he looked around, "Well never mind, you'll meet him eventually."

Camden shook hands with everyone. Disappointed that none of the men was the Te`rellean, he was eager to find his target. He couldn't imagine why the Te`rellean would be interested in this ranch way out in the middle of nowhere. They had no interest in mining or other means of making money.

"Connie, take Camden and familiarize him with the barnyard complex," Hank instructed firmly. When he spoke with his hardline tone, Connie quickly obeyed. Connie nodded to Hank, picked up his gear and took Camden over to the barn.

Caring for a sick horse, Jace was rubbing her down while Ari ran her hands over her back leg. They had just gotten the horse up on her feet when Connie stepped into the stall. "Jace, I want you to meet Camden the new ranch hand Martin hired," Connie said as Camden came around to the opening of the stall.

Jace was shocked when he saw an Emigee standing right in front of him. Immediately he warned, *"Ari stay back, Camden is an Emigee."* Jace nodded to Camden. Acknowledging Connie's introduction was essential, Jace didn't want to raise suspicion that anything was amiss; but his senses were on high alert with an Emigee present.

Ari's curiosity got the better of her. She didn't listen; peeking her head around to see Camden, she was relieved at what she saw. She said, *"Jace he's not much different than us."*

"His appearance maybe similar Ari but make no mistake he would kill us in a split second if he didn't want something," Jace said. Camden kept his eyes locked on Jace, not flinching even a little; but he was caught off guard when he heard a voice from behind the horse. Already anxious about a Te`rellean in the same space, Ari gave him a jolt when she appeared.

"Connie, aren't you going to introduce me?" Ari said with a smile. Stunned when he saw Ari; she was the most beautiful women he had ever seen. Her deep auburn hair was alluring and her perfectly flawless face was exquisite, unexpectedly gorgeous she was. That smile was enough to take his breath away.

Connie startled, surprised by her sudden appearance from behind the horse; he was engrossed by the odd interaction of the two men he had introduced. It wasn't like Jace to be so reserved. Connie was curious but managed to respond to Ari, "Sorry Miss Ari I didn't realize you were here. Miss Ari this is Camden, Camden this is Miss Ari."

Camden was speechless. Jace fumed at his reaction and became increasingly tense. His scrutiny of her was too intense by far; fire was welling up within Jace, a fire he was fighting to control. The last thing he wanted was an incident in front of Connie, but he had to protect Ari, it was essential. The growing bond between him and Ari was intensely strong, it was more than just his assignment now; protecting Ari was paramount, as if his life depended on it.

Ari said, "It's nice to meet you Camden. I hope you will enjoy your stay with us."

After a few minutes Camden regained his speech and said, "Thank you Miss Ari. It's a pleasure to meet you," he completely forgot about Jace, turned and left with Connie.

"Ari what were you thinking," Jace said scolding her. Sounding very harsh, he was more terrified for her safety knowing full well the danger the Emigee pose, especially for her.

"I was welcoming a new ranch hand," she said a little defiantly. *"Jace he seemed nice and he didn't threaten us in any way. He's not at all like I pictured."*

"Ari, please believe me when I tell you he's dangerous. His people mercilessly slaughtered our people; attempting to commit genocide, innocent men, women, and children were killed. We barely survived as a people. Please, Ari, listen to me when it comes to the Emigee." Jace pleaded, imploring her to listen but extremely agi-

tated that she wouldn't. She was a young woman strong willed and stubborn and completely independent.

"But Jace his people and our people are the same people. There has to be a way to mend the breach," Ari entreated, not fully comprehending just how dangerous the Emigee were. She had always been the peacemaker, in school and out, she believed it was possible for everyone to live peacefully together.

"If there is Ari, I don't know how, but that isn't why I'm here. My concern is for your safety. Please Ari, don't allow yourself to be alone with him or any of the Emigee, you're too important, besides, I love you. I couldn't bear it if you were hurt or killed." Jace was blindsided that he confessed his feelings so readily. Centuries of tightly concealing his emotions, his heart; then to blatantly expose them to a girl, a girl who has met only one Te`rellean in her life, it was unfair to her and opened him up to potential pain and loss. What was he thinking?

"You love me?" A little stunned by the overt confession; Ari felt as if she was going to burst with happiness. Three little words could turn her head and make her feel as if she were dancing on clouds. *"Alright, I won't be alone with Camden. I'll make sure others are around if I talk to him,"* Ari conceded, teasing him, she asked, *"You're not jealous are you Jace?"* Ari giggled as Jace scowled giving her an indignant look, she knew she was close to the truth. *"I love you to Jace."*

Camden was still thinking about Ari as Connie was showing him around the main complex. He couldn't remember ever reacting to a female the way he did with Ari. She threw him completely off focus.

***Holy Ki`lam!*** I turned my back on an enemy, he realized. What was he thinking? This girl is dangerous but so beautiful. Camden shook his head as if to clear it then he realized that she too was Te`rellean...a Te`rellean...What was going on here? Two on the same ranch, why? How did she become the daughter of humans, it just didn't make sense? He *had* to figure out the mystery of Ari.

Several days had gone by and Jace's apprehension could no longer be subdued. He was going to have to confront the Emigee to find out why he was here and how many others where in the area. The Emigee ran in packs, always moving covertly in small cells with one-member infiltrating, targeting the prey. He was going to find Camden when work was done for the day; he was determined to get answers.

Ari decided to do a little investigative work of her own. Seeing Camden putting away equipment in the storeroom by the corral, she meandered over to him. Connie was working in the corral with Andy. The perfect time to ask a few questions of her own, she thought.

"Hi Camden," Ari said. Smiling as she walked up to him, catching him off guard again.

Camden started feeling strange like someone had removed his skeletal bones from his body, he was going to mush. One look at Ari and he didn't even care. Finally, he responded with a smile, "Hello Miss Ari, how are you today?"

"I'm fine thanks. You can lose the 'Miss' Camden it's just Ari. How are you getting along? My dad says you have never worked on a ranch before." Ari asked as she was assessing his reactions.

"I'm learning a lot," Camden said a little flustered. He was having trouble ordering his thoughts with Ari around.

"Do you like the work?" Ari asked trying to figure out how to broach the subject she really wanted to talk about.

Camden could tell she was fishing for something and asked, "What is it that you really want to know Miss...uh...Ari?"

Ari was taken aback by his directness, but then again, she preferred to be straightforward. So she asked, "Why have you come here Camden you being an Emigee?"

Well, she cut straight to the heart of things. With such a straightforward, cut to the chase question, he felt compelled to tell her the truth. He knew he shouldn't tell her anything, but he was unable to stop himself, "I was sent here to determine why a Tè`rellean was on this ranch. To my surprise I found two Tè`relleans here. You wouldn't want to answer that question for me, would you?"

"I see. Whether or not I answer those questions depends on you. Who sent you?" Ari asked.

"Lare Sì`kram, our military leader," Camden said. He couldn't understand why he was giving her that information. It was as if she had him under some kind of spell.

"Are you here...to...to kill us?" Ari asked hesitantly but it was something she had to know. The people she loved most in the world were at stake.

"No, we were given strict orders not to kill anyone...at least not immediately," Camden said, "I need to get as much intel as I can get on the Tè`rell first."

"Why do the Emigee' want to kill the Te`rellean people?" Ari asked hoping to find common ground, even the smallest thread, to mend the breach between their people.

"We are a military race, we follow the orders of our leaders," he said indignantly. Soldiers never questioned the orders of their leaders. He was no different, until now, questioning the validity of the war his people were bent on.

"Have you never questioned whether those orders are right?" she asked. Questioning the morality of her actions, asking herself if she was doing the right thing had been ingrained in her from her earliest childhood memories. She believed everyone should ask themselves the same.

"No not until…" Camden fell silent. Ever since he met Ari, he had been asking himself questions, questions he never would have asked prior to coming to the ranch. Wondering how one young woman could affect him so much in such a short span of time, he was mind-boggled. A feeling of uncertainty overcoming him, he tried very hard not to answer her questions, why did he feel compelled to answer her? He couldn't explain it.

"Not until what?" Ari asked curiously. Needing to know if she could get through to just one Emigee she might be able to get through to others, open a line of communication for peace. Thousands of years of enmity, strife was too long, too long to be at war. "Not until I came here and met you. For the last several days, that is all I have been doing is questioning my beliefs, traditions, and principles," Camden said, giving in to the uncontrollable urge to be truthful with her.

"You don't have to kill Te`relleans, we have always been willing to share our world with you, after all we come from the same race."

"We are different from you. We changed when we left here millenniums ago. The world we settled on was a very beautiful world but she was deceptive. Her sun emitted a sereophasic radiation. Radiation having an insidious effect on my people, over time, it mutated our DNA. We lost our telekinetic and telepathic abilities. Some of us have retained the abilities but it is limited, only a few, a handful of my people still possess them. The worst that happened is we now die from old age. Even though we retain our self-healing ability if we are wounded, nothing can stop our aging. Our lifespan is about a thousand years. So, you see, we are no longer the same race," Camden sighed sadly.

"Even if we are two different races Camden, why can't we co-exist? Why does it have to be one or the other?" Ari asked hoping that he would see reason.

"Our DNA is not the only thing that changed, our philosophy changed too. We were invaded several times on our new world, Aurora, her resources were abundant, a prime target for invaders. In order to protect our world, we focused on military strength. The last invaders of Aurora were thwarted, but they decided if they couldn't have our world no one would. They poisoned Aurora, her land, water, air, nothing was left untouched. Only a fraction of my people were able to escape. My people went mad. Consumed with rage, seeking retribution their only solace; we were determined to have revenge for the billions of innocent lives lost, but we were unable to find the race that destroyed Aurora. We searched for two generations, two thousand years with no success. Then the leaders and consul decided to seek a new home. The madness subdued partially, but the annihilation of our homeworld left scars, irrecoverable scars. Philosophies changed drastically, our rulers promoted conquest. Conquer others for resources; eliminate anyone who would stand in their way. On our way back to earth, my people left a destructive path in its wake. Arriving here, your people embraced us at first, but then sought to eliminate us, thus the Te`relleans pose a threat," said Camden.

Connie called to out, "Camden, finish up there we have to go to round up twenty more cattle and bring them in to the corral."

Sadly, Ari glanced up and said to Camden, "I'm so sorry for what happened to your people but we weren't responsible. We should be at peace Camden…You better finish-up before Connie gets annoyed."

As she was walking away, Ari saw Jace watching her from the barn. She smiled as she entered the barn to visit Snowflake, and said, *"How long have you been there?"*

"I heard the whole conversation and to be honest with you I'm stunned," Jace said knowing the Emigee never give out information freely. Whenever an Emigee prisoner was captured, they self-terminated before the Te`rell could extract the subdural poison attached to their main artery; they would rather die than divulge any secrets.

"Why, what do you mean?" asked Ari curiously not sure why Jace was stunned.

"How did you get him to tell you his history, in great detail no less?" Jace asked, intrigued, wondering if some new ability was manifesting itself.

"You saw me. I just asked him questions. I didn't do anything special," Ari said as she shrugged her shoulders. As she thought about her and Camden's conversation, she said, *"He was rather forthcoming with information, wasn't he?"*

"I'll say…You got more information out of him than I could have. I was going to confront him after work was done, but I'm sure it would have ended badly," Jace said as he was shaking his head in disbelief.

"Did you know about everything that had happened to them since they left here?" Ari asked thinking about all the changes the Emigee endured as a people. It was no wonder they were an angry militant people, it was tragic.

"I knew some of the things but not all. They usually tell us nothing. The fact that he was talking to you was astonishing. It was almost like he had no choice but to answer your questions," Jace said. In all his years, he had never seen an Emigee respond like Camden; he would have to ask headquarters if they had ever heard of an ability that compelled others to answer them. It was amazing.

"How would that be possible?" Ari asked not convinced it was her but conceded that it was strange that he answered questions so readily.

"You are special and unique." Gently brushing away a strand of hair from her face, his fingers lingering on her skin, lost in her eyes, mesmerized. *"You are just starting to tap into your abilities. Suppressed for so long, it is possible you are developing an ability our people haven't seen since the destruction. His reaction to you was unprecedented; no Emigee reveals the smallest bit of information let alone have a whole conversation with one of us."* Spellbound Jace was completely enchanted, special and unique indeed.

"What other abilities do our people have? And why didn't you tell me about them before?" Ari asked. Intrigued about her people's abilities, she never thought of herself as special. Just an ordinary person, well she was a little special since she wasn't human, she thought, but that was neither here nor there, she was just a normal Te`rellean, that's all. What is a normal Te`rellean?

"Not all of our people have the same abilities. You know about telepathy and telekinesis which you and I both have, but others have abilities to manipulate air, water, fire, and earth," Jace said.

"Manipulating the elements, are there any other abilities I should know about?" Ari said with awe. She was just getting use to the idea of being from another

race, having telepathy and telekinesis was challenging enough. How many other abilities was she going to develop?

"Some of us have the ability to blend?" Highly attuned to Ari's emotions, Jace felt her trepidation.

"What is that?" How does someone blend, Ari thought, her mind went straight to the blender in the house and wondered how blending a person worked.

"Blending is, well it's like being a chameleon who can camouflage itself into its surroundings. Some of us can disappear into our surroundings; it's the perfect ability for covert ops." Silent for several minutes, Ari mulled this over in her mind. Her people were so focused on conflict, she thought, what about peace? Peace had to be achievable.

Jace calmingly assured her, *"Ari, it will be okay. I'm here with you. I'm not going anywhere; I will help you ease into whatever comes our way. I didn't tell you about some things sooner because you had so many new ideas and concepts to deal with, I didn't want to overload you with information and send you into a panic. You needed time to assimilate who you are, who you are not, and what you can do."*

Gently gliding his fingers over her cheek, Jace soothed her, reassured her that everything would be fine; he would be with her helping her adjust, she relaxed into his arms. Suddenly Jace turned and looked to the forest. Concern engulfed him and said, *"Ari stay close to the house."* Jace turned and ran toward the forest.

Ari started to panic and called out in her thoughts, *"Jace what's wrong? Where are you going?"*

"I'll be back, go to the house please…someone is in the forest," Jace explained.

Chapter

Eerily quiet, as he approached the forest, he scanned the area and saw nothing. The hairs on the back of his neck were standing erect. Slowly, cautiously
he moved deeper into the forest. The leaves were rustling in a swirl of wind;
a wind that had suddenly blown in from the west on a day that was perfectly
still, curious.

Eyes darting from left to right then back again saw nothing. Wondering
if he had imagined the call, he continued to watch. With the Emigee skulking
around, it was no wonder he was hearing things. Surveying the forest again,
he started to turn, about to shake it off as a case of frazzled nerves when he
was grabbed from behind and thrust to the ground.

Instantly Jace was swing his arms, fighting to regain his footing to no
avail. Refocusing his attention, Jace found himself looking up at his hare-
brained mentor grinning down on him; shock and relief swept through him
as he looked around and saw his companion leaning against a tree shaking his
head. Realizing he wasn't in danger, Jace slumped back to the ground and
started laughing.

"You scared a hundred years off my life, what on earth are you two doing
here?" Jace asked. Excited at first, it had been a few months since he had seen
his comrades, but then he became concerned. Kaazi and Alik`ram were never
sent together unless Gyasi thought there would be trouble.

"Glad to see me I see," said Kaazi grinning from ear to ear as he grabbed Jace's hand to help him to his feet.

As tall as Jace, Kaazi was broader in shoulders, massively muscular, with large sinewy arms bulging with power, and long legs, athletic and strong, giving him an intimidating air. Stately in manner with short black hair, quite distinguished, having deep dark blue eyes almost lavender, seductively enticing; with a ruggedly handsome face, square, smooth as silk, with a sleek nose which enhanced his good-looks—extremely handsome.

"Who else is going to keep you out of trouble? From what I just saw, you need someone to watch your back." They were all part of the same NOSSIC team, Kaazi the oldest team member felt it was his responsibility to look out for the rest.

Information was key to the survival of the Te`rell since it was the only weapon they were willing to use. Peaceful by nature, the Te`rell rarely used weapons to harm others. Life was precious to them, all life even the lives of those wishing them harm. NOSSIC was an agency responsible for gathering information, keeping their people informed of the movements of the Emigee, hopefully staying one step ahead of them. Protecting the innocent, safeguarding their people was the most important job any of them could do.

"Keep me out of trouble! Who's going to keep you out of trouble?" Jace asked as he raised a brow. "You get into many more skirmishes than I do." Even though Kaazi was the oldest, he was a mischievous imp, always keeping the others on their toes, a jokester.

"That's why I brought Alik`ram along, to keep me out of trouble while I keep you out of trouble," Kaazi laughed a deep hearty laugh while Alik`ram rolled his eyes and cracked Kaazi in the back of head.

Alik`ram was reserved, the quiet one out of the bunch, he liked to have his fun but he was much more subdued than Kaazi.

A tall handsome man with thick straight hair, a dark rich brown almost black, shoulder length which he kept tied at the neck. Having the same ruggedly appealing good-looks as the rest, he had an oval face with silky smooth skin, milk chocolate, and deep dark chocolate brown eyes, he was far less intimidating than Kaazi's beefy build, being about the same size as Jace.

Jace was laughing readily as Kaazi slapped him on the back almost knocking him over again, then turning serious, he asked, "Why are you here?"

"Gyasi sent us. He thought you might need some help. Intel from Isbeth informed him that Martin Lovell has been targeted by Emigee operatives," Alik`ram said with great concern. "Have you noticed anything suspicious?"

"Martin hired an Emigee a few days ago. The infiltrator, I have been on guard ever since waiting for the rest of them to show up. Why would Martin be targeted?" Jace asked trying to figure out why the Emigee wanted Martin and not Ari.

"Yes, why would my father be targeted?" Ari asked as she came up from behind them.

All of them turned at once with shocked surprise. None of them had heard her coming which was extremely unusual. Kaazi and Alik`ram stood gawking at Ari like they had never seen a girl before, while Jace said slightly annoyed, "Didn't I ask you to go to the house?"

"You were taking too long...besides I could tell you were laughing so I figured there was no danger," Ari stated as she gave him her most beguiling smile which melted away any annoyance left in him. She was not going to be put off. "What's going on Jace and who are your friends?"

"Ari this is Kaazi and Alik`ram," Jace said as he pointed to each one. "Kaazi, Alik'ram this is Ariella Lovell."

Still gawking, Kaazi suddenly burst into laughter and said, "Nice to meet you Ariella." Turning to Jace he blurted out, "How do you always get the prime assignments?" Alik`ram elbowed Kaazi in the gut.

"Nice to meet you Ariella," Alik`ram said in a much more refined manner. "Don't mind my lack-witted friend, he ran into a tree and hit his head getting here."

"Don't lie to the girl, you'll give her the wrong impression of me," Kaazi said with a wink. Ari could see he was a charmer; he probably had women everywhere falling all over him.

"I don't have to lie. She'll see your true nature for herself," Alik`ram said with a grin.

"Alright you two," Jace said as Ari watched the banter between these men, her people. Excited to have finally met more of her people she studied every inflection, every mannerism, but her excitement was curtailed by concern for Martin.

"What is going on with Martin and the Emigee? Why are they interested in him?" Jace asked centering the conversation back to a more serious vein.

Alik`ram continued, "Apparently Isbeth's boss had a geographical survey done of this mountain. It seems the results indicated a substantial treasure trove within the mountain. Zenot and the Emigee want a signed contract to drill."

"My father would never let that happen no matter what's below the surface. He loves this land too much to see it destroyed by drilling. You know… come to think of it…there was a man here a few weeks ago from some big corporation. I didn't really pay much attention to him at the time. My father never mentioned it after he left," Ari related.

Kaazi cut in," Well apparently Mr. Lovell turned him down flat because they sent in the big guns. Our old friend Hamer is here and he probably has Ja`nek and Ki here with him."

"Ki!" Jace exclaimed. "Gyasi sent you here to help me protect Ari?"

"Yes," Alik`ram said. "Htiaf and Epoh are with us too. When they heard we were coming to protect the Leg…uh to protect Ari, they insisted on coming along. They are out scouting the area. Hamer and the others must be close."

"Hold it," Ari said, confused, to many names being mentioned, "Who are all these people you're talking about?"

Jace turned to Ari and took her hand; he started to explain, "Sorry, Ari. Isbeth is one of our operatives who is working undercover at Zenot. Zenot has ties with the Emigee. Positioning Isbeth in there has been essential to our operation; it is the closest infiltration we have ever been able to achieve. Getting our operatives close to the Emigee has been nearly impossible. Because of our similarities we are easily detected, so when we can get our people into one of the companies the Emigee control without detection, well that is a major victory for us. She has been able to provide us with significant details on their business movements. Gyasi is our Lare`neg which is like a director or leader. He is the head of NOSSIC. Hamer, Ja`nek, and Ki are Emigee operatives. They are the most malicious masochistic operatives in the Emigee military. All of us have had encounters with them in the past; they are lethal."

While Jace was explaining the situation too Ari, Kaazi silently said to Alik`ram, *"Have you ever seen Jace so accommodating, so attentive with anyone before?"*

Alik`ram arched his brow and replied, *"Nope but who can blame him, look at her. She's the most beautiful women I've ever seen. She even outshines her mother, which I didn't think was possible."*

"I think he's met his match with her though. Lost his heart to her, look at the way he looks at her. He's done for!" Kaazi said with a chuckle.

"As much as I hate to agree with you, I think you're right this time," said Alik-'ram as he joined Kaazi in silent laughter. *"Who would have thought?"*

"Jace who are the other two men your friends mentioned?" Ari asked, wanting to know all her people.

"Htiaf and Epoh are operatives like the rest of us," Jace answered, patiently explaining everything Ari wanted to know.

"Why would they insist on coming along?" Ari's curiosity was bubbling over. Jace looked at Kaazi and Alik'ram for help. Kaazi just shrugged his shoulders, helpful as ever Jace thought. Kaazi loved to watch as others wiggled their way out of uncomfortable situations, he thrived on it.

Alik`ram on the other hand said, "Ari, I think they will want to explain that to you." Kaazi scowled at Alik`ram who just shrugged his shoulders and smiled.

"Oh…Okay…" she said. Changing the subject Ari asked, "Where are you staying?"

"Somewhere under the stars," Kaazi said in grand form as he raised his eyes to the heavens and spread his arms wide. Very theatrical, true to form, Kaazi was proving to be a charming rogue.

"Since you came to help me and my father, why don't you do what Jace did, apply for jobs as ranch workers? Then you can stay in the barracks," said Ari smiling at the three of them.

Jace looked at Ari then at his friends and said, "Makes sense. I'd feel better knowing that three of us are close to Ari to protect her." All were in agreement.

Chapter

14

The next morning, reflecting on her conversation with Camden, Ari was trying to assimilate the Emigee's tragic history. Something just didn't make sense to her. Why would the Emigee consider the Te`rell a threat? From what Jace had imparted to her, the Te`rell are a peaceful people who live in unity with the earth and nature. How does that threaten the Emigee? Vital information was missing. Ari decided she was going to talk to Camden again. If she did have some special ability that compelled the Emigee to answer her questions truthfully, she was going to take advantage of it too get answers.

On a mission, Ari came up behind Camden who was in the barnyard feeding the pigs. "Good morning Camden. How are you this morning?" Ari said cheerfully.

"Good morning Ari. I'm fine, how about you?" he replied with a warm but wary smile.

"I'm good. It's a beautiful day isn't it?" she said as she glanced at the sky, crystal clear and beautifully blue, then took a deep breath.

Camden nodded, looked around and said, "Yes, it is." He picked up a feed pail and dumped the contents into the trough.

"Camden…uh…why…why do the Emigee consider the Te`rell a threat?" Ari asked hesitantly. She looked intently into his eyes as if she could coax out the answers she wanted.

With no hesitation, Camden replied, "Because they have the power to destroy us." There was a mixture of fear and anger in his voice.

Ari thought about that for a few minutes then asked, "If we have the power to destroy you, then why haven't we done so already?"

"I don't know what your people are waiting for but every Emigee from the youngest to the oldest knows that the Te`rell want to destroy us," Camden replied as he remembered the stories told to him and other young children. The history lessons during his early education and his training as an infiltrator were riddled with annals of interactions with the Te`rell. All the information pointed to the planned destruction of his people by the Te`rell.

"Do you think I want to hurt you or your people?" Ari asked as she faced Camden. Her bright beaming blue eyes boring down into his soul, probing, searching for the goodness in his nature, the goodness she knew was there.

"I don't know but my gut feeling says 'no'," Camden said sensing something unique about her; she cared, truly cared about people regardless of whose people they were, her peaceful loving spirit sought out goodness in others, but she was not a normal Te`rellean. She was raised by peace-loving humans. The conflict within him was unsettling.

"But I'm Te'rellean, Camden," Ari said challenging him to realize that what he had been taught might not be true. Trying to get him to see past the propaganda of a warring people; a people veiled in shadowed truth.

"Yeah, but you said you were raised by humans and for the most part humans don't kill without a reason," he said as he continued with his work.

"Well, look at Jace. He hasn't done anything to harm you, has he? We have talked and I know he wants peace. There has to be a way to breach the rift between our people," Ari said with frustration.

"I don't know Ari; good intentions only go so far. You have to realize the amount of time we have been warring. Millenniums have passed with our people engaged in conflict and strife, continually antagonizing one another. At one point the Emigee scientists almost exterminated every living thing on the planet. That's one of the reasons our warfare is covert now. We don't want to destroy the planet while we are trying to eliminate the unwanted elements," Camden said imploring Ari to understand that what she wanted was impossible.

"We have to start somewhere. How did your scientists almost wipe out all life?" Ari asked. Her curiosity was peaked.

"We have biogenetic weapons. We introduced a virus into the eco-system which was supposed to target the Te`relleans," he said as he shook his head. Even Camden couldn't believe his leaders would condone such an irresponsible plan.

"What do you mean suppose to?" Ari asked. She was trying to suppress her astonishment at the foolishness of such action.

"Like viruses do, this particular virus mutated rapidly when it was released into nature. Many Emigee, Te`rell, and pre-humans, their grubbers, were killed. I don't know how the Te`relleans escaped but my people went into cryo-freeze. When we revived the world had changed. The Te`rell were still here but their grubbers had adapted to the virus over time making significant changes to their physiology and became the humans we have today," Camden explained. "Your people used biological warfare to destroy the Te`rell?" Ari exclaimed.

"Your people tried to exterminate mine and almost experienced the same fate. Extreme measures don't you think?" She was shocked at the extent the Emigee would go to kill her people.

Ashamed of the whole incident, Camden felt his people contemptible for perpetrating such a despicable act but it was history and the only action he had available to him was acknowledgement, thus he nodded his head in affirmation. Having had several very heated conversations with his father about his peoples' policies regarding the Te`rell and the methods they employed to achieve their goals, he was compelled to agree with Ari. He was not convinced that their methods or goals were right, so he attempted to change them to no avail.

"Camden do your people have a headquarters or base where your leaders are located?" Ari asked determined to confront these people herself. She didn't understand how naïve that notion was at present, all she knew was something had to be done.

"Yes," he said, "Why do you want to know that?" Camden asked curiously.

"I want to talk to your leaders," Ari said. She was new to this conflict it was true, but she wasn't going to sit by and do nothing. She felt it was ridiculous that two races of the same origin were engaged in hostilities.

Camden just laughed. Ari was a little annoyed by his total lack of regard, so she said, "I'm serious Camden, I want to talk to them." Camden became silent, he showed growing concern over Ari's naivety and replied, "Ari get that thought out of your head. They will kill you."

"Maybe they will Camden, but I still want to know, and you didn't tell me where they are," she said. "Where are they Camden?"

Camden was silent for several minutes unwilling to divulge this information to Ari but a strange feeling within in him compelled him to answer. "New York City, it is easy to control the humans from there," he said.

"Ari, Camden," Martin called out as he walked across the complex accompanied by her people. "I want you to meet the two new ranch hands I've hired."

They turned to see Martin approach with Kaazi, Alik`ram, and Jace. Ari smiled at their approach, but Camden froze, wide eyed and slack-jawed, he couldn't believe his eyes—two more Tè`relleans on the ranch. What was going on, he thought. What is the attraction on this ranch that there are now four Tè`relleans here?

"Camden, Ari this is Kaazi and Alik`ram. They are friends of Jace. He worked with them on a ranch in Colorado," Martin said happily. He was glad the men had ranching experience and would need little training.

"Nice to meet you Kaazi, Alik`ram," Ari said as she shook each of their hands and said telepathically, *"Be nice to Camden, especially you Kaazi."*

Kaazi grinned from ear to ear then feigned innocence by replying, *"Ari, whatever do you mean? I'm always nice."*

Brow furrowed, Ari said, *"I mean it Kaazi!"* She glared a warning at Kaazi which made his smile broader. What a hellion he is, Ari thought.

With tensions high, Camden wasn't sure what to do—continue to play the game or get the hell out of there. Ari put her hand on Camden's arm and whispered, *"It's okay Camden, they aren't going to hurt you."*

Warily Camden glanced at her then decided to take the chance, besides he didn't want to blow his cover yet.

"Nice to meet you," Camden said coldly, keeping his distance from the three male Tè`relleans.

Kaazi extended his hand to shake Camden's. Ari rolled her eyes and looked at Jace and Alik'ram for help. They just shrugged their shoulders.

Camden looked at Kaazi, then Martin and took the hand that was extended. Ari held her breath. After what seemed like hours, the two men released their grip. Ari sighed with relief. She quickly asked, "Have you two seen the barracks?" Putting her arm through her fathers, she steered the group in the direction of the barracks.

"No, we haven't," said Alik'ram as he smiled at Ari, supporting her effort to move the group away from Camden. He of all people knew the mischief Kaazi could get into if left to his own devices, lingering within the same proximity as an Emigee would be inviting trouble.

Martin stopped and said, "Ari why don't you and Jace show Kaazi and Alik'ram to the barracks. I have some things to do in my office."

"Okay," she said cheerfully and kissed Martin on the cheek. What a relief she thought, she could breathe easier with Martin heading back to the house. Instantly she turned her attention to the miscreant. "What was that all about Kaazi?" Ari asked scolding him as an errant child.

"What?" Kaazi said with pure delight. He thrived on mischievous shenanigans, eliciting untold responses from unsuspecting victims. As much as he enjoyed disconcerting his prey, he had observed over the years that true feelings and motives are frequently revealed by such antics, thus, always the covert operative, gleaning bits of information with this game.

"What do you mean *what*?" Ari said a little flustered, unaware of Kaazi's intent. She would quickly learn the tactics of the master.

"You told me to be nice. Wasn't that nice?" Kaazi said with feigned innocence.

This man is going to make me crazy, Ari thought. "I suppose it was nice to offer your hand, but you also intimidated Camden which I suspect was your motive all along," she said.

"Not only is she beautiful Jace, she's intelligent," Kaazi said with his impish grin glaring at her. Ari blushed and thought 'he is going to take some getting used to.'

Jace moved between Kaazi and Ari to distract her for the moment. Kaazi was a great person, an awesome mentor, and the person you would want on your side in a fight, but at times he comes off like a tempestuous windstorm—he definitely takes some getting used to. "Ari we are going out to the north pasture to check on the horses, would you like to come with us," Jace asked as he implored her with adoring eyes.

Feeling Jace's desire for her to be close, she smiled and said, "Sure…Snowflake needs some exercise. Why don't we let Kaazi ride Angel to the north pasture?" Jace grinned with delight. Angel was a beautiful tawny-colored four-year-old stallion. Completely unpredictable, many times over the past two years he had unseated his unsuspecting rider. One minute he was the perfect mount the next he was the devil incarnate. Jace, laughing to himself, thought he was the perfect mount for Kaazi.

"We'll get the horses Ari, give us about fifteen minutes," Jace said with satisfaction and relief knowing Ari would be accompanying them.

"Good…I have to go back to the house before we go," Ari said then ran off.

Chapter

The ride to the north pasture went smoothly much to Ari's chagrin. She was hoping Angel would teach Kaazi a lesson, but true to form Angel was on his own timetable. When they arrived, the men started their work while Ari exercised Snowflake in and around the open pasture. She noticed a couple of strays on the far end of the pasture and started riding toward them.

As she approached the tree line, a snake spooked Snowflake and he reared-up. Ari lost her grip and started to tumble backwards. After a second or two, she realized she hadn't hit the ground yet. She was levitating, floating in mid-air, but how? She wasn't doing it, she was sure. So how was she levitating? She looked toward the men she had just left but they hadn't seen what had happened.

What was going on? She looked around for an explanation. Who was levitating her? Continuing to scan the area, Ari saw two tall figures coming out of the forest, their hands outstretched. As they came close, they slowly lowered Ari to the ground.

Relieved to have her feet solidly on the ground again, she walked over to the men. "You must be Htiaf and Epoh, Jace's friends," Ari said with a smile. "Thank you for saving me."

Both men bowed to her.

"I am Htiaf and this is Epoh," the first man said. About six feet which seemed to be a dominant characteristic among the Te`rell, her people were quite tall. All of the men she met so far were of similar height. Htiaf had light brown hair intertwined with golden highlights, a head laden with lush soft curls; and large beautiful sea-green eyes could take your breath away. A handsome man with strong features, but he seemed troubled.

Ari was sensing a plethora of conflicting feelings, a troubled spirit emanating from him. His companion Epoh was about an inch shorter than Htiaf. Having the brightest fire-red hair she had ever seen, it was stunning. Wearing it straight and tied at the neck, it emphasized his bright aquamarine eyes; he also was emanating remorse and desolation. Both men were quite fit and muscular even though Ari sensed they were much older than they appeared. With all the grief and despair Ari was absorbing; she felt the need to help these two men. Too find out what was wrong, why they were in such agony was compelling.

"Nice to meet you," said Ari with a tender smile trying to comfort, console. "Alik'ram said that you both insisted on coming here when you heard they were going to assist Jace. Why?"

Epoh looked at Htiaf and lowered his head, tears filling his eyes, as if in shame. For years they had lived with the belief they had failed in their mission to safely deliver Ari, their precious cargo to the new base. The grief and the realization that the child was lost had taken a severe toll over the years.

Htiaf sighed, the tortuous heartbreak they both lived with hung heavily upon them. "Epoh and I are here to beg your forgiveness."

Ari was stunned, confused, she didn't understand what needed to be forgiven and asked, "Why do you need my forgiveness?"

Htiaf began, "Some years ago Epoh and I were traveling from our old base in Newfoundland to our new base. We were in charge of delivering a special cargo to our base in the mountains of Colorado. We were instructed to only use back roads to travel—not wanting to be discovered by the Emigee. Everything was going along as planned until we ran into a blizzard in the Adirondack Mountains. Visibility was extremely poor—we could barely see a foot in front of us. The mountain road we were traveling became increasingly treacherous as the storm worsened. One side of the narrow road hugged the mountain incline while the other side was a cliff with only a guard rail to prevent travelers from plunging into the river. With the storm's increased severity, we decided to pull over to wait and rest in the next town until the storm abated.

Looking for road signs to give us an idea of our location seemed to take hours."
Ari listened intently.

"Finally, we spotted one; the nearest town was only ten miles away. We were so relieved; but then as we continued, a tree suddenly fell across the road. As I swerved, the truck we were in went into a tailspin. When it finally stopped, the back wheels were teetering over the guard rail. Epoh and I were both rendered unconscious. When we awoke, Epoh was in better shape than I was even though he had hit his head against the window. Having some cuts on his face and hands, he had no broken bones. I, on the hand, sustained a broken arm and leg in addition to obtaining several broken ribs. He tried to get me to safety, but I told him to check the cargo first. Reluctantly, he left me in the truck. When he assessed the situation, he discovered that the truck could go over the cliff at any time. Sustained head injuries left him at a disadvantage; he was unable to use his telekinesis. So, he secured the truck to a tree on the far side of the road, the side next to the mountain, with rope we had in the truck. Once secured, he went to assess the cargo. The cryogenic orb you were in was our special cargo. Epoh was relieved to see that the cryo-unit was working perfectly. As he was securing you back in the case, he felt the truck slip."
Ari gasped.

"Knowing there wasn't much time left before the truck would plunge into the gorge, he grabbed the case to get it out of the truck. As soon as he stepped out of the truck, it lurched forward knocking Epoh to the ground. The case was thrust out of his hands. Horrified, he watched as the case plummeted into the water. Seconds later, the truck slid down the cliff. Epoh was terrified I was dead but here I am. Instead of plunging into the water like the case, the truck slammed into a cluster of trees at the river's edge. It saved my life. Our self-healing abilities did the rest; it took care of our physical injuries. But the emotional trauma of losing you has taken its toll; years of self-recrimination and shame. It has been especially hard on Epoh; he had you safely out of the truck then literally watched you slip through his fingers and plummet into the river. He has never forgiven himself for that horrible night. We searched for you for days with no success. We are begging for your forgiveness."

Ari was shocked and thrilled at this revelation. She finally had answers to the mystery of the case and her being lost from her people. Then to be miraculously discovered by Martin and Ena, she felt very blessed. She went to Htiaf and Epoh and embraced them with her whole being. Ari felt a strange flow of energy emanating from within her. It was like the energy she felt when she healed someone physically but it was different somehow.

With great care and warmth, she said to the two men, "It was an accident. I don't blame you for what happened. If you need my forgiveness, you have it but this could have happened to anyone anywhere. Please don't feel bad anymore."

Such a heavy burden was released; the two men felt incredible relief from those few words. It was as if they were lifted up from the darkness, stepping out from the shadows into the light. Shadowed truth revealed, they were released from a loathsome dismal abyss and given their first glimpse of clear blue skies and fresh clean air blowing gently over their faces. Heavy ballast had finally been lifted from guilt ridden hearts. The joy shared by Ari, Htiaf and Epoh was insurmountable. Torrents of joyful tears flowed as Epoh prostrated himself before Ari in thankful appreciation for her kind heart.

The trio caught the attention of Kaazi, Jace, and Alik`ram who had just finished with the horses. The three men rode over to join the group at the tree line.

Seeing the tears, Jace jumped down first and went to Ari, "Are you alright?" Jace embraced her and wiped the tears from her eyes. Kaazi nodded his head in their direction, Alik`ram turned to observe Jace and Ari. As was his habit, Kaazi was grinning from ear to ear with delight.

Comforted by Jacc's embrace, Ari said, "I'm fine, we're just very happy."

Tears of joy, relief surged through Jace as he turned to look at Htiaf and Epoh. They too were blubbering like babies. It was a site to see, two grown men besot by a deluge of tears. Jace started laughing, everyone started laughing; it was a wondrous day seeing the power of love and forgiveness in action healing old wounds.

After a few minutes Htiaf said, "Epoh and I found the Emigee base camp. It is on the west side of the mountain off the main trails. It is as you thought, Hamer, Ja`nek, and Ki are making use of an old cave. Only one way in or out of the cave that we could see; we scanned the area thoroughly."

"They are probably laying low until Camden reports back to them," Alik`ram said as he and Kaazi dismounted.

"This isn't their regular MO, sitting back and waiting," Kaazi said a bit puzzled. "If it were up to those three, their initiative would already be evident. The fact they are sitting quietly means someone very high up is directing this op."

"Camden wants to know why there are Te`relleans on the ranch and what their interest is here," Ari said. She had stepped back from Jace to face all the men.

"How do you know that Ari?" Alik`ram asked patiently. All eyes were intently focused on her as she answered. Conflicting emotions engulfed Ari, she was fond of Camden but these were her people.

"I have had several conversations with Camden and that's what he told me when I asked him why he was here," she said as if nothing unusual was conveyed.

Kaazi, Alik`ram, Htiaf, and Epoh exchanged glances then focused back on Ari.

"Are you telling us that he just gave you that information?" Kaazi asked. The men were dumbfounded. The Emigee didn't just give out information, they divulged nothing.

Jace stepped in and explained, "It seems that every time Ari has a conversation with Camden he is compelled to answer truthfully. It's like he wants to give her information because he never tries to leave or avoid the questions. He's drawn to her."

The four men were stunned. Thousands of years of interrogations resulting in fruitless efforts and a young woman with no training is able to achieve what the experts failed to accomplish—amazing. Every time any of them had ever tried to interrogate an Emigee, they came up empty handed. The Emigee have implants that inhibit forced removal of information from the sub-conscience. Any attempt by doctors or scientist to remove the device has resulted in the death of the prisoner. The fact that Camden was willingly giving over information was outstanding.

"What else has he told you?" Kaazi asked curiously. Hoping Ari's connection with Camden could help them finally make progress for a permanent solution to the Emigee problem. It was unprecedented that communication with an Emigee was so productive.

"We have discussed that Si`kram sent him, he's not here to kill us yet, the rightness of exterminating the Te`rell, why the Emigee feel we are a threat, the changes that mutated their DNA, philosophical changes, their history, biogenetic weapons, their headquarters…" said Ari as she rattled off the list of topics.

Alik`ram cut her off. He couldn't believe his ears. In a few conversations with Camden, Ari had obtained more information than most of them had discovered in their whole lives.

"Their headquarters? You know where their headquarters are?" Alik`ram said with excitement as the others gazed at Ari in amazement.

"Only the city, it's not like he gave me the address to the headquarters," Ari said tentatively. She didn't like the direction the conversation was heading. If she gave the location of the Emigee headquarters she would be betraying Camden's confidence, something that made her very uncomfortable. The expressions on the faces of her companions spoke volumes as to what they wanted from her. They were like kids who were eagerly waiting to be let loose in a candy store ready to devour everything in sight.

"It's more than we have now. Where is the headquarters?" Kaazi asked chomping at the bit, unable to contain his excitement.

Ari hesitated as she looked at the men anxiously awaiting her answer. What a dilemma. She should be loyal to her own race but she had misgivings about providing that kind of information to one side of a warring enemies. These were Camden's people, they were talking about. An offshoot of her own people, cousins, it was like betraying family. Ari wanted to breach the differences between their peoples not cause more dissention.

Finally, she asked, "What are you going to do with that information if I give it to you?"

"We will relay it to Gyasi at our base," Kaazi said trying to remember that Ari was new to this war and their people, but he was becoming frustrated. Anticipation was killing him; they had never been this close to knowing the location of the Emigee headquarters before.

"Gyasi...the Te`rellean director of intelligence...NOSSIC isn't it?" Ari asked as she waited for confirmation.

"Why are you hesitating to give us the city, Ari?" Jace asked gently as he turned her to face him. As he gazed into her beautiful caring eyes, usually calm and peaceful, he saw the conflict raging within her. After several moments silently beseeching her, she dubiously expressed her fears to him.

"I just don't know...what would an intelligence director who has one goal in mind...what would he do with that kind of information?" Ari said with great concern. "I would feel horrible if I gave that information to you, he relayed it to the military then, in turn, their base was wiped out. How many lives would be lost?"

A huge sigh of relief went up from the men. They exchanged glances and started laughing. Ari was completely bewildered and a bit annoyed. She didn't understand what was so funny, as far as she was concerned this was no laughing matter.

It was Epoh who finally said, "Ari, we are a peaceful people. You don't know that yet, years you have spent with the humans learning and adapting to their ways. Fighting, violence, hate, it's not our way; it is far removed from the way our people live. You are still thinking in terms of the human military, constantly at war, fighting, killing, destroying instead of talking and finding common ground. We have no military Ari. If our people didn't want to save lives, we could have destroyed the Emigee when they first attacked us millenniums ago, we have always had the means to do so, but violence is not our way. Reuniting with the Emigee is our goal but we have to protect our people in the process. The intel we gather is to warn and protect, especially since they have tried on numerous occasions to exterminate us. Our leaders have been devising a plan to hopefully unite the Emigee with the Te`rell. Whatever conflicts we encounter from them are always initiated by them. We fight for defensive purposes only. The Emigee will not be harmed by us with the information you possess."

Ari was relieved by what Epoh said, and it made sense. Camden said he didn't know what the Te`rell were waiting for, even the Emigee knew they had the ability to destroy his people. Her people want peace as does she.

"Their headquarters is in New Your City," Ari confessed, assured that no harm would come to Camden's people because of her.

"Alik`ram, do you have your com on you. I want to give Gyasi the news as soon as possible. With the location of the city, Gyasi can plan the assault, we can be there for the attack on their base," Kaazi said with all seriousness. "Way to go getting the info out of Ari, Epoh."

Ari's mouth dropped. She couldn't believe what she just heard. With shock and anger she said, "What? You lied to me?"

Frowning all four men glanced at each other and nodded; Jace, Alik`ram, Htiaf, and Epoh pounced on Kaazi as he bellowed with a hearty roar. They scuffled on the ground for several minutes each one taking his turn wrestling Kaazi, arms flailing, legs thrashing, each struggling for the upper hand, until Ari came up to him. The others moved aside so that Ari could confront her would be taunter.

"Not funny Kaazi," Ari said with clenched teeth. Glaring at him she felt a burst of telekinetic energy building. Diligently practicing her skills for weeks, she was quite proficient; she levitated him up to the highest point of an old pine tree and deposited him on the most flimsy branch she could see.

Kaazi was clinging to the tree as if his life depended on it. He called down, "Awe…come on Ari…I was just kidding." Not moving, he was frozen like a statue, hanging on to the tree for dear life.

"Nice job Ari," Alik`ram said with wholehearted approval grinning as he watched Kaazi clutching the tree which was now swaying in the breeze.

"Did you know that Kaazi is terrified of heights, Ari?" Htiaf said with a grin. He had known Kaazi for many years; he was always pulling some kind of joke or prank. Htiaf was truly delighted that this beautiful young woman wasn't going to tolerate his nonsense.

"Oh…no…I had no idea… I should probably bring him down," Ari said with concern. As she started to raise her hand to bring him back down.

"No!" Epoh said firmly and gently took her hand in his, "Let him stay up there for a while; after what he just did, serves him right."

"He'll be alright Ari," Jace said as he took Ari in his arms and kissed her forehead to reassure her.

"Come on Ari! I'm sorry! I was just kidding," Kaazi called out, "Guys! Help me out. You can get me down." The tree continued to sway in the breeze as the group moved out of hearing distance. Alik`ram looked back and made a swirling gesture in the air; several strong wind gusts whistled through the trees and he smiled. Clinging to the tree, Kaazi was paralyzed; both arms and legs were wrapped around the thin trunk of the old pine. Terrified it would break under his weight, he didn't move.

"How long should I keep him up there?" Ari asked. She got various answers, fifteen minutes, a half-hour, an hour, and forever. Epoh was really angry, Kaazi was always pulling little stunts like that and he finally got what he deserved; all the better it was from such an unlikely source. Fifteen minutes was long enough to teach a lesson and Ari had every intention of getting him down in that allotted time, but she got sidetracked when Alik`ram and Jace started showing off their skills.

Alik`ram was a windmaker. From nowhere, the wind swirled around them, forming funnel-like mini tornados. Ari was mesmerized. Leaves, twigs, and grass twirled above their heads, twisting and turning, in and out and in between the others.

"Alik`ram is showing off," said Jace grinning. As he watched attentively, a twig hit him in the back of the head. "Hey! What was that for? I was just telling it like I see it." Another twig hit him in the shoulder. A devilish grin lit up Jace's face as he looked around. Water sprang up from the ground, spinning in a tight coil, it surged at Alik`ram.

Taken completely by surprise, he was completely drenched, sputtering water.

When he mentioned sparring, Ari thought they were going to box or wrestle like they had with Kaazi, but that isn't what they had in mind.

Sparring the Te`rellean way was quite different. It was almost like dueling. The two opponents some distance apart attempted to block projectiles from knocking them off their feet. Rocks whizzing by heads, branches soaring back and forth between the two, each man blocking the other's attempt to knock him to the ground, all the while Ari was mesmerized and holding her breath. Alik`ram was trying to distract Jace with hefty gusts of wind while Jace was doing the same with torrents of water. Ari was fascinated and completely forgot about Kaazi. Htiaf and Epoh were also watching intently, calling out warnings first to Jace and then to Alik`ram. After about a half-hour of sparring, they called it a draw. Each man proved to be an expert exhibiting masterful skills.

Once the sparring was finished, Ari and the men walked back to the horses grazing near the tree line. Gradually they heard a noise, as they got closer they heard Kaazi still yelling to get down.

Ari looked up and gasped, "Oh my goodness…I forgot all about Kaazi up in the tree."

Epoh said to Ari with a twinkle in his eye, "Let me get him down for you Ari."

"Okay Epoh," Ari said as she turned to grabbed Snowflakes reins. Epoh stretched out his mind, grabbed Kaazi, and let him free fall from the top of the tree. Kaazi let out a bone-chilling scream that sent shivers down Ari's spine.

"Ahhhhhhhhhhhhhh…" down the length of the tree, about a two-hundred-foot drop. Just before he hit the ground Epoh reached out with his mind again to levitate him inches above the ground.

Kaazi turned ten shades of green. Once his feet touched the ground, he sank instantly into a ball and put his head between his legs. He wasn't able to move from that spot for some time.

Jace, Htiaf, and Alik`ram were laughing hysterically. Ari stood stunned, gawking at Epoh because of what she had just seen him do to Kaazi. It's not as if Kaazi didn't deserve what he got but to free fall from such an apogee would be terrifying for anyone let alone someone who hates heights.

Epoh casually strolled over to Kaazi and said with a smirk, "Oh…sorry Kaazi…I was just kidding." Kaazi just moaned. Even Ari joined in the laughter at Kaazi's reaction, serves him right she thought.

After a while Kaazi composed himself, returning to his normal spunky self. Htiaf and Epoh about to head back to observe the Emigee base camp at the cave said their goodbyes to Ari and the others, reassuring her that they would see each other again.

As Epoh was leaving, Kaazi called out, "Epoh…don't forget to cover up that horrendous mop you call hair, you don't want to give away your location."

Epoh snarled under his breath as he disappeared into the forest. Kaazi couldn't help laughing after that free fall stunt. For years, he had continually ribbed Epoh about the brightness of his hair especially when the sun hit it, it was like a beacon guiding, signaling to all onlookers, not very conducive for covert operations. Epoh always had to wear a hat to avoid detection which was a point of contention for him and Kaazi knew it.

The others headed back to the main complex on the ranch. True to form Angel decided he didn't want to carry a rider on the way home. He started bucking and pounding the ground for several minutes while Kaazi was attempting to gain control. Angel finally had enough. Rearing-up on his back legs, he attempted to dislodge his passenger. Successful, Kaazi lost his grip and fell flat on his back. Jace, Alik`ram and Ari encircled him with their horses. As they were looking down at him, they each smiled an ear to ear grin.

Jace said, "I see you still have a way with horses."

Ari looked at Jace and said, "I thought you told me Kaazi was an expert with horses."

Shaking his head, Alik`ram said, "Get up off the ground you're embarrassing me." Everyone including Kaazi began to laugh.

Ari couldn't remember having such a good time or laughing so much in her life. She was so thankful for such wonderful new friends and to be part of such a caring peaceful people. There was still so much that she didn't know about them, but after today she knew she would look forward to discovering other secrets as yet unknown to her. She longed for the day when she would be able to finally meet her real parents.

The day was fast approaching when she would leave the ranch and everything familiar to enter a completely new world, one far more advanced than the present one. A sense of remorse mixed with excitement surged through her, conflicting emotions to say the least but flooding through her, nonetheless.

Jace felt her turmoil and privately asked in his thoughts, *"Ari are you alright?"*

"Yes… I'm just thinking about leaving here and how much I'm going to miss this place. At the same time, I'm excited about meeting more of our people and meeting my parents. Starting college is another concern. I wish I could put college off for a while but that is the only way I will be able to leave here without Martin and Ena worrying about me," Ari said as she was trying to convince herself it would work out.

"It'll be alright. Whatever happens I'll be there with you for as long as you need me. Try to relax or I'll have to get Kaazi to lighten the mood," Jace said with a grin.

"Forget it, I'm good. I've had enough Kaazi today," Ari laughed as they approached the barn.

Chapter

Conundrum was the only way to describe this assignment. Camden had quite a week. Meeting the most beautiful woman in all creation, only to discover the unthinkable, she is a Tè`rellean. Talking with Ari was easy, very unusual in itself since he found it difficult to speak with beautiful women, always becoming tongued, but for some reason he just wanted to tell her everything, even things he shouldn't. Baffled, Camden couldn't figure out why he would divulge secret information to her.

Unable to discover the details about how she came to be adopted by the Lovell's, a human family, he was able to glean a generic overview through discreet inquires. Then there was Jace, another Tè`rellean. Why was he here? As far as he could see, there was nothing special about this ranch except Ari. What could Ari have to do with him being there beside the fact she is very desirable? To top everything else off, several days after he settled into a routine, two more Tè`relleans arrive on the ranch. What was going on there? Sure that it wasn't that they all liked ranching so much that they all converge together on this one particular ranch, even though the work was not bad. So, why were they there? It's like they called in reinforcements to maintain their position, but for what? He didn't know and didn't look forward to telling Hamer there were now four Tè`relleans on the ranch.

Traversing the meandering trails, Camden made his way off the main route on the west side of the mountain to the cave where Hamer and the others had set up camp. Ki spotted Camden as he approached the cave. Perched in the tallest pine outside the cave; he had a birds-eye view of the surrounding area. Like a wildcat Ki sprang at Camden. Not caught unawares, Camden's senses were on high alert, he felt something amiss. Before he was tackled, he was able to grab Ki in mid-air and flipped him onto the ground. With cat-like moves, Ki was on his feet poised to attack when Hamer, who had heard the commotion, came out to investigate.

"Ki…Stand down," Hamer ordered. "It's Camden…relax. Go back up to your perch." The longer Ki was out in the wild the more he took on the persona of a wild beast. "He has been getting progressively worse all week," he said under his breath, desperately hoping Camden had something significant to report so they could leave this place.

"Camden…good, come into the cave and tell us what you have learned," Hamer ordered as they took a seat around a fire in the center of the cave where Ja`nek was already seated. The cave was quite spacious compared to some of the caves he had frequented in his previous missions. Most caves he encountered were damp and musty, but this was quite dry, very comfortable. A unique opening provided protection; the rocks formed a lip that narrowed close to the opening which provided cover from predators or others seeking to gain access.

"So, Camden…what do you have to report?" Hamer asked eagerly, hoping they could complete their mission quickly to get back to civilization, roughing it with Ki was getting tedious.

Camden began, "I met the Te`rellean, his name is Jace. He is not happy that I'm there; he's very tense. When I first got there, I assumed he was the only Te`rellean on the ranch but Martin Lovell's daughter, Ari, is Te`rellean."

"What?" Hamer said. "How is that possible? A Te`rellean raised by humans."

"She is the most beautiful woman I have ever met. She is very friendly and sweet. You feel very comfortable talking with her," Camden relayed to the two men who were sitting around the fire gawking at him in disbelief, not only at the fact that there were now two Te`relleans on the ranch one of which was Lovell's daughter, but at Camden's confession about her. Their reaction to what Camden had just said could have been comical in different circumstances slacked jaws, twisted faces, furrowed brows; Hamer was in no mood to listen to how lovely the girl was. He wanted tactical information, details about why the Te`relleans were on the ranch.

"Snap out of it soldier. You're not over there to court a woman, let alone a Te`rellean woman," Hamer commanded. The thought sickened him, to actually like a Te`rellean was preposterous. Born and bred to kill Te`relleans, he wanted to exterminate them.

"Sorry sir. Several days after I was at the ranch, Lovell hired two more ranch hands. They were friends of Jace—Te`relleans. Have you ever encountered Kaazi or Alik`ram?" Camden asked hoping to glean any useful bits of information to make his job easier.

"Kaazi, Alik`ram…they are two of the Te`rellean's best operatives. Why would they send their best to an insignificant ranch in the middle of nowhere?" Hamer said as he rose and started pacing. Four Te`relleans, Kaazi, Alik`ram, two of their very best operatives, why would they send their best, it doesn't make sense he thought. "We're missing a vital piece of information. There has to be something very important on that ranch for them to be involved."

"From what I can see, it's just a normal horse ranch." Camden added.

"Let's go back to the beginning," said Ja`nek. "Who are the original occupants of the ranch?"

"From what I gathered so far, the ranch has been in Martin's family about three hundred years. He lives there with his wife Ena, daughter Ari, and his ranch manager Hank. They hire temporary help in the early spring. The ranch hands work through the end of fall," Camden explained.

"So we can rule out the temporary help. How long has Hank been working on the ranch?" asked Ja`nek analyzing every detail of Camden's explanation.

"I'm not sure exactly. It's over twenty years though," Camden replied wondering what this has to do with why the Te`relleans are on the ranch.

"Okay, we can rule out Hank he seems to be a permanent fixture on the ranch," Hamer said. Deductive reasoning was Hamer's forte, one of the reasons he was the best.

"What are you looking for?" Camden asked, intrigued by Hamer and Ja`nek's systematic analysis of the situation.

"Something triggered the Te`rell's reaction. We need to find out what it was," Hamer responded running his fingers over his cheeks down to his chin.

"Tell me more about the daughter," Ja`nek said. "She's Te`rellean and she has been raised by the humans. How old is she?"

"Connie told me she was almost eighteen; the Lovell's adopted her seventeen years ago. Apparently, the Lovell's have an anniversary party for Ari every year to celebrate her adoption. Because her birthday is unknown, they use the anniversary as a replacement for her birth date." Camden explained.

"So, she was adopted seventeen years ago," Hamer said. Something about the number seventeen years was gnawing at him but he couldn't put his finger on it.

"Did this Connie tell you anything else about the adoption?" Ja`nek asked.

"No…but Hank said that he remembered when Martin and Ena brought Ari home. They had gone on vacation to the mountains of New York with Martin's brother and they brought home a baby," Camden replied.

"The mountains of New York—the Adirondacks or the Catskills," Hamer was whispering to himself. He still had a nagging notion, pricking him like needles, but couldn't figure out why. There was something vaguely familiar about New York and years ago. "If it is the girl, why would the Te`rell seek her out now? Why didn't they seek her out before she was adopted?"

"We are still missing a piece of the puzzle," said Ja`nek. "Can you think of anything new or different that happened to the girl this year. Something one of the workers might have noticed. Or maybe an item or object she protects?" Ja`nek said as he stoked the fire.

Camden thought about it for a few minutes. When they were working with the horses a few days ago, the necklace she wore was getting caught on the horse's mane. Camden said, "She was given a pendant earlier this year, a few months ago, I think she said, by Ena. I didn't think much of it because all the Te`relleans wear pendants."

"The pendant could be a bio-detection device," Hamer said. "Our locators are implanted. As far as I know, the Te`rell don't implant technological devices within their bodies. If they were to have locators, they could be in the form of a pendant."

"This is all speculation of course," interrupted Ja`nek. Watching Hamer closely, Ja`nek was on guard; something was agitating Hamer and he didn't want to get in the way if his temper exploded.

"Yes but it makes sense. Think about it…a child is adopted by a family… the only clue to her identification is a pendant. Do you give the pendant to a baby or young child? No…you don't. The parents would wait until the child is an adult. The girl receives the pendant...who shows up—a Te`rellean," Hamer said convinced he had solved the puzzle.

"So Ari somehow activated the locator when Ena gave her the pendant," Camden concluded.

"It fits. They would send someone to train her and help her assimilate into their society," Ja`nek stated still keeping an eye on Hamer.

"So, if all this is true, why send the best operatives they have to the ranch?" Camden asked.

"There is only one reason they would do that," Hamer said. "She has to be someone extremely important to them."

It hit Hamer like a ton of bricks falling from the sky. Many years ago, he was sent to find a Te`rellean transport truck and destroy its cargo. According to intelligence reports, the truck was carrying a proto-type weapon to destroy his people. What if the intel was wrong and it was a child they were transporting? What if the intel was right and she is the weapon? He had to let Si`kram know immediately.

Hamer was still pacing, it seemed he was picking up bad habits from that boorish human, Mr. Braun, he thought. If the girl was in the truck, how did she survive? He watched the cargo plunge into the river. No one could have survived that fall in freezing temperatures unless...she was in stasis. Of course, how else would two Te`rellean operatives transport a baby? Why is the girl so important that Kaazi and Alik`ram have been dispatched?

Camden was watching Hamer pacing, deep in thought, running his hands through his hair. He would have pulled it out if it were long enough to grab, crew-cuts were a blessing, he thought.

Camden cleared his throat and said, "You really think Ari is the reason the Te`relleans are at the ranch? Besides being extremely beautiful and kind, she seems like a normal woman, nothing out of the ordinary."

"It's the only thing that makes sense. Years ago, I was sent on a mission to intercept and destroy a Te`rellean transport truck and its cargo. The intel we received was that the truck was carrying a new proto-type weapon that could destroy our people. I caught up with the truck in the middle of a blizzard in the Adirondack Mountains in New York. If the girl was in stasis, she could have survived and been found by the Lovell's seventeen years ago. All the pieces fit. We just don't know why she is so important," Hamer said as he spotted Ja`nek heading to the entrance of the cave listening carefully.

"Ja`nek contact Si`kram. Inform him of the Te`rellean girl and the circumstances of her upbringing. Request new orders," said Hamer as he barked out orders urgently.

Ja`nek scrambled to retrieve his com and went outside to get a clear signal. They had discovered the cave walls were made of some type of amalgamation of metal that interfered with com signals. They had to go up to a ridge above the cave to receive a clear communication signal from their base command.

Within minutes, he returned with orders. "Si`kram wants the girl. She is a priority. He also said to bring the human parents. We might be able to use them as leverage to obtain information from the girl," Ja`nek said. "So, what's the plan? Camden when is the best time to grab the girl and the humans?"

Camden thought about what he had observed over the past week and said, "The three of them always eat supper together in the evening around six o'clock in the main house. The ranch hands are in the barracks preparing their own meal, relaxing, winding down for the day. There is usually lots of noise in the bunk house so we should be able to get in and out without notice."

"We will arrange for our transport and will execute this plan when all the arrangements have been made. We will contact you when we have acquired everything we need. Continue to gather as much information as you can; try to get more information on the girl. Si`kram will be pleased. Now go, we have much to do," Hamer ordered. Camden returned to the ranch.

Chapter

17

Life has a way of throwing unexpected things at you; one day you are a perfectly normal human and the next you discover you are from a completely different race, Ari thought as she reflected on her unexpected life changes. Who would have thought any of this was possible, certainly not Ari. She was always the awkward one, not really fitting in, her looks and intelligence, everything about her stood out as different; the reason, she wasn't human.

Now she discovered she has all these awesome abilities, it was like she was shadowed, being suppressed for so many years, finally coming into the light. Healing, telepathy, telekinesis and who knows what else she will discover. The epitome of her joy was to realize she wasn't alone anymore, there were others of her race that have some of the same abilities. Who would have thought there were people just like her? She was so happy that she now had friends just like her.

After the excitement of the afternoon, Ari wanted to relax and spend some extra time brushing out Snowflake. Ena came into the barn searching for her, "Ari honey, I have a favor to ask." Ena was beaming with joy.

"Sure mom, what would you like me to do?" Ari asked as she turned to Ena and immediately noticed the glow emanating from her. She was beaming with delight.

"I have something very important I need to discuss with your father. Would you mind eating with Hank in the barracks tomorrow night? I'm planning to have a candlelight dinner for Martin in order to break my news," said Ena blushing slightly. Ari had never seen her mother happier than she was today; she was downright giddy with excitement.

"Candlelight, wow…it must be some news," Ari teased. "Are you going to let me in on it?"

"Of course, I am, after I tell your father," Ena said enthusiastically, re-assuring Ari that she would never exclude her. Ena's thoughts were so loud and excited Ari couldn't help but pick up her mental projections.

Smiling, immediately Ari said, "I don't mind eating in the barracks mom. You two have fun." Ari embraced Ena tenderly giving her a kiss on the cheek. Ena returned the kiss and left the barn.

Ari was thrilled; Ena and Martin were going to have a baby of their own. For years, Ena carried a silent sadness around within her. Sadness she felt since dis-covering she could not conceive a child with Martin, the man she loved with her whole being, more than life itself. It had tortured her for more years than she could remember. As soon as Ari had discovered she had the ability to heal, she took advantage of her skill. Quietly tip-toeing into the bedroom, neither Martin nor Ena were aware that Ari had gone to them one night while they were sleep-ing. Gently placing her hands-on Ena, with all the love and hope Ari had for this woman who raised her, she poured out her healing energy. Ari wasn't sure Ena would be able to conceive, but she was willing to give her the opportunity for na-ture to take its course. She was so happy it worked, she had to find Jace.

"What do you think their doing?" Epoh asked puzzling over the activity as he and Htiaf were continuing their surveillance of the Emigee's cave. They had spent several days watching the camp with nothing to report, but now some-thing was happening.

"It looks like their planning something, but what?" Htiaf said. "Damn im-plants, makes it impossible to retrieve any information when all you hear is electronic static in their minds."

"Look, Camden is leaving, and they are calling Ki down from his perch. We need to tell Kaazi and Alik`ram," Epoh said becoming quite antsy. He was not about to let anything happen to Ari this time.

"You stay here and continue to keep an eye on the camp, I'll go to the ranch and let Kaazi and Alik`ram know about the movement at the cave and that Camden was there," Htiaf said as he left their vantage point. "Stay cloaked and don't get to close."

Making his way through the forest Htiaf's agitation grew. He would not fail twice to keep Ari safe; he wouldn't allow the Emigee to get near her. Urgently, he moved like a cheetah. Finally, he saw Kaazi and Alik`ram; they were heading out to the east pasture, the opposite direction from him. Reaching out with his mind, he alerted Kaazi of his presence.

"Htiaf is over in the trees, he needs to talk to us," Kaazi told Alik`ram as they changed direction, moving to intercept his position, "He sounds anxious." As the pair approached the tree line, Htiaf transphased; talking with someone invisible is disconcerting. "Epoh and I were maintaining surveillance of the cave when we noticed an increase in activity after Camden left. Something is going on, whether they are leaving or getting ready to make a move, I don't know; but I left Epoh staked-out still, I didn't want anything vital to slip through our fingers. I will not let anything happen to Ari this time," Htiaf said with unprecedented determination.

"Camden obviously told Hamer that we're here with Jace. He has got to be wondering why," Kaazi said. "Htiaf, you and Epoh stay close to the ranch tonight but keep cloaked so no one sees you two. We'll tell Jace."

"Are you going to tell Ari?" Htiaf asked with great concern. On the one hand he felt she should be told but then ignorance is bliss. Either way he was determined, overly zealous to the point of obsession, to do everything in his power to make sure no harm came to her.

"We'll talk to Jace to determine if we will or not," Kaazi said as he scanned the area for intruders.

Htiaf started to turn to leave when he heard Alik`ram say, "Stay alert and be careful." Htiaf nodded and left.

"And be invisible!" Kaazi ordered. Tensions mounting, the Emigee would make their move soon. Time was of the essence, they needed to get Ari to their people immediately. Somehow, she was the key to peace even though he didn't know how exactly.

"We need to find Jace," Kaazi said as he turned his horse around to go in search of Jace. "Do you have any idea where he is or where he is working today?"

Alik`ram laughed, "I know exactly where he is. As we were leaving, I saw Ari running up to him as he was coming out of the vet room." Kaazi grinned and thought to himself, it won't be hard to find him then.

"He doesn't get much work done when Ari's around, does he?" Kaazi said grinning from ear to ear as he swung his horse around taking off in a gallop.

"Doesn't seem that way," Alik`ram replied laughing as he turned to keep pace.

With everyone on high alert and tensions continuing to mount, nerves felt like a rubber band stretched to the brink of snapping. Time slowly dragging on, it was maddening, with nothing amiss that night, all the men were pacing. Kaazi and Alik`ram vigilant, overtly watching the barracks and the surrounding yard. Jace always attentive to Ari was staked out beneath her window. Htiaf and Epoh were combing the perimeter around the tree line.

They met the next morning early to regroup. "What are they waiting for?" Jace growled as he paced back and forth roving about with his eyes.

"The cave is abandoned, so it has to be soon," Epoh volunteered. Anxiety was taking its toll on him with circles darkening his normally bright eyes.

"They are on the move; we just don't know when they are going to strike. I'm going to see if I can rattle some chains, spook our resident Emigee," Kaazi said, "The rest of you stay alert and report anything unusual. Protect Ari!"

As the others left, Alik`ram asked, "What did you have in mind to rattle Camden?"

"I'm just going to turn up the heat a bit, that's all," Kaazi said with a smirk.

Alone in the barn, Camden was cleaning out stalls. Kaazi quietly approached catching him completely unawares. "How's it going Camden?" Kaazi asked with a twinkle in his eye. Ever cautious when it came to the Emigee, he appeared relaxed but was anything but.

"What do you want Te`rellean?" Camden said undaunted but was unnerved by his sudden appearance. The last thing he wanted was a confrontation with this particular Te`rellean. 'Stay calm, keep it cool,' he continually repeated in his head.

"Well since you asked so nicely, I would like to know why you and your friends are here. This isn't exactly your style, to work shoveling horse droppings. What do you want here?" Kaazi asked with a gleam in his eye. He had propped himself up against the opening to the stall completely blocking Camden's escape and if that wasn't intimidating enough he was palming fire in his hand and manipulating it with his fingers. Kaazi was a blazer, a fire maker and if there was one thing the Emigee hated it was fire. A deep seated fear of fire stemming back through their history; all Emigee were terrified of fire.

Camden's eyes grew large, heart pounding, eyes focused on the flames in Kaazi's hand, but he boldly turned it around, "What are you doing here Te`rellean? Why are there four of you here on this ranch? Why did your people send two of their best operatives here to an ordinary horse ranch? There must be something very important here for them to have sent you."

"That would be *three* of our best operatives, we mustn't forget Jace," Kaazi didn't want to tip his hand and let him know there were actually five of their best operatives on the ranch. He always liked to keep an element of surprise; so, he stuck with what Camden already knew.

"So why are the *three* of you here? Let me tell you what I think. It has something to do with Ari. She is very important to you for some reason, possibly some secret weapon," Camden said fishing for a reaction.

"All of our people are important to us; she was lost, now she is found, so yes we want to keep her safe just as we would any of our people," Kaazi said as the flames grew in size, pressing ever closer to Camden.

Terror increased but Camden was not going to back down, defiantly he sneered, "We will find out why she is so important to you!"

Flames engulfed the room; Camden hit the floor in horror covering his head, gasping. What seemed like hours, the fire roared, but as quickly as they had blazed, they were gone as was Kaazi. Relieved to see he was alone again, he sighed, Te`relleans he mumbled.

Kaazi was staying close to Camden as they worked throughout the day. Camden noticed Kaazi's attentiveness and completely ignored him as if he weren't there at all, but he did try to stay a little farther away than usual. Kaazi was sure Camden's actions would provide a clue as to the timing of any imminent attack taking place. He expected Camden to respond with anxious anticipation if the Emigee were planning something soon.

Ari was in the house helping Ena prepare for her romantic dinner with Martin. Aglow with dancing candlelight, the room was breathtaking. Sweet enticing aromas from freshly cut flowers and delicious food cooking permeated the air. Soft melodious music completing the ambience played serenely in the background. Everything had to be just perfect and it was. Looking around the room, Ari sighed with pleasure. Just as she was putting the finishing touches on the table, lighting the candles and placing a rose in the center, she heard footsteps.

Ena came into the room and gasped with delight, "It's beautiful Ari, thank you." Ari could hardly contain her joy; she was just as excited as Ena.

Ari turned to Ena who was absolutely radiant—beaming with joy. "Mom you look gorgeous. You're wearing dad's favorite color—baby blue, very appropriate," Ari said as she glanced at the clock. "It's six o'clock, I hear dad outside. I'm going to sneak out quietly. Love you."

"Love you too!" Ena said as she waited for Martin.

As Martin walked in, he was stunned. Pausing as he looked around scanning the room, his eyes settling on Ena and he smiled, "What's all this honey?" He went to Ena and pulled her into his arms. "What's going on? Did I forget our anniversary?"

Ena grinned at him, "I have to tell you something," she said as she snuggled closer to Martin in his arms.

"What is it?" he asked with great eagerness as he tenderly kissed her. He couldn't imagine what had made Ena go to all this trouble. Stopping to take another glance around the room then at Ena, he noticed how absolutely radiant she was, beaming with delight.

"I'm pregnant. We are going to have a baby!" tears started flowing down her face. Martin was flabbergasted, completely stunned. Speechless, he stood gawking at Ena for several minutes. A baby, he thought, he had given up all hope of having a child of his own long ago, a miracle, what a wonderful miracle!

"A baby!" Martin said with a smile wider than the Grand Canyon. "How? Are you sure? When?" He could hardly contain his excitement.

Ena pulled him to the sofa to sit and started explaining, "You know I haven't been feeling well the last several weeks. I just thought I had a stomach bug at first but when it didn't go away, I went to see Dr. Anderson. He ran the usual gambit of blood tests which took a very long time. I was concerned when he told me he wanted a second opinion without giving me the results, but he said not to worry. So, he sent me to see Dr. Taps who is a gynecologist. By that time, I was getting really nervous because no one was telling me anything; my imagination was running rampant, the only thing I could think of was that I had cancer."

"Why didn't you tell me? I should have been there with you," Martin said mildly scolding her.

"I didn't want to worry you needlessly if it turned out to be nothing. Anyway, with all the blood test back, I finally got the results; Dr. Taps sat me down in her office and said that I was going to have a baby. Of course, I told her that it was impossible, the damage done to my uterus from the accident I had as a child left me infertile. She explained to me that she triple checked the blood work; it was conclusive—I'm pregnant! Since I didn't believe her, she asked me if I wanted to go into the examination room and have a quick ultrasound so that I could see the baby, but I felt we should see the baby together for the first time. Next week, we can see our baby together Martin. She said I'm sixteen weeks pregnant. It's a miracle!"

Martin was speechless he was so happy. "Does anyone else know?" Martin asked.

"No, I wanted you to be the first one. We can tell Ari later after dinner. She's eating with the guys," Ena said. "Let's eat so we can tell her soon."

Jace found Ari as she was coming out of the main house. She was beaming with excitement. Ari went over to Jace and said with a smile, "Well everything is set in the house. What are you doing?"

"Coming to find you, are you hungry?" Jace asked. He wanted to spend some time alone with Ari so he could tell her about what he suspected the Emigee were up to.

"No…I'm not hungry yet. I guess I'm too excited for Martin and Ena," she said. "Are you hungry?"

"Not really, do you want to go for a walk?" Jace asked cheerfully. This would be the perfect opportunity to let Ari know that Kaazi and the rest feel it would be prudent to depart to their people immediately instead of waiting for her to go to college next month. Her safety depended on getting her away from the ranch.

"Sure," Ari said, "Let's go on the south trail. It's pretty there at this time of day." They set out for the trail.

Kaazi and Alik`ram were in the barracks raising cane with Connie, Andy, and Hank. They were arguing about who was going to win the World's Series. Camden was nowhere in sight. Htiaf and Epoh were patrolling the tree line, but all was quiet. Kaazi had seen Camden go to his room so he wasn't concerned about him at the moment, but anticipation was killing him. He didn't want to be caught off-guard; the Emigee were famous for their sneak attack strategies. Unfortunately, what Kaazi didn't know was that Camden slipped out of his window to meet up with Hamer, Ja`nek, and Ki.

Chapter

Htiaf and Epoh meticulously patrolled the perimeter along the tree line. At the farthest edge of the circuit they met. For hours they had been painstakingly diligent, assessing all movement in and around the main house. Nothing absolutely nothing was happening. Nervous anticipation was taking hold, failure was not an option. They had to stop the Emigee.

"Any sign of them?" Epoh said tersely as he scanned the surrounding tree line.

"Nothing, not a glimpse of anything unusual; actually, the forest is extremely quiet for this time of day. It's as if everything is holding its breath," Htiaf said suspiciously as he glanced around nervously.

"I don't like the sound of that!"

"Epoh...look...do you see movement by the house?" Htiaf sputtered. Epoh whipped his head around scanning for movement. There they were, the Emigee, it was going down now, and they were so far away. Both men took off like a shot, trying to get to the house to prevent disaster.

"We're not going to make it in time!" Epoh shouted in panic.

"We have to, just run and stay cloaked!" roared Htiaf.

Behind the main house, the three men held position with weapons in hand. Ki was eager with anticipation, hoping desperately for bloodshed. Hamer and Ja`nek, more subdued, were on high alert waiting for Camden to get there to complete the mission. After several minutes of anxious pacing, Hamer saw Camden rounding the house.

"Camden is all clear with the ranch hands?" Hamer asked quietly, hoping that this operation went off with relative ease.

"Yes, they are occupied in the bunk house arguing about baseball." Camden replied nervously. The more Camden thought about what was happening the more he didn't like the whole situation.

"Okay…Camden you go in through the front door, we'll go in through the back," Hamer ordered. Camden nodded but was having misgivings, it didn't feel right. He liked Martin and Ena but felt a special attraction for Ari. Starting to care about her—he didn't want to see any of them get hurt. He hated the Te`rell; they were evil and wanted to destroy his people, but she was different, kind and sweet, someone he could care about. Never had he given a second thought to destroying the Te`rell until now.

Martin and Ena were at the table enjoying the candlelight dinner she had prepared when Camden walked in the front door.

"Camden, is something wrong?" Martin asked startled as he noticed the weapon in his hand.

"Martin, we don't want to hurt you so stay where you are," Camden said as Hamer, Ja`nek, and Ki appeared from the back of the house. Martin and Ena were confused at the intrusion into their home, but then became concerned at the sight of strange men coming in from the back of the house.

Hamer looked at the pair and said, "Where is the girl? Ja`nek check the other rooms for the girl." Without hesitation, he quickly went through all the rooms but found nothing.

"Ari? Why do you want Ari?" Ena asked. She was terrified not only for Ari and Martin but for herself and the baby. After so many years of desiring a child of her own, her first thoughts were to protect her unborn child from the strange men who were invading her home. She wanted to know what their intent was, why they wanted Ari, and what would happen to her and the baby?

"She's Te`rellean, our enemy, we are taking her to our leader." Hamer said coldly as if they understood what was happening and their connection to the Te'relleans.

"Who are you? What is Te`rellean? Why does your leader want Ari?" Martin demanded becoming increasingly defensive and concerned for the safety of his family.

"Ja`nek tie them up," Hamer ordered. Ja`nek went for Ena first, grabbing her roughly, he yanked her arms behind her back. She cried out in pain. Martin quickly stood up to help Ena but was met with a blow to the head which rendered him unconscious and bleeding. Ena screamed but to no avail. She was forced back into her chair after she was tied. Ja`nek then moved to tie Martin who was sprawled out on the floor.

In the barracks, Connie was knocking on Camden's door to let him know the food was done; it was time to eat. He received no answer. Kaazi ran over to the door of Camden's room and opened it only to see the open window. Slamming his fist in to the door, he alerted the others.

"Alik`ram, Camden's gone. Call Htiaf and Epoh, it's going down now!" Kaazi barked. Immediately transformed into military leader—complete seriousness ensued; when lives were at stake, he never made light of serious situations. Keeping Ari safe was certainly that.

"What's goin on?" Hank exclaimed as he reached Camden's room. He was in charge and he wasn't going to play second fiddle to those two upstarts. Determined, he wanted to know what they were talking about, especially after seeing how riled they became not finding Camden in his room.

"Hank, you and the others stay here so you don't get hurt," Kaazi ordered for their own protection. He should have realized Hank was not one to take orders readily.

"Like hell I will! Now what's goin on?" Hank demanded firmly and unmovable, he wasn't about to sit on the sidelines if there was danger on the ranch. Kaazi sighed looked at Alik`ram who just shrugged his shoulders, then conceded.

"Short version—we are here to protect Ari, Martin, and Ena from a dangerous group of people. Camden is one of them," Kaazi explained. "Now stay here!"

As soon as Kaazi and Alik`ram left the barracks, Hank hurried to his room and got his shotgun. Connie and Andy followed after him.

"What are you two lookin at?" Hank growled as he went to his rifle rack, pulled out the key from his pocket, and unlocked the cabinet. Pulling out his favorite shotgun, he examined it then he grabbed a box of ammunition.

"You got more guns Hank...give us some," Connie asked as he eyed the rest of the rifles in Hanks gun rack.

"We want to help Hank. Martin has been good to us!" Andy said with conviction as he glanced at Connie. Martin always procured that type of loyalty from his ranch hands. Giving respect and dealing fairly with others was Martin's gift.

Hank grinned and grabbed his extra rifles and ammunition. Handing one to each of the men, he nodded his approval. Loading the guns, the three men worked quickly.

Outside Kaazi scanned the area, no sign of Camden or the others. Alik`ram was running over to him from the corral. "Htiaf and Epoh are on their way. They are going to approach from behind the main house. They said they saw the Emigee enter the house," he said. "Where is Jace?"

"I don't know," Kaazi said. "Call him."

Alik`ram stretched out his mind and called to Jace, *"Jace where are you?"* He received no answer. "He's probably with Ari, he's not answering me," Alik`ram said, "Now what?"

"We check out the main house to assess the situation. You go to the right, I'll go to the left," said Kaazi.

They made their way over to the house; each of them looked in the side windows. Kaazi didn't have a clear view, he saw only Ja`nek standing behind Ena away from the rest of the group. Alik`ram saw Martin tied up on the floor with blood dripping from a gash on his head; he was starting to come around. Ena was in a chair with her hands tied behind her back and tears running down her cheeks; his heart sank. Ja`nek had his hand on her shoulder as if he were holding her down. Ki was hovering over Martin, waiting and hoping for an excuse to draw blood again. Camden was arguing with Hamer about the treatment of the Lovell's.

Kaazi met Alik`ram at the corral to get his report. Alik`ram relayed each person's position in the house. The two men heard Htiaf and Epoh approaching from behind the house. As they came into view, Epoh asked, "What's the plan?"

Kaazi said, "There are only two doors to the house. We need to take up defensive positions in the front and back. They have Martin and Ena, Ari isn't in the house. We are pretty sure she is with Jace."

"At least Ari is safe," Epoh said with relief in his voice. "Htiaf and I will take the back."

"We will wait until they make a move to leave. Remember we have to protect Martin and Ena, stay cloaked!" Kaazi ordered.

Htiaf and Epoh returned to the back of the house to take their positions behind a utility shed directly opposite of the backdoor. One on each corner of the shed, they remained poised and cloaked for the rescue. Alik`ram and Kaazi took up diagonal positions to the front door, Kaazi on the right and Alik`ram on the left. Both staying low and out of sight, waiting for the Emigee to appear.

Inside, Camden was frantic, "Why did Ki have to hit him so hard? He is supposed to be brought to Si`kram undamaged."

"Are you turning soft Camden? He's alive, besides what difference does it make, he's just a human," Hamer said as he glared at Camden. "We need to find the girl. Where is she?" he bellowed as he turned his glare to Ena. Hamer approached Ena slowly in an effort to intimidate her. Ena cringed at his approach, raising his hand to strike her; she flinched and whimpered as he landed a hard blow across her face almost knocking her out of her chair, "She's in the barracks with Hank."

Sobbing, tears rolled down her face; she felt like she betrayed Ari, her only thoughts were to protect the baby. She loved Ari, but she desperately wanted this child and would do anything to protect it. Filled with guilt she sobbed uncontrollably.

Hamer turned to look at Camden and said, "You said she would be here! Ki, find the girl. Do not harm her we need her alive."

Ki was headed for the front door, when Camden said, "I'll find Ari." He turned disappointed and mumbling until Hamer bellowed.

"No! Ki will do it. You get the human off the floor." Keeping command of the situation was essential since the op had gone awry. Hamer hated it when things didn't go as planned, it infuriated him.

As soon as Ki left the house, Hank, Andy, and Connie came out of the barracks, guns in hand. Anything but covert, the three of them drew Ki's attention immediately. Kaazi and Alik`ram couldn't believe what was unfolding before them.

"That crazy old man is going to get the three of them killed!" Kaazi thought to Alik`ram. Before either man could get to the trio, Ki was geared up ready to act.

"You there, stop and drop your weapon," Hank ordered in his usual no nonsense tone. Taken aback, Hank had never seen anyone so large; no, no, that wasn't true, the only time he had seen men like him was when the city slicker and his driver came to the ranch, but they left peacefully. He didn't think he was going to be so fortunate this time.

Ki stopped and laughed. "Puny human," said Ki with contempt as he continued to cross the yard to the barracks. Ki's spirits were soaring, there was glee in his eyes; he saw a fight coming. Even though it wasn't with the Te`rell, the blood of humans would suffice.

Hank wasn't going to let him get close. Firing a warning shot at Ki which soared by his head, made his point. Ki stopped, peered at Hank with utter delight as his eyes narrowed and became fixated on his prey. Slowly he opened his weapon. The Z-blade was his weapon of choice. A blade with many functions, it could deliver a clean cut cauterizing a wound using electric current, it could burn through a person using laser technology, and it could slice or shred a person depending on the setting used. There was no mistake, it was deadly. As sadistic as Ki was, his favorite setting was the shredder. It inflicted the most damage and resulted in the greatest blood loss. Twenty-four inches in length when opened for maximum penetration, the Z-blade had razor sharp teeth to cause massive mutilation.

Hank stepped back when he saw the weapon but only briefly. Taking aim again, this time aiming for his midsection, he fired. Ki deflected the bullet with his blade then smiled the most sinister smile he had ever seen. Hank didn't scare easily but the man in front of him was cold, demented, sending a shiver down his spine. Undeterred, Hank nodded to Andy and Connie and they all began to fire their weapons at Ki. Not one of the bullets touched the crazed wild man. Ki with his superior training and speed was able to deflect all the incoming bullets with his blade. Hank and the others were dumbfounded. Their guns were useless.

As Ki grinned and sank into a cat-like crouch, he sprang into action. His movements were lightning fast; Hank and the others didn't realize what was happening.

At the same time, Kaazi and Alik`ram saw Ki moving in for the kill. Alik`ram stretched out his mind and twirled his hand. A stiff gust of wind pushed Ki off his mark which managed to throw him astray but only by inches, just enough so that he missed the lethal stroke. Ki turned to see Kaazi and Alik`ram as Hank, Andy, and Connie lay on the ground bleeding.

In the house, Hamer and the others heard the shots fired. He commanded, "Ja`nek find out what's going on out there." Ja`nek pulled out his DM and went to the front door to see what was happening.

He yelled back to Hamer and said, "Ki has wounded the humans and he's up against two Te`relleans." DM in hand, he ran out the door toward Kaazi. The DM, a diamortic weapon, was standard issue for operatives in the field. Like the blade, the DM had multiple settings ranging from stun to bimort; the bimort, double death, not only killed its victims the setting vaporized them. The weapon was based on electrical energy, developed specifically to scramble Te`rellean neurological wave patterns. A direct hit at the lowest setting, scrambles the Te`rellean's telepathic and telekinetic abilities—it takes several minutes to recover thus they are defenseless in the meantime. Multiple hits will kill, as will, a direct hit to the head on a high enough setting.

A DM blast just missed Kaazi's head. He stretched out his hand and knocked Ja`nek to the ground as fire emerged from his hand like a flame thrower. The Te`relleans were communicating telepathically, Kaazi ordered, *"We need to immobilize them before they harm Martin and Ena. Use your MPI's to take them down."*

Te`relleans despised weapons but through the years of conflict with the Emigee it became necessary to develop and use them when absolutely essential for defensive purposes. Two types were used by the field operatives, the EP and MPI. The EP was an epiphonic device which used sound waves to disable a person. The MPI was a macropotic phase inducer which could disable or kill using transgenic power waves depending on the setting.

Lives were at stake, they needed to disable the Emigee to get close to Martin and Ena. MPI's were a last resort. The fire fight went on for several minutes lighting up the complex, flashes of red, streaks of white, sparks and debris flying at the men; flames and wind-funnels darting here and there. Swirls of smoke and dust floating in the air as the fighting raged. Each side was evenly matched, neither side had the advantage.

Watching from the door Hamer became increasingly agitated; he grabbed Martin and barked, "Camden bring the woman." They headed out the back. Htiaf and Epoh were waiting just outside the door behind the shed; weapons trained on the unsuspecting Emigee.

As soon as Hamer and Camden stepped out the door, Htiaf was ready. "Put your weapons down and let the humans go," Htiaf ordered.

Looking around unable to spot his enemies, Hamer let loose with a barrage of DM blasts, firing randomly in the direction of the voice he heard. Htiaf and Epoh with weapons discharge soaring over their heads were taking careful aim at Hamer and Camden. The last thing they wanted to do was be responsible for injuring Martin and Ena. With weapons fire whizzing by them, Hamer and Camden crouched down behind the pair using Martin and Ena as human shields. It was impossible for Htiaf and Epoh to fire without hitting Martin and Ena as the Emigee tightened their grip on the Lovell's. There was little they could do unless they got an opening.

"We will kill the humans if you don't back off," bellowed Hamer as he was dragging Martin with his DM pointed up under his chin. Tightening his grip on Martin, struggling to keep him between the Te`relleans and himself, he slowly moved away from the voice.

Htiaf and Epoh were looking for a shot but it was no use. There was no shot without harming Martin and Ena, any quick movement could trigger the DM and kill Martin instantly. Kaazi called a warning that Ki and Ja`nek were rounding the corner of the house trying to escape. Htiaf and Epoh took cover firing their weapons at the pair as they ran, Ki and Ja`nek tried dodging the weapons discharge, but took several hits to their arms and legs; nothing that would slow them down much. To be effective, it needed to be a body shot. Kaazi and Alik`ram were racing right behind them blasting their MPI's as they ran after the Emigee, determined, they had to be stopped. Ki and Ja`nek reached Hamer just in time to be transported to their hes`chala, a stealth transport vehicle which was hovering over the tree line.

Kaazi and Alik`ram reached Htiaf and Epoh just in time to see the last glimmer of the transport beam.

"Damn," Kaazi said. "What happened?"

"Hamer and Camden were using Martin and Ena as shields. We couldn't get a shot off without injuring them," Epoh said with frustration. Ari was safe but they lost Martin and Ena, they failed.

"We can do nothing about Martin and Ena right now. There will come another time and place to get them back. Come on Hank, Andy, and Connie were cut down by Ki. We need to heal them if we can," Kaazi said in desperation as they ran back to the bunk house.

Chapter

19

ontentment, one rarely finds deep seated contentment in life. Love is one of those rare precious commodities that elicit such contentment. Not selfish lust but love that seeks kindness, goodness, and patiently endures hardship. It is a gift that bears all things, believes all things, and hopes all things. Love never fails. When love is found, it must be treasured and protected that it doesn't disappear like whispers on the wind.

Jace and Ari had walked quite a long distance on the south trail. Walking hand in hand, enjoying the peaceful serenity of the evening sky's spectacular panorama, as shadows were forming on the trees and mountains, dark silhouettes shone against the receding light—stillness. Ari felt an inner peace. Aglow with happiness, being with Jace brought new meaning to her life. The feelings he evoked within her were new and enticing; tender and loving, exciting and sensual, life couldn't get much better than this, she thought. She was drawn to his warmth, his kindness; he was a haven from everything uncertain. Ari felt as if they were different parts of a whole, separate, unique, but fitting together perfectly, harmonizing as one. Deep within her soul she felt an immeasurable, irrevocable love, a love growing stronger each day.

"I'm so happy for Ena and Martin," Ari said. "Now I don't have to feel guilty about meeting our people and my real parents."

"Why would you feel guilty about that Ari?" Jace asked as they stopped and perched themselves on an old log lying on the ground.

"I don't know… I shouldn't but I guess I feel like I would be abandoning them. I love them dearly and I would never want them to feel hurt because of my desire to see my people and my real parents," Ari explained as she nestled her head on Jace's shoulder. The very nearness of her sent a rippling effect along his spine, electrifying every nerve fiber, tingling excitement difficult to contain. All objectivity lost where Ari was concerned, she was his and he would do anything to protect her.

"I think they would understand. They're good people," Jace said reassuring her that she had no reason to feel guilty. "Ari…I was talking with Kaazi and the others…we feel that it would be wise and safer for you if we went to our people soon, rather than waiting until you're ready to go to college."

"Why Jace, has something changed?" Ari asked with apprehensive gnawing within. She examined Jace intently and saw the concern emanating from him.

"Htiaf and Epoh had been watching the cave where the Emigee were camped. Camden made a visit. After he left, there was a flurry of activity. We think they are planning something. We need to keep you safe," Jace explained trying not to alarm her, but she was becoming uneasy.

"Why do you think I'm in danger? Why do they want to hurt me? Why me? I don't understand." Ari asked, frustration growing like a kettle reaching its boiling point. She felt as if she was going to explode.

"Kaazi confronted Camden today. The Emigee are baffled as to why we sent our best operatives to the ranch. They have concluded that it has something to do with you. They will stop at nothing to find out why you are being so well protected," Jace whispered as he spoke reassuringly to her. Taking her hand, he gently stroked it as he brought it to his lips to tenderly kiss it all the while sinking deeply into her beautiful blue eyes.

Calming and seductive, his touch had the desired effect; she started to relax a bit. Mesmerized by his presences, she settled into him as her mind drifted. "Why did our people send so many operatives here Jace?"

"You know why. I came to teach you and the rest came because Martin was targeted by the Emigee," he said avoiding the question.

"Yes, I know that but why did they send their best operatives?" Ari was not going to stop asking until she got a satisfying answer.

Stroking her hair, he said, "You are special Ari, special in many ways. I'm not at liberty to go into detail but we were sent to make sure nothing happens to you and to bring you home at all costs…safely. So that's why we need to go as soon as possible."

"I don't know if I can do that right now Jace. What would I tell Martin and Ena?" Ari asked as her anxiety was building again. It was too soon, no plans had been made; her parents would surely think something was amiss. Agitation welling up, Ari stood; she could no longer sit still, so she continued on down the trail, Jace followed; walking always helped relieve her tension.

"We could tell them the truth now that they have a new baby to look forward to, they will miss you but much of their time will be taken up planning for the baby," Jace said, "I will help you explain things to them."

"Do you really think this move is necessary?" Ari asked as she was contemplating the situation.

Jace stopped; he became very quiet, he felt something was wrong. Stretching out with his mind he saw smoke at the ranch swirling in the air, something was very wrong…was it the Emigee?

"Jace are you alright?" Ari could see something was wrong, but she didn't know what.

Jace shook his head. Confused, furrowing his brow, he started walking again. As they drew closer to the ranch, Jace picked up on the fire fight, flashes of white and red, blood, Hank and the others on the ground.

"We have to get back to the ranch Ari. Something has happened," Jace said urgently with concern as he started to run.

"What Jace? What has happened?" Ari exclaimed in terror as she ran to keep up to him.

"A fire fight with the Emigee, they attacked the ranch," Jace explained as he extended his mind, stretching to pick up thoughts from the others. "Stretch out your mind Ari."

"My parents, are they alright?" Ari asked frantically. Attempting to see what Jace saw, Ari gasped as she caught a glimpse of the fire and smoke.

"I can't tell the thoughts are all jumbled. Come on let's hurry," Jace said as he grabbed her hand.

Kaazi and Alik`ram were working on Hank together. Stabbed and sliced several times in the abdomen and chest, he sustained the worst injuries. Even though the whole fire fight took only a few minutes, Hank lost a lot of blood. The other two had injuries that were serious but not life threatening. A punctured left lung, Andy was stabbed in the chest twice. Htiaf was making hast to repair his lacerations, his breathing was shallow and labored. Connie was stabbed in the right side which nearly perforated his liver. He was fortunate his wound was muscular and didn't nick the liver—those types of wounds were difficult to heal, but as it was Epoh was having no difficulty using his ability to heal the shredded tissue.

Too late to be of any help, Jace and Ari came running up the driveway to the men by the barracks.

"What happened?" Ari cried. Epoh went to Ari when he finished healing Connie. He did not want to be the one to tell Ari that her parents had been taken but he was the first one done healing the humans.

"Ari the Emigee attacked, there was a fire fight. As you can see, the humans were injured. Ari...they were here to kidnap you and your human parents. Since you weren't here, they were unable to capture you but...but they took your parents. We tried to stop them...we really did...but we couldn't do so without injuring them. Hamer and Camden were using them as shields," Epoh explained with a saddened heart.

Ari listened with horror as tears streamed down her face. Epoh was beside himself, he didn't know what he could do for her. Her heart was breaking, his along with it.

"No!" she cried, "She's pregnant...what are they going to do to them?"

Jace was attempting to comfort her but she was inconsolable. Sobbing, defeated, she wanted to collapse. Holding her tight, providing solace from her anguish, he supported her limp little body.

"They will attempt to obtain information about you and us, that was their main objective; but they're original objective, the reason they were sent here was to get a signed contract, they will try to pressure Martin into signing the contract for drilling rights. The Emigee will probably try to use your parents as leverage to capture you," Kaazi said as he finished the healing process with Alik`ram.

"Jace what can we do?" Ari asked as she sobbed into his chest. Gleaning support from him, Ari was desperately trying to channel her emotions, use the power of her grief to focus on getting her parents back, but she was crushed at heart. How fragile happiness is, she thought; one minute you are flying high the next you are trying to climb out of the pit.

"Once we take care of Andy, Connie, and Hank, we will go to our people," Jace said with confidence, knowing they would have access to resources that would assist them in locating Martin and Ena.

Hank started coming around. He was looking at Ari who was leaning over him. "Ari girl you're alright!" he said with a whisper. "What happened?"

"You were wounded Hank but you're better now. You still have to rest. Kaazi and Alik`ram will help you to your room. We will talk in the morning Hank," Ari said tenderly before the two men helped Hank to his feet. Andy and Connie had already returned to the barracks to get some rest.

Before he would budge, Hank asked, "What happened to Martin and Ena?" He wasn't going to be helped to his room without knowing what had happened, near death and as stubborn as ever.

"They were taken Hank. We couldn't stop them. They were being used as human shields. We couldn't get a clear shot without killing Martin or Ena," said Htiaf with deep regret. "We will get them back. You can be sure of that Hank."

"Who were those people? Why do they want Martin and Ena? Who are you people?" Hank asked, barely whispering but he wanted to know, and he wanted to know now.

"Zenot hired them to get the fracking contract signed," Jace said. "Among other things," he said with a whisper under his breath.

"You have just been healed Hank. You need to have a good night's rest. We will talk in the morning before we leave. You will need all your strength for what is to come," Jace said as Hank went to his room with Kaazi and Alik`ram.

Chapter

Kaazi pulled into a Shop-n-Go. Htiaf, Epoh, and Alik`ram piled out of the van, stretched then headed for the snack bar. Jace gently nudged Ari who was sleeping on his shoulder. She had been exhausted, in emotional turmoil, and worried sick about her parent's safety. The trip was long and tedious. If only they could travel the quick way, it would lessen her suffering greatly, but as it was they had to move at a snail's pace since Ari had never experienced the gird. Something she would have to be trained to experience, the gird was quick but a bit disconcerting; it definitely took some getting used to.

"We have stopped to fill up. Are you hungry?" Jace asked as she straightened herself and rubbed the sleep from her eyes.

"Where are we?" Ari asked trying to clear her mind from the fog of sleepiness. Lethargy continued its grip for several minutes; gradually dissipating, she stretched to wake herself.

"We're in Grants, New Mexico. Come on, let's stretch our legs," Jace replied as he grabbed Ari's hand to help her out of the van. "How are you doing?"

"I'm fine," she whispered as big, sad puppy dog eyes surveyed her surroundings. As they headed for the store, she asked, "Jace will you grab me a bagel and a latte? I'm going to wash up." Glancing around the store to find the restroom, she spotted the sign in the back-left corner and headed in that direction.

"Any special kind of bagel—plain, blueberry…?" Jace asked, attentive to her preference. Developing an overwhelming need to comfort Ari even in the smallest ways, he felt compelled to appease her.

"Anything but onion…I don't care for onion bagels," Ari said with revulsion as she furrowed her brows and twisted her face in disgust, looking quite comical.

Jace joined the others in the shop. Htiaf and Epoh had two baskets full of junk food and soda. Jace looked at them with disbelief. "Are you guys hungry?" he said with a chuckle.

"Have to do something to break the monotony of driving," Epoh said with a grin. Alik`ram joined the group with an extra-large coffee and a large to-go bag in hand. Epoh and Htiaf went to the cashier just as Kaazi walked in from the van.

"Where is Ari?" Kaazi asked as he surveyed the room. It was empty with the exception of a couple sitting at a booth in the corner. They both had over-sized cowboy hats on which obscured their faces. Kaazi's instincts went on high alert; he didn't know why but his instincts were never wrong. "How's Ari doing?" Kaazi asked. Jace's concern for her shown in his face.

"She's putting on a brave face, but I know she's worried especially for Ena and the baby," Jace said as he ordered her bagel and latte. "We will find them Jace. I didn't tell you this before, but I tagged Martin when we were first hired. I thought it prudent to have a subdural translocator imbedded.

We will be able to track him when we get to the base," Kaazi said as he displayed his usual grin, a dazzling smile from ear to ear. Placing a locator behind his left ear would go undetected since the Emigee avoided that area on the body.

"Why didn't you tell us sooner?" Jace asked with mixed emotions. He was grateful they had a place to start but annoyed that he took so long conveying that little tidbit of information. It could have eluded Ari's fears.

"Time was of the essence. We had to get on the road as soon as possible to reach base and the tracking equipment since we were unable to travel the gird. I was sidetracked," Kaazi said with a shrug of his shoulders.

Ari appeared from around the corner and started meandering through the aisles of snack foods. She drew the attention of the couple sitting at the booth. They began to whisper amongst themselves. Kaazi caught their reaction to her and moved to secure a better vantage point to observe their actions. Out of sight, with a clear view of the pair, he was watching as the woman got up and meandered down the aisle opposite the one Ari was in.

"*Alik`ram,*" Kaazi called telepathically. "*I do believe we have two Emigee operatives trying to abscond with our girl. Cover the man in the booth, I'll take the woman.*"

Alik`ram assessed the situation and said, "*Right…got it covered.*"

The woman moved in on Ari. Pulling her weapon and just as she was about to grab Ari, Kaazi stunned her with his MPI. Catching her immediately, he took her to the restroom to deposit her in one of the cubicles out of sight.

Seeing Kaazi stun the woman, she exclaimed telepathically as she followed him to the restroom, "*Kaazi, what are you doing?*"

"*She's an Emigee Ari. Look, she has a weapon; she was sneaking up from behind you trying to get the drop on you. Her partner is over at the booth. Alik`ram is taking care of him,*" Kaazi said nonchalantly with his usual carefree attitude.

Ari was astonished at Kaazi's prowess to detect danger especially when she had had no clue as to what was happening. She gazed at Kaazi dumbfounded and said with the deepest sincerity and gratitude, "Thank you Kaazi…I…I could have been taken away just like my parents."

With a grin as large as the Mississippi River, he said, "That's what I'm here for Ari."

Htiaf and Epoh were at the van when Kaazi, Ari, and Alik`ram left the shop. Jace was waiting for Ari just outside the door with bagel and latte in hand taking in the sunshine and surveying the lay of the land.

"They will be out for several hours. We'll be miles down the road by then," Kaazi explained to Ari as Jace glanced around to determine what was happening.

"Who's going to be out for hours?" Jace asked wanting to be brought up to speed on what they were discussing. "Those two people at the booth were Emigee operatives. The woman tried to grab Ari," Kaazi said as they were walking back to the van.

Jace was very quiet when he handed Ari her bagel and latte. He couldn't believe what had just happened; he was so distracted by his feelings, trying to please Ari, that the danger to her completely eluded him. Stunned, two Emigee in the store, missing imminent danger was something that had never occurred to him in his life, he was always the first one to recognize danger, not miss it completely. She could have been lost to him, kidnapped like Martin and Ena, killed even; it was unthinkable. His feelings for Ari were throwing his judgment off, but what could he do about it. He remained engulfed in self-incrimination, thus, deriding himself with disparaging thoughts for the proceeding hundred miles.

Ari too was immersed in thought. She couldn't help but long for her parents return; feeling completely responsible for the Emigee capturing her family and injuring her friends, she was submerged in guilt. Hank the dear old man almost got himself killed trying to protect her family. That following day was extremely difficult, but she was compelled to explain the events that had occurred to Hank. He took it as well as could be expected when she went to speak with him in the barracks before she left.

"Hank, how are you feeling today?" Ari asked gently with great concern. She knew he would make an attempt to put on a brave front for her sake but she could tell he was weary.

"I'm fine Ari girl. Don't you fret about me," Hank said with conviction, but it was lacking in his stance. "You want to tell me what last night was all about?"

Ari didn't know how much she should reveal. So she started with what he had already been told hoping he would leave it at that. "Zenot wants a signed contract to frack on our land," Ari said cautiously, but she should have known he would want complete details. It wasn't in his nature to accept simple explanations and let it go.

"That might be true but something more was going on. The weapons those guys had were nothing like I've seen before. They were right out of a sci-fi movie. The one with the blade called us "puny humans" implying he was something other than human. Kaazi and Alik`ram—who are they really? They healed my wounds. I should be dead not sitting here talking to you," he said wearily, still slightly pale. Hank implored Ari to tell him the truth, his eyes beseeching her. Unable to bear up under his scrutiny, she began to melt. Hank might be a simple ranch hand but he was very intelligent. Ari loved and respected him too much to lie to him; she decided to tell him the truth.

Ari glanced around the barracks. With no one was in sight, she began, "Hank, did mom and dad ever tell you the circumstances surrounding my adoption?"

He locked eyes with Ari and said, "Martin told me that they found you abandoned by the river they were camped by and that you were in a strange case."

"Hank, if I tell you the truth you have to promise me that you won't tell anyone," Ari said with unyielding conviction. This was a secret which needed protection.

"Nothing you say Ari will go any further. I won't tell another soul," Hank promised, he was telling the truth, he would carry the secret to his grave.

"Kaazi, Alik`ram, Htiaf, Epoh, Jace, and I are not human, we are a race known as the Te`rell. Our people were the first inhabitants of earth, the original race. The other four men are from a race known as the Emigee. They are an off shoot of the Te`rell. The history is long and complicated. After they returned to earth from exploring the galaxy, they became invaders and were bent on total conquest and the annihilation of my race. Last night they came to abduct not only my parents but me also," Ari explained slowly and calmly.

Hank was expressionless. The revelation of two races of people who predate humans was a shock, but he was desperately trying to assimilate the information. He finally said, "So you're not human?"

"No, we are similar, obviously, but not the same; we have been living among humans for thousands of years. The Te`rell are a very advanced race and so are the Emigee which has prevented our detection," Ari said calmly with a reassuring tone.

"Hank, we will be leaving today to go to my people. It's the only way we will be able to get my parents back. I am going to need you to take care of things here on the ranch. Can you do that for me Hank?" Ari asked, hating to put that kind of responsibility on him just now but he was the only one she could trust to oversee the ranch, to make sure it continued to function. She would get Martin and Ena back; the ranch, she was determined, would be just the way they left it when they got back. Hank would see that it ran smoothly.

"Ari you know I will do whatever it takes for Martin and Ena and if taking care of the ranch is what is needed then I will do it with pleasure, but I can't let you go off on your own after those crazy mad men," Hank said firmly. The thought of Ari going after that wild man-made Hank tremble, that was saying something, Hank did not scare easily.

"Hank... you don't have to worry about me. My friends Kaazi, Alik`ram, Htiaf, Epoh, and Jace will protect me, as will my people. I'm going to find a way to get my parents back. My people are the only hope of getting them back safely… Hank, I *have* to go!"

Hank lowered his head; the realization that she wasn't a little girl anymore hit him like a kick in the gut. Looking up with tears glistening in his eyes and he said, "You be careful, Ari girl." Smiling at her, he took her in his arms, and hugged her as if he would never let her go.

"I love you Hank. I promise everything will be alright. I will find Martin and Ena and bring them home," Ari said with intent and conviction.

"I love you to Ari girl. Don't worry about the ranch Connie, Andy, and I will take care of things here," Hank assured Ari as she left to search out her people.

Chapter

The van swerved to the right to avoid an enormous crater in the road which would have surely broken the front axle of the van if they had hit it full force. Arms and legs flailing in mid-air as the unsuspecting occupants in the back of the van were taken by surprise. Coffee cups and soda cans were catapulted from one side of the vehicle to the other splashing their contents through the air, a deluge of wet, sticky liquid rained on the discombobulated passengers, which started a flurry of expletives.

"Hey...what are you doing up there Alik`ram? You want me to drive," snorted Kaazi as he was jarred awake from the motion, soaked with soda, and completely tousled.

"You alright Alik`ram?" called Htiaf, hoping he wasn't falling asleep while he was driving. Alik`ram just shook his head indicating he was fine.

Attempting to settle everyone, Epoh said, "He was avoiding a huge crater in the road. Believe me; hitting it would have been much worse!"

The van became quiet again. Ari privately asked Jace, *"Are you okay? You have been quiet for a long time."*

"I'm fine Ari...I've just been thinking," Jace said, knowing full well he was not fine. Over the last hundred miles or so, his constant companion had been disparagement and reprimand, an ongoing conversation with himself which was driving him into despair.

"What have you been thinking about?" Ari asked thoughtfully, snuggling closer to Jace. He stiffened without realizing it, but Ari felt it, she knew something was wrong.

Jace wasn't sure he wanted to brooch the subject now or ever. After several minutes of silence, he figured it was as good a time as any to try and explain his feelings, his emotions were such a jumble. *"We will be with our people by afternoon; you will meet your parents, the consul and others, and you will want to spend time with them. The rest of us will be trying to get a line on Martin and Ena. So we won't be seeing each other anymore after today. Besides, you are someone very special to our people, our leaders will be very excited to see you and will keep you occupied a great deal of the time,"* Jace said, not entirely sure he wanted to continue.

"What are you trying to say Jace? Are you saying you don't want to see me when we get to the base camp?" Ari asked as her heart sank. To lose her parents and now Jace, it was too much—too much emotional turmoil for one person to handle. A hostile abduction was bad enough but losing three intimate connections, the three people she loved most in the world within such a short span of time, she wasn't able to bear that kind of lose.

"No…No…I'm just saying we probably won't see much of each other. Besides Ari, I need to focus on protecting you and finding a way to get Martin and Ena back. At the café, you were almost abducted…I didn't even see it coming! If they would have succeeded…I don't know…I don't know what I would have done! I can't fathom the thought of someone hurting you. I need to focus my attention back on protecting you," Jace lamented, it was coming out all wrong, she had the wrong notion it was written all over her face, but it was too late.

"Jace, the incident could have happened to anyone, Htiaf and Epoh didn't notice anything at the store either. You can't blame yourself for something that almost happened. After all these months, you made me believe you cared about me. Were you lying? Were you just being nice to me because I was your assignment? If you don't want to be around me just say so, don't make excuses. Your assignment is over! You won't have to see me anymore if that is what you want…starting now," she said as she moved forward in the van and asked Epoh if she could sit in the front with Alik`ram. If he didn't want to be around her, now was as good a time as any, she thought.

Jace whispered, "Ari…" but she ignored him which gained him several looks of curiosity from the others. Overwhelmed by what just happened, Jace spiraled lower and lower into the lowest depths of despair, into a pit never to find his way out, he was alone.

Ari too, felt suddenly very alone in a van full of people, her last thread of hope being torn away. She curled up in the front seat turning her head to gaze out the window. Her vision blurred, tears glistened in her eyes, silent torrents slide down her soft reddened cheeks; enveloped by darkness and despair like the treacherous gloomy thunderheads rolling in with threatening malevolence. Ari withdrew into herself as she tried to focus on meeting her real parents and her people, anything but Jace, but the ache in her heart was like a malignancy growing increasingly painful, threatening to consume her like an inferno. First Martin and Ena were taken and now Jace was pushing her away. It was too much for her to bear. Her sorrow swept through the van like gale-force winds and was being felt by all; heads turned to Jace looking for an explanation, but he just swung his body around giving them his back as he was consumed with shame. A heavy thickness befell the comrades as they rode in silence the rest of the way.

Stopping at Kingman before they turned north on route 93 quelled the mood. A mixture of misery and anticipation permeated the air, two conflicting moods made for a very unpleasant ride. The anticipation, excitement to get home, was growing the closer they came to their destination; but Kaazi couldn't tolerate the sadness percolating in the van one more second. It wasn't in his nature to be melancholy, so he decided to take it upon himself to cheer her up. Piling out of the van, Jace and Epoh headed for the convenience store, Htiaf started walking around the parking area under the guise of stretching his legs, while Kaazi and Alik'ram filled the gas tank. As soon as Ari left the van, Kaazi approached her.

"You couldn't take it anymore could you?" Kaazi stated as he sought to gain Ari's attention. Ari blushed; she thought he was referring to Jace.

"What do you mean?" she asked slightly embarrassed at the thought of being confronted by Kaazi, her feelings being so transparent.

"Alik'ram's driving of course. You couldn't take it anymore could you? That's why you went to the front, you were getting queasy?" Alik'ram came up from behind him and cracked him upside his head which lead Kaazi to display his signature grin.

"Very funny you oversized behemoth," Alik`ram snorted. He knew Kaazi was trying to lighten the mood. Ari had been sinking lower into depression for more than an hour. Eternally grateful that Kaazi was attempting to cheer her up; he couldn't stand to see a woman unhappy.

"Behemoth...who are you calling a behemoth? I'm just large boned," he said with a grin that could charm a hop-toad. "Ari...do I look like a behemoth to you?"

Ari laughed despite herself, she just couldn't keep a straight face when Kaazi was around.

"Oh...oh...never-mind that...back to the subject at hand...tell Alik`ram that his driving makes you queasy, be honest now," he said with a chuckle.

Denying queasiness she said, "No, it wasn't Alik`ram's driving."

"Are you sure? You're just trying not to hurt his feelings. Seriously, Ari who's driving is better mine or Alik`ram's?" Kaazi asked with an innocently sincere face trying to get Ari to pick between the two of them.

Alik`ram played along and said, "Tell him the truth Ari he needs to hear that his driving is horrible." After filling the tank, the three of them headed toward the store as the banter continued.

Ari didn't know what to do; all she could think was these two big oafs' were going to get into a sparring match at the gas station. She tried to defer by saying, "I don't know Kaazi... I slept the whole time you were driving."

"See, I told you I'm the best driver!" Kaazi blurted out with excitement as he jumped out in front of Ari and Alik`ram.

"How do you come to that conclusion when she said she was asleep?" Alik`ram retorted as he shook his head and glared at Kaazi.

"My driving lulled her to sleep of course," Kaazi said as he cradled his arms as if he was rocking a baby.

Alik`ram cracked him in the head again and Ari burst into laughter as she stood between the two men and put her arms around both of them. Their ploy to cheer Ari up was working.

Jace fumed as he watched the interaction from the gas station window, his heart sank ever lower into the abyss he was already wallowing in, unable to find any relief. As he felt the rage building within, he knew it was his own fault. He should have handled it better, explained his feelings to Ari, but that was no excuse. Now he had to watch as others vied for Ari's affections. After all that Kaazi and Alik`ram and him had been through in the past, how could they treat him like that…stealing Ari away from him. No Jace thought, 'I pushed her into their waiting arms.' It didn't matter; he still wanted to go over and deck Kaazi and Alik'ram. Instead, he turned to sulk as he browsed through the aisles paying no attention to what he was picking out. He needed to focus on protecting Ari, he tried telling himself—it didn't help. Feeling the loss of not having Ari close, the pain he experienced from not identifying the danger, his mood was not quelled; it was intensified. He finished inside the store and headed back to the van.

"Let's go!" Jace barked to Kaazi, as he threw him a murderous look then hopped into the van.

Kaazi smiled as he thought to Alik`ram, *"Hum…something seems to be bothering Jace…I wonder what it could be?'*

Alik`ram laughed, *"As if you didn't know…Are you trying to make him jealous?"* Alik`ram furrowed his brow at Kaazi attempting to grasp his motive; he knew Kaazi was up to his old tricks.

"Whatever do you mean?—Why would I want to make Jace jealous?" He grinned with the innocent pretense he was famous for; he had a plan and he was going to initiate the caper.

"Yeah that's what I thought," said Alik`ram. It was inevitable, Kaazi was up to mischief; heaven help anyone who gets in his line of fire.

"Someone has to show him how stupid he's being about the incident in Grants… He'll figure it out though…In the meantime, I'm going to have some fun with him." Kaazi said in no uncertain terms.

"What about the incident in Grants?" Alik`ram asked, he wasn't sure what the problem was since everything turned out fine in Grants.

"Jace's feelings were so transparent I couldn't help but pick up on them when I was in the back. He thinks that because of his feelings for Ari he has lost his focus and ability to protect her. The dunce told Ari they wouldn't be seeing each other at base camp. So she thinks he doesn't want to be with her anymore," Kaazi relayed rolling his eyes. It annoyed him that Jace was being ridiculous about what happened. No one can catch everything, that's why they worked in teams, what one person didn't catch another would. His people learned a long time ago that teamwork was the best check system available for field operatives.

Jace mucked things up; Kaazi would make sure he learned a valuable lesson from his mistake.

"Oh brother, you're really going to rub it in good, aren't you?" Alik`ram asked cringing at the response.

Kaazi just grinned, that was the only response Alik`ram needed to start feeling sorry for Jace. When Kaazi took action, he was ruthless and very believable.

On the road again, Htiaf was driving with Ari in the front passenger seat. The others sprawled out in the back of the cargo van occupied with various tasks. Epoh was levitating a soda can. Kaazi was rummaging through his bag while Alik`ram was stretched out resting. Scrunched in the right corner of the van, Jace was coiled like a viper ready to strike if his prey came close, stewing in his misery.

As Ari was gazing out the window, she turned to ask, "How soon will we get to the base camp?"

"We should be there in about two or three hours," Htiaf replied. Returning to her reflections, she stared out the window as the van fell silent.

Chapter

22

Reaching Willow Beach, Ari was able to get her first glimpse of the Colorado River. Under different circumstances, she would have been thrilled but these were desperate times, she was just relieved to have the long ride over so that they could start looking for her parents. The area was beautifully rugged but quite barren. With a nagging persistence, she found herself missing the luscious greenery of her home with the myriads of trees, bushes, and the abundant variety of other foliage and flowering plants, but the area did have a certain appeal with its wide open expanses, extensive and breathtaking, the natural meandering of the river through the massive rock formations framing the passageway was awe-inspiring.

Parking the van at the Willow Beach Marina, Htiaf let out a long sigh. As soon as they had stopped, the men scrambled out of the van. There was an excited anticipation among them; shortly they would be among their own people—home. Kaazi attentively went over to assist Ari from the van. Being so close to home, he didn't want an unexpected incident at this point; the others too were scanning the area for signs of trouble. Not picking-up on any potential problems, they all started walking toward the souvenir shop. After such a long trip, Ari wanted to freshen up before meeting her people.

Kaazi stayed close to Ari, to his delight the bantering continued back and forth. Like an annoying big brother whose sole purpose was to torment his little sister, he was providing a greatly needed distraction much to Jace's dismay. Jace was miserable, wanting desperately to take back his ill-spoken words from the morning; he was at a loss as to how to make amends. It didn't help that Ari was avoiding him. Starting to realize that he had trapped himself into a situation that was unbearable; he felt a certain trepidation. Loving Ari more than he thought possible since they had only known each other a few months, but when two people connect in spirit, time means nothing. Such a connection, spirit to spirit, transcends even love, it makes all things possible—it is eternal and ever so rare. How could he have just thrown that away?

In the souvenir shop, Ari found the ladies room and disappeared from the men. She was grateful for a few minutes to herself. Kaazi was great as a distraction but her heart yearned to be with Jace. She felt like her heart was being torn to shreds. Only this morning Ari felt secure and confident that they would get Martin and Ena back from the Emigee, but that was because Jace was at her side, now she felt lost and alone with too much uncertainty about the future and she didn't like it. Tears began to roll down her cheeks again. She wished this morning never happened, if she could only go back in time, but she couldn't go back, it did happen, so she would have to make the best of a bad situation.

Looking at herself in the mirror, she gave herself a stern talking to, 'You have to buck up,' as Hank would say. 'You have to stay strong for Martin and Ena.' Wiping the tears from her cheeks, she did just that as she continued her pep-talk. 'You can do this without Jace, you're strong.' The others would help, besides she was having fun with Kaazi, he made her laugh like they did back on the ranch; it would have to be enough to get her through.

Ari was just finishing, pulling her thick golden red locks up into a ponytail, when she heard a knock on the door and a muffled voice, "Ari are you alright? We're ready to leave now."

She called out, "I'll be out in a minute." Ari took one last look in the mirror, straightened the ponytail perched from the top of her head that flowed to the middle of her back, sighed, and left to find the men. Kaazi was waiting for her around the corner.

"Well don't you look nice," Kaazi commented knowing Jace was in the very next isle. Laughing to himself, he could feel the jealousy building in Jace. Served him right for being ridiculous, Kaazi thought.

"What are you talking about? I put my hair up, put on a pair of jeans, and a light-weight cotton shirt because it's hot," Ari replied rolling her eyes as she headed toward the door.

"Ari don't you realize you could wear a box and make it look good?" Kaazi said with his signature grin.

Ari laughed and said, "Well maybe someday I'll just make that kind of fashion statement."

Kaazi and Ari met the others by the door while Jace trailed behind like a puppy with his tail between his legs. The group left the souvenir shop walking toward the pier. It had been explained to Ari that they would be taking a boat down river to a bend just north of Monkey Hole. A ravine was their destination, a short trail in the hot desert which they would be hiking along to reach the entrance of their secluded base.

The Te`rell regularly used Willow Beach to access the base when their usual mode of transportation, the gird, was unavailable, thus they had an arrangement with the marina to store two of their boats. Htiaf was in the process of retrieving one of them. Approaching the pontoon boat, Kaazi jumped in first then steadied Ari as she stepped in; it was large enough to hold the six of them easily. Reminding Ari of riding the rapids, the boat was large, yellow and made of thick rubber; she hoped they weren't going to run into any white water; she didn't think so because the boat was motorized, but she never knew what to expect these days. As they started down river, Ari felt at ease, a peacefulness she hadn't felt for several days. Attributing the calming effect to the water as they were slowly meandering down river, she felt a new serenity. The multi-colored canyon walls painted in rustic earth-tones were majestic, awe-inspiring, steep in areas rising straight heavenward from the river's edge. It was as if portions of the wall had been sliced and hacked by hand allowing passage through the vast desert wilderness. Deep vertical grooves permeated the layers of earth accentuating the rustic-colored sediment. While other areas, were carved and whittled away by the elements, projecting the primitive ambience of the canyon. It made a person feel quite small in relation to the magnificent scene nature brandished—very grandiose.

A short time after setting out from the marina, they approached the bend in the river which was their destination. On the west side of the river, a finger-like projection of land formed a small inlet. Epoh turned the boat into the inlet.

Kaazi and Alik`ram were the first ones out of the boat. The inlet's surrounding area was the perfect place for an ambush. They scanned the area for intruders while Htiaf was assisting Epoh with the boat. Jace held out his had to Ari so that he could assist her out of the boat, the boat shifted unexpectedly with a jerking motion. Jace lost his balance and fell backward into the river. Ari let out a little startled scream, "Jace are you okay?"

Jace was completely humiliated and grumbled, "I'm fine." The others were snickering amongst themselves while Kaazi wore his signature grin.

"Did you jerk the boat Kaazi?" Jace demanded to know, his anger rising, building to the point of explosive fury. Kaazi was just the person he wanted to unleash his pent-up emotions on since his attentiveness to Ari was pushing him to the edge.

"I don't know what you are talking about Jace, I was scanning the area," Kaazi replied innocently, still grinning. Kaazi went over to the boat, put his hands on Ari's waist and lifted her out placing her on dry ground.

Before Ari could say thank you, rubble from the rock slope was disturbed. All of the men gathered around Ari to protect her. A tall copper-skinned man stood stern faced glaring at them. A pair of emerald-colored eyes just like Jace's was peering down at them with intense scrutiny. Poised with authority, he had the same dark ebony hair with just the perfect amount of soft waviness that Jace had in his hair, Ari thought. The two could be related, both were ruggedly handsome, both with similar builds. The man standing before them appeared to be somewhat older which was hard to determine since they all had the appearance of adults in their twenties.

The men froze, speechless as the man approached. Advancing ever closer to Ari, her heart started to pound with anticipation. Finally he said, "This must be Ariella. My goodness… young lady you look just like your mother…except for the eyes. Those belong to your father." Then he smiled, took her hand and kissed it in a show of affection as if she were a long-lost family friend.

Relief swept over Ari, he wasn't as stern as he first appeared to be. Jace made the introductions. A new realization occurred to Jace as he introduced her to Gyasi. She was going to be surrounded by many Te`rellean men once they get back to the city. He was having difficulty with Kaazi showing Ari attention, what would he do if others did the same? How would he manage, especially with her upset with him? Jace was desperately trying to figure a way out of the hole he had dug for himself.

"Ari this is Gyasi, the Te`rellean military leader and my father. Gyasi, obviously, this is Ari," Jace said solemnly. Gyasi took one look at Jace and raised his left eye brow, expressing great interest at his present condition, soaked through and dripping water everywhere. The scene before him would no doubt be explained later.

"Ariella have these miscreants been behaving themselves?" Gyasi asked. It was quite obvious that something was going on and it appeared none of them was going to be forthcoming with the information. Gyasi knew them well enough to be assured of mischievousness on their part.

Ari had to laugh, "Well sir, for the most part they have been good. A couple of them have proved trying at times."

"Really…well…you will have to tell me who I must chastise for their indiscretions," Gyasi said with a smirk as he glanced at the five men before him. They all drew a breath in sync.

"Well… enough of this. Let's get you to base camp so you can meet our people," Gyasi said with delight then added, "I'll deal with the rest of you later."

Kaazi wasn't smiling anymore. As a matter of fact, all of the men became unusually quiet. It was difficult at times to know when Gyasi was serious or when he was joking; on more than one occasion, every one of them had been on the receiving end of his sternness. It was rather peculiar the men felt uneasy around Gyasi. Never cruel or violent, he just projected the mien of authority. Obviously, he was someone not to be defied due to his position among them. All the men had the utmost respect even reverence for the man, especially since he was one of the oldest of the Te`rell.

The group had a short jaunt to the entrance of the camp. Gyasi and Ari were engaged in conversation while the others followed behind in silence. Gyasi stopped about a half mile up the ravine, bent down to pick up a rock; he handed the rock to Ari and said, "Toss the rock at the canyon wall."

Ari took the rock and tossed it at the wall. The rock hit the wall and fell to the ground. Curiosity peaked, she asked, "Was something supposed to happen?"

Gyasi smiled at her and instructed, "Place your hand on the wall now."

Ari looked at Gyasi—hesitantly she reached out her hand to touch the canyon wall, but there was no wall. It wasn't solid. Ari's whole hand disappeared into what appeared to be solid rock. She glanced up at Gyasi wide eyed with astonishment.

"This is our holographic defense barrier. From this side, it reflects the surrounding landscape and is impregnable. The only ones that can pass through are the Te`rell—the barrier is specifically keyed to Te`rellean physiology which can't be artificially replicated," Gyasi explained.

"Is it possible to let others in if they aren't Te`rellean?" Ari asked with great curiosity.

"It is possible but rarely done. There is too much at stake to risk the safety of our people to let outsiders in the camp. Are you ready to go in and meet your people?" Gyasi asked.

Ari's eyes widened with excitement, anticipation and trepidation. She took a deep breath and said, "I'm ready."

When Ari stepped through the barrier, she had no idea what she would encounter. What she saw took her breath away. Base camp was a serious misnomer. When she thought of base camp, she imagined tents, cots, temporary field equipment like what is portrayed on the television. What she saw was a city—not just any city, it was magnificent. As she stood at the access point, she beheld a long street made of irregular geometric slabs of slate in a variety of soft earth-tones. The slate exhibited subtle wave-like patterns of grey, rust, beige, blue, green and black hues intertwined like delicate threads within the rock. She was enthralled, never having seen anything quite so exquisite as what she beheld in front of her. Walkways on both sides of the street were made of clean, snow white marble, pristine, glistening as the sunlight bathed the stone. The buildings lining the street sparkled and glistened—natural precious stones, raw and unprocessed, composed the outer façade. Structures, textures, and symmetry echoed the harmony of nature's beauty in this glorious city. She saw one structure on her right comprised of Alexandrite—a translucent yellowish green mineral. Many other buildings were made of unprocessed amethyst with various shades of purple crystals; almandine with its deep red and black crystals. Still others were constructed of various types of Chalcedony such as green Aventurine, yellowish-red Binghamite, Bloodstone, Fire Agate, Holly Blue, Jasper, Sardonyx and other beautiful rocks and minerals. Ari had never seen anything like this before—she was in awe.

"Oh my…I…I never expected anything like this in my wildest dreams. This is the most beautiful place I have ever seen. How is it possible that the city is made up of such expensive material?—Is…is that gold…and diamonds?" Ari asked as her gaze jumped from one object to the next, fascinated with the aesthetics of this incredible city.

"Our construction materials are very expensive in the human world, it's true, but you're not in the human world anymore Ariella. I'm sure Jace explained to you that we come from the earth. She provides us with everything we need…in great abundance. We have mastered the art of creating various types of rocks and minerals; she allows us to manipulate base elements that she provides for us. It is a simple task to create gems, precious metals, and other minerals," Gyasi answered.

"I have so much to learn about our people," she said. Amazement didn't come close to how Ari was feeling at that moment. The city was incredible, beyond imagination, and the most beautiful thing she had ever seen.

They strolled down the sidewalk of the main road to the center of the city. A very large tower occupied the center space, tall like a monolith, cylindrical, narrowing at the top. Gyasi had explained that the city was laid out in the pattern of a snowflake. The tower was at the center and eight main streets like the one they had walked down extended outward from the center like the branches of a snowflake, delicate and beautifully intricate. Each street was designated with a specific purpose such as, medical research, scientific research, covert intelligence, geological and earth science research, agricultural research, education, recreational activities, and medical care. The central tower was the nexus of the community, the control center, as well as assembly center.

"There will be plenty of time for you to learn about our people. Right now however, several people would like to meet you," Gyasi said gently but firmly.

Chapter

23

Wide-eyed and holding her breath as they entered a voluminous vestibule, Ari was in awe. The entrance to the central tower was amazing, exquisitely constructed with the same natural beauty exhibited throughout the city, it was breathtaking. The main vestibule was designed with Turquoise and Amazonite that glistened with clear crystalline Quartz as accents, exhilaratingly beautiful. As sunlight spilled in from expansive vaulted windows, the ambience was that of an illusion, a chimera; it was fanciful with light dancing off crystal, like fireflies on a summer's eve, flickering here and there. At the center of the vestibule stood a spectacular water fountain, made of clear sparkling blue topaz, shaped like an iris. As water flowed from the center down the petals and leaves into the bath, it formed a pool at the base. Around the fountain, several benches had been placed for those who wished to enjoy the peaceful, serenity of the water feature.

Ari and the others proceeded to a dais or platform to the right of the fountain on the main floor. Vivid coloration of the dais caught Ari's attention; she moved to get a better look. The base of the dais was solid but appeared to have pulsating images changing and forming into three dimensional figures. So realistic was the spatial view that Ari reached out to touch the figures but was blocked; continually amazed at her people's technology, she laughed. The pedestal next to the platform housed the control panel. Once all were on the platform, Gyasi waved his hand over the light on the panel; the group was transported to the leader's chambers at the top of the tower.

Sitting behind a small desk conversing with several other people was the leader of the Te`rell, Ashi`nat. When he glanced over as the group transported in, he became transfixed on the beautiful young woman standing in the middle of the group. Ashi`nat stood up; he was a very tall man, muscular with broad shoulders, beautiful cobalt-blue eyes, just like Ari's, and golden-brown hair. A ruggedly handsome man with a straight aquiline nose and a strong square jawline, regal; he had the aura of nobility.

"Ariella, welcome home," Ashi`nat said with a smile as he came around his desk to embrace her.

Ari was stunned that a leader would be so welcoming to a stranger. She felt something more from this man, not just a friendly welcome to a long-lost subject, familiarity, a familiarity one feels with intimacy. She stepped back and gazed into his eyes. Glistening there, she saw the tears of joy only a parent could feel for a long lost child. A stark realization engulfed her as she drew breath—she was the daughter of the Te`rellean leader. Why didn't Jace tell her? He should have told her so she could have been better prepared, the implications were enormous.

"Ariella…I see recognition in your face. Do not be upset that you were not told your real identity, knowing could have put you in greater danger than what you have experienced. Your true identity needed to be kept secret while you were out of our protection, but there are other reasons also for not telling you sooner," he said in earnest.

"You are my father?" she said hesitantly as she took in every inch of his face, examining it closely so as never to forget it. As the realization began to take root deep within her, a smile began to form on her face that rivaled Kaazi's signature grin and with all the love within her she embraced her father for the first time.

Ashi`nat was elated. Everyone in the room was ecstatic—overcome with tears of joyful happiness. At long last his precious child had been returned to him, healthy, strong, and so very beautiful, but for the reunion to be complete they had to wait for his mate. As he held his daughter, he whispered, "Your mother will be here soon, in the meantime, I would like to introduce you to some other people who are very eager to meet you and who you will be working with in the future."

Ari nodded and said, "Okay." Experiencing an overwhelming feeling of belonging and acceptance, she was thrilled to be meeting her father's friends and workmates. She released her father and turned toward the group, but she never completely let go of him, keeping his arm entwined with hers; needing the security and strength she felt emanating from him.

Ashi`nat drew Ari to a short woman, short for her people, about five foot six inches, with straight platinum blond hair elegantly pulled back in French curl rolls crossed in the back and secured with an aquamarine hair clip then left to flow effortlessly down the back of her petite frame. This was the first of her people who didn't exhibit the usual height she had seen thus far. She had a kind face with a pert little nose and rosy lips, but her most impressive feature was her pale blue eyes that appeared like crystals—sparkling and intense, observing every detail of her surroundings.

"Ariella…this is Diza, she is a member of the leadership consul and one of our oldest citizens," Ashi`nat said before moving on to the next person.

Diza nodded with a warm appealing smile and said, "Welcome home Ariella."

"Thank you," Ari said as if she was speaking to a queen.

"Ariella this is Zuka, he also is a member of the leadership consul," Ahsi`nat said making the introductions. Zuka was taller than Diza but not as tall as her father. His eyes were like Nephrite Jade; his face was round with a subtle chin. Ari sensed he had a reflective spirit—not one to make a snap decision. When he smiled at Ari, she sensed genuine relief and joy.

"We are so very glad you have returned to us safely Ariella. We were all extremely distressed when we thought you were lost to us seventeen years ago," Zuka said as he glanced at Htiaf and Epoh.

Several other members of the leadership consul were introduced. Ari began to feel a little overwhelmed, repeating their names in her head to remember them, she wasn't quite sure she would succeed. Relieved when Ashi`nat reached the last member, she sighed inwardly.

Gyasi interrupted and began, "Ashi`nat we will take our leave now. I'm sure my companions would like to get started with their endeavor to find Ariella's adoptive parents."

"Yes…yes indeed. We own Martin and Ena a great debt of gratitude for taking such good care of Ariella all these years. By all means find them…and Gyasi…make this your highest priority," Ashi`nat said.

Ari looked at her father as tears flowed down her cheeks, "Thank you," she said, so grateful for his understanding and help.

Each man approach Ari to take their leave. She hugged and kissed Htiaf and Epoh who were both in tears. Kaazi and Alik`ram were next and Ari started laughing when she heard Kaazi say telepathically, *"If you need an escape from all this leadership mumbo-jumbo, just give me a call Alik`ram and I will steal you away for a while."*

Alik`ram heard what Kaazi thought to Ari and cracked him in the head for saying such a thing to the leader's daughter. Kaazi just grinned from ear to ear. Ashi`nat and Gyasi just rolled their eyes for Kaazi's antics were well known.

Jace was next. Ari stiffened as he approached. She did not hug Jace. Ari offered her hand and said, "Thank you Jace for all your help. I wish you well in the future."

Jace was deflated. He said telepathically, *"Ari, I'm sorry I hurt you but I have to focus on protecting you. I couldn't live with myself if anything happened to you."* He wished she didn't take what he said to mean he stopped loving her. If anything, he was doing this because he loved her so much. Why couldn't she understand that?

"You have made your stand perfectly clear," she said, moving closer to her father she said nothing more to him.

Ashi`nat and Gyasi raised a brow as the rest of the group suddenly became preoccupied with anything from papers to counting tiles on the floor.

"We will be at NOSSIC," Gyasi said as he turned to leave; followed by the friends Ari had been accustomed to spending night and day with since she discovered she was Te'rellean, she felt a bit sad until her father redirected her attention.

"Ariella, I have one bit of business to take care of with Diza and Zuka and then we can spend the rest of the day together," Ashi`nat said before he went to his desk. Zuka and Diza followed him; the other members of the consul had left. Ari sauntered over to the window for a birds-eye view of the city.

The city was even more spectacular from the top of the central tower. As she moved to the next window, she realized her father's office was a rotunda, circular with enormous windows, which offered a 360-degree view of the city. Slowly Ari moved from window to window taking in the spectacular vistas.

Having a partial view of the city, she was able to see several of the main arteries fan out from the central tower. The stone facade from the outlying buildings made of various rocks and minerals glistened in the sunlight. She was amazed that this magnificent city was concealed within the confines of a holographic barrier. Her people were truly advanced. With all this advanced technology, she wondered why her people didn't just take control; rid the world of its corrupt governments, to bring peace to an unstable world.

As she moved to the next window, her father came up from behind her and said, "Well that's done now we have the rest of the day to get acquainted."

She looked around the room to discover they were alone. Ari smiled nervously as Ashi`nat gestured for her to have a seat.

"I'm sure you have many questions. I will try my best to answer them. Some questions though will be better answered by your mother," Ashi`nat said lovingly. They sat opposite of each other, facing one another. Ashi`nat made use of a plush office chair while Ari made herself comfortable on the sturdy chaise.

"When I was looking out the window admiring the incredible workmanship of our people, I was wondering why our people, who have vastly superior technology from the humans and even the Emigee, haven't just taken control of the world scene and made changes?" Ari asked.

"Well you are your mother's child. You just cut right to the heart of things, don't you?" Ashi`nat chuckled and flashed a dazzling smile upon Ari.

Ari shrugged her shoulders and smiled. There was so much to learn about her people, who better to learn from than the leader of her people, her father. Ari felt she needed to make up for lost time, especially if she was going to help Martin, Ena, and her people. She had to get down to the deep issues surrounding the conflict between the Emigee and the Te`rell.

"To answer your question, we have to delve into our history. I don't know how much Jace has told you so jump in anytime you don't understand something or have a question. My father was the leader when the Emigee arrived back on earth. The humans were not on the scene yet. My father met with the leader of the Emigee and his consul. At first there seemed to be mutual cooperation and a willingness on their part to reintegrate into our people. To be completely integrated, both sides agreed that a reversal of the mutations the Emigee had undergone was essential. Scientist on both sides set to work on a cooperative effort to reverse the mutations.

There was an accident and several people were killed on both sides due to the impatience of the Emigee. The differences between our people are immense, our main characteristic is peacefulness and we are very patient, whereas, the Emigee due to their mutations and militant background are just the opposite. They wanted immediate results, instant gratification, even after our scientists had explained that it would take years to find a permanent solution. After the incident, we attempted to start again but the Emigee leader had retribution in his mind due to the loss of his mate who was one of their chief scientists. His grief led to our current status—war and conflict.

The Emigee attacked without warning, wiping out most of our people. Only a few thousand of us survived. With our cities devastated and population significantly reduced, we had no choice but to go underground," Ashi`nat explained.

"When you say underground, do you mean you actually went under the ground or you just lived in secret?" Ari asked wanting to make sure she understood him correctly. Sitting on the edge of her seat, she listened intently.

Ashi`nat chuckled, "Actually, both—for a time we lived in an area in Turkey called Cappadocia. Humans have discovered several of our abandoned cities such as Tatlarin, Derinkuyu, Ozkonak, Mazi, and Kaymakli. Of course, those are not the names we called them. Humans have given our cities names of their own. We had to live underground until we were able to obtain the resources needed to rebuild our technology. The devastation was complete, we had nothing, almost everything was destroyed; it took a great deal of hard work through hardship and pain to regain our technology and way of life; tirelessly we worked to get to the point you see here today. So much was destroyed from the attack. It took many millenniums to recuperate to our current status. The fact that we don't die unless mortally wounded has helped alleviate delays in our technological growth, but the loss of life cannot be undone.

The Emigee have caused several set-backs inhibiting the recovery of our civilization. One of the biggest ones was the biological warfare they used as they attempted to exterminate our people. We are still trying to figure out the best possible solution to resolve the consequences of that fiasco," Ashi`nat said as he shook his head.

"What do you mean? What consequences?" Ari asked.

"Humans…they are not even supposed to exist. We are still trying to understand why they exist and weren't wiped out by the virus. Let me back up a little. In order to expedite the recovery of our race, our scientist experimented with the genetic manipulation of an ape-like animal called a gorba. The gorbas stood about five feet tall, had protruding lips, a large nose, and a slightly larger forehead than chimps. They were very intelligent creatures—curious but greedy. They would horde food, trinkets—really anything they could get their hands on. Some of our scientist had been researching their behavior and found that if trained properly, behavior modification, they made excellent workers. Since our population had been depleted, we needed a labor force; it was suggested that the gorba be used as a domesticated animal workforce. The gorba were trained using the behavior modification techniques, it took months to complete. As it turned out, the success rate was not great, approximately 50%, but after all they were just animals. It became apparent that more was needed. Our scientist attempted to alter their genetic make-up to increase mental function enough to alleviate some of the problems we were facing with their cognitive functions.

Our scientist had tremendous success with this process. After a while, we reach sufficient numbers to build above ground cities again. The gorba gained increased understanding and improved fine motor skills. We never could eliminate their need to horde, but they turned out to be great pets.

In the meantime, thousands of years had gone by with only small skirmishes with the Emigee, mostly because they couldn't find us and we stayed away from them. It was an almost fatal mistake for our people. We should have spent more time negotiating with them. We had no idea they were so determined to completely wipe us off the face of the earth. It was only by chance that one of our scientists discovered their plan to release a virus into the environment meant to target our DNA. We had to move quickly to save our people. It was determined that under the protection of the holographic barrier our people would go into stasis until the virus became inert. The sensors would continue to monitor the environment until it was safe for our people. It took many thousands of years for the virus to become extinct," Ashi`nat explained.

"Are you telling me our people were in stasis for thousands of years? That must have taken a lot of power to sustain the equipment and what about repairs. How was the equipment maintained? What do our people use as a power source?" Ari asked completely astonished at what she had learned.

"Yes, our people were in stasis for many thousands of years. You're right it did take a tremendous amount of energy to power the equipment for so many years. Because we have an intimate knowledge of the earth and advanced tools, we were able to tap into the geothermal energy of the earth's core. To maintain the equipment, we had just reestablished several artificial intelligence programs at that time. We transferred the program into an artificial intelligence matrix which would be able to execute programmed tasks, thus, our AI's were able to make adjustments as needed. With everything in place, our people went to sleep.

The world was a completely different place when we emerged from stasis. Instead of wiping out the gorba like we had assumed would happen, the virus had mutated within their physiology propelling them into modern day humans, sentient beings; they infested the earth. Their rapid proliferation was outstanding—one we are still researching. Much like the gorbas, humans have developed into very greedy, selfish beings. Humans like the gorba take advantage of the weaknesses of others of their species. The Emigee have exploited that tendency to promote their own agendas. Don't get me wrong, they have some virtuous qualities too, such as their ability to love, show kindness, compassion, and at times even generosity; at times I'm amazed at their ability to love. On the other hand, they have exhibited equal capacity for hatred, violence, greed, and selfishness; just like the gorbas they display animalistic qualities.

Because of their development into sentient beings we have been in a quandary as to the correct course of action to take. Our people don't force our way of life on other sentient beings. If we did, how would we be any different than the Emigee? That is why we haven't changed the world forcibly," Ashi`nat explained.

"Well from what I have seen, the world would be a much better place if there was a central government made up of peaceful people who are interested in caring for the needs of others instead of the greedy pursuit of money and power. I have done research on different types of governments when I was preparing for college before I found out who I am. It seems to me that every type of government conceivable has been attempted yet they have all failed. Is there nothing we can do to bring the world into balance?" Ari asked.

"Well that is the problem. Our society was ideal, and we have achieved a measure of what was once lost. I personally don't believe the humans as a whole will ever be able to overcome their animalistic behavior and predisposition for greed and violence. Some are capable of living peacefully; but the majority, exhibit the same qualities as the Emigee. Unfortunately, I believe that human society, as we know it, is going to come to a catastrophic end which will wipe out billions. We have been preparing for such an event. In the meantime, we are attempting to counteract the Emigee's plans in any way we can, but there is only so much we can do without infringing on the free will of sentient beings," Ashi`nat said.

"I don't understand…we have the ability to stop the violence, yet we don't," Ari said.

"Let me try to explain it this way. Consider this about societies: bees or even ants make a great example. Each bee or ant goes about working at their specific job for the good of the hive or hill. You come along and see that the hive or hill is in an inconvenient location. You attempt to move or change the hive or hill. What happens? The bees and ants swarm to protect what is theirs. Some become violent and aggressive. They don't want relocation…they don't like to be disturbed. Unless you wipe them out completely they will continue to fight against you. Same goes with humans…they don't like change. It is never easy for them to accept. Only a few adapt. If we forced our ways on others there would be rebellion, even though our ways are for the betterment of the earth. This sounds horrible Ariella but the violent and greedy population needs to be eliminated in order for any real progress to be made to ensure a return to a peaceful balance and harmonious relationship with the earth," Ashi`nat explained.

"When you put it that way, I see your point," Ari conceded but was not happy with the realization that violent, greedy traits had to be eliminated. She was beginning to understand the problem.

Chapter

shi`nat's office had several pieces of artwork which Ari was admiring. Left alone for several minutes she began examining one rock sculpture made of zoisite. The miniature monolith was simple but elegant with the various arrays of purple, pink, white and black mineral deposits and veins which formed random patterns of lines, spots, swirls and freckles throughout the greenish-blue core providing a natural beauty unmatched by any human art form that Ari had seen. One simple symbol was carved into the structure, the same symbol that was on her pendant, the identifying mark of the Te`rell.

As she was admiring the sculpture, Ashi`nat entered the office from the platform. "I'm sorry about the interruption. I like to be informed of any interaction with the Emigee," he said as he approached Ari.

"I imagine you are kept quite busy then, from what I've been told about their activity, they continually try new ways to eliminate us," she said as she ran her fingers over the sculpture.

Remorse engulfed Ashi`nat, he regretted that Ari was being pulled into their conflict with the Emigee, but he was ever so thankful that she was home again, home where she belonged. "Where is my mind, I'm so excited about you being here my manners flew out the window. Are you hungry or thirsty?" he said with a slight blush, completely embarrassed by forgetting common courtesy and hospitality.

Ari chuckled slightly, "I'm not hungry but I would like a drink if it isn't a problem."

"You can have anything you would like, my dear. The monolith you are admiring will gain you access to our food and drink syntech. If we don't have what you like we can program the molecular composition into the processor for you," Ashi`nat explained.

"What do I do?" she asked as she ran her fingers over the sculpture admiring the smoothness, the sleekness of such a beautiful work of art; gently she traced the outline of the symbol.

"Touch the center," Ashi`nat said. As soon as Ari touch the center, the monolith changed to reveal a console, a computerized display to input requests for food or drink. Ari was impressed and examined the console closely.

"Would you like something from the console?" Ari asked her father.

"No thank you," he said, "but you get whatever you would like."

Ari wasn't hungry she just needed a drink of water. "Um…I don't know our language…I can't read the panel," she said a little embarrassed.

"Oh…of course…I'm sorry, I will program English into the console for you," he said as he moved to input the information. "There you go. Now it will display Te'rellean and English."

As soon as she had her drink, she went to sit down again. With a flash of light, the transport was activated. A very tall beautiful woman with red hair and deep emerald green eyes stood on the platform, almost a mirror image of Ari. Her gaze immediately fell upon Ari. Ashi`nat approached her with a smile and held out his hand to her. He drew her close as they strolled over to Ari.

"Ariella, this is Ayotal, my mate and your mother," Ashi`nat said with genuine pride at having this lovely woman as his wife. It was immediately apparent the two shared a deep intimate connection of spirit.

"Ariella, I can't believe you are really here after all these years," Ayotal said as she embraced Ari longingly. "You are every bit as beautiful as I had imagined you would be."

"Thank you," Ari said as her heart accelerated out of control. She had been longing for this moment ever since Jace had told her that her parents were alive and they wanted to see her. She could hardly contain her excitement, but she tried, "I could say the same about you. I never imagined that we would look so much alike though, except for our eyes."

Ayotal laughed a sweet kindly laugh, "Yes…you have your father's eyes and his golden highlights in your hair. It makes for a stunning combination."

"Ariella…now that your mother is here, we would like to explain a common practice done within family groups among our people. We use our telepathic abilities to bond to one another. We would like very much to reconnect our bond with you since we have not done this since before you were put in stasis," Ashi`nat explained hoping she would not shy away from such intimate contact.

"Are you willing to bond with us Ariella?" Ayotal asked. For years she had longed for the familial bond so integral to Te`rellean families, she had never completely given up hope that Ari would return to them, to be reunited. Since it was discovered that Ari was alive, the desire to bond had become intense, she loved her daughter profoundly.

There was almost nothing she wanted more than to complete the bond with her parents; but she was feeling a slight trepidation. She hesitated momentarily because of Martin and Ena. Wondering if it would change the way she felt about them, she was in turmoil; she didn't want her feelings for them to change.

Sensing her hesitation Ayotal said reassuringly, "It will not affect how you feel about anyone else."

Thankful for her honesty Ari said, "I love Martin and Ena very much and would never want my feelings for them to be in conflict…but…yes I definitely want to reconnect with my real family…with both of you. What do we do?"

"It is very easy, we place our palms together. Since there is only the three of us I will be connecting with you through your left palm while your father connects with you through your right and then he and I will complete the circuit. Close your eyes and relax," Ayotal said tenderly. Eager to make the connection she glanced at Ashi`nat, the excited anticipation radiated from her eyes as they sparkled.

Ari felt nothing at first then gradually she felt warmth—love. Energy began to flow freely between the trio. Ari was being shown images and feeling the emotions of her parents as Ayotal gave birth and greeted Ari into the world. Unparalleled happiness and love permeated Ayotal at the first sight of her new daughter. The joy was overwhelming, the love shared between Ashi`nat and Ayotal was endearing. Her birth was the culmination of their love and brought both parents great unsurpassable joy.

Progressively Ari was shown the first six months of her life before she was put into stasis. The immense tenderness and devotion of this family was projected into Ari's heart and mind. It was incomparable, like nothing she had ever experienced before. The sense of belonging, of being home was strikingly clear. This experience was truly a gift and Ari drew strength from it.

Ayotal thought to Ari, *"If there is anything you would like to share with us from your life we would love to experience it with you. Just think about the memories you want to share."*

Ari was thrilled at the prospect of sharing her life with her parents. Ari immediately thought about the ranch with the horses, mountains, Martin and Ena, her favorite places on the ranch, and Hank. She was able to project the love and happiness she experienced through her years of growing up on the ranch. She showed them everything, the happy joyful times and the sorrow she felt when Martin and Ena were captured. There was one image she did not want to display, she wanted to keep it to herself, but it kept flashing through her memory. She was trying to push it out, but it was impossible since she was so new at experiencing this level of intimacy. Jace was there in her mind and heart. She couldn't help but show her parents every interaction she had with Jace from the first time she met him, to the kiss, to this morning when he said he wouldn't be seeing her again. The sadness she felt took over and she stopped projecting her thoughts.

Ashi`nat and Ayotal said nothing for a few minutes as they glanced at each other, understanding and love in their eyes. Ari, who had broken contact, went to the window to look out over the city, quietly longing for Jace.

"We have known Jace for a long time Ariella. He has never shown an interest in a woman until now. He might be having difficulty contending with an abundance of new emotions he has never had to cope with before meeting you. Believe me when I say, you have not seen the last of him," Ashi`nat said with concern and compassion for his daughter's feelings. Te`rellean emotions, when experiencing them for the first time, especially when love was involved, were intensely erratic. Shaking off the memories of his first experience with those feelings, Ahsi`nat shivered and smiled at Ayotal as she gazed at him in her all-knowing way.

Ayotal went to the window with Ari and put her arms around her, "Let me tell you a story. The first time I met your father I was a little girl. Ashi`nat was working with his father laying out plans for our new city. We were living in the mountains of what the human's call Nepal. Founding the community was of high importance, since we had just moved there, everyone was busy establishing the boundaries of the new city and planning buildings and housing complexes. I was gathering wild berries with some friends when I saw him perched on a ledge speaking to several builders or what you would call engineers. He was spectacular—handsome, intelligent, and kind. I knew from the very first time I laid eyes on him that he was my mate, even though he didn't know I existed...yet. Several hundred years of growing, emotional ups and downs passed before that occurred. Our people have the advantage of time, thus, we are a patient people. Things will work out for the best. We know it is difficult for you to change your thinking, it is very different thinking in human terms now to suddenly change to Te`rellean terms, but with time you will adjust. It will get easier."

"Jace is a good man; try not to take what he said as a rejection of you. It was very apparent that he was quite distressed when he said good-bye earlier," Ashi`nat said as he moved to the window to embrace the two women he loved more than life itself.

"I will try not to," Ari said with sadness in her voice. With all that she had seen and the people she met within the last few hours, she was beginning to feel the strain, she was exhausted.

"Let's go home. You have had several very traumatic and exhausting days. You will feel better with some food and sleep," said Ayotal, motherly instincts taking over.

Ari agreed, her head was swimming with everything she had seen and experienced. She could definitely use a shower and a bed. The images of her parents flooded through her mind. The love and intimacy within her family was far exceeding even that of Martin and Ena. She was finally home where she belonged. It was as if shadowed truth was being slowly revealed to her. Even though she loved Martin and Ena immensely and they loved her, she never felt the depth of emotional intimacy she felt with these two strangers who weren't strangers at all.

The connection to her family and her people was complete. There was still so much she didn't know. She wondered if they had anything like colleges in the city. She would have to do some catch up learning but then she thought about what her mother said, there was plenty of time. Her people are patient and even though Ari had never really been impatient she was not as patient as her people.

Chapter

Sunlight danced gleefully, reflecting off the fine crystalline formations of the inner veneer. Shimmering brightly, the sun sparkled in the sleep chamber Ari was given, she woke with a sense of complete contentment. She couldn't remember ever having such a restful night's sleep. As she stretched, Ari took a good look around the room; she had only briefly glanced at it the night before. Last night she was too exhausted to notice anything except the bathroom. Of course it was beautiful as was everything she had seen so far; she decided that she would have to learn how her people constructed such beautiful structures.

She was in a spacious room; the chamber had more than enough space to meet her needs. The bathroom was off to the right—her own bathroom, how nice is that, she thought. As she looked around, she noticed a door to the left. Curiosity peaked, she hopped out of bed to explore; as she opened the door, she discovered a room which was lined from top to bottom with various types of storage space—armories, chests of drawers, shelves. It was enough space to store everything Martin and Ena, Hank and all the ranch hands owned, along with all of her things, with space to spare. She was sure the suite was not large enough to accommodate such a large area, but here it was; it defied explanation. It was enormous. She would have to remember to ask about it, but it made sense after all, her people lived many lifetimes; she was going to have to acclimate to the longevity of her life. As she was exploring, she heard a knock on the door and went to investigate.

Ayotal was standing outside the door and greeted Ari, "Good morning Ariella, How are you feeling this morning?"

"I feel good. I must have really been tired last night. I don't remember ever getting such a restful night's sleep," Ari said as she moved aside allowing her mother to step into the room.

"Our sleep modulators are equipped with sensors. They monitor our physiology, adjust the environmental parameters to attain optimal physical homeostasis, thus, providing us with restful sleep," Ayotal explained. So many things Ashi`nat and she took for granted, common place, but to Ari everything was a new experience. She wanted Ari to feel at home, comfortable, but she couldn't help feeling slightly anxious for her.

"It was wonderful," Ari said, "Everything I've seen, the barrier, the city, the transport, the architecture, now this; it's mind-boggling!" They chuckled together for a few minutes. Ayotal peered out the window allowing the sunlight to permeate her flaming red hair, accentuating her exquisite features.

"I have cleared my schedule for the day. We can do whatever you would like today, but first, are you hungry?" Ayotal asked always tending to the practical needs.

"Yes, I am. I will get dressed and be right out," Ari said with a smile. She quickly made her bed and put her clothes on after she freshened up. Hurrying out to the main area of the living quarters which was basically one large open room with a kitchen and dining table, a sitting area, and office space—simple but functional. She noted that her people valued natural simplicity. Elegant décor was how she would describe Te`rellean style, rather than the pretentious opulence and grandeur for which many humans strive. Her parents were sitting at the dining table conversing when she entered.

"Good morning," Ari said as she greeted them with a smile and a kiss. She went to the food console and obtained a bagel and latte which had become her favorite breakfast food over the past few days.

"Your mother tells me you had a restful night," Ashi`nat said grinning, "I've become so accustom to our sleep modulators that when I have to leave the city, I don't sleep if one is not available."

"Yes it was wonderful," Ari agreed, settling into her chair, taking a bite of bagel, and a sip of latte. After a long pause, she asked, "I was wondering if you both could answer a question I have been wondering about for a while now… why was I put in stasis…why for so long?"

Her parents looked at each other knowing that explanations were inevitable, so Ashi`nat began, "The stasis was supposed to be a short-term temporary measure. Your mother and I had to manage a crisis in one of our smaller cities in South America. The Emigee were causing them trouble. As leader, I had the responsibility of dealing with the problem. Your mother is our hierophant—she is like a human religious leader but different. Religion really has nothing to do with what she does. She educates our people on the old ways of living in harmony with the earth and each other. It is the most important duty in our city. The Emigee had killed several of her assistants assigned to that city. With their deaths the city was in chaos. It was imperative she accompany me to re-establish our organizational and educational structure. Since there were no replacements qualified at that time, new people had to be trained who had only the very basic qualifications. We knew it was going to be time consuming."

"We would have taken you with us, but the situation was unstable and dangerous. The barrier in that city had been damaged by an unexpected geological disturbance, probably initiated by the Emigee. If there was a working barrier in place, we would have brought you with us. We did not want to risk you being injured or killed. It was my idea to put you in stasis because I didn't want to miss a minute of you growing up," Ayotal lamented recalling the turmoil she felt leaving Ari.

"We were away in South America for over a hundred years. Once we solved one problem, ten more became apparent with the help of the Emigee. When you were lost, we were just establishing a new camp in Colorado and had requested special transport for you to be brought to us since the stasis unit could not be transported on the grid. The transport pads between the old camp and the new one were malfunctioning, and no aerial transports were available so transport by truck was arranged. We were devastated when we heard about the accident. Htiaf and Epoh were likewise traumatized. We searched for days to no avail; we were unable to find any sign of you. We always held out a glimmer of hope that you would return to us someday…and you have. For that we are eternally grateful, even though we missed out on your childhood," Ashi`nat said reflecting on the whole situation, longing for the day when the Emigee would no longer cause such chaos and destruction.

"To have lost someone you love is heart-wrenching, it must have been very difficult for you. I know I'm struggling with losing Martin and Ena. I'm just glad we found each other again," Ari said. Ari was very happy to have answers to some of those nagging questions that had been plaguing her. Now that she knew the circumstances behind the unexpected events in her life she could move forward and concentrate on finding Martin and Ena and her future.

"Is there any news about Martin and Ena?" Ari asked eager for any information. Even a small tidbit as to the location of the Emigee and where they were holding them would be better than letting her imagination run rampant.

"We have sent alerts out to all of our operatives, but we haven't received any information yet. Don't worry, we will find them, but it could take some time," Ashi'nat said with reassurance offering her hope. "I must be on my way. I will leave you two alone to talk. I'm sure your mother will be able to answer all your questions. I'll see you later. Love you both." Ashi`nat embraced both women and kissed them tenderly then left for the central tower.

"What would you like to do today?" Ayotal asked. To finally have an opportunity to talk with Ari after years of separation filled Ayotal with excitement, her heart was going to burst, she was so utterly happy. For years she had her husband and work to occupy her time since the accident, but the longing for her child was a constant companion.

"There are so many things, I don't know where to start," Ari said perplexed.

"Well let's go to the education center, I'm sure it will spark much interest," Ayotal said. Ari nodded her agreement as they left the suite.

It was only a short distance to the large complex in the middle of one of the main thorough ways named Enlightenment Row. Te`rellean life centered on walking from one destination to another whenever possible, any opportunity to be outside with nature was a boon. Ayotal felt the same; she loved nature and an opportunity to enjoy her surroundings. As they walked, Ari embraced everything she saw, every building, every person, and every child as they made their way to the center. The whole street was devoted to education. Ayotal was continually explaining points of interest as they entered the main complex.

"All of our young children starting from the age of six months are brought here for Kaa-tee`. This is when they are evaluated for ability, strength, and potential. As Te`relleans coming from the earth, we all have some natural ability to manipulate certain elements of the earth such as wind, water, fire, or the earth itself. Most everyone has mastery over one of the elements. Very few have the ability to master all four. As a matter of fact we have not had anyone who was able to master all four in over seventy-five thousand years. It is quite rare. Before the destruction, those who could control all four elements were more common but that was a long time ago," Ayotal explained.

"So each one of our people can control an element?—How?" Ari asked— her curiosity was peaked.

"Some can manipulate one, others can manipulate two, and still others have the ability to manipulate three. Any of our people who have been able to control all four are different. They become one with the elements. It is quite fascinating actually. My grandfather was the last to have this ability before he was killed. Our mentaplex system, the specialized organs Jace told you about, is how we connect to the elements of the earth. Let me show you," Ayotal said as they walked over to the water fountain in the center of the lobby.

It was a large granite rock formation with a variety of foliage growing through the cracks in the rock. It looked like a natural waterfall from pictures Ari had seen of places like Hawaii and the South Pacific islands. As Ari was standing there, she watched the water stop flowing straight down. It started rotating and flowed up, it formed a face which smiled at her, and then it circled around the whole lobby which concerned a few people who obviously didn't want to get wet. As they looked around nervously to find the culprit, they noticed that it was Ayotal who was performing the demonstration, and all seemed to relax.

"Amazing…is that the only element you can control?" Ari asked intrigued at what she was watching her mother demonstrate.

"No, I am one of the few who can control three of the elements as is your father. I have mastered water, fire, and earth. He has mastered wind, water, and earth. We balance each other nicely," Ayotal said as she returned the water to the fountain.

"What is involved with Kaa-tee`?" Ari asked. Thrilled to be at the education center, she wanted to know everything about her people, their abilities, and their routines.

"Children are brought here to the center and a physical examination is done to determine the structure of the mentaplex. First let me explain the mentaplex in more detail. An organ about the size of your fist, it is diamond shaped if laid out on a table. Anterior to the spine in the lower thoracic region, thus its location is right in the core of your body. Intertwined along the neural tissue, fibrous tendrils are outstretched to the base of the brain where a small organ called the epicort is located. From the epicort, if a person is able to control one element, a single tendril transverses the outer layer of the brain to the frontal lobe. A person capable of two has two tendrils extending to the right and left side of the brain. For people able to manipulate three, there are three tendrils which transverse the outside surface of the brain to the right, left, and center. The rare individuals who are able to manipulate and control all four elements are different. The tendrils extending out of the epicort do not transverse the outer surface of the brain; these tendrils are burrowed through the center of the brain and are intertwined throughout the entire brain structure into the tissue," Ayotal explained as they strolled through the center.

"So...it is based on physical structure," Ari said trying to understand the physiological function of the mentaplex and epicort.

"Partly...all the structures must be in place yes...but the person must be willing to learn how to access the ability. The Kaa-tee` is what determines willingness. The children play games specifically designed to identify a willing spirit," Ayotal said as they stopped at a room full of children playing games. She pointed to the room; Ari looked in through the window to observe the children.

"The children are so young how is it possible to make that determination at such an early age?" Ari asked skeptically.

"You are still thinking in human terms. We are not human. Our children are different, abilities manifest very early. We have a ranking scale: M1, M2, M3, M4 based on mentaplex structure. Capability is ranked by N for not willing, W for willing, E for eager, and I for independent. I am rated M3W—I have three tendrils to control three elements and I am a willing participant. Your father is M3E—he has three tendrils and is eager to participate which is a higher level than me. A person's willingness to use the ability is essential in determining his or her ability to master the control of an element. Would you like to know what you are rated?" Ayotal asked. Smiling, she could see Ari was more than eager to know what she was rated which pleased Ayotal.

"You had me tested before I went into stasis?" Ari asked. Her eyes lit up with excitement. She definitely wanted to know what her potential was for manipulating the elements. It could be useful in helping her people against the Emigee, she thought.

"Yes we did," Ayotal said grinning.

"Yes...I want to know what I'm rated," Ari said eagerly. "You are rated M4I," Ayotal said as she assessed Ari's reaction to her rating. She noted Ari's immediate realization that she had the highest rating possible.

"Are you sure? Has the evaluation ever been wrong?" Ari asked not at all sure that was an accurate assessment. She had never been able to control any of the elements even by accident, not like she had inadvertently moved objects or healed things.

"Yes, I'm sure... and no the test has never been wrong," Ayotal confirmed. She saw the uncertainty in Ari's expression. What Ari failed to realize is that the Te`rellean children had the benefit of guidance from a young age.

"But I can't control the elements," Ari said a little concerned at her inability to manipulate the elements.

"Ariella...our children are trained from the time the evaluation is complete to tap into their abilities. You have never had that opportunity. It doesn't mean you can't achieve the skill with a little training and practice. I have assigned all my duties to my assistants so that I will be able to teach you myself, if you are willing to learn," Ayotal said reassuring her that she was more than capable of using her natural talent.

"Yes...I want to learn but...you are an important person to our people. Can you really leave your duties to others?" Ari asked. She was grateful for the opportunity to be trained and master her skills, but she didn't want to be selfish and take her mother away from her people when she was such an integral part of their life.

"The work is routine anyone of my assistants can handle it and if an emergency occurs I will be available. Right now there is nothing more important than preparing you to reach your full potential. For those that possess the ability to control all four elements, there are four trials that must be completed to maximize the effectiveness of their skills. So, you can attempt the trials to assist you in your role as Legate," Ayotal said. "You can choose to complete the trials or not, that decision is up to you."

"What is this Legate you are calling me?" Ari asked hoping for a better understanding of what it means to be Legate.

"The Legate is a position of great importance. It literally means messenger, but it entails more than delivering a message. The Legate provides a demonstration as to the validity of the message by use of all four elements, elemental oneness it's called. My grandfather was our last Legate soon you will be the next. You are an extraordinary person Ariella, your father and I have complete confidence in you; you will be fine don't look so worried," Ayotal said beaming with confidence.

"Does it show that much?" Ari asked.

"Just a little...I promise it will be fine. I have confidence in you. Shall we get to work?" Ayotal asked as they disappeared into one of the training rooms.

Chapter

Jace was at the same computer console he had been at for over a week trying to discover clues, any clues, as to the whereabouts of Martin and Ena—no success. Beyond tired, he was completely exhausted. It was as if they had vanished off the face of the earth. Kaazi said he tagged Martin but there was no sign of the implant's signal anywhere. Frustrated, running his hands through his hair, Jace sat back to clear his head for a moment, hoping for a flash of insight.

Staring at the numerous NOSSIC monitors surrounding him, a monitor for every aspect of covert operations, he was able to see almost every known Emigee operative's current location but that was not the objective. A command center, complete with technically advanced surveillance and tracking equipment in front of him and he had found nothing on Hamer's location or Martin and Ena's whereabouts. The Emigee must be keeping them in a shielded location, but where, he asked himself. Fatigue was taking its toll; he was at a loss for new ideas. His mind wandered back to the ranch, like a proverbial light bulb he thought—Zenot had a stake in the operation at the ranch perhaps Hamer took them to one of Zenot's holdings; he should check their records.

Kaazi and Ali`kram approached Jace as they wander into the control room, Kaazi asked, "Any progress?"

"No… what about you?" responded Jace, frustration evident in his voice.

"Nothing—they must have Martin under a jammer. We have checked with every operative in North and South America. They haven't seen or heard a thing," said Alik`ram as he took the seat opposite of Jace.

"What about Htiaf and Epoh they were checking with the operatives in Europe and Asia. Have you heard from them?" Jace asked wanting to make sure all bases were covered.

"No…haven't seen them yet," said Kaazi. Just as he finished answering Htiaf and Epoh entered the NOSSIC control room. "Let's ask them, they just walked in," Kaazi said and the other two men turned in the direction Kaazi was pointing.

Htiaf and Epoh caught sight of Jace and the others and moved in their direction. Frowning, Epoh asked, "Have you had any success?"

Alik`ram responded with frustration, "No…how about you two?"

"None of our operatives in Europe or Asia have seen or heard anything but they remain vigilant," said Htiaf. Epoh and Htiaf had run out of options and were desperately hoping that by meeting with the team alternative action could be implemented.

"What about Africa…has anyone checked with the operatives there?" asked Epoh. A deep voice from behind the group answered.

"Nothing from the operatives in Africa," said Gyasi. "I have just come from seeing Ashi'nat; he urgently wants this matter seen to and resolved immediately. Ariella asks about the progress we're making on finding her adoptive parents every night."

"Have you seen Ari?" Jace asked his father. Everyone turned to Gyasi for his response, none of them had seen her since the day in Ashi`nat's office.

"Yes, I've seen her," Gyasi said. He, in his usual reserved fashion, only responded with brief concise answers. This he did for two reasons; he was able to gain insight from facial and emotional responses and it drove his operatives crazy—it was fun.

"How is she?" Epoh asked. The past week had been busy, but he missed seeing and talking with Ari.

"Fine," Gyasi said. The men were anxiously awaiting any tidbit of news about Ari; they were almost holding their collective breath.

"What has she been doing?" Htiaf asked hoping to glean more information than Epoh received.

"Training," Gyasi responded. Keenly watching, he realized Jace was hanging on every word spoken as if he had a vested interest. This intrigued Gyasi, he suspected there was more to Jace's relationship with Ari than he was letting on.

"Training for what?" Kaazi asked having the misconception that she was training to become a field operative like them.

"The Trials," Gyasi said. With that response, Gyasi received five confused and comical reactions, faces twisted and distorted, brows furrowed; he wished he had a recorder to capture the moment.

"What trials?" Alik`ram asked what they all wanted to know.

"The ancient trials of oneness," Gyasi said. Never did Gyasi expect the reaction that occurred. All five men responded in unison, reacting almost violently, in complete disbelief.

"Why!?" all five men exclaimed at the same time.

"Why? So she can truly be the Legate for our people. Why are you so surprised? You all know the responsibilities of the Legate; the trials are part of the responsibilities of her position. In order to achieve her maximum potential as Legate, she must successfully complete the trials," Gyasi said, chastising the men for their surprised response, the men for which he was responsible. They should have known that.

"I just thought she was an M4, I didn't realize when I took the assignment that she was going to go through the trials…M4's, they don't have to go through the trials…it's not mandatory…it's crazy…why would she do that…" Jace said extremely distraught at what could happen, so much so, he was rambling.

"Well according to Ayotal she is a very adept, quick to learn new abilities. She has gained control of earth and fire already and it's only been a week," said Gyasi finally providing more than one-word bits of information.

"Well there is a huge difference between having control over an element and becoming one with it. What she is going to attempt is dangerous, she could be killed," said Kaazi. Even care-free Kaazi had his reservations about Ari participating in the trials, he was usually the first one to take the most dangerous venue but not when the trials were concerned.

"Yes…she could, but her great-grandfather was able to survive the trials," Gyasi said. Reminding them that success usually followed in hereditary lines. It was true that was not always the case, tragedy did strike at times, but compared to what could be gained it was worth the risk.

"Yeah but several others have attempted and died in the process," Jace said with fear in his voice, Ari could die without him ever making things right with her.

"Well the decision has been made, you really need not worry about Ariella; she is being trained by the best, Ayotal herself. It has been many years since she trained a student, but because the student is Ariella, she has reassigned her duties so she can devote herself to her daughter's training. Ariella has the best instructor we have," Gyasi said, "Now back to the task at hand. We have all our operatives actively searching for the Lovell's—any other ideas?"

"I had a thought. Zenot wanted a signed contract from Martin to frack on his land…Hamer has dealings with Zenot…Zenot has many holdings. It's possible they took Martin and Ena to an abandon mine site or other site they own. I think we should start searching the records for property not currently in use by Zenot," Jace said trying to stay focused but not succeeding. Over a week now he had tried to put Ari out of his mind and focus on finding Martin and Ena, but it was impossible she permeated his soul, she was in his mind, his heart, his entire being. It was like trying to stop breathing, unrealizable; he just couldn't stop thinking about her, longing for her. He needed Ari, she was his life, his essence; it was inconceivable to continue to live without her in his life.

"Good idea, I'll talk to Isbeth to see if she can provide us with the most updated information on Zenot property," said Gyasi. A strange glint appeared in Kaazi's eyes when Gyasi mentioned Isbeth, no one seemed to notice except Alik`ram; he chuckled silently to himself thinking things would become interesting if Isbeth became actively involved in the search.

"We should also look at Emigee property sites that we know about, the ones currently in use and the ones they have abandoned," said Kaazi attempting to redirect his thoughts to the subject at hand. Every time Isbeth was mentioned his mind wandered, stern discipline and training over the years had him again focusing his attention on the matter at hand.

"Gyasi have our operatives been able to locate the headquarters of the Emigee in New York City yet?" asked Alik`ram.

"No…but New York is a big city. They're still looking," said Gyasi. "Kaazi, you and Alik`ram start searching for potential prospects among the Emigee property. Htiaf, you and Epoh start searching the Zenot properties we know about for potential prospects. If anything looks like it would be a

good spot to conceal two people, we will send our people in to check it out…
Jace I would like a private word with you if you don't mind." Every man looked
at Jace then at each other but didn't say a word.

Jace followed behind his father quietly still thinking about Ari and the
trials, and asked, "What is it, father?"

"We haven't had a chance to talk since you've been back with you being
here day and night. Don't think I haven't noticed. Let's take a walk," said
Gyasi trying to determine how he was going to broach the subject he wanted
to discuss.

The two men left NOSSIC and started walking down the street called
Hidden Cloak toward the central tower. Gyasi began the conversation by asking Jace, "How are you?"

Jace curtly said, "I'm fine." Without realizing it, Jace was mimicking
Gyasi's tactics for answering questions he didn't want to respond to.

"I can see something is bothering you…do you want to talk about it?" said
Gyasi trying to coax Jace into opening up, to talk about whatever was torment-
ing him.

"Nothing is wrong, and I don't want to talk about it," said Jace so preoccupied he didn't even ascertain the oxymoron, something he was usually quick
to pick-up on.

"Well there is something I would like to ask you. You spent a good deal of
time with Ariella; do you think she will make Kaazi a good mate?" Gyasi asked
deciding to try another approach, anticipating Jace's reaction, he braced himself.

"What? No…absolutely not! Why…what did he say…does he have intentions toward her? I will incinerate him!" Jace said angrily under his breath.

Gyasi hadn't expected such a volatile response. His brow went up immediately as he waited for Jace to calm down, "So you have finally met someone
who interests you?"

"Yes…but…" Jace tailed off and didn't finish what he was thinking.

"What's the problem Jace?" Gyasi asked a little confused by his reaction.
As far as he could see, it would be a very good match, not now of course they
needed time to get to know each other better, but sometime in the future.

"There are a lot of problems," said Jace. He did not like where the conversation was heading and he certainly didn't want to discuss his shortcomings
with his father.

"Like what?" Gyasi said, not letting it go; he wanted Jace to face the issues troubling him, deal with them, not to run away from them. It was apparent the issues centered around Ari. It was not difficult to ascertain how Jace felt about her. Gyasi was determined to get him to realize confused, scrambled emotions were an inevitable part of the process all Te`rellean males worked through during the initial stages of a bonding. If dealt with directly, the outcome could lead to a long healthy union of two spirits.

"She is the leader's daughter for one," he said knowing that was just a lame excuse and had absolutely nothing to do with the real issue.

"And you have been friends with both Ashi'nat and Ayotal for many years. They love you like a son," Gyasi said. "That's not a problem it's an excuse."

"We were at a convenience store on our way here. The Emigee almost grabbed her and they would have if Kaazi and Alik`ram weren't there. I didn't even see it coming because all I could think about was pleasing Ari. I lost my focus—instead of looking for danger I was worrying about bagels and lattes," Jace said with disgust as he turned away from his father.

"We all lose our focus occasionally but that doesn't mean we stop living or loving or taking chances. We readjust our thinking to accommodate our new interest and maintain our alertness. The incident could have ended badly but it didn't thanks to friends. Friends who care for us," Gyasi said relieved to be making headway, he was finally talking about what triggered his discord.

"But what if I lost her…what if they hurt her…She is strong, but she has no idea how to deal with the Emigee. I could not bear it if I lost another…" Jace didn't finish.

"…another person you loved…like your mother…She would be the first person to tell you to take hold of life, make mistakes and learn from them—live life to the full. Grab love when it comes your way and never let go of it! We lost your mother, but she would not want you to forsake loving someone Jace," Gyasi said as he reminisced about the incredibly high-spirited, beautiful woman he had loved and lost, still longing for her. Both he and Jace were devastated when she was killed; recovery was slow, painstakingly so, it took years.

"It's too late; I already told Ari I wouldn't be seeing her once we got here. You saw her reaction to me in the Leader's office. She doesn't want to see me after what I said to her," Jace told Gyasi, lamenting that decision.

"Yes…Ashi'nat and I both saw the interaction between the two of you. It was quite apparent there was more than friendship going on between you two. How close did you become Jace?" Gyasi asked hesitantly. If they made a connection bond, it would explain the unusually severe distress he was experiencing.

"So close that it hurt to pull away from her. I almost initiated the mental bond. I couldn't be that unfair to her. I was the only one of our people she had ever had contact with, how could I bond with her knowing she was limited to just me?" Jace said recalling the intensity of his feelings for her.

"Are you sure you didn't make that bond? Your reaction earlier when I mentioned Kaazi was quite explosive," Gyasi said as he arched his brow.

"After I told Ari I wouldn't be seeing her, Kaazi and the others knew something was wrong and tried to make her feel better. Well it seemed to work. Several times I saw Ari and Kaazi together…laughing and joking. He's one of my best friends but I want to rip his head off when I see him with Ari. Is that normal? That can't be normal," Jace said shaking off the image of holding Kaazi's head in his hands.

Gyasi chuckled to himself and said, "Unfortunately it is very normal. We are a peaceful people except when mating and meeting up with a rival."

"Is Kaazi interested in Ari?" Jace asked, suddenly very anxious about the two.

"I don't know to be honest with you. Maybe you should go and talk with Ariella. Don't sever all lines of communication with her. She needs friends," Gyasi said as they approached the garden on the northeast side of the central tower facing Enlightenment Row, the street where all of the educational training centers were located.

"What if she won't talk to me?" asked Jace. Knowing she felt slighted when they spoke in the van, it would serve him right if she never talked to him again.

"You won't know unless you try will you?" Gyasi said. "Think about it Jace. From what I can see, she is a rare beauty and much stronger than you give her credit for."

Jace didn't say anything in reply; he sat down in the garden contemplating his dilemma. His father had raced off to a meeting. Alone in the lush green oasis of the central tower in the middle of the southwestern desert, his mind wandered to a secluded garden by a lake. Luscious velvety green foliage caressed the landscape just as a soft fluffy blanket securely wraps around an infant. Flowers dancing in the breeze filled the air with sweet smelling aromas.

A beautiful woman, graceful and lean, with long dark hair freely blowing in the wind sat with her young child in the midst of the blossoms. Carefree and innocent they played their naming game, the child's favorite, name the flowers. Jace felt safe, at peace among the blooms with his mother. Whenever he was troubled, he would often recall the scene to find a measure of peace.

Glancing around the garden he saw every kind of flower imaginable in full bloom, asters, gladiolus, lilies, azaleas, pansies, and roses were just a few he remembered from long ago. Loving flowers with their fragrant aroma as he did, he wasn't familiar with all their names but he did enjoy them immensely. Desperately he was seeking solace in the serenity of the garden among the flowers that once offered security and peace; but in the early morning light, he found that it was eluding him. He hadn't known peace since before that horrible last day in the van. He tried to bury himself in his work, but Ari continually imbued his thoughts, penetrating his barriers.

Talking to himself under his breath Jace was now attempting to gird himself up, muster up courage to try to recover what he so blatantly discarded… 'You have to buck up man—go talk to her. Tell her you're sorry for being an idiot. If you don't someone else will seek her out—Kaazi will vie for her affections. You can't let that happen. What is stopping you? You have always gone after what you want—what's different now? You're afraid she's going to reject you like you rejected her. I didn't really reject her—he argued. I just told her we wouldn't be seeing so much of each other. How do you think she took that—as a rejection you idiot. How can you face her after that…buck up and be a man. You love her…show it.'

Jace's thoughts came to an abrupt halt as he saw Ari walking down Enlightenment Row…with Kaazi, that slug. He's supposed to be working on the Emigee property list not walking with Ari. Jace was ready to go after them when he heard people behind him.

Htiaf, Epoh, and Alik`ram were standing there when Jace turned. They all fell silent when they saw the expression of anger on Jace's face.

"What's wrong?" Epoh asked. Jace was always even tempered, the last person to become angry at anything. Something must be terribly wrong, he thought.

"Nothing…I just need to beat someone to a pulp," Jace said as he glanced back in the direction of Enlightenment Row where Kaazi and Ari had been.

"Who do you want to beat?" asked Htiaf, now growing as concerned as Epoh. This was just not in Jace's nature.

"Do you need help?" Alik`ram asked suspecting the culprit to be Kaazi.

"No, I don't need help…now get out of my way so I can find the slug," Jace said angrily.

Unexpectedly from behind the men, Kaazi approached and said, "Who's a slug?" Kaazi wearing his signature grin greeted his companions happily which just pushed Jace over the edge. Jace dove for Kaazi getting in several good jabs before the other three men had Jace suspended in mid-air above Kaazi using their combined telekinetic abilities.

"What is your problem Jace?" asked Kaazi as he remained on the ground looking up at Jace suspended in the air with fists still clenched. His friends had no intention of releasing their grip as long as Jace was fuming.

"Let me go so I can beat that slug to a pulp!" Jace growled, stabbing Kaazi with daggers propelled from his eyes.

Kaazi picking up on Jace's thoughts realized this was about Ari and decided to have some fun with him. No mercy to be shown to the pig-headed fool, he thought.

"Jace calm down and tell us what this is about," said Epoh, he was not about to let the team be torn apart by some petty misunderstanding.

"It's about Ari," said Kaazi with his signature grin firmly in place, which just infuriated Jace all the more. Alik`ram gave Kaazi a hand up from the ground.

"What about Ari?" asked Htiaf as he glanced between the two men; he was beginning to understand.

"Kaazi's making a move on her," Jace snarled. Overwhelming feelings of possession engulfed him, the desire to defend what was his was overpowering.

"She's fair game," said Kaazi. Jace's ire was growing, Kaazi could feel it; he was so easy to mess with it only took a little salt to rub in the wound to get him in a tizzy, they all could see that he was miserable staying away from Ari, everyone except Jace. He decided he was going to push the issue.

"Not for you she's not!" Jace growled. Frustrated that he couldn't get his hands on Kaazi, he felt as if he were going to explode in mid-air his anger was so consuming.

"We thought you were staying away from Ari to focus on Martin and Ena. So, why are you angry if other's show interest in her?" Kaazi asked, rubbing the wound.

"She's not right for you…You just stay away from her!" Jace ordered vehemently.

"Giving orders now are we. Well…I like Ari and unless she's mated to another, I will continue to seek her out," said Kaazi unconcerned at Jace's warning.

"Let me down so I can pummel him," demanded Jace.

"I think we have heard quite enough," said Htiaf. By now, it was evident that Kaazi was taunting Jace, a little was fine but this was going too far, Htiaf thought.

"You know Jace, you hurt Ari very much when you told her you weren't going to see her once we got to the city," said Epoh, chastising him for causing her pain.

"Why the renewed interest in Ari? Is it because Kaazi is seeking her out?" Alik`ram asked driving the point home.

"No…I never stopped being interested in Ari. It's just when the Emigee almost grabbed her in Grants I realized I could have lost her forever and I couldn't deal with another loss. If it wasn't for Kaazi and Alik`ram, the Emigee would have her now. I was more focused on pleasing Ari than on looking for danger—I failed to protect her. I never would have been able to forgive myself if something happened to her so I decided to focus my attention on the job of protecting her and finding Martin," Jace confessed, completely forlorn.

"How's that working for you?" Kaazi asked with a grin, getting one more jab in before he confessed.

"Let… me… down… and… I…will…show…you," Jace said as he struggled.

"First of all, puppy… I like Ari but only as a friend. I have had my sights on another for some time. Besides the fun I have had trying to get you to realize you have been a pig-headed fool for staying away from Ari, was amusingly diverting. I saw how well the two of you are suited to each other, that kind of affinity comes along once in a lifetime…who am I to stand in the way? As far as your inability to protect Ari, you are forgetting covert op basic training 101: NO ONE PERSON CAN DO EVERYTHING! That's why we work in teams, block-head. Now can we stop all this nonsense and get back to work?" Kaazi confessed.

"You have no interest in Ari?" Jace asked his hopes soaring at Kaazi's revelation of another love interest.

"Only as friends," said Kaazi reassuring Jace that he had nothing to worry about from him.

"You have been messing with me from the beginning?" asked Jace. He should have known it was just the thing Kaazi would do to get his point across.

"Yup!" said Kaazi as he started laughing. Jace smiled a grin bigger than Kaazi's signature grin; he was so relieved.

"You can let me down now. I'm not going to do anything except go see Ari," Jace said. They slowly lowered Jace to a standing position.

"Are we all friends again?" said Alik`ram, glad that was resolved.

"Yes," said Jace, "As long as Kaazi stays away from Ari we're good." Kaazi laughed his deep hearty laugh then everyone joined in. Kaazi grabbed Jace, gave him a hug and a slap on the back.

"Why are you all here?" Jace asked realizing they were supposed to be at NOSSIC.

"We found a prospective site owned by Zenot, but it was also a former Emigee camp. We wanted to tell you and see if you wanted to join the op," said Htiaf who was also relieved the hostilities were ended.

"When are you leaving?" Jace asked. Absolutely he wanted to be part of the op but he had to talk with Ari first. He wasn't about to leave without trying to make amends.

"We probably won't have everything together until tomorrow," Alik`ram said. Always vigilant about mission preparations, Alik`ram triple checked plans and supplies which was the reason for the delay.

"Yeah, I'll join you. I need to take care of some business first. I have to talk to Ari before I do anything else," Jace said.

"Go and set things right with her. We will be at NOSSIC putting our strike team together," said Alik`ram.

"Grovel if you have to," said Kaazi his signature grin firmly in place.

"I'll see you all back at NOSSIC when I'm finished," Jace said as he left his companions to face the woman he loved.

Chapter

As the men headed in separate directions, Jace excitedly ran down the street. So happy Kaazi had no interest in Ari; he would be flying if he could, soaring higher and high, it was as if he was floating in mid-air. Searching for Ari in the main education center, he headed for the training rooms. After checking several rooms, he saw Ari working with fire, manipulating the fire in her hands. No easy task—if she lost her concentration for even a moment she would get burnt. Quietly he opened the door and stood silently watching her. The more confidence she gained working the fire compelled her to became more daring, making the fire dance and swirl around her, high then low, twisting, turning, like a dragon circling its prey. Intensely focused on the flames, she was feeling the control, then, she saw Jace, the fire surged fueled by her emotions. It roared like a lion seeking to intimidate its prey. Jace didn't wait another minute.

"Ari, I would like to talk to you," said Jace as the fire closed in on him, darting in, out, and around him.

"Why…you said we wouldn't be seeing each other," Ari said as she continued to manipulate the fire, menacingly encircling Jace. Her emotions were ablaze as was the fire she was controlling.

"Ari…I made a mistake telling you we wouldn't be seeing each other… I was afraid," Jace confessed trying not to anger her. Upsetting someone when they were manipulating fire was dangerous to one's health, in particular his.

"Afraid...afraid of what Jace?—afraid of me?" Ari asked as she tried to keep her mind focused enough on the fire so as not to hurt either of them. It was becoming increasingly difficult. He was stirring her emotions, emotions she needed to restrain.

"No not afraid of you...afraid of losing you. I couldn't bear it if something happened to you especially if I was supposed to be protecting you. When the Emigee almost grabbed you in Grants, I was so preoccupied with pleasing you I didn't even see the danger. If it wasn't for Kaazi and Alik'ram, they might have taken you; you would be lost to me. I couldn't bear that so I made the decision to focus on the job of protecting you, making sure you were safe, but that's not working much better. I think of you day and night, I can't sleep or eat; I hate not talking with you. Ari, I miss you so much it hurts. Please forgive me. I'm sorry," said Jace pleading with her as he poured out his heart.

Ari was ecstatic, so happy at his admission; her emotions exploded in delight, intensifying the already voluminous fire that still encircled Jace. The heat from the fire blazed ferociously. Ari decided to take advantage of the situation and said, "So, am I just supposed to forgive you for breaking my heart the way you did?"

"I'm sorry Ari, I never meant to hurt you," Jace lamented feeling the pain and remorse of his actions, along with the heat from the raging fire.

"What did you think would happen when you told me we wouldn't see each other?" Ari said. She wasn't trying to get revenge; she just wanted him to realize what he had done to her, the pain, the loss, the despair she felt as a result of his mistake. She never wanted to feel his absence again.

"I don't know Ari, I guess I wasn't thinking. I'm an idiot," Jace said as the fire roared furiously and went out.

"Yes...you are Jace," Ari said with a faint smile turning her back to him.

With the fire safely extinguished, Jace immediately went to Ari and took her hands in his; he affirmed, "I am really sorry Ari. Do you forgive me?"

He pressed his lips to her hands gently, tenderly kissing them, sparking an excited tingling shared by both, the amour they shared was rekindled instantly.

"Yes Jace...but don't try to separate us again. I couldn't bear it, being away from you was like losing part of myself—my heart. If it weren't for the distractions I've had this past week, I would have lost my mind. You are my heart

Jace, so deeply entrenched in my heart you are that the two have become one; it's unthinkable to live without you. I know my heart, I know who and what I want. You must understand, I would have waited a hundred years or longer for you to come to your senses," Ari said from the depths of her soul as she embraced Jace and kissed him gently. Passion flared, fervid heat blazing, the separation had taken its toll. They were engulfed in frenzied bliss, consumed by need. Reaffirming their love for one another, intertwined in spirit, their joy was boundless. Unexpectedly the depth of their reunion was interrupted by a "hum hum" coming from the entrance. Slowly, painfully, Jace and Ari looked to see who the intruder was—of course it was none other than Ayotal coming to check on Ari's progress.

"Jace, Ariella…am I interrupting anything?" Ayotal said straight faced but she was smiling on the inside. She was thrilled Jace had finally come to his senses. Ariella had been so unhappy without him this past week.

"Um…Ayotal…uh…good morning…I…ah…I needed to talk to Ari before I left on a mission. We have a lead we want to check-out on a property owned by Zenot which was used as an Emigee camp," Jace said, red-faced and flustered, but trying to maintain a measure of composure.

"When are you leaving Jace?" Ari asked startled at the news, but intensely curious as to the details.

"Our strike force is leaving tomorrow," said Jace still holding Ari. After the week of torture he had put himself through, he wasn't about to let her go quickly.

"Who is going?" Ayotal asked equally as curious for the details of the mission.

"Htiaf, Epoh, Kaazi, Alik`ram, me and a few others I'm not sure about yet," Jace replied realizing he really didn't know much about the details since he had been so preoccupied with Kaazi.

"Since Jace will be leaving tomorrow, why don't you take a break and go for a walk around the city gardens," Ayotal told Ari. She knew how dangerous these missions could be, it was always good to spend time with the people you loved and cared for before embarking on perilous operations. Tragedy could strike at any time.

"Thank you, mother," Ari said eagerly. Wanting to spend time with Jace after their week of separation, which seemed like a year, was exactly what she needed and desired.

"Ayotal...Ari is making great progress with her control of fire. I was very impressed and nervous at the same time as the fire danced around me, very closely," Jace said with a smile.

Ari nudged Jace as her cheeks flushed. Glancing at her mother she shrugged her shoulders. The look was all it took for the imp to feign innocence.

Ayotal raised a brow and laughed to herself thinking that Ariella was certainly a spunky little thing. She said to Jace, "Well I guess it was a good thing you came to apologize to her then instead of making her upset...right Jace?"

"Yeah," he said with a smile, shaking his head quickly as he squeezed Ari lovingly.

Ari and Jace took their leave and headed out into the street. There was increased activity outside, a flurry of activity, the time when her people would bring their midday meal outside to enjoy the numerous gardens, fountains, parks and ponds throughout the city. If there was one thing Te`relleans loved, it was nature and being outside. All aspects of nature and the resources the earth provided were fundamental in their daily lives. The core of their essence embraced even the miniscule aspects of earth's life-force.

Jace and Ari walked to the central tower then circled around past Hidden Cloak to Jolly-Romp Road, the area of the city where their people went for enjoyment. As they walked Jace pointed out the different types of activities that could be undertaken such as arts and crafts. There were artisans galore—painters, sculptors, pottery masters to name a few. The artwork was magnificent. Jace revealed that some of the artisans had been mastering their craft for thousands of years. As they continued walking further, glorious music delighted the ears; nothing like the noise humans call music. It was as if the musicians were one with nature and they emulated the very essence of life on earth. The spirit of the music carried one to new levels of tranquility.

"This is wonderful Jace thank you for sharing it with me," Ari said, thoroughly enjoying her time with him.

Jace steered her to a bench surrounded by flowers and trees near a pond. The music continued to flow effortlessly on the breeze. "What have you been doing the past week?" Jace asked wanting to close the rift between them.

"Reading, spending time with my parents, worrying and crying, it's been a very hard and busy week, but mostly I've been training with my mother. Apparently, I am rated an M4I which I am told is greater than my great-grandfather. I'm going through the exercises children go through after they find out their rating. I'm actually having fun exploring my potential," Ari said a little embarrassed that she was working on children's exercises, but she knew it was the best way to start the exploration of her abilities. She found herself quite adept at the training.

"My father told me that you are also training for the trials," Jace saying trying not to show his displeasure and weariness about such a pursuit, not quite succeeding.

"Yes, that's all part of it," Ari said. She had come to the realization that going through the trials was the best way to help her people with the Emigee problem.

"Do you know how dangerous the trials are?" Jace asked, his concern clearly showing through his control.

"Yes…mother has told me that some of our people who have undergone the trials don't make it through," Ari said, attempting to express the end result of the trials for a few unfortunate individuals gently.

"They died Ari! They didn't just fail the tests hoping to try again. They can't try again because they are dead. The trials are dangerous! You can be Legate without putting yourself in danger; no one will think less of you. Are you sure you want to attempt the trials?" Jace blurted completely discomposed at the prospect of Ari's death.

"Jace I know there are risks but I have never shied away from a challenge before, I'm not about to start now. Your support would be welcome though," Ari said hoping with all her heart that Jace would stand by her decision, support her in the work she was determined to accomplish, and love her even though he didn't approve of her path.

"Yes…but you have to remember your challenges up to this point have been in the human world, not ours. Our world is much more dangerous, some peril is blatant while other threats are insidious. Ari you have no idea what awaits you!" Jace roared.

"I know you are worried about me, but that is why I'm taking things slow and learning everything I can. I feel compelled to move forward Jace, to help our people but especially to help Martin and Ena. I miss them so much. My heart breaks every time I think of Ena and the baby, scared and possibly hurt and Martin, who knows what he would do to protect her and the baby. I want them back. I just want to do my part and I would like your support," Ari declared.

"Ari you will always have my support. I just want you safe and with me," Jace said. Safe was foremost on his mind, he vowed to do whatever it took to keep her safe and out of the hands of the Emigee.

"Do you think I will not worry about you when you are gone on the op tomorrow? I know it's something that must be done. Besides if I succeed in the trials, I may be able to assist with the Emigee problem. I want the earth restored to the way it is supposed to be, our people safe, not having to worry constantly about being exterminated, and Martin and Ena home safe on the ranch. How that will be accomplished, I don't know, but I fear there will be much death and tragedy before it's over," Ari said. The longer she was with her people, becoming part of their lives, learning their ways, adapting to her heritage, the more she was determined to solve the conflict.

"You're going to worry about me?" Jace said with a grin as he nuzzled her shoulder.

"Of course, I'm going to worry about you. I want to go with you but I know I'm not ready for anything like that yet," said Ari assuring Jace she wasn't going to do anything to endanger herself needlessly.

"Yet, what do you mean yet?" said Jace as he put his arm around her, and she relaxed into his shoulder.

"Don't think you're going to keep me safe and protected forever. I'm just smart enough to know when I'm not ready to go along with you. Mother says I'm an exceedingly quick study, just as you once told me," said Ari. In order for their love to grow and flourish, Jace was going to have to accept that she was competent and determined. To have an active part as Legate, she would have to reach her maximum potential. She knew that these emotions were all new to him and had become overwhelming, but he was going to have to find a way to reconcile himself, make adjustments in his thinking to accept her path or they were going to be doomed before they began.

"You are, if your demonstration with the fire was any indication, I'd say you've definitely taken control of the ability," said Jace with a chuckle. From the time he met her, he knew she had great potential and she would do great things, but he just wished he could get these nagging feelings, panic, worry, possessiveness, under control.

"What is your level of ability Jace?" Ari asked out of curiosity.

"I'm rated M3I," Jace said, "I can control air, water, and earth."

"I haven't attempted air or water. Mother said earth and fire prove to be the most challenging for many people. I can see how that would be the case. Earth has so many components to control and fire well I've been burnt several times. I've always tried to get the hard things out of the way first before I start on the easy," said Ari as she laughed at her quirks.

"Don't underestimate the power of air and water. When forced into certain forms they can both be formidable forces. Watch the water," Jace said as the water started to swirl into a whirlpool sucking leaves down into a vortex. A few minutes later the water changed form. A miniature waterspout formed dancing on top of the water spinning faster and faster sucking debris into it. "Think about the destructive power of the wind and water on a larger scale, hurricanes, tornadoes, they can cause massive destruction."

"The power of wind and water, in the wrong hands, could cause extensive loss of life, homelessness, starvation, illness, and countless other maladies. It's a good thing that the Emigee don't have this power. Can you imagine the destruction they would cause," Ari said as she shivered.

"Are you alright?" Jace asked feeling her shiver. Realizing she was recalling the night that Martin and Ena were taken, he drew her closer, protectively reassuring her everything was going to turn out for the best.

"Yes, I'm fine I just can't stop thinking of Martin and Ena being held captive. Who knows what kind of torture they're going through," Ari said venting her fears about their fate, realizing that the longer they were held captive the greater the chances of them not surviving. Urgency had been a permanent driving force within Ari since Martin and Ena were taken.

"We'll find them Ari. I promise you, we *will* find them. No matter how long it takes we will never give up," said Jace not only for Ari's sake but to reaffirm his own desire to rescue the Lovell's. He had enjoyed working on the ranch; Martin and Ena were extraordinary people and didn't deserve to be caught up in their conflict.

"I know Jace. It's just frustrating," she said trying to muster up some of that patience her people were known for, but it was proving difficult.

"Come on, let's walk," he said as he grabbed her hand and headed down the road past the artisan shops. "Have you seen much of the city?" Jace asked in an attempt to divert her attention.

"No not really. I've been too busy with training although I am getting to know my way around Enlightenment Row," Ari said confidently.

Exploring was one of her favorite things, so he decided to show her around the city. "Well let's take a walk around the central tower," Jace said. "Most people say the city is laid out like a wheel with spokes, others say it's like a snowflake, but I like to think of it as a flower, delicate and beautiful, with the central tower as the center and the streets are like petals extending out from the center. You already know Enlightenment Row. All our educational needs are met in those centers."

"Yes, the library and training centers have an extensive data base. Of course, it would with millenniums of knowledge stored in them," Ari said in awe. Thinking about the wealth of knowledge in the library, she felt it was fortuitous that Te`relleans had long lives because it would take her forever to sift through such voluminous amounts of information.

Jace laughed, "Yeah it boggles the mind sometimes. Now you have been introduced to Jolly-Romp Road. Did you like our recreational area?"

"Are you kidding? It's magnificent, like nothing I've ever seen before, and the music was wonderfully soothing. I could have been completely captivated by it if I didn't have so many other things to worry about," she said hoping that she would be able to return there soon.

"Okay, central tower is right in front of us, if you turn left the next street is called Crop Circle. Can you guess what we do down that street?" Jace asked as he chuckled.

"Well let me think…something to do with agriculture maybe," she said as she joined Jace in laughter.

"Very good; we have research and development facilities and farmland which grow our food," Jace said.

"I find it fascinating that we are in the Nevada desert and we are growing our own food. Our protective barrier is amazing," Ari said. So many aspects of Te`rellean living fascinated her and there was so much more to learn.

"Next is Panacea Way. Venture to guess what we do down this street?" Jace asked teasingly.

"Hum…panacea…that has something to do with medicine, right?" Ari asked as she was delving into the recesses of her memory.

"Yup, all our medical research is done in the medical centers and laboratories. Occasionally, a child is born with defects that need to be corrected;

our doctors and scientists have been able to fix most infirmities that occur. Mostly what our doctors are working on is the Emigee genetic mutation problem and how to reverse it, but that problem has proved difficult. I don't know if we will ever solve that problem," Jace explained.

"I'm sure that if a solution can be found we will find it," Ari said with confidence as they continued around the tower to the next street.

"Here we have Boffin Lane. What do you think?" Jace asked curiously.

"Boffin Lane…I don't have a clue. What is done there?" Ari asked. She had never come across a word like boffin; there were no clues to glean by the name.

"Boffin is an old English word for scientist, it's archaic now. So Boffin Lane is where all our scientific research and development is done. You have seen some of the advancements we have achieved," Jace said proudly. Even with the destruction of their original civilization, they had remained an advanced, educated people.

"Advancements…are you kidding me…what advancements? Our people live in the stone age!" Ari said as she laughed with Jace.

The next street is Reflection Haven. We put into practice what we have learned in the meditation centers. With our daily lives being so unpredictable, we refocus our selves here and strive for oneness with the earth even though most of us will never achieve that goal we can gain a certain level of connection to her. It is refreshing to be centered and in tune with nature. Our connection with the earth is symbiotic in nature, but the humans and the Emigee have disrupted the balance of nature. By our meditation, we help the earth regain a small part of its balance. A more permanent solution must be found or they will kill her," Jace said sadly. Through the years Jace practiced meditation, he felt a strong connection, like he was being drawn to the meditation chambers, it felt almost compulsory.

"Do you go there regularly?" Ari asked Jace; seeing that he was passionate about the destruction and damage being done to the earth.

"When I am here in the city, I am very regular but this past week I have been a bit distracted," Jace said with a smile.

"Really…hum…well let's just forget this past week. What do you say?" Ari asked as she shook off thoughts of the horrendous week of being separated from her parents and Jace.

"Sounds like a good idea," Jace said as they approached the next street. "This is a tough one...the next street is named Fault Line...any ideas?"

"If I had to venture a guess, I'd say study of the earth—all things geological," Ari said as she grinned.

"It also includes our manipulation of the minerals, rocks, gems of the earth and how we construct our buildings. I know you were impressed when we first arrived seeing the spectacular raw beauty of our stonework," Jace said watching Ari as her face lit up with excitement.

"Impressed...more like bowled over...you never prepared me for how beautiful the city was. I was expecting a camp with tents, crates, and equipment like a boot camp or something like that. I wasn't expecting a gorgeous sparkling city," Ari said. Taking note, she decided she would have to explore this area in much greater detail when she had the time.

"We are almost finished. You know Enlightenment Row," he said as they walked past. "Last but not least is Hidden Cloak. This is another one that is tough to figure out," Jace said with a laugh. "This is where I spend most of my time. Our main intelligence center is called NOSSIC. The others are there preparing for the op tomorrow. Would you like to see it?" Jace asked. Hoping she would like to see where he spent most of his time, he watched her intently. The desire to share everything with Ari from the most insignificant aspects of his life to the most important was growing ever stronger as if it was as urgent as the need for air.

"Are you kidding? Of course I'd like to see," Ari said excitedly. "I'd like to see the others too. I haven't seen anyone except Kaazi this morning, when I ran into him literally, and he walked with me to Enlightenment Row."

"Well...let's go see NOSSIC," Jace said, trying not to think about this morning and seeing Kaazi and Ari together, as they walked down Hidden Clock.

The pair entered NOSSIC. Ari paused as she took in the scene before her. Huge ceiling to floor wall monitors which displayed every country on the planet. Some screens showed airline flights, while others had red, green, blue, and yellow dots still others had massive amounts of computer data. There was a large area to the left that looked like a communications center. Several areas in the center of the large room had numerous sleek pillar-like consoles with flashing displays that Ari couldn't even image what their purpose was. At the far-right end of the room, she saw a group of faces she was familiar with, instantly her heart leapt with excitement. Jace walked her over to her friends.

Everyone's face light up with eagerness; hugs went out to everyone who came to Ari. An explosion of happy voices engulfed the room, everyone talking at the same time. Ari felt grateful and very secure with such good friends. She felt as if she had come home to her family when she was with this rag-tag bunch.

"I've missed you guys," Ari said with a smile.

"We've missed you to, we have been trying endlessly to find some clue as to Martin and Ena's whereabouts," said Epoh as he hugged Ari again.

"We finally found one and we are going to Wyoming tomorrow to check out a lead," said Alik`ram attempting to reassure Ari that everything that could be done was being done to get the Lovell's back.

"Are you getting along alright Ari?" asked Htiaf as he assessed her with his kind tender eyes. She appeared much happier than the day he left her in Ashi`nat's office which was a relief.

"Yes, I've been doing a lot of catch-up training. The kind you learn when you are children," Ari said. "It's been fun actually."

"I don't remember that training being fun," said Htiaf with agreement coming from the others.

"Well it's about time Jace came to his senses," said Kaazi as he approached with a grin on his face. "He's been a miserable cuss without you Ari." Four hands reached out and cracked Kaazi on the head then everyone burst into laughter.

"Yes…yes…I'll admit I have been miserable. But I'm fine now," Jace said as he squeezed Ari's hand.

"Is everything set for the op?" Gyasi asked as he approached the group. The three men grew quiet and became very busy looking at computer screens while Kaazi responded to Gyasi's inquiry.

"Everything is set; Danek and his team are setting up the temporary transport pad. We will meet them there in the morning at 0500 hours," Kaazi said very serious, mission ops were a serious business; he never treated the details lightly.

"Good, Jace I see you are giving Ariella a tour of NOSSIC," Gyasi said with a smile. "What do you think Ariella?"

"It's very impressive," she said in awe. "I just hope they will be successful in finding Martin and Ena tomorrow."

"We will find them no matter how long it takes," Gyasi said. "I'm glad you are all here. Ashi'nat and Ayotal would like you all to come for evening meal. I expect to see you all there," Gyasi said as he left the group.

Chapter

28

Lying in bed the next morning, Ari was recounting the wonderful day she had the day before. Together with Jace again, she was so happy and relieved. Exploring parts of the city she hadn't seen before was exciting; but it was even more special since she was with him. Dinner was fun and relaxed. Learning a few more things about her parents from their friends that she didn't know was intriguing. They were just like the others—laughing and joking and even Gyasi let his hair down which surprised Alik`ram, Htiaf and Epoh; he had quite the sense of humor. Kaazi has a kindred spirit in Gyasi. Never showing it, she thought, was probably due to his authority, afraid to let those he worked with see that he was just as free spirited as them. And Jace, her heart swelled with happiness thinking of him; he said that if all went well, they would be back tonight or tomorrow at the latest.

Talking to herself she said, 'Better get to work and try and keep my mind off the op. I need to keep working and train for the trials. Mother said I have already completed the training for control of earth, and it wouldn't be long before I'm done with fire, then two more to master. I wonder what the trials will really be like, to become one with the earth. How do you become one with something? I'll have to talk to mother about that aspect of the trials. It would be helpful if my great-grandfather was here so I could get firsthand information. Well, all in due time…time to get up.'

Kaazi's team met the others in Wyoming. The whole mission team met for the first time that morning. Consisting of Kaazi as mission leader, Jace, Htiaf, Epoh, Alik`ram formed the main team, Danek's five man team, plus a team of operatives lead by Dirk provided support; his team had just come back from doing a sweep of the area around the Lovell Ranch. Dirk's team found no evidence that Martin and Ena were still in that area. A total of fifteen men were setting up to sweep the property just west of Smoot, Wyoming, thought to be used by the Emigee and owned by Zenot.

Smoot was a perfect place to hide. A small town cradled in between two mountain ranges—secluded. The property was close to the base of the western mountain range. As they drove to the site, they noticed the deceptive façade; it had the appearance of a ranch with several large buildings on the property. They would have to search each building separately after they determined how many people were on the ranch. It was just before dawn—they still had the cover of darkness when they arrived at their destination.

Kaazi, in charge of the op, started giving orders as soon as they disembarked from the two cloaked vans. Taking cover in a grove of trees with an excellent vantage, the men piled out. Kaazi ordered, "Danek send two men to scout the compound perimeter." Danek immediately dispatched his men.

Kaazi continued, "We go in from both directions. There are three buildings Danek you and your men take the building on the left. Send two men around back to cover any rear exits. Dirk you and your men take the building on the right. Divide your men accordingly. My team will take the center structure. Htiaf, Epoh, you make your way around to the back and enter from there. Alik`ram, Jace and I will go in from the front. Does everyone know what they are supposed to be doing?" All the men nodded.

The scouts returned after several minutes to report. "There is a perimeter fence, a guard house at the gate with one guard on duty. We saw no other guards and no back exit," said one of the scouts.

"Okay so my team will take out the guard. Danek update your men and get ready to move out," Kaazi said. After a few minutes of gathering their gear, they set out. "Alik`ram take out the guard," ordered Kaazi. The wind started to swirl, gently at first, gathering dust as it grew larger. It surrounded Alik`ram, engulfed him so he was no longer visible. Caught completely unaware, the sentinel was mesmerized when the swirling dust cloud entered and consumed the entire guard house. Alik`ram used his weapon to render the man unconscious. After he was down, Alik`ram made the wind dissipate as he bound the guard. The way was now clear to proceed. All three teams moved in with weapons in hand to immobilize any unexpected sentry. Danek's team headed to the left, Dirk's team went to the right while Kaazi's team went straight to the center structure.

Htiaf and Epoh split each taking a side to meet in the back. Htiaf went to the left while Epoh went to the right of the very large grey structure resembling a warehouse. The building was solid, made of concrete block. There were windows in the upper wall. Even though the men were tall, the windows were too high for them to see inside. They reached the door, but it was locked. Kaazi reached into his pocket for a small oblong case resembling a cigar holder. In the container, there were tiny cylindrical filaments the diameter of a strand of hair and the length of approximately ten inches. Removing one of the filaments, he inserted it into the keyhole; the filament instantly wrapped around the locking mechanism, within seconds there was a click. Kaazi reached for the handle and slowly opened the door. He saw two men in the center of the room surrounded by a warehouse filled with boxes. The men were playing cards, eating and drinking, apparently doing anything they could to stay awake and alert, thus they were trying to past the time more quickly.

Kaazi said, *"Alik`ram, you and Jace go right and I'll go left, let me know when you are in position. I want to stun them at the same time,"* Jace and Alik`ram nodded and moved around into position. There was an open crate on a small table as they approached their optimal location. Jace nudged Alik`ram to check out the crate; they were full of Emigee weapons and there were hundreds of crates.

"Kaazi we are in position. The crates are filled with Emigee weapons and the warehouse is filled with these boxes," Jace said knowing that even though it wasn't the primary reason for their mission, they could not lose an opportunity like this to cripple the Emigee military by destroying a weapons stash.

"When we secure the guards, we'll sweep the warehouse then destroy the weapons," Kaazi said. *"I'm in position. Take out the guards."*

The unsuspecting guards fell instantly after being hit with the immobilizers. Alik`ram said, *"Spread out, Jace there is a room on the second floor, check it out. I'll check the rooms down here."*

Jace went upstairs, Kaazi searched his side of the warehouse, while Alik`ram searched the rooms downstairs. On the second floor, Jace entered what appeared to be an office. A map was hanging on the wall with several cities marked in red with numbers next to them. Jace checked the desk to see if anything else was there. He found computer crystals which he put in his pocket. No clue as to the whereabouts of Martin and Ena. Jace grabbed the map, folded it and secured it in his vest then left to find the others.

"Did you find them?" Jace thought to Kaazi and Alik`ram hoping they had better success than he did.

"Nothing here," said Kaazi as he finished searching his section of the warehouse. The only thing he had found was more boxes of weapons; it looked like the Emigee were arming several military factions.

"No, just storage rooms on my side," said Alik`ram disappointed. They all knew it was a long-shot but it was the first conclusive evidence that the Emigee were directly connected to the Zenot Corporation.

"We have the guards outside," said Epoh, *"They are still out cold. Htiaf is watching them."*

"Danek, did you find anything?" said Kaazi as he stretched his mind to contact Danek for an update on his target building.

"We found a chemical lab over here and several data crystals which we retrieved but no one is in here," Danek said. The crystals were a boon, but he would have rather found the Lovell's.

"Destroy the lab," Kaazi said. Danek answered with an acknowledgment.

"Dirk, did you find anything?" Kaazi asked as he stretched out his mind to Dirk.

"It looks like some kind of medical research lab in this building," he said. Knowing the history of his people, the fact that the Emigee had a secret medical research facility scared him terribly.

"Is there anything we can use?" Kaazi asked hoping to gain insight into what the Emigee were up to next. A secret medical facility only meant trouble; they needed to know what kind of trouble.

"There are numerous data storage units here. I'm going to need more help re-trieving them. Martin and Ena aren't here," he said urgently. Hundreds of data crystals were being kept in several large storage units; in order to retrieve them, it would take at least eight people.

"I'll send Danek and his team to help. When you're finished retrieving the data, destroy the lab," Kaazi said. He wanted the whole facility destroyed which would hamper whatever plan the Emigee had in store of for them, at least for the moment.

"Danek, Dirk needs help with retrieval go help him after you destroy the lab," Kaazi ordered.

"Jace, Alik`ram, Martin and Ena aren't here. We need to leave, now; set the ex-plosives. Light it up," ordered Kaazi.

As they left the warehouse several minutes later, they saw the buildings to the left and right engulfed in flames. The center building exploded seconds after Kaazi, Jace and Alik`ram left the building. Htiaf and Epoh raced from around the building and met up with the others. Just as they started toward the perimeter exit, a hes'chala, one of the Emigee stealth transports, appeared hovering over the compound, just like the one in which Hamer escaped with Martin and Ena.

Emigee operatives appeared directly in front of the team glistening into formation as they were transported down from the hes'chala. Dozens of Emi-gee swarmed the area. Kaazi and the others were trapped. Weapons blasting from the front and sides of them, an inferno of fire and explosions behind, they were cornered with no escape route in sight. They took cover behind a tractor and other farm equipment which was apparently used to divert pas-sersby from the real purpose of the compound.

"Do you see Dirk or Danek and the others?" Kaazi asked looking around. They were nowhere in view, he mentally sent out a telepathic SOS to anyone who could hear him.

"This is not good, they are coming around trying to flank us," said Alik`ram assessing the moves of the Emigee. They were in trouble, outnum-bered and if they got out flanked, they'd had it; it would be all over.

"Jace, Epoh shore up our flank, we'll cover you," said Kaazi. Jace and Epoh moved to an old farm truck to the left to shore up the flank while the others provided cover fire. The MPI blasts were hitting their targets but were having little effect.

"The MPI's are useless change to T-bat," ordered Kaazi. The Te`rell never killed unless absolutely necessary. T-bat was the Te`rellean equivalent to combat using their natural abilities.

A massive explosion from behind them sent flares into the air. Alik`ram took advantage of the fire using his ability to manipulate air to keep the fire and debris from falling on them and sending it toward the Emigee. The wind propelled the flaming debris like missiles at the Emigee which caused them to retreat. They needed to do something quickly or they were going to be over run. The Emigee would eventually breakthrough due to the extreme number of them. Kaazi using his skill with fire as a flamethrower was sending streams of flames in the direction of their enemy scattering them on the ground. Htiaf shook the ground making it unstable for the Emigee forces while Jace and Epoh were shoring up the flank.

Noticing an old well toward the back of the property, Jace focused on manipulating the water. Chunks of ice were pelting the Emigee who were trying to out-flank them. In the meantime, Epoh was diverting the blasts from the Emigee DM weapons with telekinesis until the hes'chala starting firing. Several blasts bombarded the area around them, with each shot they were getting closer. It was all he could do to maintain a protective shield over them to avoid being hit. They were in trouble and if they didn't get help soon, they were all going to die. It seemed like hours had gone by, under siege with no relief in sight. Where were the others?

Suddenly two vans roared through the gate catching the Emigee off guard. Danek's team in one and Dirk's in the other. They blasted through the center of the Emigee which sent them scattering in every direction taking cover. Then the vans circled around one to the left the other to the right dispersing the enemy. As they roared through the center again chasing the Emigee operatives, they maneuvered the vehicles for easy extraction. Dirk moved his van to retrieve Jace and Epoh while Danek retrieved Kaazi, Alik`ram, and Htiaf who were still providing cover for the others. Jace and Epoh made a run for the van. An Emigee operative spotted them and took aim at Epoh as they were racing toward the van. Jace saw it coming, a direct head shot, so he pushed Epoh out of the way only to be hit by the blast. Dirk's team pulled Jace into the van and continued to fire providing cover for Danek's team retrieving Kaazi and the others.

Once in the van Kaazi barked orders, "Shields on...engage cloak!" The vans vanished from sight.

Inside Dirk's van two of the men were assessing Jace's wound. Epoh thought to Kaazi, *"Jace has been hit; he needs all of our healing abilities—NOW!"*

About a mile down the road with the vans cloaked and shields on they pulled into some brush to provide cover while they lowered the cloak. Lowering both the shields and cloak just long enough for the two vans to connect enabling the vans to cloak and shield under one barrier, they got to work. Quickly the men set-up a portable table and placed Jace on it, face down in order to have direct contact with the wound. Jace took a direct hit to his back from an Emigee DM, the Emigee diamortic energy blast destabilizes electrical functions of the Te`rellean victim and unless healing takes place immediately the victim dies. Jace was fortunate to have had the vest on. It absorbed some of the blast.

"Where is the mooka?" Htiaf called out eager to initiate the healing.

"Take off his vest and shirt!" ordered Kaazi. Jace's vest was removed but the shirt was fused into his skin, charred and scorched. Grabbing a knife, the fabric around the wound was cut away leaving only the fused portion.

"Quick, grab the E-line. We need to dissolve the fabric before we can begin," said Dirk. Kaazi grabbed the E-line and applied it on the fabric fused to Jace's back. E-line was an enzyme specifically designed to remove foreign material from wounds in order to promote healing; it was essential nothing be between the wound and the healing energy, E-line worked instantly.

"Rinse the wound quickly," said Epoh as he was watching Jace turn ashen. The neurological electrical impulses were shutting down, they needed to hurry.

"Okay we're ready!" Htiaf exclaimed. All fourteen men stood around the table with their arms out straight and palms facing the mooka as it levitated over Jace's wound. Every man had his eyes closed focusing all his healing energy into the mooka. The mooka began to glow and concentrated healing energy flowed into Jace's wound. Nothing happened, the wound was not healing. The men focus their concentration further into the mooka, still nothing happened. They were going to lose Jace!

"We have to connect," said Kaazi, "normal healing isn't working. I will initiate the link; once it is established, I will connect to the person to my right and move around the table." Telepathic connection was a last resort healing process; it formed a more intense focused method of projecting healing energy through the mooka into a wounded person. If this didn't work nothing would. After several minutes of using the focused healing, it appeared to be futile, but then, slowly the edges of the wound began to regenerate new tissue. It was a painstakingly slow process, but it was working.

Finally after an hour of intense mental concentration the wound was healed enough to move him back to their base camp. The men reach their camp completely exhausted, mentally and physically. They started to transport all the data and supplies back to the city. It was decided that all of the men would return to the city to sift through the massive amount of information they retrieved.

Several men were monitoring Jace, when he reached a certain level of stabilization, he could be transported back to the city; he was next to go. The transport pad was set to coordinates for NOSSIC; it was not possible to change so Jace was transported there where he would be taken straight to the medical facility to undergo intensive regeneration to recover from his wound. Epoh went with Jace; he felt obligated to him for saving his life. If Jace hadn't pushed him out of the way, he would have taken a direct hit to his head—no one recovers from a direct blast to the head. Jace saved his life and risked his own, he owed him everything.

Gyasi was waiting at the transport platform. He accompanied Jace and Epoh to the medical facility. Transportation from NOSSIC to the med-plex was expedited since Jace had not regained consciousness completely—he was in and out of wakefulness.

"Does Ari know what happened?" Epoh asked Gyasi.

"Word was sent to Ashi'nat as soon as we heard," Gyasi said, "She should be here soon."

Chapter

Serenity and peace of mind, something most people seek to discover in a world full of worry and dread. Te`rellean life was no different, as a matter of fact; they needed it more than most. Under constant threat from the Emigee, life was stressful, thus the Te`rell were centered on maintaining balance.

Sitting on a mat in a large room with no windows Ari was alone with her thoughts. Randomly placed candles were flickering around the room providing a luminescence in the sparsely furnished chamber that glowed, muted and hazy in certain places, glimmering in others. A water fountain was the only object in the room, used as the focal point for meditation. Made of pink and white granite with flecks of black pigment, it glistened in the faint glow of the candle's light. The stones formed a circle with one side elevated into several tiers. As the water trickled down the rock formations into the pool below, stresses and tension flowed away from the body. The soothing flow of water was just what was needed to ease a troubled spirit. The last several weeks had been unusually trying. First Ari had suffered the loss of her adoptive parents, capture at the hands of the Emigee, then estranged from Jace, and if that wasn't bad enough, to almost lose him at the hand of the Emigee's weapons fire. It was just too much.

She continually relived the moment her parents told her that Jace had been wounded during the Wyoming op. Her heart felt like it was being torn from her chest. She raced to his side at the med-plex only to find him unconscious. Seeing him lying in bed helpless was agonizing. Days pasted before he regained consciousness, but she sat by his side gently caressing his brow, whispering softly, encouraging him with words of strength, love and hope. Never once did she give up hope. Her strength she imparted to him, to support and carry him through the endless darkness to the light. When he finally awoke, she was overjoyed. To be able to gaze into his beautiful green eyes again brought tears to her own, the joy was overwhelming.

"Ari…what happened?" Jace croaked-out in a raspy voice as he opened his eyes, groggy and blurred; he blinked in confusion.

"You were hit with a DM blast. You are very fortunate to be alive," Ari said calmly but inside she was being ripped apart by the knowledge he could have been lost forever; she would never let him see that fear.

"Epoh is he…" Jace whispered as he trailed off. Afraid of what the answer would be, he kept silent.

"Epoh is fine. He's been here ever since they brought you in. He just went to stretch his legs a bit," Ari assured him. In such a vulnerable state, she was seeing a very sensitive side of Jace, how much he cared for his friends. The extent of what he would do to protect those he cared for endeared him to her all the more.

"Jace, how do you feel?" Ari asked. He continued to have a slightly ashen appearance, much improved from when he was first brought in, but still not his normal skin tone.

"Ah…sore…and tingly all over," he whispered with a frail voice trying not to moan, not wanting to concern her; he put on a brave face.

"Do you need anything?" Ari asked as she held his hand. Physical contact with Jace was vital to Ari at the moment. It helped her affirm that he was alive and healing, that he was going to be okay; she needed to feel his presence, his warmth, his energy. She couldn't explain why, it just made her feel more secure; she felt it was essential to maintain contact with him.

"No… how long have you been here? How long have I been here?" Jace asked weakly, a little confused, fuzzy and unclear, having lost all sense of time.

"You were brought here after the op, late afternoon. You have been unconscious for over a week. Me, I've been here since shortly after you were brought to the med-plex. Your father, my parents, and the others have taken turns popping in to see if there was any change, "Ari said. There was a slight hint of strain in her voice which Jace picked up on immediately.

"You must be exhausted," Jace said with strained concern, "Why don't you go home and get some rest?"

"I'm fine...I'm not going anywhere," Ari said firmly already taking on the tone of Ayotal, strong and forceful. Her strength was growing but Jace knew that if she didn't have a means to release the stress she had endured these past few weeks, she would be harmed, snap like a twig, perhaps irrevocably.

"If you won't go home and get some rest, will you do me a favor?" Jace asked knowing she wasn't going to like what he was going to suggest but it was for her own good.

"Of course, what do you need?" Ari said. Her desire was to please him and assist in his recovery; she would do whatever he wanted if it would help.

"I don't need anything except to rest and get my strength back. I need you to go to the meditation center and find a way to release all the stress you have endured lately. This is very important to me. I want you to take care of yourself while I'm here. Knowing you the way I do, I don't want you to wear yourself out taking care of me. I know you must have been very upset with me being wounded and everything that happened before we came to the city. You need to release all those bad feelings and replace them with good ones. What helps me when I'm stressed is to seek oneness with the earth, find a connection to her, she has a lot of positive energy," Jace said as he pressed her hands to his lips; pleading with his eyes, tenderly urging her to find a release for all the stress she had endured, she melted under the warmth of his urging.

"I can't do that...I don't know how," Ari said, never having attempted meditation; she was at a loss, she just didn't know how to start.

"There are Entas at the centers who will be more than willing to guide you," Jace said. He wasn't going to let lack of experience be an excuse for her.

"But..." Ari said desperately searching for an excuse to evade the issue.

"No buts," Jace countered. "Please do this for me."

Seeing his sincere concern for her compelled her to capitulate. Besides, she melted like butter under the searing gaze of his pleading eyes; no one could withstand that kind of pressure. She would attempt meditation—for him. How could she say no to that plea?

Every day for a week since Jace had asked her to meditate; she had been seeking to ease her troubled spirit. The relaxing calmness of the flowing water had helped immensely, but Ari knew deep in her mind and heart the thing troubling her spirit the most was a problem with no easy solution—the Emigee. They had kidnapped her parents and they continually plot to exterminate her people. Something had to be done about them. She knew her purpose in life was to find a way to resolve the issues between her people and the Emigee. Ari was not about to let any of the people she loved be harmed by them again. She would survive the trials and somehow bridge the rift between two peoples.

With so many worries, the hardest thing for Ari to do at the center was to quiet her mind. It took all her focus and concentration to get even the smallest measure of silence in her mind, but she was learning. Of course, Jace was right about coming to the center. Even though she had far from mastered meditation, it had helped her alleviate some of her anxiety. She wasn't able to concentrate at all today though. Jace was being released from the med-plex that afternoon, she was just too anxious. Just deciding to give up, she headed over to see him. Her excitement couldn't be contained.

Chapter

30

"I can't stand being cooped up. Is he ever going to come?" said Ki as he paced back and forth like a caged animal, eyes wild and crazed. It had been three weeks since they grabbed Martin and Ena. Si`kram still hadn't shown up to interrogate the prisoners. If he had to stay in this secluded compound in the middle of nowhere much longer, he was going to explode. If he could just pound someone, let off some steam by interrogating the prisoners just a little would improve his mood, but he was forbidden. Oh how he hated that word—forbidden.

"Si`kram will be here when he gets here. Do you want to go up against him? Remember the last person who questioned his actions, he was sliced and peeled like a banana," said Hamer recalling the incident. The soldier corrected him about the location of an upcoming mission, obviously the wrong thing to do, unfortunately he was one of his best men too; but he paid the price with his life just because Si'kram was in a bad mood.

"I'm going to walk the perimeter," Ki growled and stormed out of the room.

"He's going to go off the deep end if we stay here much longer," said Ja'nek. Tolerating Ki when he felt like a caged animal was horrendously tedious, not to mention dangerous; the best way to manage was to stay away from him.

"Well, there isn't much we can do about it, is there, especially since Si'kram wants to do the interrogation himself. All you two have done is moan and complain since we got here. You must realize, this is our punishment for not capturing the girl. So live with it!" snarled Hamer. "Go feed the prisoners!"

Ja'nek grumbled his way out the door and headed to the kitchen.

Martin and Ena were being held in a large room devoid of furniture, except for two wooden bunks with extremely thin mattresses and table. The mattresses felt as if they were made up of crinkled newspaper. Loud, noisy, and hard, not the best place for a pregnant woman to rest. Two large windows covered an entire wall of the room, large enough to climb out of except, they were barred. The bars were solid and strong, not a weak spot in sight. Martin had tried several times to loosen them to no avail. Three weeks they had been kept in this room. The one called Hamer said they were waiting for a man named Si'kram to arrive—the only information he would provide. Besides being imprisoned, they had not been mistreated much physically except for a few shoves here and there for which he was thankful, especially for Ena's sake. He couldn't help but wonder why this was happening. Martin's mind continually relived the night they were captured. It started out with the miraculous news of Ena's pregnancy and ended with their capture by these thugs.

Martin had so many questions—why did they want Ari? What is a Te'rellean? Was Ari alright—did she escape? He had to find a way to get Ena away from here but how? He had no money on him if they did escape—he didn't even know where they were except by what he could tell by looking out the window. It was cold outside, high in the mountains with snow on the ground, a lot of snow. If they could get away, they would freeze, exposure to the elements this high in the mountains was a certainty. The only clothes they had were thin—made for summer. In her condition, Ena wouldn't last long without warmth. Martin glanced over at Ena resting on one of the bunks. His gut wrenched with fury—this should be a happy time for her, planning a nursery, making all the preparations she never thought she would get the chance to make. Her joy was stolen—someone would pay for this he vowed.

The door lock clicked, Ja'nek entered with food for Martin and Ena.

"How long are you going to keep us here?" Martin demanded. Frustration growing, he contemplated rushing Ja'nek, but considering his size he thought better of it which made him furious. "Answer me!"

Ja'nek glared, his eyes were on fire, but he ignored Martin and placed the food on the table next to the door. As he turned to leave, Martin grabbed his arm. Out of frustration and instinct, Ja'nek wrenched his arm away and back-handed Martin across the face sending him flying across the room landing solidly on the floor. Ja'nek snarled at Martin and left the room. Picking himself up off the floor, Martin was so frustrated he punched the closed door which woke Ena.

"Martin what's wrong?" Ena asked as she sat up to see what was happening.

"I'm sorry I woke you," he said, "I'm just so frustrated and I punched the door when the guard brought the food."

"Oh Martin…are you alright? Your hand…let me see it," Ena said as she moved to examine Martin's hand—red but no broken bones she thought. As she lifted her eyes to see Martin, she noticed that his face was red and beginning to swell.

"What happened to your face?"

"Oh…nothing," he said.

"Martin…tell me what happened!" she demanded.

"I grabbed the guard and he back-handed me that's all. It's just so frustrating. Held here for three weeks—waiting. They don't say anything—no reason, no questions—nothing. It's driving me crazy!" Martin exclaimed, running his hands through his hair, yanking it in agitation.

"Martin, you can't do that, he could have killed you," she cried.

"I know, I'm sorry, I'll try not to do that again," he said to reassure her.

"Let's try to look on the bright side; at least they haven't tortured us. I pray Ari is okay," Ena said. "Do you think we'll ever get out of here Martin?"

"Somehow we'll get out of here and get home. I don't know how but we will, I promise you," Martin said as he put his arms around her. He knew he had to keep telling Ena that to keep her hopes up, give her something to look forward to, but he was beyond frustrated and losing hope of escaping. Once their leader showed up, he was sure they were going to die. Somehow, he couldn't let that happen. "They brought food, honey. You should eat," he said tenderly.

"Aren't you hungry?" Ena asked watching every move Martin made. Worrying about him, she hoped he wouldn't do anything risky. Trying to stay calm for the baby's sake, she felt compelled to pray continually.

"No not right now, I'll eat in a bit," Martin said as he moved to the window. The amount of food they had been getting wasn't nearly enough to sustain them both. He always let Ena eat first so that she would take enough for her and the baby. Martin had been slowly losing weight; he had been adjusting his belt accordingly hoping Ena wouldn't notice.

Out in the yard he saw the crazy one with the dangerous eyes pacing back and forth like a caged lion. It was evident he wasn't dealing with the situation any better than Martin, but when a wild animal is backed into a corner, he becomes lethal. He would kill us without so much as a blink of the eye, Martin thought. Afraid for Ena and the baby, he was desperate to find an escape. Watching from the window, Martin scrutinized Ki as he pulled out his blade and started swinging at the wind. Each slice was purposeful and deadly.

Something caught the attention of the man out in the yard. He was looking up but Martin was unable to see what it was that caught his attention. Suddenly out of thin air a craft appeared and set down in front of the man. On one side of the vehicle, a large cargo door opened. Martin watched as huge muscular men disembarked from the transport and started to unload cargo. Martin thought, with the amount of cargo being unloaded, they were going to be there a long time. Despair started to seep into his soul.

Over a month, he had been waiting over a month now, waiting for the shoe to drop right on his head. Stewart Braun, once a self-confidant, ruthless, self-made multi-millionaire reduced to a sniveling, squirming bundle of nerves. Over the last month he dropped fifty pounds and went completely gray from stress, anxiety, and fear. The dark circles under his eyes gave testimony to his inability to sleep. His sanity was teetering on the brink. Constantly on guard, always looking over his shoulder for that behemoth to reappear to pummel him within an inch of his life; it was taking its toll on Stewart.

Why did he ever get involved with the bankers, Stewart thought—greed, plain and simple greed. Now look where it got him, he was a nervous wreck. He suspected they were into high stakes ventures, but he had no idea how dangerous these people were and what measures they would take to achieve their objectives. If only he could escape...disappear, but they have people everywhere. They would find him—he was doomed.

Isbeth was at her desk and noticed Stewart. Day by day she had watched this man change from an arrogant, self-centered boar to a scared child needing protection. Pulling at her heart-strings, she couldn't help feeling pity for the man. Vigilantly she had been staying close to Stewart for several reasons. When she was finally able to determine how Hamer and Stewart were connected, she felt that staying close to him would be prudent, the best way to obtain intel on the whereabouts of Martin and Ena. All major expenditures come through her on their way to Stewart for final approval. If Hamer and the Emigee were using Zenot as a cover, money would be needed to maintain a secret facility. Clues to the location where the Lovell's were being held had been almost non-existent. To uncover even the slightest little tidbit of information would be a windfall.

Pacing—the man was pacing again. He was going to have to replace the carpet in his office if he continued pacing. Getting up from her desk, she moved to Stewart's door.

"Stewart, can I get you anything? Have you eaten today?" Isbeth asked. Over the past month their relationship transformed from businesslike to friendship—more accurately, custodial care, with Isbeth taking on the role of caregiver.

Stewart jumped, letting out a little squeal like a piglet when grabbed from behind, as she spoke. Immediate relief appeared on his face when he discovered it was Isbeth at the door. "Oh...Isbeth it's you. No...no, I'm not hungry," he said, a jittery bag of nerves.

Isbeth took her motherly tone with him, "Now Stewart...you have to eat something. Look at you...you've lost so much weight already I hardly recognize you."

"I know...I'm...just not hungry. If I did eat, it probably wouldn't stay down long," Stewart lamented. Eating used to be one of his favorite pastimes.

"Well... try to relax. Everything is running smoothly," Isbeth reassured him. Actually, the employees had never been so relaxed. Stewart isolating himself resulted in increased productivity.

"I will let you know if anything urgent develops," Isbeth said attempting to reassure him.

"Have you had any contact from Mr. Hamer?" Stewart asked tentatively as his voice trembled; he hoped never to hear from that monster again.

"No," Isbeth said as she left the room.

While she was talking to Stewart, accounting dropped off the monthly reports. Usually she hated going through the piles of endless expenditures, but this month she was hoping to find some clue as to the location of the Lovell's. As she sat down and started sifting through the stack of papers that had to have a hard copy signature, her anticipation soared.

Chapter

Blistering hot, the sun was relentless, searing the landscape. Ari wasn't used to this kind of weather. The ranch would get warm but nothing like the dry scorching heat of the desert sun. All this time within the barrier, the climate was comfortably regulated. She had forgotten they were living in a desert, but this was the perfect place to practice for the trials, quiet, peaceful, and no one to watch her. She felt as if she were under a microscope back in the city. Her people were lovely and warm, but she would catch individuals watching her. Picking up on their whispers was becoming disconcerting. She so wanted to succeed but the intense scrutiny was making her nervous and tense thus inhibiting her performance.

Finding a place to practice away from the city, a place very secluded was imperative. Deciding that she needed to try something different, she found herself alone in the desert. Walking along the canyon wall in the ravine, the same one that she traveled to reach the city; the ravine was perfect. She decided to start practicing on something small. There was plenty of dirt and rocks to manipulate, they surrounded her, they could be found everywhere, and the seclusion was evident. Now, she hoped she could relax practicing by herself.

Ari had been working on refining detail. Very proficient at manipulating large bulky masses of earth, that was easy, the problem she was having was detailing. After many attempts to fine-tune her skill, the results were comically disfigured. She definitely needed to refine the detail aspect of her ability. It was as if she were a sculptor who couldn't quite get that precise image she had in her mind to form within the stone she was manipulating. In the city, she was getting advice from everyone, but it just wasn't working. Everyone's technique was different, she was just getting confused. Here by herself with no prying eyes she hoped to find a little peace to concentrate. Focusing her energy, she tried to etch out the detail, the manipulation she was hoping to achieve was arduous; she worked tirelessly. Slowly, painstakingly, with controlled effort, she was striving to maximize the detail in the rock with the image she envisioned in her mind, but it was proving elusive.

Ari was determined to master her ability. If she didn't, there would be no way she could survive the trials. Ari struggled for hours attempting to get the details right. She was close but still the details weren't quite right. In a moment of utter frustration and anger, she levitated the boulder, the one she had been working on, and flung it into the rock wall, then slumped to the ground against the opposite wall.

Jace came running up the ravine, "Ari, what are you doing out here? I've been looking for you everywhere."

Ari just looked at Jace. Frustration plastered all over her face. He sighed then went to her and sat down beside her.

"What's wrong?" Jace asked with concerned as he wrapped his arm around her and drew her close comforting her tenderly.

"I don't know Jace…what if I'm not good enough to master earth completely. I have become really good at manipulating bulky masses of earth, but I can't get the detail I want."

"You know you have performed with unprecedented ability, skill, and speed. Give yourself a break you have only been working on this for a few months. Not everyone is able to master both bulk and detail and those who do spend hundreds of years perfecting the skill," Jace said reminding her how much progress she has made in such a short span of time.

"I don't have that much time. Martin and Ena need to be found, our people need to find a solution to the Emigee problem, and I need to do my part," Ari said urgently as if she were going to jump out of her skin. She was pushing herself to fix all the problems they faced and being completely unrealistic.

"We will find Martin and Ena. We will find a solution for the Emigee problem. I promise you that you will be instrumental in the process...in time!" Jace affirmed hoping that she would realize everything comes in due time.

"They have been gone so long. Nothing, we have nothing on their whereabouts. Jace, she's going to have a baby, she needs to be with her family and friends, not to mention prenatal visits. What if they have been tortured... starved...sick...! I can't stand it! I have to do something!" Ari cried as tears flowed abundantly down her soft rosy cheeks.

Jace held her tight feeling her frustration, her helplessness, but his team had been searching day and night for months trying to glean any useful information from their field operatives to no avail. It was as if Martin and Ena disappeared off the face of the Earth. Determined never to give up, they would find the Lovell's, he hoped.

They sat in silence for a while, finding comfort in each other's arms. After several minutes, Ari asked, "Jace, why were you looking for me?"

"Oh...I was so glad to find you...I forgot. Ayotal was looking for you. She has something to give you," Jace said slightly embarrassed, as usual when he was around Ari she consumed him, every thought, action, even the reason for searching for her. Irrevocably in love, he was overwhelmingly captivated by her presence.

"I suppose we should head back," Ari said as she stood up and pulled Jace with her.

As she was starting to move away, Jace pulled her back, pressed her back against the canyon wall and encircled her. Gently putting his cheek next to hers, he whispered, "Nothing will stand against us, we will find them, we will help our people, and we will do it together." Tenderly he kissed her sending shivering tingles pulsating down her spine.

Walking back to the city, Ari asked, "Do you know what she has for me?"

"No...she didn't say," Jace said.

Back in the city, Jace and Ari found Ayotal at the education center. She was conversing with her assistants when they approached. Ari gave her mother a hug and kiss on the cheek.

"Oh...there you are. Where have you been?" Ayotal asked as she greeted the pair.

"She was outside the barrier in the ravine," Jace said hoping that Ayotal would caution her as to the dangers of going outside the city.

"I wanted to practice without so many people around," Ari said, "Everyone has such high expectations of me, but I'm having trouble perfecting detail."

"I see, you wanted to work without the pressure," said Ayotal, "Well maybe this will help you."

Ayotal went to her desk and pulled out a book from one of the draws. It was an old black leather-bound journal very well preserved. The Te'rellean symbol on the front was raised and embossed with gold. She handed the book to Ari.

Reaching for the book Ari asked, "What is this?"

"Your great-grandfather's journal, he wrote his experiences down in this journal after his trials. It was his desire that if anyone in our family was rated an M4 the journal might assist in preparations for the trials," Ayotal explained hoping Ari would find it beneficial. Ari's eyes lit up like sparklers on the fourth of July.

"I'm heading over to NOSSIC, I want to see if there are any new developments," Jace said as he kissed Ari on the cheek. "I'm sure you will be occupied for a while."

"Okay, I'll see you later," Ari said as she started to open the journal. Suddenly, her excitement disappeared.

Ayotal noticed the instant change and asked, "What's wrong?"

"Um…I can't read this," she said as she showed her mother the journal. "It's in a different language."

Ayotal laughed, "I forgot. My grandfather wrote it in code so no one would be able to read it unless they had the key, which I have here. You see he didn't want those who were rated less than an M4 to be able to decipher the journal."

"So you haven't read this?" Ari asked, looking for confirmation. She would be the first person in her family to read the journal. The excitement was back in full force.

"No…my father and I have kept it safe until the right person came along," she said, as she reached into her pocket for the key. "The key fits into the back cover of the journal. It will translate the journal into any language you choose. Then, you read the journal just like any other book."

"I'm going to go home now and start reading. I'll see you later," Ari said, enthusiastically as she immediately raced to the door, she couldn't get home fast enough she was so excited.

Chapter

Martin was holding Ena on the bed, the new one Hamer had move into the room; the baby was actively moving in the womb making its presence known. After weeks of pleading for better sleeping accommodations, Martin was shocked when Hamer had a more comfortable mattress brought in which was large enough for both of them. Grateful for the new mattress, Martin could now comfort Ena readily, quelling her fears. Being imprisoned, he had too much time on his hands, it necessitated that he occupy his thoughts. Consumed, he spent every waking hour comforting Ena and trying to devise a way to escape.

Having made some progress with the one called Hamer, talking with him, he had obtained a few tidbits of information, thus trying desperately to put all the pieces together as to who these people were and what they wanted. The one called Ja'nek was more difficult; at times he also relaxed his demeanor. Intemperate, his mood was the gauge; Martin was usually able to determine their treatment. When he relaxed, he would bring more blankets and warm clothes for them and when he was stressed, he would often forget to feed them. The other one stayed away, for which Martin was thankful. The dangerous one, crazed man as Martin came to refer to him, had found an outlet for his frustration—blood-letting. Martin made it his routine to keep an eye on him from the window. Months they had been there, he couldn't believe they were still alive and still being held captive, he was at the end of his rope, desperately try-ing to remember that as long as they were breathing there was hope of a res-cue; this supposed military leader Si'kram still hadn't made an appearance, he wondered if he ever would.

Prowling the yard as usual, Ki had relieved some of his rage by hunting. Even though, he would rather be hunting Te'rell, should be hunting the Te`rell, the huemul, cougar, and bears had to suffice. It was getting more dif-ficult for him to find prey in the area—he had killed everything he came across earlier in the month but at least he was occupied, outside combing the moun-tains, instead of standing guard over lowly humans. He thought, if Si'kram didn't come soon, he would have to confront him—not something he wanted to do. Si'kram was too much like him, hot-tempered and eager to annihilate. He didn't know who would come out the victor if they came to blows.

A hes'chala appeared above Ki, which startled him since the next supply de-livery wasn't due until next week. Scrambling to get out of the way, he moved just before the hes'chala landed. Martin heard the commotion and went to the window to see what was happening in the yard. A very large muscular man dis-embarked from the transport, massive, intimidating. His hair was very short, re-sembling a military crew-cut but shorter, white with remnants of brown randomly scatter on the sides. He was fearsome—dangerous. His face was battle worn. Something glistened from the right side of his face. Martin couldn't quite make out what it was until the man came to a halt right in front of Ki. Using one of his beefy arms, he swung around striking Ki in the jaw sending him to the ground, no easy task unbalancing the massively built wild man. At that moment, Martin got his first terrifying glimpse of Si'kram. The right side of his face was met-allic—a metal plate imbedded into his head. The usual location of the right eye was occupied with an artificial eyepiece which was terrifying—sinister.

Martin saw Hamer and Ja'nek rush out into the yard only to come to an abrupt halt when they saw what was happening. Si'kram raised his right hand and both Hamer and Ja'nek fell to their knees and clutched their throats as if they were being strangled. He was not one of the Emigee who retained their telekinetic abilities; Si'kram had been implanted with mechanical devices which converted thought waves to kinetic energy, thus allowing him limited telekinetic skills. Martin became very fearful. He could not let Ena know what was happening. So he closed the shades and went back to her.

Out in the yard Si'kram, still holding Hamer and Ja'nek, snarled, "Hamer you disappoint me. You know what happens to soldiers when they disappoint me...my ishta exact punishment."

Hamer and Ja'nek turned stone cold. The ishta, Si'kram's elite guard, underwent extensive training to master the techniques in pain administration. They knew how to inflict excruciating pain in ways unimaginable to ordinary people; they would not stop until ordered to do so. Compassion and understanding was foreign to them. The only purpose, their only focus, was to deliver vehemently agonizing pain; it was like food for them, needing it to sustain them. Hamer and Ja'nek had seen others being punished by the ishta—helpless to intervene they watched the sadistic pleasure the ishta derived from the torture. It was repulsive.

Hamer quickly said, "Si'kram...we beg your forgiveness for not bringing the girl. She was not on the farm when we grabbed the humans."

"I don't want to hear your excuses," he growled as he glared at them, tightening his grip.

"No excuses Lare ...a solution...I believe we can get her to come to us," Hamer offered in desperation, coughing and choking out the words.

"How is that?" Si'kram snarled. If there was one thing he couldn't tolerate, it was incompetence in his soldiers. Hamer had never let him down before, until now.

"Call her," Hamer croaked out as he was gasping for breath. Easing his grip on Hamer's throat, he decided to listen to his solution.

"Call her? How are we going to do that, do you have the Te'rellean's telephone number?" Si'kram said sarcastically, not taking him seriously.

"No, but we have her adoptive parents. She did grow up as a human and as such she probably has a cell phone. We can implant her father to access the information, then contact her," Hamer said grasping at straws, even the tiniest bit of reprieve would give him the opportunity to mend the rift between his team and Si'kram.

Si'kram was silent for several minutes, which was driving Hamer and Ja'nek mad, teetering on the edge, ready to fall over the precipice but clinging to hope. Finally, he turned to face Hamer and said, "You ALL will receive fifty lashes, then we will call the girl."

Fifty lashes—a reduced punishment—the pain was going to be excruciating but would eventually end. They would survive for the moment. The lashes would be administered not by a whip of rope or leather—no, the device to be used was made of a metal that was abundant on their former homeworld—hanzol. Hanzol is stronger than steel, flexible, and highly conductive. The Emigee were ingenious at finding new and improved ways of inflicting pain. When the whip made contact with skin the thin filaments would bore into the pain receptors and discharge a near lethal jolt of electricity to incapacitate. It also released chemicals into the victims system which amplified the sensation while inhibiting the victim's natural response to pass out. So, the victim had no hope of relief until the punishment was complete. The recovery time ranged from five to seven days depending on the individuals and their stamina.

All three men were tied by their wrists, their arms were hoisted in opposite directions maximizing skin surface on the back and arms. The ishta took their places as Si'kram stationed himself to watch. He was a hard man and didn't like to be disappointed. The only regret he had was he would have to wait another week for them to recover to put their plan into action. Through the years he had learned to be patient though, so another week wouldn't matter much.

The ishta were perfectly synchronized as they wielded the hanzol whip. Ki, Hamer, and Ja'nek each made it through twenty-five strokes without any indication of feeling pain. Throughout the millennium the Emigee had developed physical stamina out matched by none; this punishment would have killed anyone other than an Emigee. Ki was the first to buckle to the tortuous pain being inflicted. Begging and pleading for mercy, he only added to the ishta's enthusiasm. Hamer and Ja'nek groaned with each lash as their endurance decreased. As they approached fifty lashes, they could no longer contain their screams, the pain was unbearable. They collectively thought that death was preferable.

When it was finally over, Si'kram ordered them to remain tied until sunset, which was five hours away. Si'kram disappeared into the compound. The three men were slumped down hanging from their tied wrists, conscious and exhausted as the wind was whipping, tearing at their open wounds, pelting snow and ice at already sensitive skin in the freezing cold of the harsh winter.

Chapter

After Ari had read her great-grandfather's journal several times, she still was unable to fathom becoming one with the earth. How does that happen, she thought? Her great-grandfather, Ea'nal, wrote of his experiences with each of the trials. The trial Ari was interested in at the moment was the trial of earth. He wrote:

> *"Nothing could have prepared me for the trial of earth. I went through all the traditional training from the education centers. Hours I spent practicing my manipulation and control exercises. When I made my decent into the trial chamber, I was confident that I would succeed. My two companions accompanied me to the external chamber to wait and bear witness to either my success or failure. As I entered the trial chamber an eerie sensation permeated my being, straight to the soul.*
>
> *As I waited the air became thick and it was becoming difficult to breath. I should have probably engaged in meditation, but I was experiencing a lot of agitation. Becoming unsettled, I started examining the walls of the chamber. There was nothing unusual—just carved out walls, smooth to the touch except for one area to the right of the door in the far corner. An oval shaped elevation was in the wall with several crystals protruding from the center. The crys-*

tals were white and when I touched them, they started vibrating or pulsating.

The room started to get warm. I became dizzy, my vision blurred, and I fell to the floor unable to move. I had made a telepathic connection to the earth somehow. Visions of the earth, minerals, plant and animal life raced through my head along with the destruction brought from the Emigee and the humans. It is hard to put into words the horror that was shown to me but it touched something deep inside me—I knew I had to find a way to change the damage being done to our mother earth. I don't remember anything after the visions even though I know other things happened. My companions heard roaring, banging, and screaming—I don't remember anything occurring to account for those noises. The one thing I do know is that the trials seem to be different for everyone who attempts them. My predecessor experienced something completely different. The trails are completely individualized. With basic skills intact, one faces their own character. After the trial was over, I had new abilities…"

The journal was helpful in that it explained what happened to Ea'nal up to the point of seeing the visions but it didn't explain how to become one with the earth. She was slightly less frustrated but too much depended on her success. Ari needed to talk with Ayotal. Not having far to go, Ayotal was just entering the door when Ari rounded the corner and met her.

"How was your day?" Ari asked sweetly. Bombarding her mother with countless questions as soon as she walked in the door was rude, thus, Ari was trying to exercise patience.

Ayotal raised a brow in her all-knowing way and said, "Thankfully uneventful, how was your day?"

"Fine, I've been practicing and reading. Mother did Ea'nal ever talk to you about the trials?" Ari asked, she couldn't wait any longer.

"A little but because I'm an M3 he knew I would never be able to fully comprehend the trials," she said sadly, remembering her conversations with him so many years ago.

"Did you ever discuss oneness or how to become one with something? This aspect of the trials still eludes me," said Ari trying not to let her frustration show, but she was not successful, her mother saw right through to the core of the problem.

"Ah…I see you are still frustrated. Well maybe this will help you. Ea'nal didn't tell me how to become one with the earth, but he did say that no one knows how to become one with the earth before the trials begin," said Ayotal recalling what her grandfather had told her when they were walking the path to a lake in Nepal.

"Really?" Ari asked disappointment in her voice, "So a person can't really prepare for that aspect of the trial."

"Later in his life, I overheard him talking with another M4. Ea'nal was explaining that it was his belief that everyone experiences the trials differently because not one person is exactly the same. We each bring different thoughts, feelings, and values to the forefront when we endeavor to reach our goals thus the trials can't be the same for everyone," Ayotal said, offering hope.

"So if the trials aren't the same for everyone, becoming one with the earth is different for everyone," Ari said as she reflected on what her mother told her.

"Ea'nal also said that it's a combination of things like desire, ability, motive, and a few other things I can't remember that initiate oneness. It can't be forced he said. I don't remember anything else," said Ayotal, searching Ari's face, hoping that even a little of what she explained would help.

"Where is the trial chamber?" Ari asked, changing the subject; the location of the trial chamber was something she had been meaning to ask but hadn't had the opportunity until now.

"Actually there are four trial chambers. Each trial has a distinct separate chamber location. They are located in areas where our oldest cities once stood. The underground city the humans call Derinkuyu in Turkey was once a center for earth trial preparation. After the destruction, it became one of the refugee cities we set up to escape the Emigee. Once we had abandoned the area, it was found by the humans who claimed it as their own. Derinkuyu, according to what the humans have found, is a complex with eleven floors. Unknown to them, there are actually fourteen levels. The twelfth level is hidden—it is where the trial chamber is located," explained Ayotal.

"Will we have difficulty gaining access to the chamber?" Ari asked, wondering if they would have to travel the human way.

"No…we have our own entrance," Ayotal said, reassuring her they would have no difficulty accessing the chamber when she felt she was ready.

"When can I attempt the trial?" Ari asked anxious to move forward and undertaking the trial would bring her one step closer to accomplishing her goals; at least she would be doing something productive until they found where Martin and Ena were located.

"When you feel you are ready...do you...are you ready?" Ayotal asked, curious as to the expression Ari displayed, one of pure determination.

"I've made a lot of progress this week with my detail, it's not perfect but it is better than it was besides, Ea'nal said you can never be completely prepared. Reading the journal has helped somewhat and since the trials are different for everyone...I...I'm as ready as I'll ever be," Ari said with conviction, completely determined to go through with the trials and succeed.

"If you are sure, I'll make the arrangements," said Ayotal as she embraced Ari, "I knew you would want to attempt the trials quickly, as hard as you have been training in your endeavors, you could do nothing less. You are a remarkable young woman."

Ari smiled and said, "I come from two very extraordinary people."

Chapter

Si'kram was enjoying a warm fire in what was the Zenot executive suite. It had many luxuries. Humans do love their luxuries, he thought. Not caring much for such things himself, he could take them or leave them, but if they were available, he would take full advantage of the amenities. The suite resembled a cozy ski lodge with a massive stone fireplace, high ceilings with enormous log beams, and a wall of windows to admire the spectacular panoramic vistas. Southern Chile was truly beautiful—even Si'kram had to concede that fact.

"Bring me Hamer," Si'kram ordered one of his ishta's who quickly obeyed. As beautiful as it was here, Si'kram wanted to conclude his business. Pressing matters with the Umbra were calling him elsewhere—something about inciting protestors to violence. Humans were always squabbling about something.

"Lare," Hamer said. Almost fully recovered, even though it had been less than a week since Si'kram had him and his two companions punished for not delivering Ari to him; he had always been a quick healer. The only remnant of his ordeal was a slight limp.

"I want you to implant the man with a SIRD. I want the information now," Si'kram ordered, he had been patient long enough.

"Yes Lare, I'll see to it personally," Hamer said as he went to inform Ja'nek and Ki that the interrogation was starting. Hamer had never liked humans, he had always thought of them as animals, a lower species, until he met the Lovell's. These humans weren't like the ones he had known in the city; Martin and Ena were exceptionally caring people and had been kind to him even after he had forcibly taken them from their home. Unexpectedly he found himself liking them, they had courage not like other humans, they didn't deserve any of this, but what could he do to change the situation—nothing. He was a soldier, an Emigee soldier who always did his duty, it was all he had ever known; he had to follow orders.

"Come with me," Hamer said after he walked in the room. Watching the two say their good-byes was tearing at him, it felt as if a knife was stabbing at his heart, he had never felt that way before and he didn't like it. These abnormal, obscure feelings were compelling him to just let them go, but how could he even consider such a thing? These conflicting feelings needed to be checked immediately.

Martin and Ena reached for each other. Martin embraced Ena and whispered, "It's okay...it will all be okay...don't worry...I'll be back soon."

Ena broke down; tears flowed down her face like torrents. She was terrified. He kissed her gently then left with Hamer. Hamer was starting to hate the whole thing. Maybe he was getting soft with age, maybe it was the lashes, he didn't know for sure, but these were actually nice people not like the usual humans he had to deal with—greedy, selfish low-life's. There was real love within them, not just for themselves but for others—a rare quality, something that was lacking in his life.

"I will try to protect her if something goes wrong," Hamer said to Martin as they walked through the corridor.

"Thank you," said Martin looking up at Hamer with surprise and gratitude, "Where are we going?"

"To see Si'kram," Hamer said, hoping the implantation would go smoothly, Martin would give Si'kram the information he wanted, then he could be back with Ena quickly.

"Why did he have you whipped?" asked Martin no longer able to contain his curiosity.

"We failed to retrieve the Te'rellean, your daughter. He was disappointed, he does not accept failure and he loathes being disappointed," said Hamer, attempting to drive the images of Si'kram's face out of his mind, the pleasure he derived while he sat watching him and his team being whipped was chillingly debase and sadistic.

"Why does he want Ari?" Martin asked, taking a protective stance, continually gleaning any information he could to understand the conflict between the Emigee and the Te`relleans.

"Because the Te'relleans wanted to keep her safe; he wants to know why," Hamer said as he opened the door to the suite to deliver him to an uncertain fate. Martin was brought before Si'kram who studied him for a moment.

"We can do this the easy way or the hard way. It's up to you," Si'kram said to Martin.

"Do what? Why have you brought us here?" Martin demanded harshly; he was having difficulty containing his anger after being held captive for over two months. Hamer cringed inwardly, if Martin only knew how much Si'kram despised humans he wouldn't have been so flippant, he hated mouthy people, he had the tongues of others cut out for less.

"The human has spirit…" As much as he admired spirit, Si'kram was not going to tolerate an arrogant human, so he asked, getting right to the point, "does your daughter have a cell phone?"

"Yes…why?" Martin asked a little confused. After all this time having them imprisoned, he wanted to know if Ari had a cell phone; it didn't make sense to him.

"What is her contact number?" Si'kram asked, becoming irritated, he was effectively exercising his patience; he was unaccustomed to being questioned, especially by a human. The number, he wanted the number and he wanted it NOW.

"I don't know. If I need to talk with her, I just push speed dial on my phone," Martin said. Determined, he was not willingly going to give him access to Ari, he stood firm. She was safe from this sinister man, he wasn't about to give him any information to jeopardize her safety.

"So we are going to do this the hard way," Si'kram said as he signaled for his ishta to hold Martin. "Hamer, the SIRD," he said. Reluctantly Hamer inserted the SIRD into the base of Martin's neck. Martin struggled briefly as his eyes rolled back into his head from the initial burning sensation, it was like red-hot needles penetrating his spine then shooting to his brain.

"What is your daughters contact number?" Si'kram asked after having been assured the SIRD was in place.

Martin straightened up and said, "I told you. I don't know. I use speed dial."

Si'kram looked at Hamer fiercely and demanded, "Why isn't the SIRD working?'

Hamer was dumbfounded. Present when the SIRD was being tested, it was found to be initialized and operational for implantation. Starting to get nervous, Hamer rechecked the SIRD, but everything was working perfectly, there was no reason for it not to work. Becoming increasingly anxious, he was at a loss, he didn't want to risk disappointing Si'kram again. Enduring another lashing would be intolerable. Hamer knew he needed to give Si'kram a reply, but he was unable to offer a viable explanation, all he could say was, "I don't know. It was initialized, ready, and active, it should be working. I will get a replacement." He hurried to bring a replacement SIRD.

Martin took the opportunity to ask Si'kram, "Why do you want Ari, she is just a seventeen-year-old girl?"

"She is Te'rellean. They are the enemies of my people," Si'kram said. His hatred was ingrained in him from childhood. One of the scientists working on the initial project to eliminate the mutations the Emigee had developed over the millennium was a blood relative. Ven'tash was passed from one generation to the next; it was the responsibility of every generation to continue the fight, to fulfill the blood oath of revenge, to destroy their enemies until the last one had been destroyed.

"She didn't know she was different until a few months ago. She knows nothing of these Te'relleans," Martin said trying to appeal to the better nature of the man.

"Maybe but they know of her. They sent five of their best operatives to protect her...why? Why her? What makes her so special? I must have an answer," growled Si'kram hoping that discovering the answers would provide him with an advantage, an advantage to finally destroy the Te`relleans.

Hamer had returned with a new SIRD. Moving toward Martin to implant it, Si'kram raised his hand and motioned him over so that he could inspect the SIRD. Assessing the device himself would assure success. Satisfied that it was precisely calibrated and in working order, he handed it back to Hamer; after getting approval, he implanted the device in the base of Martin's neck.

"What is the number to contact your daughter?" Si'kram asked again, hopeful that he would finally get the needed information.

"I told you already, I don't know the number and even if I did I wouldn't tell you," Martin repeated the same response for a third time. The Emigee were astounded, the ishta, were whispering among themselves, unable to believe what they just witnessed. No human was able to circumvent the SIRD; but no other human had ever been tagged with a Te`rellean locator before, it rendered the SIRD inert.

Darkness fell over Si'kram as his face reddened; a menacing shadow befell the room as his true nature came to light. Si'kram approached Martin and backhanded him across the face sending him flying across the room. "Pick him up and hold him," Si'kram bellowed as he landed an agonizing blow to his mid-section. With his patience spent, his mood turned vehemently lethal.

The force of the blow was so strong, it felt as if his fist had torn a hole straight through his body, from his front to his back, pulverizing all tissue and organs in its way. Martin was sure he had an open space where he took the punch. Unable to breathe or catch his breath for several minutes, he slumped between the two ishta.

"How is this human resisting the SIRD?" Si'kram demanded, frustration brewing; he started pacing. After several minutes, he turned and hissed, "Well it looks like we will have to take drastic measures to obtain the information I want." Si'kram motioned to the ishta. Martin was taken outside and tied like the others had been. Because humans cannot withstand the type of punishment an Emigee can endure, the ishta had to modify their tactics.

As the ishta were discussing different types of torture to inflict, Martin whispered to Hamer, "Don't let Ena see this." Hamer looked at Martin, the realization of his concern was evident; he made an excuse to go into the compound. Still puzzling over the SIRD, he thought, 'I don't understand why it didn't work, they always work on humans. Now Martin is going to be tortured, it would have been so much easier if the SIRD just worked, no pain, no fuss, he should be back in the room with Ena by now.' As he entered the room, Ena questioned him with her eyes but said nothing. Ordering Ena to gather her supplies, he removed her from the room under the guise of her weekly bathing time.

By the time he returned to the yard, the ishta had decided on their course of action. The ishta chose the Dolorous, a creature native to an island on their home world. The Dolorous had an affinity for neuro tissue. In its dormant stage, it is approximately an inch in length, half an inch wide when it is coiled, and a beefy-red color. It burrows into the skin and attaches itself to the pain receptors of nerve cells. Once attached to the neuron, the Dolorous uncoils spreading hundreds of hair-like tendrils along nerve tissue, feeding and repro-ducing. During the feeding process, pain stimulants are release at the pain re-ceptors sites which serve a dual purpose, to prolong the life of the cell as well as inflicting agonizing pain. Fiendishly they won't kill a person but once im-planted the pain inflicted is tortuously excruciating, a person begs for death just to end the torment. This type of torture was typically used for races other than Emigee who lack the stamina to endure more severe tactics. Removal is possible but rarely done, most of the time the leader forgets about the victim after they have the desired information; and the ishta won't remove the crea-tures without a direct order leaving the victim writhing in agony. The ishta sadistically revel in the suffering of others.

Martin was praying for the strength to endure. He had to be strong for Ena and the baby, he had to protect them, and he certainly didn't want to give his captors the satisfaction of seeing him defeated. Martin stood strong and determined.

Chapter

After months of sifting through mountains of invoices, she found nothing, Isbeth was frustrated. She was sure that she would come across some clue as to the whereabouts of the Lovell's. The Emigee must not be holding them at a Zenot facility, she thought. It was the only conclusion she could come up with as she was finishing the second month's accounts reports for Zenot.

Andrew, one of the junior accountants, reluctantly approached Isbeth's desk and hesitantly cleared his throat. "Uh…Miss Benjamin…ma'am…these reports were supposed to be brought to you last month for signature by Mr. Braun. Um…they… were misplaced…uh…sorry ma'am." Well aware of how Isbeth reacted to incompetent performance within the organization, Andrew was waiting for the bomb to drop; his heart was racing, sweating, and holding his breath, he looked like he was going to pass out at any moment.

Isbeth raised an eyebrow and scowled at the young man which sent him scurrying in retreat. She opened the file folder Andrew had delivered, normally she would have chewed his ear off with a good tongue lashing, but she was hoping to find a clue in these new bills. Astounded, she couldn't believe her eyes, there before her were at least twenty expenditures for the facility in South America near Bertrand Lake in Chile, a facility that had been closed for five years. No plans to open the facility had been discussed, Stewart always informed her of such events. As she was reviewing the expenditures, she noted a few very peculiar items that had been purchased, items that would never have been supplied for normal Zenot operations. Isbeth finally hit pay dirt, she was ecstatic. It would be the perfect place to hold prisoners—quiet, secluded, and abandoned. She had to contact Gyasi!

Chapter

After long anticipation, the day finally arrived, the day of trial. Ari was eager and ready to undergo the trial of earth. Painstakingly she had intensified her meditation and practice sessions over the past week; she was as ready as she ever would be—do or die! Having no other alternative, Ari knew she had to succeed—failure was not an option. Departing the city, the transporter pad glistened; the foursome appeared in a cavern. What an awesome way to travel Ari thought.

Attentively glancing around the cavern, Ari was enthralled by the habitat, a piece of her history, the history of her people, and she was in the midst of it all. Jace was a bundle of nerves. Having confidence in Ari and her abilities was never the problem; he had never seen anyone with such extraordinary natural ability. The nervousness wasn't because he doubted her ability but from fear, fear of losing her. Unable to bear the thought of life without Ari—life would be meaningless and empty, devoid of any pleasure which terrified him, but she was focused, determined. Attempting to have faith in that wasn't easy, Jace struggled to put on a brave face for Ari's sake, endeavoring to support her, but she was the one who comforted him.

"Jace...it will be fine. Try not to worry," she thought to him as she gently squeezed his hand. What a magnificently beautiful woman she is, he thought. Deeply filled with love for her, he was amazed; never in his wildest imaginings

did he believe it was possible to have such intense tender, loving feelings, feelings he only surrendered to when Ari was close. As such her affinity for calming him, reassuring him, especially during bleak circumstances, was like a tranquil serene spirit flowing through him, wrapping him in the warmth and safety of her soft loving arms, something for which it was impossible for others to achieve.

Ari glanced around the ruins of the cavern at Derinkuyu. Amazed at her people's stamina, their ability to survive the devastation of their civilization and then to rebuild from almost nothing. Ari's imagination took over as she felt the cavern walls. It was as if the rock formations quivered as she touched them, wanting to reveal all their hidden secretes. She felt a slight breeze rush over her—echoes of the past. Instead of becoming anxious which would be the typical reaction, Ari felt a sense of peace and contentment.

As Ari was caught up in reflection, Ayotal and Kaazi checked the surrounding area and the barrier to assure the integrity and secrecy of the three lower levels had been maintained. The control panel display indicated a slight fluctuation in the barrier's integrity which needed to be corrected before they could continue.

"Kaazi, how long do you anticipate the repairs will take?" Jace asked as he walked up to the panel.

"We should have the barrier back to maximum efficiency within the hour. Go check the secondary unit, it's at the far end of this level just outside the external chamber," Kaazi said. He knew there was nothing wrong with the secondary unit. Giving Jace something to do was prudent because his incessant hovering was going to make him jumpy. With Jace occupied, Kaazi got to work on the primary barrier system.

"The AI should have greeted us when we arrived," Kaazi said as he opened the primary maintenance panel.

"Yes, I noticed that too. I'm searching the database for the AI's program to see if there is degradation," responded Ayotal. "Ah…it looks like…hum… the fluctuation in the primary system caused the AI to go offline."

"So repairing the primaries should fix the problem," Kaazi said.

We really should have a better maintenance schedule on the barrier system, he thought. Before the humans became technologically advance, there was no need for frequent inspections, but things are different now, especially with humans poking around in the upper levels, the barrier should probably be checked more frequently.

Ayotal had moved to another terminal reviewing the data from the sensors in the city above. Arduously she downloaded the data for the scientists back at their base city. She noted several new archeological digs the humans had initiated. One of which caused a collapse on level seven; due to this incident, Ayotal's attention focused on the structural stability of level twelve. The structural field was intact, but she strengthened it nonetheless.

With everyone occupied, Ari opened up her senses to the city. Images came to her slowly at first then as a raging flood; it was as if the air rippled like water when a pebble was tossed in, hazy and distorted, eventually clearing. Visions of men, women, children, chaos, mayhem, destruction; she saw her people wounded, charred and bleeding, agonizing in pain, dying. Despair penetrated the inner recesses of her soul like a fierce raging storm, stabbing, tearing at her very being. The scene changed as her people struggled to survive. Despair transformed to determination, then hope. Visions of children playing, adults working together to rebuild their shattered civilization, happiness regained. What Ari noticed the most was that her people displayed no need for revenge; to the contrary their feelings were of compassion and determination to heal the wounds that would cause the outsiders, a group of militants ravaged by years of hardship, to act in such a vicious destructive way. But how could they help? What could they do to heal such a gaping wound?

Jace meandered back to the group and reported, "Secondary systems have been maximized. Is there anything you need Kaazi?"

"No, I'm almost finished with the primary systems. See if Ayotal needs help," Kaazi said providing another distraction for him.

Jace moved over to the console that Ayotal was working at and asked, "Do you need assistance Ayotal?"

"No Jace, the download is almost complete. I'll be finished within minutes. Check on Ari, she has been very quiet," Ayotal said as she glanced over to her daughter.

Jace turned around to locate Ari; she was seated by the old winery. She appeared to be meditating. Jace took a seat next to her which interrupted the flow of visions from the city. It was as if the city could sense another's presence as could Ari. She reached out her hand to grasp Jace's and thought to him, *"Jace, are you alright?"*

"Yes, I'm fine," he said attempting to alleviate any doubts she might have.

"I just had the most wonderful experience," Ari said full of wonder. She had made a connection to the city to glimpse the past, she had no idea her people were able to undergo such visions.

"What kind of experience?" Jace asked. He yearned to share with her, to be an active participant in every new experience; knowing that it was not always going to be possible, he felt that any experience he could be involved in was crucial and should be treasured.

"Ever since I arrived, I've had this feeling. It's hard to explain. It's like the city is calling to me. When I opened my mind to my surroundings, I began to see visions of the devastation, the pain, the suffering our people endured after the first attack. Wounded and dying people—I felt their despair. Gradually, I felt the determination of our people to rebuild as they struggled to survive. Right here within this underground city I experienced it just as if I had lived it. Eventually our people regained their hope for the future. They never gave up. The experience was incredible," Ari explained thoroughly enthralled by what she had seen and felt.

"It sounds as though you had a vision flash. I have heard of them but few people actually have experienced them," Jace said in amazement.

"These vision flashes... are they common among our people or is this a rare occurrence?" Ari asked wanting to know everything she could about this newest milestone in her developing abilities.

"Before the attack, the vision flashes were common among those who were rated M4, but the number of those who have them now has decreased significantly," Jace replied. Only a few M4's even exist, among them only a small percentage, have ever experienced a vision flash.

"There is so much history in this place, it is as if these walls are alive and want to tell me the story," Ari said as she ran her fingers over the stone.

"Well I don't know about that, but maybe you unknowingly made a telepathic connection to the very fibers of time. Time is relative and the continuum is like a flowing river, it's possible you tapped into that stream. It's only theory; some obscure reasoning's debated at the education center, but I wouldn't know since I've never had a vision flash. With your unique abilities surfacing rapidly, it wouldn't surprise me," Jace said as he speculated on what Ari had told him.

Ari and Jace turned their attention to Kaazi as he announced that he was finished with the primary system repairs. Touching the control panel, he activated the AI. At approximately the same time Ayotal confirmed the download was complete. They both approached Jace and Ari as a transmorphic image appeared before them.

"Greetings, I am Iets, how may I assist you?"

Ayotal responded, "We are here as witnesses. Ariella, my daughter will undergo the trial of earth. Make the preparations."

"As you wish, is there anything else I can do for you?" asked Iets.

"No, that will be all," said Ayotal. Iets bowed slightly and hurried to complete his task.

"Everything is set to go. Are you ready to undergo the trial Ari?" Kaazi asked, his carefree demeanor suspiciously missing. Concerned about Ari, this was the first time he had been involved in any way with the trials, never having known an M4 personally before he was a bit anxious; everyone knew the risk she was taking and the consequences if she failed, he wanted to be close at hand to lend support.

"I'm as ready as I'll ever be," she said, anticipation causing a few jitters, but she was confident and determined to continue.

Iets reappeared and said, "All the preparations have been made. You may enter the external chamber at any time."

Ayotal acknowledged Iets and then directed her next comments to Jace and Kaazi. "Boys wait for us in the external chamber," Ayotal ordered. Jace and Kaazi nodded and moved to the chamber door.

"Ari...I just want you to know how much I love you and how proud I am of you. I have faith in you and your abilities. You will succeed and you will be our true Legate," Ayotal said. As she embraced Ari, a torrent of emotions exploded between the two. After several minutes, they walked slowly to the external chamber.

Ari whispered, "Even though we had been separated for so many years, these last few months have been incredibly important to me, I never imagined I would actually meet my real parents. It has been a privilege to get to know you and father, to know what special people you are, it's like a dream come true. I know who I am, who my parents are, and who my people are; I have never known such peaceful contentment in my life. It is as if I have new meaning to my existence, a new life set before me. Only one thing is missing, and I am hoping this trial will help me recover them." Ari wiped a stray tear from her cheek as the two women embraced again and entered the external chamber. Iets was waiting for Ari to provide direction.

Those in the external chamber were there to meditate and witness the outcome of the trial. When Ari entered the trial chamber, Ayotal would position herself on the right side of the door, Kaazi on the left and Jace would be positioned in front of the door. The three would form a triangle which signified part of the Te'rellean symbol—a symbol of strength.

Directing Ari to a small room designed for trial preparation, Iets explained the ritual. She washed systematically completing the trial preparations which included dressing in the trial ra'bo made of fine muslin the color of desert sand. The ra'bo clung to her body as if it was a second skin. Her hair was secured in one long braid which was draped down the length of her back. When she was finished with her physical preparation, she took several minutes to empty her mind in preparation to enter the trial chamber. The others were deep in their own meditation when Ari entered the external chamber.

As she entered the triangle formed by her three witnesses and faced the entrance to the trial chamber. Ari took a deep breath and spoke the traditional announcement:

"I am Ariella daughter of Ashi'nat and Ayotal. I seek oneness and unity with our mother earth, provider of strength, sustenance, and life. I endeavor to be worthy."

As soon as she was finished, the trial chamber door opened. Ari confidently entered the room. Once in the room, the door immediately closed. Darkness, complete darkness engulfed her. Senses struggling to compensate, comprehend even the slightest stimulus, but nothing, there was absolutely nothing. Unable to see through the darkness, she reached out with her mind attempting to make a connection. She sensed nothing—no presence, no vision flash, just blackness. She felt emptiness—a complete void of thought, emotion, life. Ari made her way to the wall of the chamber and started feeling her way around. Her great-grandfather's journal spoke of a raised area in the chamber with protruding crystals to the right of the door. Making her way to the corner her grandfather described, she found nothing. A little confused Ari felt her way around the whole chamber. The walls were carved smooth—not a raised area to be found.

The journal explained that her great-grandfather experienced the same thing—nothingness, nothing occurred for a while when he entered the chamber. Ari decided to sit and meditate to clear her mind of all thought. She had been practicing and was becoming quite good.

Waiting outside in the external chamber, Ayotal and Kaazi continued their meditation. Jace, on the other hand, was attempting to meditate. His anxiety level was slowly rising with the passage of time. Diligently he attempted to restrain his emotions but several hours into the trial, just waiting, he was losing control. Usually his control was perfect, but nothing was normal when he was dealing with his feelings for Ari. Unbalanced and off-kilter was how he felt, like a yo-yo with its ups and downs. At the moment, the intensity and uncertainty of not knowing what was happening to her was maddening.

Suddenly, with a burst of emotion, Jace exploded intrusively into the thoughts of Kaazi and Ayotal, *"How long is this supposed to take? It has been hours!"*

Jumping, his intrusion startled Ayotal who quickly regained her composure and in her usual calm refined manner explained, "Since I have never been involved in the trials before, I have no point of reference. The information I researched from the ancient database was limited. It set no time limit... Put simply, it stated 'It takes as long as it takes.' Not very helpful, but it is all I know Jace. Try to relax...I know it is easier said than done but...Ari is gifted. Have faith that she will endure the trial and come back to us one step closer to fulfilling her role as Legate."

Before she finished and Jace could respond. A loud thud was heard in the trial chamber as if something was slammed against the door. The three witnesses stared at the chamber door then at each other with overwhelming concern.

"The database said that we would hear disturbing sounds from within the chamber," said Ayotal as her anxiety started growing.

As soon as the words came out of her mouth, the door began to shake and rattle as if caught in an earthquake. All immediately stood in unison as Jace raced to the door.

Kaazi grabbed his shoulder to stop him from entering. "You're not supposed to enter while the trial is in progress," Kaazi said which gave Jace pause. Ari would be upset if the trial were interrupted.

He slumped back—he knew Kaazi was right, but Ari needed him. Hating the helplessness, having no idea what was happening to her in the chamber, he started pacing. She could be hurt—she could be dead. No he couldn't think like that, she was fine. Talking to himself continually, he had to purposefully remind himself that she was fine and this would soon be over; though he didn't really believe it. Jace was terrified that he would lose the woman he loved because of this silly trial. Despair flooded through Jace like a raging river unrestrained and wild.

Ayotal sensed what Jace was feeling and embraced him, attempting to restrain the consuming doubt overcoming him. Slowly he began to respond to her comfort and strength when suddenly they heard bloodcurdling shrieks and screams coming from within the chamber. For what seemed like hours, Ari's three witnesses stood frozen in horror, unable to fathom what they had heard. Coming back to his senses first, Jace pushed the door to the chamber but to no avail—he couldn't open it. Kaazi realizing what Jace was doing went to the door and started pushing with him—nothing. The door wouldn't budge.

Kaazi said, "Let's try TK." The combined effort of Jace and Kaazi failed to open the door. Ayotal joined the efforts to use telekinesis but was unsuccessful; the power of the earth was greater than their combined strength. The door was not going to open. All the while the terrifying shrieks and screeching, along with what sounded like whipping wind as if a tornado was vehemently seeking to find an exit from the room, was emanating from the chamber. The actuality was that they were helpless to rescue Ari; simultaneously reality overtook them like a tempest. Shock and terror engulfed them as they stared at the door.

Tirelessly Ari had sat for hours meditating. Emptying her mind of all thoughts and emotions, all except one—hope. A great stillness came upon her as if she had taken on the great void she felt when she first entered the room. Time past as she sat on the floor of the chamber, some moments as fast as a twinkling of an eye then in other instances as if in slow motion. Measuring the passing of time by her breathing, she attempted to even the pace, but it seemed like it was being controlled by an outside source…but how could that be?

After a while, the chamber felt like it was getting warmer. Ari noticed a faint glow within the walls, floor and ceiling. Large mounds of dirt, rock, salt, and metals surrounded her. It was as if Ari was witnessing the formation of them at the beginning, the beginning of time. Periodically, heat radiated from the mounds of earth altering with episodic cooling. The cycle repeated several times. From each of the mounds, tentacles emerged. The appendages consisted of the different substances making up the mounds—each one was unique. They reached for Ari to make contact. Instantly, as they touched her, Ari convulsed. Her mind exploded with sensations—brightness, hardness, softness, darkness, hotness, coldness. She was overwhelmed by the experience. If there was a purpose for this experience, she didn't understand what it was, but she was determine; determined to find it. Searching the inner most regions of her mind, body, and soul for comprehension, she was unable to attain what she sought. Stretching her mind, reaching outward, probing the mounds, one thought smashed into her—'You are us.' The pain she felt from that impression knocked her over.

'You are us'—what does that mean? Ari thought. Desperate to know, but she had no idea. It was as if a million tiny red-hot needles were probing her mind, searching. Never having thought such agony was possible, she was inundated with new hellacious sensations which enveloped her as if thousands of fire ants were dissecting each and every cell in her body. Distantly she heard a terrifying screech, startling her until she realized she was the one screaming. The assault of her mind and body intensified. It raged violently on like a tornado, an F5, twisting and turning her form.

Just when Ari felt she could endure no more, the mounds surrounding her began pelting her body with dirt, sand, salt and metals—the entire composition of the mound joined the assault. Ari knew she was going to die; she would never survive such an onslaught. She surrendered body, mind, and soul to the forces, to the greater power.

Jace continued his attempts to open the door to no avail. Ayotal and Kaazi drew him away from the entrance in an attempt to comfort him. Reliving the death of his mother over and over again in his mind, he was sinking into despair. Grievously mourning his mother Jace was consumed with sadness for centuries, losing Ari would be worse. He slumped to the floor, limp and deflated holding his head in his hands. All he could do was wait.

The three had spent the last hour in silent meditation listening to the horrific sounds from behind the chamber door. Suddenly there was silence, the three looked up and glanced at the entrance waiting, then at each other in anticipation. Several moments later, the door to the trial chamber opened. Expecting to see Ari walk out at any moment, it was if time stopped. Unable to contain their exuberance a moment longer, they enthusiastically rushed to the doorway. As they breathlessly searched the dark chamber, each anticipating seeing Ari first, they were stunned—the room was empty. Horror filled their hearts—Ari was gone. Gone, how could she be gone? Where did she go? How was it possible for her to leave the room when they were so vigilant?

With a horrific screech Ayotal cried, "She failed? It's not possible. I had never seen anyone with such extraordinary natural abilities before...my daughter...I never would have let her attempt the trial if I had thought for one second she would die!" Tears surged like floodgates releasing their swell after torrential rains.

Jace and Kaazi just stared at Ayotal both in shock, neither knowing what to say or do.

"This isn't right. I don't believe it, I won't accept it!" Ayotal choked out as anger rose swiftly within her along with unprecedented guilt. She lost Ari when she was a baby and by some miracle they were reunited. Life could not be that unfair as to take Ari away from her again especially after they had just been cementing their relationship after years of separation.

Kaazi had never seen Ayotal any way but self-assured and composed. Now she was beginning to frighten him. If she lost her way, it would have devastating effects on their people. He understood the loss she was feeling, but he also understood the importance of a strong spiritual leader—the role she played. Getting her back to Ashi'nat was imperative, she needed his strength and assistance more than ever, he would help her. Jace, on the other hand he didn't know about. Doubting he was going to be of any use; since the door opened, he just stood there with a blank look on his face—complete catatonic shock.

After several hours of waiting, entering and re-entering the room to see if Ari had returned, Kaazi decided that he needed to take them back to the city; he gathered the equipment and supplies they had brought and placed them on the transport pad with the help of Iets. It was going to be up to him to get them back to the city, to deliver the bad news. With both Jace and Ayotal being emotionally devastated it was the only thing he could do. Kaazi hated being the bearer of bad news especially when the hopes of so many would be dashed to pieces. Dread filled his heart. No one would ever be the same. Finally he gathered Ayotal and Jace and with a glimmer of light they disappeared.

Chapter

NOSSIC was buzzing with activity, anticipation of the outcome of the Legate's trial high on everyone's mind. Alik`ram and Htiaf were manning the communications control center attempting to obtain the latest updates from field operatives around the world. As frustrating as it was for them, they never once wavered in their diligence to find some thread of information that would lead to the location of the Lovell's. Martin and Ena deserved their help and both felt strongly that they owed them all the effort they could muster to see them rescued.

Epoh was sifting through all the field reports from their operatives for the slightest inkling of something out of place that would warrant investigation. Only two or three had been discovered thus far which were assigned to teams for inspection. Epoh felt at times that this was going nowhere, and they would never find Martin and Ena but then he envisioned Ari happily embracing the Lovell's which was incentive enough to continue. She would be so happy if they found the Lovell's and brought them to safety. Overcome with sadness when he thought of Ari, the unhappiness she would feel if something injurious was to happen to her adoptive parents was heartbreaking. He just loved Ari and wanted her to be happy; he knew for that reason alone that he would never stop looking for the Lovell's no matter how many reports he had to sift through.

Gyasi was right on time, as he was every day, to retrieve his morning report. Formidable and intimidating Gyasi was, demanding the highest standards from his operatives, but there wasn't one person in NOSSIC that he didn't take the time to greet or converse with each day, he cared about each one enough to give them the respect they deserved. This little act of respect and attention endeared him to all who worked closely with him at NOSSIC; Gyasi commanded such respect that the members of NOSSIC would do anything for him.

As Gyasi approached Epoh to ask if he had anything new to report, Alik`ram called, "Gyasi...Isbeth is on the com...she says it's urgent!"

The control room became very still and quiet. Each operative was holding a deep inhaled breath as they patiently waited to hear Isbeth's urgent news. The team was desperate for good news—something—anything to give them hope.

Gyasi moved to the communications center, "Put her on speaker," he ordered. "Isbeth...what do you have for me?"

"I've been monitoring Zenot's accounts. Special accounts have to be signed by the CEO, so they come through my desk. I came across several large expenditures for supplies—food, furniture, security equipment, and maternity clothes," Isbeth said as she grinned. Having a competitive nature, she was excited to be the first one with solid evidence, clothes for a pregnant woman.

"Maternity clothes...an odd expenditure for Zenot Corporation," Gyasi said, hope rising deep from within, finally a solid lead, he thought.

"Indeed...the location from where these expenditures originated is a facility that has been closed and abandoned for several years," she said with excitement. If the facility had been reopened, Isbeth would have known about it, she reviewed the updated statistics after she discovered the new expenditures and found that the facility had not been reopened, according to inside sources, they had no intention of reopening anytime soon.

"Really? Are you going to tell me where this facility is located or are you going to keep me in suspense?" he smiled letting out a sigh. Isbeth was one of his best operatives, hard-working, dedicated, but high-maintenance and impish. She held a special place in Gyasi's heart.

"Only if you are really nice to me and let me go with the team that is going to investigate," she said as the imp in her got carried away. Even though Isbeth knew the chances of her going on the op were slim, she was going to take a shot anyway; she desperately needed some time away from Stewart.

"Isbeth!" Gyasi said in a stern tone but they both knew he was not angry.

"Okay…okay…the facility is near Bertrand Lake in Chile, South America," Isbeth squealed. Immediately there was a flurry of activity within the control room as operatives started the verification process of this new piece of information.

"Good job Isbeth, very well done…as for you going on the mission, don't you think you will be recognized?" Gyasi asked trying to get Isbeth to realize that her cover could be compromised.

"Awe… come on Gyasi…it's so boring here. I need a little excitement," Isbeth's pleas were falling upon deaf ears. Bottom line, it was essential she stay where she was, at least for the time being.

"You are needed where you are for now. You are well aware we need the intel on the human-Emigee connection and…" before Gyasi could finish Isbeth cut in with a tirade of her own.

"Yeah…Yeah…I know. My position at Zenot is the closest infiltration to the Emigee we have ever had. I'm going crazy here…nothing is happening! I haven't seen the bankers for months or the Emigee operatives. As a matter of fact, I haven't seen anyone except Stewart. This is insane…I'm starting to act like Stewart…climbing the walls I am… You've got to get me out of here…" she continued for several more minutes before Gyasi interrupted her.

"Well I can see you need a little diversion…What can I do to help?" he said and took several minutes to think about it. "I know…I'll send Kaazi to you as soon as he gets back…that ought to calm you down." Gyasi displayed a huge grin for all to see. Knowing that Isbeth and Kaazi had unresolved issues as did everyone in NOSSIC, the rapscallion he was turned the tables on her. His remark had the desired effect; Isbeth was stunned into complete silence. Quickly Gyasi said, "Take care Isbeth, I'll talk to you soon." He signaled for the com to be terminated and started laughing with half the staff snickering with him.

Alik`ram grinned at Gyasi and said, "That shut her up. How long do you think she will fret about whether you were serious about sending Kaazi?"

Gyasi laughed and said, "I don't know but it will distract her long enough for her to realize that we can't risk her discovery. The intel she provides is too important. Alright enough nonsense…we have work to do, Alik`ram,

Htiaf, Epoh…I want a detailed analysis of the terrain, the complex, enemy forces, etc…and find out who we have in that area of South America. You know what we need…this isn't your first op, so get to it. I want a strategy meeting at early call tomorrow morning in Ashi'nat's office. I'm going to inform Ashi'nat now.

Ashi'nat's office in early morning offered a spectacular view of the city as the sun rose over the horizon. The crystalline structures glistening as the first rays of light danced throughout the city was breathtaking. Beauty personified as the city came to life each day. The respect for life, art, and beauty was evident in all aspects of Te'rellean culture. One just had to look around to appreciate the history and heritage here, Ashi'nat thought. Each morning he would look out over the city and reflect on what was lost, what was gained, and what was about to be established. It was uneasiness that Ashi'nat felt this morning; unsure if it was the news Gyasi delivered yesterday regarding the Lovell's or something else completely. Years he had relied on his inner voice, his intuition, to guide him. It was always correct, as if it had some intrinsic knowledge of rightness. When things were not as they should be, he would know like one knows thick dark gloomy clouds looming on the horizon are precursor to a threatening storm. His foreboding was starting to concern him.

Gyasi was the first to arrive interrupting Ashi'nat's thoughts bringing him back to the present and the situation at hand.

"Greetings…you are well Ashi'nat?" Gyasi asked. The two had been friends for centuries. Ashi'nat didn't have to answer for Gyasi to know something was troubling him.

Ashi'nat replied, "I am well Gyasi and you?"

Gyasi raised a brow to acknowledge to Ashi'nat that he wasn't accepting his assertion of being well. "I am well…but you…what is wrong?" Gyasi asked. Knowing his friend as he did, he knew the subtle nuances that most never recognized, the faraway look, the tilt of the head, and the subtle change in his tone. Being friends for millenniums had its advantages.

"Never could hide anything from you or Ayotal…you both know me to well. An uneasiness I cannot shake off, something isn't as it should be; the feeling has been growing, looming, preparing to descend and consume like a specter in the shadows," Ashi'nat expressed his concern with dread.

"Do you know the source of this dread?" Gyasi asked. Knowing Ashi'nat's record of accuracy gave him concern now. As far as he could recall, Ahsi'nat had never once been wrong.

"No...that's the problem...I'm unable to determine the enigma," he said. The others started to arrive for the meeting. Danek and Dirk arrived from Wyoming. Final clean up to ascertain the activity of the Emigee, what they were doing with the secret base they had destroyed, and their presence, if any, along with the number of soldiers left behind had just been completed. Htiaf and Epoh arrived next. These two were very lively and ready to get started. Lastly, Alik`ram arrived grinning with excitement. Greetings were exchanged by all. The men took their seats and waited for Gyasi to initiate the meeting.

Before Gyasi started, he whispered to Ashi'nat, "We'll talk about this later...see if we can figure out what the problem is about." Little did Gyasi know that information would be revealed sooner rather than later.

Gyasi pulled up a geographical map of the area around Bertrand Lake. The facility was located in rough terrain. It certainly wasn't going to be as easy to maneuver around the area as it was for the Wyoming op.

"The accessibility to the facility is troublesome," Gyasi began. "Our field operatives have determined that there is only one road into the facility, located here. It is more like a dirt trail than a road. The problem is that it is winter in South America and the snow has made the road inaccessible. The only way in is by transmobile, helicopter or hes'chala, and transport."

"We need to take into account that Ena is pregnant. So we will want the fastest way out of the area that we can manage with a pregnant woman," Epoh said. According to what Ari had revealed to him, Ena was very pregnant, approaching her seventh month.

"The fastest way is by transport, but she is human and pregnant. Is it safe to use the transport grid?" said Dirk.

"We need to check with the healers," said Ashi'nat.

"Yes, but the facility has some type of disruptor field which interferes with out transport pads," said Htiaf. The disruptor field completely shuts down most Te`rellean technology making it impossible to use inside the field. If the transport were to be used, they would have to be well out of range of the disruptor field or we need to disable it first which would draw attention to the team.

"We can set up the pads outside the disruptor field," said Danek.

"We can use snowmobiles instead of transmobiles, they won't be affected by the disruptor field because they are human machines which are based on Emigee technology," said Alik`ram. "Since the transport pads are the best way to retrieve the Lovell's, have the field operatives designated an escape route and an appropriate location to set up the transport pads?"

"They are scouting the area…I'll have their report later today," Gyasi said assuring the group that all bases were being covered.

Before he said another word, the transport beam glimmered. Ayotal, Kaazi, and Jace appeared drawing everyone's attention to them. Greetings filled the air until Ashi'nat moved toward Ayotal and saw that something was wrong. As he glanced at each of them, he sensed something was terribly wrong. Jace was staring blankly into space; Kaazi was unable to look Ashi'nat squarely in the eyes—not like Kaazi at all; strange but not what caught his attention. Ayotal, the most significant of all, was angry and pacing—completely uncharacteristic. Uncontrollable tears were pouring down Ayotal's cheeks, tears of despair—she never showed her vulnerability, especially never to the public.

Alarmed Ashi'nat said, "What's wrong? Ayotal what happened?"

She stopped, turned toward her husband with horror on her face, attempting to explain, unable to even whisper a word, her lips moved but nothing was spoken. Beside herself with grief, she was unable to utter a single word.

That uneasy foreboding plaguing him, increasingly looming over Ashi'nat today, was finding its place in reality when his expression turned stone cold.

"Where is Ariella?" Ashi'nat asked urgently, instantly panic spreading like wildfire through dense dry brush surged through him then to the others in the office, as if all were one, a gasp was heard as realization overtook them all.

No one said a word for several moments. It was Kaazi who finally answered, "She's gone."

"What do you mean she's gone?" Ashi'nat demanded. Gyasi reached for Ashi'nat; he made contact just in time to restrain him.

"Come sit down and explain to us what has happened," Gyasi said ushering them over to the furniture trying to maintain a semblance of calm. Kaazi related everything that took place. All were focused intently on the words spoken, but shock and disbelief soon enveloped Ari's friends and family.

Kaazi finished the sordid tale by saying, "When the trial was over and the door to the chamber was opened, we expected to see Ari walk out. She didn't so we went into the trial chamber to see if she was injured and needed help. When we entered the room…it was empty. We waited for a while; we were all in shock, hoping that by some miracle she would reappear, but after some time had passed, I decided it was best to come home. Jace hasn't said anything since the trial ended. Ayotal, well I thought it best to bring her to you," he nodded to Ashi'nat.

The room was silent; each person was processing what had happened in his own way. Tears flowed freely, there was no shame, expressing the loss of one loved so dearly was a tribute, an expression of how deeply she touched each of their lives. After some time, Gyasi was the first to speak.

"We need time…this meeting is over…we will finalize the tactical plans in a few days. Ashi'nat, take Ayotal home. Kaazi…thank you for bringing them home safely. If I am needed, I will be at home with Jace."

Slowly everyone departed from Ashi'nat's office to find a private place to reflect. A great sadness fell upon those who knew Ari, each desperately missing her, her smile, her laughter, the sweetness of her spirit, all trying to accept what had happened, searching for understanding. Her cheerful, lively spirit would be absent, gone, leaving each one to mourn in their own way. All determined in their hearts to honor her memory by finishing the task they set out to accomplish—rescuing the Lovell's.

Chapter

Time a relative concept, passing quickly when having fun or busy, then at other moments moving at a snail's pace, unusually slow. Minutes seemed like hours, hours seemed like days, days seemed like months; time was at a standstill as the city grieved. With all hope gone, it felt like months had been lost when in reality it had only been a week since Ari had vanished from the chamber. There were some who refused to believe she was dead—died in the trial chamber never to be seen from again. Others threw themselves into their work, using it as a distraction to avoid the pain of such a great loss. Still others withdrew into themselves, building barriers deep into the obscure, dark, indistinct regions within, to protect their very existence from cruel oppressive pain that would never be healed—to excruciatingly traumatic to acknowledge. As time crept by, most adjusted, moved forward, sadly, facing life without Ari.

Attempting normalcy, Gyasi was meeting with Ashi'nat to finalize the rescue plan. With final approval, the operatives would set out before dawn the following day. Most of the operatives were eager to complete the op; they were looking for any way to pay tribute to their lost Legate.

"The plans look complete…it's a good plan…let's hope we find the Lovell's safe and unharmed," Ashi'nat said nodding his approval to implement the plan.

"How is Ayotal?" Gyasi inquired. He had not seen much of Ashi'nat and Ayotal the past week having issues of his own with Jace to occupy his time.

"After the first day, she changed; it was like flicking the proverbial switch. For some unknown reason, she has reverted back to being in expectation of Ari's arrival; she continues to refuse to accept that Ari did not survive the trial. I'm worried that she isn't going to accept the reality of the situation. My biggest fear is that she is losing her mind. She is going on as if Ari went on some assignment or vacation and will be home any day. Honestly, I thought she would slowly come to accept this tragedy, begin the healing process, but it is just not happening. She has me very worried," Ashi'nat said as he circled his desk.

"How are you holding up?" Gyasi asked seeing the turmoil so evident in his countenance. Dark circles were starting to appear under his eyes, not a good sign. Ashi'nat rarely allowed stress to affect him in this way, always being the strength for everyone else, but the evidence was clear. Ashi'nat was in crisis.

"As well as can be expected I suppose, part of me wants to believe Ayotal is right, but then, there is the realization that there are only two known outcomes to the trials—you live or you die. I have never heard of anyone disappearing after the trials, only to reappear later, which only solidifies my belief that she is gone forever. My heart breaks knowing we had such a short time together. All I have now are my memories," sighed Ashi'nat as tears were welling up in his eyes, changing the subject he asked, "How's Jace?"

"You should take some time, you and Ayotal, go, heal, your assistant can handle things for a while and I'm always here. Both of you need time to reflect. As for Jace, for the first few days, he didn't eat, drink, sleep or even acknowledge my existence. Staring off into space was the only thing he did, lost in a void, an abyss of darkness, consumed by lonely despair. As time went by with no change, I decided something drastic was needed, so I formed a telepathic link with him. It was really rather scary, the things I found in his mind. At first the image I received from the link was black," Gyasi said as he shivered, remembering the feeling as if it just occurred.

"Black? What do you mean black?" Ashi'nat asked, never having heard of an instance where a link was black.

"His mind was a black void…that must be how traumatic shock is symbolized and projected in the mind," Gyasi said, he had no other explanation for what he saw.

"What did you do?" Ashi'nat asked with great concern. Gyasi and Jace were like family and nothing was more important than family.

"I stayed in his mind maintaining the connection and just spoke to him softly, quietly, sustaining a comforting presence. After a while, the image of a void changed, transformed into an extremely high wall of thick rust-colored bricks which encircled him. Around the bricks was a wide raging river. The river was surrounded by a fortification of mountain-like rock. If that wasn't bad enough, the rock fortification was surrounded by a thick dense forest. Jace had put up so many barriers I didn't think I would ever be able to reach him. Protecting himself from the pain of losing Ari was as essential to him as breathing, especially after what he experienced when his mother died. It took me a few days being linked for him to open a pathway so I could reach him, I really didn't think I was going to be able to sway him." Gyasi explained, shaking off the memory.

"With so much pain and Jace withdrawing into himself, it's a miracle you had an impact at all," Ashi'nat said in amazement. "It so unfair, to be given a glimpse of this magnificent creature and then to lose her as quickly as she came to us, there has to some purpose to it all."

"Recovery will be slow, the depth of his love for her from what I was able to discern was immense. I barely scratched the surface; he is guarding those feelings with his life. Protecting his heart is his focus, he will have those barriers up for a very long time, but he is at least functioning. Coaxing him gradually, I was able to help even if it was just a little, he went back to NOSSIC yesterday; he wants to go on the op to rescue the Lovell's. Unrelentingly determined to face the Lovell's, he feels Ari would have wanted him to explain the reason why she wasn't there. I know that is probably true, but I have my reservations about letting him go," Gyasi said. Afraid for Jace, the ordeal was still too fresh, he would have preferred Jace to wait before going on an op, but Jace wouldn't hear of it.

"As well you should…you don't think he will do something to put himself in harm's way do you?" Ashi'nat asked. The last thing they needed was for one of their own to inflict injury on himself or deliberately place himself in harm's way.

"The thought had crossed my mind, but I spoke with Kaazi and the others and they are going to look after him. I'm worried about all of them…in all my years at NOSSIC, and as you know there have been many, I have never seen my operatives affected to this extreme," Gyasi confessed. Something about

Ari, her kindness, strength, her capacity to love and show honor to others, it touched people to their core, an extraordinary young woman.

"Do you think they are stable enough to undertake the mission?" Ashi'nat asked worried that their grief would interfere with the mission. Having a safe and successful op was of the highest priority, if they needed more time, he would gladly give them the extension.

"They are determined to go tomorrow…that is one thing I'm sure of and I don't think it possible to hold them off any longer," Gyasi said admiring their dedication.

"So be it…you have my approval," Ashi'nat sighed. After a long silence he turned toward the window to look out over the city and said, "I will talk with you tomorrow. I might even stop by NOSSIC."

Gyasi's brow rose, "What a surprise that would be for NOSSIC," he said with a grin then left, leaving Ashi'nat alone in his office.

Very rarely leaving the compound these days, Kaazi was at NOSSIC with Alik`ram when Gyasi arrived. The pair was busily studying the plan, meticulously combing every detail to determine if they prepared for all conceivable scenarios. The best strategists devised this plan, but Kaazi, more secure in his own abilities, reviewed and examined the plan repeatedly; he was determined this op go off without a hitch.

"We have final approval for this op," Gyasi said. "Is everything ready for deployment?"

"Yes…we were just checking to make sure we didn't miss anything," Kaazi said relieved to have final approval. He was ready, as was his team.

"Have you seen Jace?" Gyasi asked wanting to spend time with him before he left tomorrow.

"He was here earlier…I believe he went for a walk," Alik`ram replied hesitantly.

"Do you know which direction, I need to speak with him," Gyasi said. Both men shook their heads 'no'; Gyasi sighed and turned to leave. Outside, he stretched out his mind in an attempt to find Jace. Starting to walk, he intensified his search of the area with his mind, but he was unable to locate him. His search range wasn't great, he was never very good at that particular skill, but he diligently searched for his son even with his limited reach. As he approached the meditation center, he started sensing Jace. The closer he came to the center the clearer the image became.

Jace was in the garden of loneliness peering into the pool of insight. Remembering his quandary when his wife was brutally taken away, viciously murdered, Gyasi didn't approach him; he went to the other side of the garden and sat alone for a while. Jace was deep in thought. Reflecting back on the last several months, the joy he had felt for the first time since his mother was taken from him. Joy wrapped up in one very lovely woman. Ari had become an integral part of his life, entwined into the very fabric of his soul, reaching into the threads of his very being, connecting deeply with his spirit. Happiness and love was the epitome of existence with Ari. How would he ever be able to live without her?

Now, he felt numb as if all emotions and feelings had been anesthetized. Nothingness, devoid of all sensation, completely stolid; not happy or sad, he felt absolutely nothing. It wasn't normal, he knew it, but he supposed it was better than the gut-wrenching agony he felt when his mother died. This respite from feeling he was sure wouldn't last, when the pain did surfaced, he was certain it would be worse than being consumed by fire, delving into a bottomless pit of despondency. He just hoped the numbness lasted until the op was over.

After a few minutes, Jace looked around wondering how long he had been lost in thought as he glanced up to the sky; the sun was on its downward decent. Whether his father was finished with his meeting with Ashi'nat or not, he wasn't sure, but he decided to go in search of him. Noticing the figure sitting in the shadows across the garden, he sensed familiarity. Without seeing the man's face, he knew it was his father. Jace approached Gyasi and asked, "How long have you been here?"

"For a little while...I didn't want to disturb you. I haven't visited the garden of loneliness for several years. It felt amazingly refreshing to sit and meditate for a while. I used to come to the garden every day when we lived in the old city, but the previous site was a bit smaller, it is quite beautiful here," Gyasi said as he reflected on old memories.

"Do we have final approval for the mission?" Jace asked, not that he was really curious; he assumed his father would expect him to ask if the mission was a go. It was difficult to become enthused about much of anything at this point, especially when he dreaded the task at hand when they found the Lovell's.

"Yes…I've already been to NOSSIC…everything is ready for tomorrow," Gyasi said, his eagle eyes assessing Jace, his reactions, mannerisms; he was still not comfortable sending Jace on the op, but if he tried to stop him, he was sure Jace would find a way to be in the thick of things, part of the team.

"When this op is over and the Lovell's are rescued, I want a deep under-cover assignment that will last for years…preferably something that will keep my mind busy and active," Jace said, no feeling, no emotion, just blank emp-tiness which worried Gyasi to no end.

Gyasi thought about what Jace said and knew it for what it was—an escape. He was not going to agree to this request, what Jace really needed was to be around those who loved him not to isolate himself. Gyasi had seen too many friends isolate themselves after some traumatic event in their life which only led to their destruction. Jace wasn't going to be one of those people, not if he had anything to do with it. So he replied, "We will discuss this after the Lovell's are safe and everyone returns."

"Fine…but I'm serious father," Jace said, determination and stubbornness exuding from the inner recesses of his character with defiance in his stance.

"I know you are…now…have you eaten yet? Let's get a bite," Gyasi said as they left the garden.

Later, in the evening, Ayotal was in Ari's room putting fresh flowers in a vase. She was preparing it as if Ari would be returning home anytime. Ashi'nat stood in the doorway watching his wife as she was fussing with the flowers and humming a tune. What was he to do? How was he going to help her if she wouldn't acknowledge that Ari was dead? Ayotal smiled brightly at Ashi'nat when she caught a glimpse of him from the corner of her eyes.

"How does that look?" she asked, waiting for her husband's approval.

"It looks beautiful love, but do you think we can have a word? I would like to speak with you about Ariella," he said. Extremely concern at his wife's in-ability to accept the fact that Ari did not survive the trials, he was afraid he was going to lose her as well; she was losing touch with reality.

"Of course, what is it?" Ayotal asked as she sat on the bed. Ashi'nat brought the chair over from the desk to sit facing her. Taking both hands into his, he began caressing them with each stroke of his thumb. Pausing, he brought both hands to his lips and gently kissed them.

"I think we should close up Ariella's room and seal it like we did the first time we lost her," he said gently, hoping that if the room was sealed she would move on with her life, put this dreadful experience behind her, behind both of them.

"Why would we do that when she will be home soon?" Ayotal asked looking a bit confused. After the initial shock wore off from the trial, something changed.

Grieving at home a few days after the trial, Ayotal had been alone out in her private garden. A place secluded and peaceful, desperately seeking to make sense of what happened, but it didn't make sense, nothing about it made sense. As she attempted to meditate giving herself over to the melodious symphony of nature, one of her favorite pastimes; the breeze blowing, the leaves rustling, the birds singing, and hundreds of other sounds engulfed her, all floating on the wind. As it was, attempting to meditate with a troubled spirit proved elusive. An endless deluge, again tears had begun streaming down her cheeks, it was as if they would never stop, her heart was broken and throbbing mercilessly.

In an instant, a tear had fallen to the ground, a single tear. As it hit the surface, it was as if the earth quivered. When the tear was absorbed, a ripple was felt through the whole garden. Seconds later, Ayotal felt a warmth embrace her as if she had soft warm arms around her to comfort and sooth her providing much needed relief. Amazingly she was consumed with consolation, feelings of happiness and contentment—her solace. Echoing's on the wind, she heard whispers, faint wistful whispers—a sense of Ari. Looking around to see if she had imagined it, she saw nothing, but was left with a peaceful notion that everything was alright.

"Ayotal, the ancient accounts state that there are only two outcomes in the trials—success or failure, life or death. There is no recorded history of someone disappearing then reappearing," Ashi'nat reasoned. He wanted Ari to be alive as much as she did but the reality was, she was gone and they both needed to face the fact they would never see their child again.

"This is true. I have been over the ancient texts several times myself, but on the other hand, they don't say it can't happen. Besides Ariella is extraordinary, her outcome could be completely different," Ayotal explained having complete confidence she would be 'home soon.'

"My love, there has been no sign of her for over a week. I don't want it to be so but we can't avoid the evidence. She died in the trial...we need to put this behind us and the only way to start doing that is to close up this room," he said pleading his case.

"Ashi'nat ...I understand what you are saying to me, but I want you to listen to what I am saying to you, I can't explain it but I know just as sure as the sun will rise in the morning that Ariella is alive. Sure, when we first discovered that Ari had disappeared from the trial chamber, I was devastated... hurt...angry...but after I was home and the shock wore off, as I was meditating a warm, homey, secure feeling enveloped me. The same feeling I get when Ari is around. It is like part of her reaching out to me to let me know she is fine and will be home soon. I don't know why she disappeared or where she is now but I know and feel she isn't lost to us," Ayotal cried, pleading for her husband to understand. "Join with me and feel what I know."

"I know you believe that but isn't it possible this feeling you have is your mind tricking you into believing something that isn't true to compensate for the pain? After all, we are no strangers to the pain of losing a child," Ashi'nat reasoned.

"Anything is possible but join with me so you can know what I know," she urged.

She reached her mind to his; immediately he experienced the absolute assurance that Ari was alive. Unable to determine its source, Ayotal was right; there was no doubt in her mind that Ari was alive. Being that as it was, he was more cautious and needed more proof than just his wife's feelings. If she was alive and he hoped with all his heart that she was, where was she and why hadn't she come home?

"Alright, we don't have to close the room now, we will wait longer. I hope you are right, and she will come home to us," Ashi'nat conceded, experiencing Ayotal feelings, but still doubting its certainty.

"She will come back to us," she said as they embraced.

Chapter

39

"Of all the luck, I can't believe the timing!" Ki spewed as he was ranting, pacing back and forth in the yard outside the compound, waving his arms resembling a menacing wild beast out of control ready to devour anything in his sight. Disappointment didn't even come close to what he was feeling. Looking forward to the diversion, seeing the human suffer and wither in pain would have provided some much-needed entertainment in this god-forsaken wilderness. At least it would have brought meaning to the horrid exile in this secluded desolate winter wasteland. Being of the same mind as Si'kram and the ishta, he reveled in making the human suffer to retrieve the information he wouldn't relinquish. Unable to withstand the anguish of boredom any longer, Ki picked up his weapon and headed up into the mountains, he needed to kill something, anything, and fast before he went mad.

Hamer was heading down the corridor to the prisoners. The timing of Nadroj's arrival was impeccable, it couldn't have been better. Martin was spared the torturous agony of the Dolorous to the ishta's dismay but even the ishta did not cross Nadroj, the Supreme Commander of the Emigee. Disappointed, their plans thwarted, they would have to be satisfied with the injuries already inflicted, small consolation but nonetheless it was all they would have, at least for now. Ecstatically pleased, he would never forget their surprised expressions when the hes'chala appeared above them prior to inserting the Dolorous into

Martin's semi-conscious body. Their maniacal plans circumvented. After the hes'chala landed and the Supreme Commander disembarked, the ishta slithered back into their hole to await further instructions.

Ambushed was what he felt when he discovered that Nax`el and Camden were one in the same. Played as a fool, something he abhorred and didn't forgive easily; Hamer had not realize that Nax`el, Nadroj's son, went by an alias. Certainly, it was a surprise to see Camden with Nadroj; he didn't know whether to be furious or elated. Never approving the kidnapping, he was sure it was Camden who enlisted the aid of Nadroj, but it was puzzling, why would Nadroj go along with Camden? It was no secret that Nadroj despised the Te`relleans, and with Martin and Ena so closely connected to the Te`relleans he couldn't see the reason behind saving Martin. Hamer glanced down the corridor behind him and wished he knew what was going on behind closed doors. Uneasily curious, he wondered what the fate of the prisoners would be—life or death, unfortunately he surmised death.

The three men were sitting at the table, Nadroj at the head of the table with Camden at his right side. Silently intimidating, Nadroj sat with his sternly focused eye on Si'kram. If there was incompetence from an unseasoned soldier, it was to be expected, Nadroj would understand, but incompetence coming from a seasoned military leader, one he had been closely associated with for about seven hundred years was incomprehensible and completely intolerable. What made it worse was he was considered a friend.

"What was occurring here before we arrived?" Nadroj demanded in an authoritative calculated deportment.

Si'kram glared at both men; he loathed his authority challenged especially in the presence of underlings. Pausing for several minutes, gathering a semblance of control, he stiffened then looked Nadroj squarely in the eyes, "The human was immune to the SIRD. We have never encountered such resistance from a human before, so my ishta were about to implement another means of retrieving the needed information."

Nadroj listened to Si'kram's explanation with skepticism. Fixated, he knew that Si'kram and his ishta thrived on inflicting pain on others; Si'kram loved to watch others wither from excruciating pain; it was as if he was regenerated by the malicious manipulation. For almost as long as he had been the leader, Nadroj observed Si'kram and the ishta's obsessive appetite for inflicting horrendous interrogation tactics on the Te`rell who were unfortunate enough to be captured; it was appalling even for him.

After a brief pause, Nadroj stated, "I see...Si'kram you are an extraordinary military leader. You have served our people well for many years. So why have you mucked up this situation so badly? Kidnapping the adoptive parents of a Te`rellean was not authorized. The girl is who I want not her parents. She is the priority. A Te`rellean who is so important to her people, they had sent their best operatives to protect her. A Te`rellean who escaped your best operatives! How was that possible? If that's not bad enough, you have a human woman held captive, one that I have no interest in, and you torture her husband. Where has it gotten you?—nowhere! Even if they were useful, did you ever consider that with this form of treatment you were alienating everyone involved, forcing them to put up stronger barriers?"

"I did what I always do...I used proven tactics of interrogation," Si'kram said defiantly becoming uneasy as he watched Nadroj's every move.

"You have to change your tactics! When strong emotional bonds exist between people like the Te`relleans and the humans, subtle tactics need to be used. Our circumstances have change Si'kram and so must our interrogation strategies. We are no longer facing an enemy as warriors in blatant physical confrontation. We face them covertly by using power and control, a more insidious method of warfare. Attacking from within, manipulating people and corporations, economies and government through banking, financial trade and laws...this is where your focus should be, not on physical warfare. Face it Si'kram, if you don't change your tactics, you will be obsolete," Nadroj explained urging his companion to comply.

"I am a soldier, born and bred for war, physical war. How am I supposed to change now after eight hundred fifty years of fighting, tactically maneuvering the humans into position, positions which make it conducive for them to want to destroy each other?" Si'kram growled.

Nadroj was becoming annoyed, but he maintained stealth-like composure, not once giving any indication that he wanted to snap Si'kram's neck. Nadroj was one of the few Emigee who retained the power of telekinesis; he was quite capable of ending this ridiculous confrontation at any moment. Learning through the years that patience was extremely beneficial, more so than an outright attack, manipulating events to his advantage then he could deliver the deadly blow. Si'kram was still useful, he just needed to be reigned in, controlled.

"I am well aware of your military record Si'kram, your expertise initiating wars. You have what…about 980 wars that you can claim credit for igniting… quite impressive but humans are evolving…yes, they still like to destroy themselves but they do it with money, power, greed, manipulation…covertly so that no one is the wiser until it is too late. Very effective tactics actually," Nadroj said.

"Fighting reduces the population of the humans, they multiple like vermin," Si'kram protested.

"True but we have a solution to that as you know—the virus will be ready within the next few years which will significantly reduce the human population to less than 200,000, a much more manageable number. When the virus is released, we will be one step closer to claiming victory over the Te`rell. Their pets, those pitiful humans, have unwittingly assisted them in blending into the general populous. As the humans are reduced to a handful of individuals throughout the world, the Te`rell will be much easier to identify, locate, and eliminate. I live for that day Si'kram. I will not have anyone jeopardize the plan," Nadroj snidely barked. "Now, tell me what information you were trying to retrieve from the human?"

"My operatives had the idea to retrieve the Te`rellean girl's cell phone number in hopes of luring her here to rescue her parents," Si'kram said hesitantly.

"That would get Ari to come for sure," Camden said, speaking for the first time. "There is nothing she wouldn't do for her parents…she loves them very much."

"She would put herself in danger for them?" his father asked with astonishment, assessing any little piece of information he could exploit.

"Without a doubt," Camden said. "I have her number and I will give it to you if you give me your word that you will not harm Ari."

"Why do you protect her Camden?" Nadroj asked annoyed to have limitations put on him, not that it would make a difference, if he chose to rescind his word no one would question his reasons.

"She is a very lovely person, kind and good. I don't want to see her hurt… I mean it!" Camden demanded, boldly speaking up to his father was very uncharacteristic.

"I see…very well you have my word, she will not be harmed but I can't say the same for any other Te`relleans who might get in the way," Nadroj said. "Give Si'kram the number."

Excitedly, a new sense of anticipation filled Camden, the opportunity to see Ari again. Giving the number to Si'kram, he left to find Hamer. After leaving the room there was an extremely long and awkward silence, Si'kram was looking at the small piece of paper with Ari's number on it and Nadroj staring out the window contemplating his next move, like a chess master, was formulating his strategy.

"Nadroj…what do you want me to do with the humans?" Si'kram asked.

"Yes…you have to clean up this mess don't you…I suppose there is no other choice…you will have to kill them after the girl presents herself. Hum… I suppose she will want to see them first…after that you can eliminate them," Nadroj said half talking to Si'kram and half talking to himself.

Nadroj's habit of talking to himself out loud while talking with others was disconcerting to say the least. Those who were close to him knew how to respond and Si'kram had hundreds of years of experience with the Supreme Commander. Nevertheless it was unsettling, most people had no idea how to respond, it was open to misinterpretation which could be disastrous.

Apprehensively jittery, Si'kram was steadily becoming uneasy; tension was building inside him like a boiling pot at the brink of eruption. He wondered how he lost control. Nadroj was right about one thing, times were changing. It seemed as though his people were losing their strength, their spirit. As warriors, they were driven, the need for conquest and blood was at the very center of their existence. Living here on this world was affecting all of his people. The Emigee were losing themselves, their identity; the very idea of losing one's strength as a warrior was loathsome, an unthinkable dreadful outcome. Somehow, he had to prevent that from occurring, but how?

Chapter

Explanations were inevitable, the reckoning was coming. A matter of time before his true identity was discovered, the question was how would they handle the truth? Refusing to put it off any longer, Camden found Hamer on the other side of the complex near what was now the prison cell. Ja'nek was with him in the room across from Martin and Ena. His comrades were having an intense conversation. As he approached, the men were becoming quite heated, but the two immediately became silent as Camden entered.

"Hamer…Ja'nek…good to see you," Camden said as he cautiously entered the room.

"Nax'el, the Supreme Commander's son, have you come to lord your power over us?" Hamer snarled boldly, knowing that going against the ruling family could cost him his life.

Camden knew this confrontation was unavoidable; he had to atone for his deceit if he was to regain the trust of his team. Preferring not to explain the situation, such explanations would expose too much of himself to the scrutiny of others, he felt he had no choice. All he had wanted was to be accepted for who he was, not whose son he was; he could not control the circumstance of his birth. Camden just wanted others to see him, not as the son of the Supreme Commander, but as a person, someone of value, on his own merit, a person of skill and intelligence. He understood why the men were angry, they felt betrayed, but that was not his intention. Somehow, he would have to make them see his side.

"Why did you lie to us?" Ja'nek asked pointedly, beating around the bush was not the soldiers way neither was it his.

"I did not lie to you," Camden said calmly hoping they would give him an opportunity to explain before they flew off the handle.

"You called yourself Camden when your name is Nax'el. Sounds like a lie to me. What were you doing spying on us, reporting back to your father on how bad this assignment had gone?" Hamer barked, emotions surging. The mission had gone from bad to worse, now he was convinced that is was just wrong.

"First of all my name is Camden, Nax'el Camden. Most of our people don't know my second name and I like it that way. It provides me with an opportunity to be myself instead of what people expect me to be, the Supreme Commander's son. I did not spy on you that was not my intent. I wanted to become a member of your team, to gain your respect, the respect of the best operatives our people have, I still do," Camden explained calmly with sincerity which had both men listening.

"You were against taking the Lovell's from the beginning. Are you telling us you didn't run right back to daddy with a bad report?" Ja'nek asked as he sneered at Camden, visibly displaying his disbelief.

"It's true, I was and still am against the kidnapping, but it was Si'kram who removed me from this op. Separating us and sending me on some fictitious, tedious, unimportant mission to Greenland was his intention, to cause dissent among our team. As soon as I returned home, my father told me that he was leaving to intervene in an op that had gone wrong, to go clean up a mess that Si'kram had made in South America. When I asked about the mess, he told me it was something about kidnapping humans. Obviously, it was the Lovell's, who else could it have been, I wanted to come myself to see what had happened," Camden continued to explain hoping that they would understand.

"You said nothing about the team to anyone?" Hamer asked skeptically, brows furrowing in disbelief.

"No...not to anyone...I would never betray the team," Camden exclaimed.

"Hum...good otherwise son or no son we would have to exact punishment," Hamer said. The tension in the room started to dissipate.

"What has happened? How are the Lovell's?" Camden asked. Ja'nek and Hamer glanced at each other with a weary expression focused on Camden.

"When your father and Si'kram were in conference and the ishta received word that the Dolorous implantation was cancelled, they were enraged. Their bloodlust had no outlet. On the verge of insanity, they had to have retribution, their rage exploded onto Martin. Besieged by the ishta, fist slamming into his face, back, and ribs like bricks, this fragile human was beaten to within an inch of his life. It took several of our best soldiers to get the ishta off Martin. He's in the room with Ena. She is doing everything she can to care for his wounds, but there is very little she can do to make it better. He is in dire need of medical attention, but I doubt that will be approved, if we only had the healing ability that the Te`rell possess we could help. Ena has reached her limits; the stress is taking its toll on her. I'm afraid she is going to deliver early, possibly lose the child," Hamer said with deep sorrow in his voice. Having grown fond of the humans over the last few months, the last thing he wanted was to live with this tragedy.

"Deliver early? A child?" Camden asked somewhat confused, he had no idea Ena was with child.

"She's pregnant," Ja'nek said clarifying the confusion. Still feeling guilty about kidnapping a pregnant woman, he was qualmish about the whole matter. Pregnant women were highly respected in the Emigee culture, to harm one was unthinkable.

"Pregnant!" Camden said in disbelief. "She didn't look pregnant when I last saw her."

"She had just found out when we grabbed her. That's why the girl wasn't home, Martin and Ena were supposed to be having a romantic dinner so Ena could break the news to him," Hamer said remorsefully.

"Can I see them?" Camden asked, more like pleaded. Wanting to see for himself the damage the ishta had done.

"Why? Why do you want to see them?" Ja'nek asked, having become increasingly protective over the past few months.

"I want to reassure them that I am going to do everything I can to obtain their release," Camden said. Not knowing how, he was determined to find a way to get them released.

Martin was lying on the bed; Ena was replacing the cool cloth on his head. His body felt like it had been run over by a freight train. Martin's face was swollen to twice its normal size. Swollen shut, his left eye was puffed up and oozing, with his right eye swollen just enough to form a slit for him to peer up at Ena. Several shades of red and purple permeated the swollen skin, deep indigo around the eyes getting lighter at the edges. Ena could barely look at him without breaking into tears. Gently she placed a cool cloth over his eyes and nose to reduce the swelling and provide much needed relief. Sure the nose was broken, cut and off center, slanted to the right, she could barely lay the cloth upon it without him moaning in pain. When Martin attempted to talk, the lacerations on his lips broke open and bled only prolonging its healing, stitches were needed, but it was difficult for him to stay silent. Ena was terrified that Martin had internal bleeding and that he would bleed to death; she tried to push that thought to the back of her mind and focus on the present but seeing him that way was impossible ignore. All her efforts went in to making him as comfortable as possible.

"You need to rest," Martin muttered through swollen lips, speaking in whispers.

"Shhh…I'm fine, lay still and sleep," Ena whispered back. With every breath he took, pain surged through his chest, sharp, throbbing pain, it was excruciating. Martin knew he was not going to make it out of there alive. Ena and the baby were the only thought in his mind, what would become of them? His heart was breaking at the thought of leaving the love of his life and their unborn child alone to an uncertain future. Martin was never a religious man though he always tried to do good, be honest, and treat others with respect which earned him an excellent reputation. Seeking a higher power was never a high priority, until now. Martin searched deep within himself for the words to express what he felt, his most sincere and desperate desire for Ena's safety. Not understanding why he felt that prayer was the answer, the need to implore a higher power for help was overwhelming. It didn't matter, without reservation he released his deepest fears and anxieties, hoping without hope that he was being heard, this he did continually as he was being cared for by the only women he ever loved, his Ena.

Ena was changing the water when she heard a light tap on the door to her prison cell. She turned to see Hamer and another man walk through the entrance. After all this time, she had developed a strange relationship with Hamer. Even though he was her captor, he was very kind to her and Martin.

She could see the distress in his eyes at having to keep them imprisoned. He was always bringing little things to make her stay more comfortable. Limited to what he could provide for them, he did bring them extra food when possible along with a few personal items, and books and magazines.

Hamer crossed the room to Ena who appeared very weary and said, "How are you holding up? Can I get you anything?"

"I'm just tired. Hamer he's not doing to good, is there any way you can get him some pain medicine or medical help? I'm afraid he has internal bleeding and if he does, he is going to die…I can't bear the thought of losing him," she whispered, pleading her case, hoping Hamer could help.

Hamer was twisted up inside, his gut wrenching; listening to her desperate plea for help, knowing there was nothing he could do. Turning to Camden hoping for a solution, he found none; he was at a loss just as much as Hamer was for now.

"We will try…Ena do you remember Camden, he was one of the workers Martin hired…he has come to assist in obtaining your release. Camden was against the kidnapping from the beginning, but like the rest of us he had no choice," Hamer explained. Ena glanced at Camden and nodded in recognition. She remembered Camden and the work he did on the ranch, he seemed like a nice young man until that frightful night when she and Martin were taken from their home, the night that should have been the happiest of their lives together, the night she told Martin she was having his baby—something thought to be impossible, but now a reality.

"Is it possible? How can you help Camden?" Ena asked urgently with hope in her voice, hope she thought lost.

"Si'kram did not have approval for this operation. He acted without the Supreme Commander's knowledge. Nadroj arrived just in time to stop Si'kram's plans," Hamer explained trying to comfort her.

Camden continued, "Nadroj is my father and the Supreme Commander, I may be able to influence his decision regarding what to do next. Unfortunately, I can't guarantee anything specific."

"It's hope, more than we had a few minutes ago. Martin and I have both resigned ourselves to the fact that we wouldn't be getting out of here alive, but you have given us a thread of hope. Thank you for trying," Ena said as she hugged Camden and Hamer.

Camden's heart was being ripped to shreds seeing Ena in her current state. Unable to bare it any longer; he needed to leave the room before he lost control. Hamer watched him as he inched his way closer to the door. Before he followed, he handed Ena a new book for her to read. She thanked him then turned back to Martin. Hamer and Camden took one last look then left the room.

"She looked frazzled. It can't be good for the baby," Camden exclaimed, "There has got to be something I can do to help."

"I'm afraid the decision is not yours but your fathers to make," Hamer said as he walked away leaving Camden alone to contemplate what he saw.

Running down the corridor, Camden went in search of his father. After a thorough search of the complex, Camden went back to the hes'chala and found his father in his quarters. Camden shook his head and laughed inwardly, he should have known he would be here. It was the only place he felt secure and comfortable. Full of memories, memories of his beloved Shanty, his mate, her loss had consumed him for years. Blaming the Te`rell for her death, he was adamant about avenging her with their extermination. Camden rarely came to his quarters'; it was too much of a reminder, a reminder of the loss he felt. The suite was just as it had been when his mother was alive. Establishing a shrine to her, he knew his father would never change a thing in the place where they lived and loved. It was twisted; his father was bent on revenge. No matter the outcome of the war with the Te`rell, he would never get her back. Letting go was his only hope but he was so consumed with vengeance he couldn't see clearly. Sad really, if revenge wasn't his motivating force, his living quarters would have been heartwarming actually, to know his father felt such deep and lasting love for a woman.

Nadroj's quarters were spacious considering they were on a transport-space vehicle, similar to the human version of air-forces one. The design was sleek and angular with modern looks, clean lines. Geometric figures would be the theme of its furnishings. Sitting at his workstation, a large rectangular desk, cylindrical legs, built-in computer consoles at both ends, with several master control pads divided into several specific categories between the monitors, these pads could be concealed with the push of a button. They were concealed by descending into the desk and covered by what looked like smooth gray crystal which formed a chic tabletop. Nadroj was engrossed, intently reading reports on the screen.

Nadroj was stunned as he looked up. To see Camden standing in the doorway was unusual, he always avoided reminders of his mother. "Camden...what a surprise...what can I do for you?" his father smiled as he motioned him over to the chair on the opposite side of the workstation.

"I must speak with you about Martin and Ena. What are your plans with regard to them?" Camden asked urgently. Frowning at his obvious anxiety, Nadroj was baffled.

"Martin and Ena? Who are...oh...the humans Si'kram has imprisoned. You heard the plan. Si'kram is going to contact the girl to set up a meeting. We are using the humans as a lure," he said unsure why he had to repeat the plan when Camden was at the meeting.

"Yes, I know all that...what are you going to do with them when they are no longer needed? I would like your permission to take them back to their home," Camden said earnestly.

Nadroj didn't quite understand why Camden would be pleading for humans. He was curious though so he asked, "Why would you want to do that? What are these humans to you? Humans are of no importance."

"I disagree father, the Lovell's are very good people. I don't want to see them hurt, besides Ena is having a baby," Camden said.

"That is neither here nor there my boy; it's not as if she was an Emigee woman having a baby; that would be a different matter altogether. Because of the mess Si'kram has made of this whole situation, it has been decided the humans must die as soon as we get the girl here," Nadroj decreed, his decrees were final.

"Please change your mind father, let me take them home so they..." Camden was interrupted by the firm loud bellow of his father.

"Camden...why are you questioning my authority...the decision has been made and will not change. I have been patient with you because you are my son and the future ruler of our people, but I will not be questioned...Is that understood? Put things in perspective Camden, our people and their survival is what is important, it takes precedence over all other concerns. Humans are nothing; they are slaves, nothing more, a means to an end. Start acting like the next leader of our people." Nadroj declared in the tone Camden had known and hated from the time he was a child, his 'I have spoken' tone that meant 'this discussion is over, and I don't want to hear another word about it.'

Distressed, Camden left the room to seek solitude. Si'kram was coming up the corridor to give his report to Nadroj. Si'kram would never give him information before he gave it to Nadroj, so he waited until Si'kram entered his father's room before he turned back to the closed door and began to listen to the muffled voices. With the Emigee's heightened hearing ability, he was able to make out everything they were saying without too much straining; they were talking about normal routine activities. As he listened for a few more minutes, he heard Si'kram say the Te`rellean girl wasn't answering her phone but he left a message and he would try again later. Camden was relieved to hear that Si'kram hadn't been able to get in touch with Ari; it gave him more time to figure out how to save the Lovell's.

Urgently, Camden set off to find Hamer. After a thorough search of the complex, he finally found Hamer battering a punching bag in the training area. Pounding the bag mercilessly, he tried to alleviate his anger. Taking out his frustrations was all Hamer was consumed with at the moment which was even more frustrating. He was not one to sit idly by and do nothing, he needed action.

Camden broke into Hamer's concentration. "My father has decided that the Lovell's will be killed after they get Ari in their clutches," he shouted to Hamer. Hamer's focus was redirected to Camden; he turned, gripping Camden with a blazing glare, holding him motionless, he felt a slow heated anger growing within.

"Did you think it would be otherwise?" Hamer sneered, how naïve Camden was to think he could change the mind of their leader, even if he was his father.

"Yes…I thought he would at least listen to me but his mind was already made-up, the decision a foregone conclusion, determined between Si'kram and himself, no discussion allowed!" Camden hissed. "We need to do something!"

"Do something? What do you propose…go against the Supreme Leader?" Hamer exclaimed as he watched Camden nod his head acknowledging that was exactly what he had in mind. "Are you crazy, do you know what will happen if we are caught?"

"I know it's dangerous but my father and his pok'too are wrong. Are you going to help me or not?" Camden asked, adamant in his conviction.

"Pok'too…that's pretty bold calling the leaders of our people pok'too…" Hamer was silent contemplating what he would do. Exposing Camden could get him points in identifying a traitor to Si'kram and the Supreme Commander or he could go along with Camden and help. Living dangerously these days, at least in his thoughts, he felt uncertain. The capture of the Lovell's had him questioning the validity of the Emigee agenda. If he questioned one decision, he had to question others. The bottom line was did the current leadership have the best interests of the Emigee in mind? Hamer didn't think so, not anymore; he would listen to Camden.

"Did you have something in mind? How can we save them?" Hamer asked, his curiosity peaked, if there was a way to save the Lovell's, he wanted to know.

"Well, I don't know we have a little time to figure it out. Si'kram has not been able to get in contact with Ari yet," Camden said. "Do you think Ja'nek will assist us?"

"I know he doesn't like the fact that the Lovell's are captive, but I don't know if he would willingly go against the Supreme Commander or Si'kram. I think we should just keep this between us," Hamer said. "Let's throw some ideas around to see if it is even possible to help them."

Chapter

Anticipation was high; finally, with definitive information on the location of the Lovell's, NOSSIC teams were ready. High in the snow-covered mountains of South America, Kaazi and the other operatives were taking their positions to execute their rescue mission. Several days of repeated delays to get all operatives in the proper positions had everyone frazzled. Due to a violent blizzard which rolled in just after the transport pads were positioned, the mission had to be postponed. Once the storm was over, the pads had to be dug out from under five feet of new snow. The operatives themselves took refuge in thermal tents and had to dig out from the snow in the aftermath of the blizzard as well. It made for one of his more interesting ops, Kaazi thought. Jace was focused intently on rescuing the Lovell's although he didn't relish the idea of having to inform them Ari was dead. He could barely accept it himself. Nonetheless, he knew Ari would want him to break the news to her adoptive parents himself.

The Emigee couldn't have found a better location for a secret base with the facility surrounded on three sides by mountains leaving only one access point by land; of course, air transport was always an option. Unfortunately for them the disruptor field eliminated the possibility of an air attack. The plan devised was a solid one, having to rely on split second timing all the operatives involved were the very best and had years of experience pulling off successful ops. Kaazi was waiting for all teams to relay their readiness. Danek and Dirk's teams were responsible for setting primary explosives at the base of the mountains behind the facility where the fuel and generators were located. With the generators disabled, the disruptor field should be eliminated.

Secondary explosives would be set in the facility after the Lovell's were rescued. Kaazi's team which included Jace, Ali'kram, and a few others for back up were to gain access without drawing attention to themselves, find the Lovell's, set the explosives and escape. Waiting at the snowmobiles outside the perimeter fencing was Htiaf and Epoh. They were to guard their escape vehicles, so everyone made it to the transport pads safely.

It was decided that the op would be implemented at 0300 hours; everyone except the night guard would be sleeping—hopefully.

For days, Si'kram had been on edge ever since Nadroj arrived then the raging blizzard swept through. He didn't know if it was because he hated the violently whipping wind howling eerily through the mountains with snow striking like razor-sharp claws, or if his uneasiness was due to not having been able to reach the girl yet. Nadroj would not be put off indefinitely. Even though Nadroj had achieved a measure of patience over the years his temper, when unleashed, was lethal. Deprived of sleep these last few days, in turmoil, his agitation was consuming him. Well, if he couldn't sleep, no one else would either. Rousing his men, all but the gate guards, to put them through drill training would ease the tension. It was one way to work off the pent-up anxiety that had been plaguing him since the storm. Si'kram always engaged in combat drills with his men to assure he was at the peak of his ability.

Si'kram's soldiers reluctantly formed up, all the while grumbling to themselves, they wouldn't dare utter a complaint aloud; Si'kram would dole out severe punishment at such insubordination. Secretly hoping for a complaint so he could inflict his merciless punishment on an unsuspecting prey to relive his anxiety, he was disappointed when no one said a word. For two hours without rest, they trained leaving only the minimum guard posted outside. Security of the complex was at a minimum, one on the right side of the entrances and the other on the left side. Normally the perimeters would be attended to by no less than six soldiers.

◆◆◆

Kaazi couldn't believe it, only two soldiers on guard. This op is going to be a snap, he thought.

"Is everyone in place?" Kaazi asked as he got affirmative responses from Danek and Dirk who each had their operatives spread around the perimeters of the complex, forty men total.

"We are ready Kaazi," Jace said as he was waiting with Ali'kram and the five operatives making up his team.

"All clear here," Epoh answered, guarding the snowmobiles with Htiaf and several operatives to assure escape was possible.

"Execute plan," Kaazi ordered as he joined Jace, Ali'kram, and the rest of his team. Making their way down the left side of the mountain slope to the perimeter fence, one of the men cut an opening to gain access. Ali'kram gathered the wind into a funnel cloud and took out the guard on the left first then move to incapacitate the one on the right. With perfect control neither man knew what hit them, others moved in to secure them. Recon done before the blizzard hit indicated an interesting target, Jace noted a window with bars, the only one with bars in the whole complex. It seemed the obvious place to gain entrance to free the Lovell's. That was the target, the window with bars.

Making their way to the target, tensions were high. Reaching their mark, Ali'kram worked quickly taking the e-sive filaments from the cylindrical container, wrapping them securely around the bars covering the windows. Within seconds, the bars were dissolved. Both Kaazi and Jace attacked the window, securing the e-sive filaments to the glass by pressing it firmly in place. Flawlessly they worked, quickly forming the large rectangle that would allow them access to the room beyond. Again, within seconds the glass dissolved allowing them entrance into the interior room. Darkness permeated every inch of the inscrutably still room. The team entered quietly through the window; Kaazi leading followed by Jace and Ali'kram. The others brought up the rear, two holding position at the window and the others took up posts at the door.

Kaazi and Jace approached the bed and slipped their hands over Martin and Ena's mouth; unwilling to take the chance that the Lovell's would inadvertently alert the guards. Ena was immediately awake staring into Jace's eyes.

He said, "Shhh…we're her to rescue you." The fear in her eyes immediately turned to relief. Jace removed his hand from her mouth and said, "Are you alright?"

"I'm fine but Martin is hurt, they beat him. I think he's got internal injuries, I'm sure he is bleeding. I don't think he is going to make it," she said as she began to tear. Jace looked over at Kaazi for confirmation.

Kaazi was moving his hands over Martin to determine the extent of the injuries he had sustained. "He has several broken ribs, broken nose, bleeding around his lungs and stomach, a small perforation of his small intestine. He is going to need all of us," Kaazi said as he turned to Ali'kram and asked for the mooka.

Jace explained to Ena that they were going to heal Martin and reassured her that he would be fine. A flood of relief surged through her, so much so that she grabbed Jace and hugged him tightly. After a few minutes, he guided her to a chair so that she could sit while they were working on Martin.

Gathering around Martin who was lying unconscious in bed, the team focused all their healing energy into the mooka. Slowly the mooka directed the regenerative energy into Martin repairing damaged tissue and broken bones. Not anticipating this delay, concern escalated. Having to heal one of them was going to take time, they were risking discovery; naturally it was causing a great deal of anxiety among the team. His injuries were extensive; to heal such injuries could not be rushed. Kaazi felt the apprehension in the men. Urging them to focus on the healing, he reassured them that it was the right thing to do. Martin responded well to the mooka's focused healing energy. After what seemed like hours, Martin was completely healed and awake.

"What's going on? Who are you People?" Martin asked. Fear was welling up within him, especially since he couldn't see Ena.

"It's okay Martin," Ena said as she raced to his side. "They are here to rescue us. Some of them even worked for us on the ranch, Jace, Kaazi, and Ali'kram. Do you remember them?"

"Um…yes…yes, I remember. How am I able to sit up without the pain?" Martin responded, full of unanswered questions, he glanced around the room until his eyes met Kaazi.

"Martin, I know you must be tired, but we have to get you and Ena out of here…NOW! Do you have coats?" Kaazi asked in an urgent whisper.

"No, we are never allowed outside," Ena said.

"Hurry…get dressed…put the warmest clothes on that you have and wrap yourselves in blankets. It's very cold outside," Kaazi urged. Then he turned to focus his attention on the team. Gathering by the window to receive new instructions, he immediately rattled off orders.

"Si'tee, you and Lok take Martin and Ena to Htiaf and Epoh and wait for us there. The rest of us will set the explosives within the complex then follow. If we aren't back within fifteen minutes get the Lovell's to safety," Kaazi ordered.

The wind was whistling as it carried snow spiraling into the air. Dancing gracefully upon the thermals, the snow sparkled in the moonlight, glistening like stardust in a child's fantasy. Htiaf was pacing back and forth, every few minutes stopping to look toward the complex, anxiety building. The longer it took to retrieve the Lovell's, the greater the risk of discovery.

"What's taking so long? It shouldn't be taking so long!" Htiaf said more to himself than to Epoh. His uneasiness was escalating as his patience was losing ground.

Epoh trying to reassure his friend said, "There is no sign that they are in trouble, no additional guards deployed. Any number of things could have delayed them. Maybe the Emigee invited them to tea."

Htiaf stopped his pacing, turned to look at Epoh laughing on the snowmobile, and burst out laughing himself. What a thought sitting down with the Emigee and having a civilized conversation. All Htiaf had ever known about the Emigee is their violent, militant nature. The fact that they wanted to exterminate the Tè`relleans had become the reality of their existence. Blaming the Tè`relleans for their current circumstances was unfounded. His people were peaceful. They never did any harm to the Emigee, all those millennium ago his people and the Emigee were one people. The explorers chose to leave earth to seed the galaxy, to settle on other worlds, to forge a new existence. No one forced them into leaving their home. Because this one group of explorers out of all the others was met with tragedy and hardship, they blamed us, their forefathers for their misfortune, thus wanting to exact revenge. If they would only sit down and talk over tea, we might make a start for peace and possibly reunification, he surmised.

Epoh broke into Htiaf's reflection, "Look Si'tee and Lok are coming back out of the window. Jace is handing Si'tee a blanket...why would he be handing Si'tee a blanket?"

"Look closer... it's a very pregnant Ena!" Htiaf said as he tapped Epoh on the shoulder.

"Jace is handing another blanket to Lok, it must be Martin," Epoh said. "I wonder why Lok is carrying Martin...he must be injured."

"That must be why it was taking so long...healing one of them was not part of the plan," Htiaf concluded as he watched the operatives help the Lovell's toward the snowmobiles.

As soon as the Lovell's were out of the building, Jace and the team started placing explosives throughout the building. Kaazi, Jace, and Ali'kram took the east side of the complex while the others went to the west side. The place was like a maze. The trio planted the charges at junctions to inflict the most damage and to cut off access points. As they went down a long corridor, they noticed a light at the end of the hallway. Muffled voices were coming from the room. As they approached the door, they were stunned. Through the narrow rectangular slits of glass embedded in the door, the trio watched the Emigee train for combat.

"*It's 0400, the middle of the night, and they are up training!*" Ali'kram thought to the others.

"*We didn't plan for that!*" Jace projected back.

"*Let's set the rest of the charges and get out of here,*" Kaazi conveyed to the others.

As they set the last explosive and started back toward the Lovell's cell, an alarm went off suddenly. Instantaneously they started running, the Emigee were flooding out of the training room from several directions, weapons in hand, ready for battle; they swarmed the corridors. Swiftly making their way through the halls, almost to the cell and escape, they came face to face with Ki as he was racing toward them shouting the warning, "THE PRISONERS ESCAPED...INTRUDERS...THE PRISONERS ESCAPED... THE TE'RELLEANS ARE HERE!"

Ki had been out, up in the mountains, when he came across the camp of Te`relleans. They had spread out through the whole area; he had difficulty returning to the facility. Dressed in a white parka, blending into the landscape was his saving grace. To get back, he had to duck and hide, several times he was almost discovered, but the fresh snow provided the cover he needed to return and sound the alarm.

Grinning as he drew closer to the Te`relleans, Ki was ready for a slaughter. Drawing his blade for battle his eyes gleamed, delighted now to have real adversaries to kill. He lunged forward. Kaazi was the first to encounter Ki, blocking his attack he threw Ki back into the wall. Undeterred Ki sprang back with his cat-like reflexes and sliced Ali'kram in his right arm. Jace stopped to help Ali'kram while Kaazi was trying to hold off the horde of Emigee that had caught up to them with fire. Again, Ki lunged toward Ali'kram, the blade directed toward his heart, but was deflected by Jace. Anger filled Jace, levitating Ki in the air he threw him into the Emigee behind him being pelted with a barge of fire.

Suddenly, a voice bellowed, "I want them alive!" Having been awakened by the alarm Nadroj and his guard had entered the complex to see what was happening.

Kaazi, Jace, and Ali'kram had not noticed his arrival; they were trapped between the Emigee leader and his soldiers. A hopeless situation with diamortic weapons trained on them. Even with all their skill, they wouldn't survive close proximity hits from DM's. With the sudden appearance of Nadroj and the split-second distraction it afforded, a lone soldier maneuvered into position grabbing Alik`ram. Out of options for the moment, they offered little resistance with Alik`ram captured.

Kaazi quickly projected his thoughts to Htiaf and Epoh, ***"Get the Lovell's to safety...NOW!"***

"We can't just leave them!" Epoh said to Htiaf, urgently looking for agreement.

"You heard Kaazi we need to get Martin and Ena out of here," he barked. "Danek and Dirk are still here. When an opportunity presents itself, they will attempt a rescue. Now let's go!"

By this time, the Emigee soldiers were pouring out into the yard surveying the perimeters for intruders. As the snowmobiles started, one of the guards shouted, "There they are...get to the hes'chalas." Several soldiers were running to the transports ships to follow in pursuit.

Htiaf and Epoh were racing to the transport pads with Martin and Ena in tow. Htiaf had to travel slower than Epoh since Martin was weak and having difficulty hanging on to him. Ena was gripping Epoh tightly knowing that for the sake of the baby she needed to escape at any cost, but her heart was drawn to Martin. Struggling to hold on, she could see him wavering. The rest of the team held back a bit attempting to take out those following on snow vehicles. After what seemed like hours on the snowmobiles, the hes'chalas were seen in the sky, gaining ground, the transport ships would catch them within seconds.

Epoh could now see the transporter pad, freedom and escape. Just then, a hes'chala was hovering above them and sent out a pulse wave that shut down the snowmobiles. Epoh and Htiaf frantically attempted to restart the engines to no avail...they were dead. So close to freedom, about 100 yards away, they could make it, hope surged.

Htiaf shouted, "Let's make a run for it!" He grabbed Martin, half carrying half dragging him; they headed toward the transporter pad. Epoh and Ena were also running, although Ena could do little more than waddle. The snow was so deep; sinking with every step they took, the snow was sucking them in like quicksand. Struggling against the elements, the snow, the wind, and the cold was taking its toll on Martin and with the added weight of the baby Ena's breathing was labored. Trudging through, the only thought in her mind was escape, she pressed forward with Epoh's help.

"We are almost there...about fifty more feet," Epoh encouraged her as he helped her through the snow. Behind them she could see Htiaf dragging Martin, the snow was to deep and the trauma to his body had been severe, he was just too weak, but he was determined, trying to catch up to them, refusing to give up. She noticed how much Martin was struggling to stay upright, forcing himself to move forward. Her heart went out to him, she was struggling herself; she knew there was nothing she could do to help except to keep moving forward.

With a loud thunderous roar, the hes'chala landed between them and the transporter pad. Immediately, there was a flood of Emigee soldiers surrounding them. Martin slumped to the ground in defeat, Ena raced to his side, while Epoh and Htiaf stood over them protectively.

Epoh watched the Emigee intently, sure that they would be killed. To his surprise, they were ordered into the ship.

"This is unexpected," he thought to Htiaf as he helped Ena to her feet, *"I thought for sure they would kill us and take the Lovell's back."*

"Yes...I agree. This is not the way they usually handle situations like this," Htiaf thought to Epoh while he was carrying Martin. Once in the ship, they were placed in a small room which looked like a dining area with two long cold metal tables, rectangular in shape with metal benches. Comfort was not the motif for Emigee dinning, cold, hard functionality. No room for comfort in the lifestyle the Emigee soldier, apparently, they were accustomed to militant simplicity, at its best. Exhausted Martin was helped to one of the tables to rest.

"Now what happens?" Ena asked looking for some kind of reassurance from her would be rescuers, but none came.

"I assume we are being brought back to the complex," Htiaf said as he was examining Martin.

Chapter

Surrounded by the enemy, time and unforeseen occurrences befall us all. Plagued with problems from the beginning, this op had gone from bad to worse. What were they going to do now? Kaazi, Jace, and Ali'kram were taken to the combat training room where the other members of his team had been brought. Surrounded by Emigee soldiers with firearms trained on them, the others immediately inquired about orders when Kaazi entered the room.

"Do nothing for now, there are too many of them. Our telekinetic abilities cannot ward off so many weapons unless we are in formation. I doubt very much they will allow us to get that close to each other. Stay alert when an opportunity presents itself be ready!" Kaazi said.

Nadroj and Si'kram approached Kaazi, Jace, and Ali'kram. Behind the two Emigee leaders were Hamer, Ja'nek, Ki, and Camden. Ki was salivating profusely, wanting to tear the trio apart, bloodlust pulsating through his body, restraint barely containing his faculties. Hamer and Ja'nek standing firm, no clues as to their opinion, not that it would matter with their leaders in the forefront, but Camden was visibly distressed, about what, they could only imagine.

"Who are you?" Nadroj asked in a calm methodical tone. None of the team answered. Nadroj knew who they were and why they were there.

Nonetheless, Si'kram pointed to the trio and mockingly sneered, "Te`rellean operatives…huh…these are supposed to be their best…this one is Kaazi, team leader, arrogant and cocky…not so cocky, now are you?" The Emigee soldiers bellowed with laughter at the humiliation Si'kram was attempting to inflict.

"This one is Ali'kram, skillful and quiet, quite a capable soldier, but not good enough today…" Si'kram jeered, Nadroj glaring intently.

"This one is special, he has feelings for the girl and she for him. Jace is his name," Si'kram said as he began to thoroughly examine him. Jace was fuming, being reminded of Ari, the reason she was so determined to attempt the trials was because of them, it was too much, especially, since this op went so terribly wrong; he didn't even know if Martin and Ena had escaped.

"Easy Jace…he's just trying to rile you into doing something stupid," Kaazi cautioned as he projected his thoughts.

"Ah…we will be able to use this one as leverage against the girl," Nadroj arrogantly announced to his soldiers.

Jace could stay silent no longer, "What do you want with Ari?" he demanded arrogantly.

"The boy has spirit…I like that, so I will tell you why I want the girl. Years ago, we obtained information that the Te`rell had a weapon that would destroy my people. We sent out our best soldiers to find and destroy it. We were assured that the truck in which it was being transported was destroyed, completely," Nadroj relayed as he gave a pointed glare to Hamer.

"What does that have to do with Ari?" Jace demanded impatiently.

"Earlier this year, we discovered an unusual set of circumstances revolving around a young girl raised as a human but is in actuality a Te`rellean. Somehow, the Te`rell discovered she was alive and sent their best operatives to guard her…I had to ask myself why…why would they do that…what is so special about this girl?" he explained as he shrugged his shoulders, "If she was that important to the Te`rell, then naturally I must have her. The obscurity of these circumstances makes me conclude one thing—she is the weapon!"

Jace was beyond restraint, beyond consolation, "Well you can't have her… she's dead!" he shouted. Just as the words left his lips, Martin and Ena were brought into the room followed by Htiaf and Epoh. Ena gasped at hearing Jace's words. She clutched Martin's arm.

"Who's dead?" Ena blurted out. Epoh moved to help support her. "Well… well…well…it seems our prisoners haven't escaped after all," Nadroj jeered, "Well my dear it seems your Te`rellean daughter is dead."

Tears instantly streamed down Ena's face. She flung herself into Martin's arms as he attempted to console her, his heart breaking too. The site of this one human couple had an amazingly profound effect on those around them.

The plethora of emotions stirred many of the Emigee soldiers to question the wisdom of their actions especially Hamer, Camden, and Ja'nek. Years of hardship and misfortune before the Emigee returned to Earth had made them cold and rigid in their outlook. Since returning home, circumstances had changed. They have made good lives for themselves here with little interference from the Te`rell. It's even possible their claim to peace is valid and should be explored, many of them thought.

"How touching…but since the girl is dead, they really aren't of any use to us anymore are they…" Nadroj said speaking out loud more to himself than anyone else.

Panic embraced the Te`relleans; Martin and Ena were in mortal danger now that their usefulness had ended. Htiaf and Epoh moved closer to the Lovell's in a protective stance. Heightened tension was noted among the Emigee. Alik'ram and Kaazi were surveying reactions trying to determine if any of the Emigee felt strong enough to oppose Nadroj. To their surprise, there were.

"Kaazi…did you notice the reactions of Camden and Hamer?" Alik'ram projected.

"Yeah…I saw the jaw tighten and the fist clench. We might have possible allies in those two…Ja'nek's reaction to Nadroj was not as severe, but I got the impression he didn't like what he heard," Kaazi replied.

"Take them to the yard and have them eliminated," Nadroj ordered. If he couldn't have the girl, there was no reason to keep the humans alive any longer. He could be finished with this business by the end of the day, move on to more pressing business.

"What about the Te`rell?" Si'kram asked wanting to have an opportunity to interrogate them, then enjoy the satisfaction of watching them suffer under the ishta's skillful torture.

"Eliminate them too! I want this mess behind us…I have more important matters to deal with.

"Father...please...reconsider...Let me take the Lovell's home. They can't hurt us if we let them go," Camden pleaded as he glanced at Hamer.

Gruffly with disgust and irritation Nadroj barked, "No...we have had this discussion before, and I will not have it again. They must be eliminated. Not another word before you embarrass yourself and me." Camden was silenced, dismissed without another thought. His anger blazed at the injustice. Martin and Ena didn't deserve this end. He had to do something... but what?

"Nadroj...would it not be prudent to interrogate the Te`rell before we eliminate them?" Si'kram asked, hoping for the opportunity to break one of them.

"Do what you want with them Si'kram but make them all watch the execution of the humans. I want them to realize just how much they failed in their plans," Nadroj growled.

"*This is perfect,*" Kaazi projected to is team. "*They are going to take us outside to watch the execution. We will be away from the building, we can execute the contingency plan, stay together as much as possible,*" Kaazi ordered.

"*Jace are you okay...I know this has been hard on you, but you need to focus now. We are only going to get one shot at saving them,*" Kaazi thought to Jace.

"*I'm fine now. I'll do whatever it takes to save them,*" Jace said in reply. Gaining control over his emotions, he chastised himself for letting Nadroj get under his skin. Ari was still an extremely sensitive topic for Jace to deal with; the constant jeering and chiding from the Emigee only fueled his volatility.

As they were being herded out into the yard, Martin and Ena embraced, he whispered to her, "I'm sorry about all of this Ena. I would give anything if things could be different."

"Shhh...there is nothing you could have done Martin," she said through tears.

"I want you to know that you are the love of my life, my heart, my soul, my whole reason for existing. Our years together have been the happiest of my life. Living without you would be futile; you give meaning to my existence. I love you now and for all time, even death will not be able to extinguish our love; you are my life," Martin said from the depths of his soul as he embraced Ena with all the intense passion he felt.

Tears streaming down her cheeks she held tight to Martin, as if gaining strength from the love they shared.

"My only regret Martin is that we won't be able to share our child. The child I have longed to give you; the miracle growing in me from a lifetime of love and passion. This child should be the culmination of our love and existence, our legacy. To be snuffed out before even being born is unthinkable. I love you Martin, more than I can possibly express with words, I will love you for an eternity," whispered Ena tenderly, compassionately from the depths of her heart.

Out in the yard, the Emigee soldiers pushed the Te`rell to the side as they marched Martin and Ena to the execution wall, actually a hanger door where supplies were kept. Several soldiers stood in front of them with weapons in hand.

Nadroj stepped forward and asked, "Any last words?" He had a passion for the dramatic.

"Your cruelty and injustice will be your downfall. Those who cannot show love and compassion are destined for ruination and defeat. You have failed, you just don't know it yet," Martin said boldly, holding Ena in his arms.

"Nice words…but you could not be more wrong. A glimpse of the future that you won't be around to see I will give you. My people have control of the world governments, financial institutions, and military powers. We have manipulated them to our advantage for thousands of years. Our plan is to wipe out your friends the Te`rell and significantly reduce the population of humans by controlled genocide. Transforming the human population into a slave race, we will be the masters. This is what is in store for the very near future you won't be around to see," Nadroj taunted. Nodding to Si'kram, he signaled to finish it.

"*Get ready…this is our chance!*" Kaazi warned. All teams were ready and waiting.

"Soldiers…take aim," Si'kram commanded, "FI…"

Before he could finish saying the word, the ground began to tremble around the soldiers in the firing line. Trying to keep their balance and carry out their orders was no easy task, they were rocking back and forth, unstable, some falling to the ground. Earth snaked and twisted upward around the soldiers like creeping vines until they were completely encased in hard clay-like soil. They felt as if they had been entombed in solid brick. Panic struck the Emigee as others rushed to free them.

"What's going on?" said Jace. He had never seen the earth react in such a focused manner before, neither did his companions.

"I don't know," said Kaazi watching intently, looking around for any sign of an outside presence.

"Kill the humans," Si'kram ordered. Several men responded to the order, took aim and fired their weapons toward Martin and Ena. Before the blast reached them, a flat reflective crystal barrier formed between the Lovell's and the Emigee, deflecting the energy blast back at the soldiers.

"What is happening?" Nadroj shouted, losing his long-controlled patience. Soldiers dashing here, running there, all were trying to avoid being hit with the ricocheting energy blasts.

"It's the Te`rell, they are doing this!" Si'kram barked using the Te`rell as a scapegoat. As with any prejudice or conflict, enemies on opposing sides were at fault, whether it was true or not didn't matter.

"I don't think it's them. They are just as surprised and confused as we are," said Camden. Watching Kaazi, Jace and the others, Camden realized they had no idea what was happening.

"Kill the Te`rell!" Nadroj ordered in the pandemonium. Only a few of the Emigee heard the order since the others were distracted by a series of explosions behind the complex.

With the generators down, the disruptor field collapsed. Secondary operatives took up positions on whiff-jets and hover platforms for an aerial assault. Blasting the Emigee with a barrage of fire streams, wind funnels, and ice balls, they provided cover for the operatives on the ground. With the chaos that ensured, Kaazi, Jace, and the rest of the team were able to defend themselves.

Hamer, Camden, and Ja'nek attempted to reach Martin and Ena to free them but were unable to get close to them. The crystal barrier was protecting them from the stray weapons fire which was being deflected. As the Te`relleans were protecting themselves, random energy blasts were coming from all directions. Danek and Dirk's teams were moving in to help Kaazi's team who were in the midst of the fighting, but the Emigee were in such chaos they didn't need the help. The earth was selectively encircling the Emigee soldiers, wrapping long, hard clay-like tendrils around their legs, up their bodies, to immobilize them. Even Si'kram was caught by one tendril as he attempted to free his men.

As the fighting continued, no one noticed the lone figure walking through the gate; the white parka blending into the landscape was an effective camouflage. Boldly, the mysterious figure stood in the midst of the Te'rell and Emigee who gradually focused on this intruder. Who was this person with the audacity to approach the fighting alone with no apparent weapons? The weapons fire decreased to a minimum, only a few Emigee were not contained by the earth, the Te'relleans stopped fighting to discover the identity of this enigma.

The hood of the parka was lowered revealing beautiful red hair with golden highlights. Everyone in the complex gasped. Jace was shocked at seeing the beautiful face of the one person he thought he would never see again. A torrent of emotions surged through him, he was so happy to see her; there were no words to express how he felt the moment he saw her standing in the midst of the complex.

"Ari…you're alive!" Jace projected to her. He was elated but she was in the midst of fifty Emigee soldiers even though they were mostly subdued.

"Yes…Jace…I will explain everything to you but first we must get my parents to safety."

Ari turned her attention to the Emigee, Nadroj in particular. She boldly looked at Nadroj who was momentarily stunned by her beauty. His entire life had been filled with beautiful women, human and Emigee alike, but he had never before seen anyone who personified beauty as she did, perfect were her features, he was mesmerized.

"Who are you?" Nadroj asked, intrigued by her presence.

"I am Ariella Lovell. I've come for my parents."

"So, the Te'rell lied…they said you were dead." Nadroj sneered confirming in his mind that the Te'rell could not be trusted.

"They did not lie…they did think I was dead, but obviously I'm not," Ari said, "Why are you fighting?"

"We have a long history of fighting. We fight to survive."

"The way of peace is better. Can we not live in peace together?" Ari asked hoping he would listen and reason with her. Watching his manner, she thought that it was a lost cause, but she would try.

"It is not possible. Too much has transpired between our people for us to have peace…No, we must destroy the Te'rell and their human pets," Nadroj growled letting his pride overrule his reason. Hatred, it was the only thing he had left, it had to burgeon so his people could flourish.

"We were once one people... we can be one people again. Let us work together in peace to benefit both our peoples," Ari pleaded. She would find a way to make peace with these people, but this man, their leader was not going to listen to reason.

"Who are you that you can negotiate peace for your people? You didn't even know you were Te`rellean until earlier this year," he sneered mockingly at her.

"What you said is true. I didn't know that I was Te`rellean until this year. Nonetheless, I am the Legate to my people' from the time I was born, it is what I am," she said courageously, embracing her true self, accepting her role as peacemaker.

"Legate...my people don't need your peace. We have our own plans and they don't include peace with the Te`rell," Nadroj growled. He raised his hand and then closed his fist. "This is what I think of your peace."

Clamped like a vice, the air was cut off from her lungs; a tightening grip around Ari's throat was slowly starving her lungs, suffocation; the precious air she needed to survive—gone. Gasping for air, she felt the life draining from her body. With no relief, a feeling of dizziness overtook her as if she was teetering on a precipice about to fall. Dirk and Danek had been watching the exchange and realized before anyone else what was happening, that Nadroj was squeezing the life from Ari. The others went to her side to see what was wrong. Immediately, Dirk and Danek set-off the secondary explosives which distracted Nadroj long enough to release his hold on Ari.

Relief surged through Ari along with much needed air. She was not going to give him a second chance to attack her. The ground moved under Nadroj as tendrils wrapped themselves around him, securing his arm and covering his mouth, to ensure he could not hurt anyone or bark orders. Ari went over to Nadroj, stood before him defiantly and looked into his eyes. The meaning was clear. He had not seen or heard the last of her.

"We will have peace! You will leave my family alone and you will call off your people from Zenot!" she said with conviction. Ari then turned and walked over to her parents. The crystal barrier fell as she approached them.

"Ari!" her parents cried. "They said you were dead." Ari embraced them, relief surged through her, after months of worry to see them alive and well, she was overcome with joy, as tears filled her eyes.

"I'm fine…are you two okay?" Ari asked as she held them tight, happiness filled the air. As she placed her hand on Ena's swollen belly, she was so thankful they were alive, and Ena was still pregnant.

"We are fine," Martin said. "Actually, Hamer and Ja'nek have been taking very good care of us this whole time. Now, Ari was shocked, but the shock turned to hope. If two notorious Emigee operatives could display such kindness to her parents perhaps there was hope for peace between their people.

Kaazi, Alik'ram, Htiaf, and Epoh were waiting their turn to welcome Ari back. Jace was standing back a little to let the others see her. Epoh grabbed Ari and hugged her so hard she gasped.

"I missed you to Epoh," Ari said as they laughed together. It was so good to see all of them; it seemed as if she were gone for months. Each of them embraced her to welcome her back from the dead.

Each asking questions as to what happened, where she had been, how she knew to come here.

"I promise I will answer all of your questions, but let's get my parents to safety first," she said as she started coaxing her parents to move toward the exit.

"Those were some neat tricks you picked-up." Kaazi said as he gave her his signature grin.

"Liked that did you?" She said as she returned the grin.

With a swift cat-like pounce, Ki with blade drawn jumped toward Ari poised to kill. The team as one using their collective TK flung him into the building. Landing forcefully into debris from the explosions, surprise emanated from his face as he looked down at his chest. Protruding from the center was a metal pipe dripping with blood. Impaled, he had been impaled by the Te`rell were his last thoughts as he went limp, a fitting end to such an evil maniacal foe.

"Let's get out of here," shouted Kaazi, "Grab Nadroj and Si'kram, we will take them back with us."

"They're gone," yelled Alik`ram looking around hoping to spot them. Nowhere to be found; only Emigee soldiers still encased in earth were left which filled the whole complex.

"Never mind, let's get out of here," said Kaazi.

Danek and Dirk arrived with snowmobiles. "Anyone need a lift?" Dirk asked. Kaazi started barking out orders. Htiaf and Epoh helped the Lovell's onto the snowmobiles. Jace approached Ari and embraced her for the first time. Too emotional for words; he took her hand and led her to one of the snowmobiles to ride together.

"Hurry, let's get out of here!" Ari said. With a roar, several snowmobiles with attached sleds sped away leaving the Emigee immobilized by the earth unable to do anything but watch as they disappeared over the horizon.

Reaching the transport pads, Ari was finally able to relax a bit. Holding on to Jace, savoring the moment, she never wanted to let go. It seemed as if she hadn't seen him in years. Struggling with his emotions, she felt the turmoil within him, trying to give him time to adjust, she remained silent. Suddenly, a loud scream permeated the air which startled everyone into silence, then instantly to high alert.

It was Ena, she had been walking to the transport pad with Epoh's help when she clutched her belly, screamed, and fell to her knees in the snow.

She called out, "Martin…" then passed out. Martin hurried over to her. He checked her all over; she was breathing. The blanket had fallen open; he noticed she had blood on her pants—it was the baby!

Ari raced over to them, "What's wrong?" she cried.

"It's the baby…she is bleeding!" Martin said tears in his eyes. He was terrified; after all these months of captivity, they were free. This was not supposed to happen, she had to be alright—she just had too.

"We need to get her to the med-plex," Ari said. "Jace can you set the transport to send us directly there." He nodded as he hurried to set the pad. Epoh picked Ena up while Htiaf helped Martin. Ari and Jace were already on the pad. The six of them glimmered out of sight.

Chapter

Arriving at the med-plex in a glimmer of light, Jace started barking orders. "We have a bleeding pregnant woman here. We need assistance!" Hurrying off the grid platform, Jace scanned the area, "Epoh put her on the hov-bed."

Epoh carried Ena over to a stretcher as the medical staff approached. They moved swiftly, as they were assessing the situation. One of the staff turned her attention to Martin and he began a tirade of chatter.

"Slow down and tell me what happened," she said encouraging him to calm down so she could determine the problem.

"She has been under a lot of stress throughout her pregnancy. We were finally rescued, and she collapsed. She's bleeding!" Martin said frantically as he explained what happened to the woman.

"We will take care of her, check the status of the baby, and run some tests to determine what's wrong. When is she due to deliver?" one of the doctors asked as she approached.

"She isn't due for two months," Martin said tears filling his eyes. A mountain of conflicting emotions bombarded him, the culmination of all that had happened to them, the captivity, torture, worry, injuries, this was the last blow; it was all collapsing in on him in full force. Losing his grip, his control, he felt it was all sliding away. If something happened to Ena or the baby, he wouldn't be able to go on, he knew it; he was afraid, no not afraid, stone cold mortified.

"Martin…we can wait over here," Htiaf supportively guided Martin into a waiting area. Weak, pale and diaphoretic, Martin was frail and debilitated. Htiaf was worried about him, not having had time to rest and recuperate after the healing, he could relapse.

"Can I get you anything…something to eat or drink?" Epoh asked noticing the same.

"No…I'm okay," Martin said as he shook his head. Holding his head in his hands he was too worried to think about food or anything else for that matter. Minutes seemed like hours, what was taking so long, he thought.

Jace stepped in and firmly insisted, "Epoh…get Martin soup and a sandwich. It's essential that he eats since we had to heal him; he hasn't had anything to eat or drink since and he needs to get his strength back, he needs rest too." Having a feeling they would be there a while, he decided to get some food for everyone.

Ari was consoling Martin when she noticed Jace watching her. She smiled at him but could tell he was upset.

"When Epoh comes back with the food, I want you to eat. After the healing process, your body needs food and rest," she explained to Martin who just nodded in agreement.

Ari went over to Jace, took his hand and lead him to a private corner in the waiting area. Feeling the turmoil he was experiencing, it was so prevalent she was sure everyone else knew the pain that consumed him; she wanted to put him at ease, comfort him.

"What can I do to make this easier for you Jace?" Ari asked. Her eyes big and bright, lovingly gazing at Jace, intently coaxing, pleading for him to open up to her. She was terrified that he would withdrawal from her completely, guarding himself from the pain, the pain of losing her, so much so, that he overtly pushes her away.

"There really isn't anything you can do Ari. It is something I have to work out for myself…I thought you were dead…you can't imagine what that did to me…I nearly lost my mind. What happened to you?" Jace asked wanting to know everything.

"When I was in the trial chamber, I felt like I was going to die. It was as if I was being torn apart from both the inside and outside. I didn't know what to do except keep resisting. It wasn't until I surrendered myself to the earth that I was able to make the transformation. The transformation is incredible; every cell in my body changed. My guide explained that those who survive the trial go through a transphasic metamorphic cellular alignment," she explained.

"Your guide…who was your guide?" Jace asked, never having heard about any kind of guide before from those who had undergone the trials.

"My guide is an ancient woman from before the invasion of the Emigee. She has instructed all who have been successfully transformed. Her name is Lark," Ari said.

"Lark…you were with her this whole time? Why didn't you let anyone know you were alive?" Jace asked trying to remain calm.

"Yes…I was with Lark this whole time. When I was with her, time seemed not to exist. I had no conception of time and didn't realize how much time had elapsed. To me it was like a blink of an eye. Honestly, Jace, even though she showed me many places, I assumed I was still in the trial chamber," Ari said as she continued to explain what had happened to her.

"So, you thought we were out in the external chamber still waiting for you," Jace said with a touch of bitterness that Ari couldn't have mistaken for anything but resentment. She sighed; she knew he was hurt and wanted to fix it but didn't know how.

"I'm sorry you were worried…" Ari started to say when Jace exploded.

"Worried…I wasn't worried…I was devastated…in shock…out of my mind that I had lost you!" He said through clenched teeth, seething but trying very hard to keep his voice down so as not to concern the others. He could have used his telepathy, but he was to upset for that kind of connection with Ari just then.

"I'm sorry Jace…I didn't do it on purpose. I had no perception of how much time went by," Ari said emotions spewing.

"You didn't do it on purpose? I beg to differ…you were determined to go through the trials knowing full well that it was possible you wouldn't survive. You didn't care about anyone but yourself and going through the trials!" Jace exclaimed in full fury, unleashing the full extent of his pain on Ari.

"What are you talking about…I didn't care for anyone but myself. I went through the trial of Earth for our people, not myself. You know full well that to truly be the Legate I have to complete all four trials. I didn't make up the rules. Our people have suffered enough. If I can help end the war between us and the Emigee, I have to try. I have three more trials to complete, Jace. How are you going to handle them? You know that just because I survived the trial of earth doesn't mean I will automatically survive the others. It is something I have to do, it's my duty to our people; it's my responsibility as Legate to complete what I have started. If we are going to continue to have a relationship, you have to find a way to deal with what I must do," Ari said with determination. This was not turning out how she wanted it to, but Jace had to understand that she had an obligation to help her people the same as he did.

"Well, maybe you should do it without me by your side. I can't stand by and watch you kill yourself!" Jace exclaimed, his emotions riding high. He didn't want to explode at Ari the way he was, but he couldn't help himself. Loving her so much, the thought of anything happening to her was unthinkable. It made him furious; he knew the obligation she felt toward their people, he felt the same way, but the path she was determined to take was dangerous. Once she got an idea in her head, it was impossible to change. Being pushed to the limits, he just didn't know if he could bear it. He needed to leave, go and calm down, think about everything that has happened and what will happen. Standing up, he looked at Ari and said, "I have to go…I need to think." Jace didn't wait for a response. He walked out the door just as Kaazi, Alik'ram, Gyasi, and Ari's parents were entering the med-plex.

Ari was close to tears as she watched Jace leave the building. Kaazi was the first to notice and went to her.

"Is Jace being and ass again?" Kaazi said with a frown which made Ari pause. She looked up at him and smiled. Gathering her into his arms, he held her and comforted her.

"He's hurt and he's blaming me," she said as the smile disappeared. Gyasi heard what she said, not surprised at Jace's reaction, he knew the turmoil of losing someone who means everything to you.

Ashi'nat and Ayotal rushed over to Ari and embraced her. Joy filled their eyes and happiness their hearts. She was back among her people, friends, and family.

"We are so relieved you are alive!" Ashi'nat said, "Your mother never doubted that you would be back."

"It's good to see you," Ayotal said, "You gave us quite a start when the trial door opened, and you were not there. We had never heard of someone disappearing from the chamber." Ayotal said as she was holding Ari in her arms.

Martin was watching and listening to everything around him as he was sitting with Epoh and Htiaf, but his mind was with Ena. What was taking so long, he thought. He needed some answers. Epoh sensed his increased agitation and decided to go in search of the healers.

Ari brought her parents over to meet Martin. Ashi'nat greeted him, "Mr. Lovell, I'm pleased to meet you. I'm sorry we have met under such difficult circumstances." Ashi'nat extended his hand in friendship which Martin accepted. He continued, "I can't tell you how grateful Ayotal and I are that Ari had such loving people to raise her. Ari has told us all about you and your wife…" Before Ashi'nat could finish, Epoh came back with the doctor.

"Mr. Lovell, your wife is fine, her water broke, and she is in the early stages of labor," the doctor explained.

"She's not due for two months, though," Martin said, concerned that it was too early for her to deliver.

"It's not uncommon for twins to be born early. Both babies have strong healthy heart beats," the doctor explained.

Martin was stunned, "Twins? Did I hear you say twins?"

"You didn't know she was carrying twins?" the doctor asked.

"Ahhhhh…NO! We were kidnapped before we had a chance to have any prenatal visits or ultrasounds," Martin said as a frantic panic and excitement slowly crept over him. He glanced to Ari who was smiling from ear to ear as she shrugged her shoulders.

"Well, there are definitely two babies there and they are both doing well," the doctor explained.

"Can I see her now?" Martin asked anxiously. The doctor smiled and led him off to see Ena.

"You must be exhausted?" Ayotal said to Ari as she watched. The joy of knowing Ena and Martin were safe disappeared from her face to be replaced by sadness and distress.

"I have a lot of things on my mind," Ari said as her mind drifted back to Jace.

"Speaking of which, Ashi'nat, Gyasi, there is something we have to discuss immediately," Kaazi said as he signaled Htiaf and Epoh to join them. Ayotal and Ari went to the garden outside the med-plex.

"During the rescue, Nadroj revealed his plans for the future. He was very confident we would not escape so he taunted the Lovell's with his plans for the future," Kaazi explained.

"What did he say?" Gyasi asked.

"He confirmed what we have suspected. The Emigee control the world's governments, financial institutions, and military powers. They have been manipulating them for thousands of years. He didn't mention specifics but there is a plan in the works to commit a controlled genocide, to significantly reduce the human population, thus transforming them into a slave class. We already know they want to exterminate us that hasn't changed. When he was taunting the Lovell's, he used the term 'very near future.' Something big is in the works and it will be soon," Kaazi explained.

"We must inform the consul," Ashi'nat said. "Gyasi check with our field operative to see if they have any information with regard to medical research, biochemical research, and genetic research. We do have operatives in all the major companies, right?"

"Yes, we do…we didn't want another incident like the one that transmutated the gorbas and nearly annihilated all of us when the Emigee unleashed the last virus," Gyasi said. He couldn't believe they would be foolish enough to set loose another virus.

"I want as much information as possible gathered to present to the consul when we meet," Ashi'nat said, he suspected that foreboding feeling he was having was going to have enormous repercussions.

"Kaazi, you and Alik'ram go to NOSSIC and start contacting our operatives. Take Htiaf and Epoh with you. Set up teams to gather information within the medical field but also setup teams to investigate the Emigee's influence in the governments with their military and the financial institutions controlling the world economy. I don't have to tell you the implications of an economic collapse among the humans—it would be utter chaos."

"That's exactly what the Emigee are hoping for, I'm sure," said Alik'ram having seen similar situations before, but this would have to be on a much grander scale.

After Kaazi and the others left, Ashi'nat and Gyasi lingered in conversation. While out in the garden, Ayotal was with Ari.

"I don't understand why Jace is blaming me for trying to help our people!" Ari exclaimed, emotions stirring.

"I don't think he really blames you for wanting to help our people, after all that is exactly what he has been doing for years," Ayotal said consolingly.

"I know he feels hurt but where is the anger coming from?" Ari asked as she struggled to understand.

"When the chamber door opened and you weren't there, Jace went into shock. He was speechless; he completely shut down mentally and emotionally. Ari, he didn't speak to anyone for days. We were all extremely worried about him. He shut everyone out, even Gyasi. Your father told me that Jace had subconsciously erected numerous barriers within his mind to keep everyone out, but especially the pain he felt. Gyasi didn't think he would be able to reach him, but eventually, Jace did allow a small line of communication with him, it was his lifeline," Ayotal explained.

"Like I said, I know he feels hurt, I obviously didn't know the extent of the hurt, but shouldn't he be relieved or happy that I'm not dead instead of angry?" Ari asked, desperately trying to make sense out of Jace's feelings.

"Everyone expresses their emotions differently. I think his anger comes from knowing how close you came to dying and him losing you. He knows you are determined to complete the trials and take your place as Legate. The danger involved is great, he knows that too. If you choose to continue in the path, your life will be subject to great perils and he is afraid for you, for himself, and for our people. Jace is still young...he's only five hundred and twenty-three. He has never dealt with the emotions of being in love with someone and building a relationship of mutual trust and respect. He's a good man; he will struggle to come to terms with his emotions and hopefully you will both be able to live with the results," Ayotal continued.

"I hope you are right. I don't want to lose him," Ari said. "He has got to understand how important it is to me to continue with the trials. Our people deserve peace and an end to the war with the Emigee."

"Yes...it has been such a long time. I can scarcely remember a time when I felt really secure and at peace. The war has taken its toll on all of us but especially on our world. Our home needs to be restored to balance. The Emigee and humans have destructively ruined the natural balance and beauty she provides. Time to heal is what is needed," Ayotal lamented.

Ashi'nat appeared in the garden, searching for his family. He approached the two beautiful women sitting on a bench under a miniature willow surrounded by a glorious array of dynamic color. The garden's flowers were in full bloom, delighting the senses, filling the air with sweet floral aromas meant to satiate the soul. The two people he loved most in this world before him, no man could be happier. He was more determined than ever to find a solution to the Emigee problem.

"Here you two are," Ashi'nat said with a loving smile. "Is everything alright?"

"We're fine," Ari said as she stood up from the bench to embrace her father.

"We were just discussing the nature of relationships," Ayotal said as she winked at Ashi'nat. "…and how our feelings can get a little mixed-up."

"I see," said Ashi'nat, knowing full well that last comment was meant for him, something Ayotal never let him forget since he himself let his feelings disrupt their relationship when it was in the its infancy. He quickly changed the subject. "Ari…I assume you will want to stay here until after the delivery."

"Yes…I want to be there for Martin and Ena," Ari said as she smiled lovingly at her father. After so much time in captivity, she wanted to be there, loving and supporting the two wonderful people who found her and loved her all these years.

"If you can get Martin to leave Ena, he can stay with us," Ayotal offered, tenderly caressing her cheek.

"Thank you for being so kind to them…I love you both so much," Ari said as she embraced them.

"We love you too. We will leave you so you can be with the Lovell's for a while," Ashi'nat said as he took Ayotal's hand, said their good-bye's and left.

Ari remained in the garden for a while reflecting on everything that had transpired. Her mind drifted back to the trial chamber, the moment she surrendered to the earth. Her body was exhausted from struggling to keep the barrier up to protect her from the onslaught of debris pelting her. She could still feel the stinging, clawing, ripping forces attacking her skin. She knew she was going to die but instead of giving up she embraced the onslaught, drawing it into her, when she did, the agonizingly painful assault stopped.

The earth with its diverse components continued to engulf her but it no longer inflicted pain. All Ari's senses were caressed, massaged with feather-like softness. Skin began to tingle as she watched her cells change from flesh to soil, then diamonds, then rubies. Continually changing until she truly was one with the earth.

The transformation was amazing; she felt the earth's pulse from its formation to the millenniums of peaceful existence with the Te`rell, through the destructive invasion of the Emigee. The devastation inflicted when the Emigee scorched the earth causing the imbalance within her. Radiation from their weapons seared the beauty of her surface. Over time our life-giving earth was slowly healing herself, then the Emigee discovered other destructive means to keep her unbalanced—the virus. Not only did it effect the Te`rell and the gorba, it furthered the destructive imbalance of the earth, mutating its natural fauna and flora. Throughout the ages the Emigee have been finding new ways to exploit the earth using the mutant gorba as the means to an end with their intense need to horde. Instead of using only what is needed, the humans have fought wars to possess resources others have, ripped open the earth to find her treasures, polluted the idyllic habitat which supported thousands of creatures some of which have become extinct. Something needed to be done to restore earth's balance; she is desperate to heal, to be returned to paradisiacal conditions.

After Ari felt all the anguish portrayed from the earth, she saw a beautiful woman walking toward her in the desert. The woman was tall with a slender frame, pale skin—a silky ivory. Her hair was a silvery white flowing down her back to below her knees. A natural curl, ringlets, gave her the appearance of a young child but this woman stood with the presence of authority, wisdom emanated from her face. No, this was no child—she was as old as the earth. When she smiled, her crystal blue eyes reflected the sun, just as she was radiating warmth and brilliance from her heart. Ari blinked her eyes, awed to see this incredibly beautiful woman standing above her in a gown so stunning it defied words. Iridescent splendor flowing down the length of the woman's body, the material was sheer and thin which gave the appearance of wings when caught by the wind. Several layers of deep rich bold iridescent colors, like a rainbow, dazzled her eyes.

Stretching out her hand she said, "Hello Ariella."

"Hello," Ari said, "How do you know my name?"

"You announced it at the beginning of your trial," said the woman as she chuckled to a bewildered Ari.

"Oh…I guess I did, didn't I," she said as she giggled to herself.

"My name is Lark. I am guide to those who successfully complete the trials. I was the first to become one with our precious world. I was guided, now I guide others," the woman explained.

"Lark…where did you come from and how did you bring me here?" Ari asked as she looked around. "Where is here?"

"I come from the earth, our life-giver. You were brought here to be taught. We are in what the humans call the Sahara Desert. I must show you the change, the imbalance which the Emigee and the humans have caused. It is one thing to see images of our world in your mind, it is quite another to experience the changes by use of our senses," Lark explained as she waved her hand. Instantly the landscape changed from a dry barren sandy desert to a lush green humid savannah teaming with wildlife. Ari looked around in amazement, the desert, transformed into a paradise.

"Press your hands into the soil Ariella. Feel the texture, the mineral content, the life living within," Lark instructed, encouraging Ari to explore, learn, feel.

As Ari placed her hands into the soil, she discovered her hands dissolved like salt in water stretching deep, feeling the pulsating life beneath the surface. Fascinated at what she was discovering, she transformed herself and submerged deep into the soil, becoming one with it. She was able to see the creatures who found safety under the earth, rodents, snakes, and insects. Her favorite was the meerkat family she saw; she stayed to observe them playing until she heard her name. Ari resurfaced and as she did she realized just how much she had been transformed. She was able to not only become soil but traveled through it. Overwhelmed by her discovery, she gazed up at Lark in astonishment.

Lark never tired of that first look of realization at what the trial survivors had become. She greeted Ari with a wide grin and waved her hand again, the desert was back, dry and dusty.

"This is the result of the Emigee invasion. The radiation from their weapons has killed almost all life here. Look for yourself," Lark instructed, and she pointed to the sand.

Ari pressed her hands to the ground again and felt something completely different. She felt dry lifeless sand with no substance, no moisture for life. She went deeper and found minimal animal life, none of the richness she felt before. Below the surface was the same as above the surface, a barren wasteland where nothing lived. Tears came to Ari's eyes as she searched for life; sorrow at the loss filled her.

"Listen to what I say Ariella, this is what the whole earth will become if the Emigee and humans are not stopped," Lark warned, "I do not usually appear to trial survivors face to face; it is usually in images where I instruct them. You are different, special, I will instruct you face to face."

"What can I do?" Ari exclaimed, she knew she had a purpose but what could she do against such a great enemy.

"Keep doing what you are doing…stay on the path…become Legate… our world is depending on you," she said.

"Ariella…" the medic called. Ari looked up and saw a medic standing at the entrance to the garden.

"Yes…" Ari responded after recalling that she was in the garden at the med-plex.

"The Lovell's would like you to come to the delivery room," he explained. Ari followed him out of the garden.

The trickle of water flowing from the fountain, the candle light flickering throughout the room, the whisper of the wind through the window all had a soothing effect on Jace as he sat on the mat in the center of the sparsely furnished room. Desperately he needed to get his emotions under control. Yelling at Ari like he did was unthinkable and completely inappropriate. Showering her with love is what he should have done, showing her just how much he missed her, how much she meant to him, instead of bombarding her with his anger. The feelings she stirred in him were so diverse, it was like being on a rollercoaster with all its ups and downs, twists and turns, it was no wonder he was in turmoil. She evoked the deepest love, passion, and intimacy he had ever experienced in his life. Life would have no meaning without her sharing it with him, her presence, her exuberance, her determination; she made the day a little brighter with her glorious smile.

On the other hand, that same determination to push forward, giving no consideration to her safety was driving him mad. Jace just wanted to keep Ari safe, protect her from danger, sorrow, and tragedy. Anything having to do with the Emigee was bound to end badly, result in calamity. Already having endured so much as a result of their treachery; he just wanted to shield her from more heartache. Ari was determined to face the Emigee head on by completing the trials, thus putting her life in danger. Anger boiled within him at the thought of losing her to the Emigee.

Hearing a noise from the back of the meditation room, Jace turned slightly to see what was scratching. Teta was there perched on a rod. Jace smiled at her; he hadn't seen her for a while, but she always knew when Jace needed a friend. Immediately, a feeling of familiarity, closeness, friendship, came over him. Jace called her to him, she obeyed instantly flying over to his shoulder. She immediately started pecking him as she always did when she wanted seeds. Reaching into his pocket where he kept a small pouch of seeds for Teta when she came around, he grabbed a handful. Spreading the seeds out on the mat, Teta hopped down to retrieve them. She had a calming effect on Jace and he forgot his troubles for a moment.

After several minutes of watching Teta, Gyasi knocked on the entrance to the meditation room. Jace already knew who it was without turning to look.

"Jace," Gyasi said hesitantly. "Are you okay?"

Jace replied, "No, father I'm not!"

"Is there anything I can do? Get you something…talk…anything?" Gyasi asked as he slowly entered the room, moving closer to Jace.

"The problem is I don't know what's wrong with me," Jace said with all sincerity.

"What do you mean?" Gyasi asked as he moved toward the mat and sat down next to Jace. Teta cawed as he sat down providing a warning not to interrupt her meal. Gyasi got the message and moved slightly to the right of the bird.

"I should be showering Ari with love, showing her just how much she means to me but what do I do? I blow up at her, yell at her, displaying my hateful rage," Jace lamented, "Why did I do that, what is wrong with me?"

"Is that what happened at the med-plex?" Gyasi asked, remembering how Jace stormed out without even a greeting.

"Yes…I was so angry!" Jace explained, "I knew I needed to leave before I did irrecoverable damage."

"Well that was probably a wise move," Gyasi assured him. "What is it that you were so angry about? Certainly, you're glad Ari is alive, aren't you?"

"Of course, I'm glad she is alive…I'm ecstatic she's alive. I'm afraid she's not going to stay that way! I know she is going to continue with the trials, continue with trying to solve the Emigee problem, continue in her quest to help our people…all with no regard to her own safety. How can I get her to stop?" Jace exclaimed, sincerely seeking an answer.

"I see…you don't want Ari to continue with the trials to help our people with the Emigee problem when it is a dangerous, risky business because she could be hurt or even killed. That is a perfectly understandable reaction with regard to someone you love. Let me ask you a question. How do you think Ari felt when you went off on the Wyoming op and were injured?" Gyasi asked as he watched Jace's reaction.

Jace became flushed and warm, struggling within himself between anger and embarrassment. After a few minutes, he managed to sputter, "Well…I suppose she wasn't happy that I went…she was very worried when I was injured… but that has nothing to do with this situation."

"Doesn't it…what's the difference?" Gyasi asked as his brow rose, "You and the others went in search of her adoptive parents. You don't think she felt responsible for you being injured?"

"First of all, I'm a field operative…it's my job to implement covert operations," Jace said, still flushing as his father was homing in on a few very pertinent points.

"Yes…it is your job. Why do you do such a dangerous work? You could work at anything, why do you pick the dangerous work?" Gyasi asked. He wanted Jace to examine his motives, to see that his motives weren't much different than Ari's.

"You know why…the Emigee have plagued our people for so long we need all the information we can get in order to solve the issues they have with us," Jace said. Hearing himself say the words was like hearing an echo of the things Ari had expressed to him on many occasions; he was not happy with his growing awareness that he and Ari had the same goal.

"Oh…so you do a dangerous work with little regard for your personal safety to solve the Emigee problem so our people can be safe. Is that right?" Gyasi asked.

Jace frowned, realization creeping in on him and said, "…Yes…"

"The let me ask you this, what makes you so angry with Ari when you are both doing the same kind of work but in different ways?" Gyasi asked pointedly. Jace was getting the point but didn't want to concede.

"It's different…she's a woman…" Jace said grasping at any excuse he could come up with even lame excuses.

"Is that a valid reason Jace? Do you really feel that Ari is not capable of accomplishing the same type of work as you?" Gyasi asked, knowing full well he was driving the point home.

"No…she is the most extraordinary person I've ever met. Her abilities, as new as they are to her, have become exceptional. She survived the first trial… she can probably do anything she set her mind to…but…" Jace conceded. Ari was an incredible young woman with outstanding abilities; he knew she was more than capable.

"But…what?" Gyasi asked hoping to finally get to the bottom-line, the real and true reason Jace was in turmoil. If he acknowledged the real issue and not suppress it, he would be able to work through it, deal with it, and conquer it.

"Uh…I don't want to lose her!" Jace whispered, tears welled up as he felt a tugging at his heart.

"I know and the fact that you lost your mother doesn't make this any easier, but Jace she was as strong willed as Ari and very capable. Your mother taught me that to love someone is to support them. Support their goals…their likes…their dislikes…even if they are not the same as yours. It took me quite a while to adjust, but when I did our relationship was enhanced beyond compare. A deepest sense of oneness between us developed enhancing the respect and love we felt toward one another…Respect Ari's abilities and desires, love her with every breath you take, cherish the time you have together. Surrendering to love, you will be happier than you can possibly imagine," Gyasi said recalling the love he shared with a very special lady.

"But the pain," Jace said as he clutched his heart.

"Embrace the pain, let love soothe it. It will vanish," Gyasi explained as he stood up disturbing Teta again. "I'm going to leave you to meditate; I will be at NOSSIC if you need me." Gyasi gave Jace a huge and a slap on the back. He left Jace sitting on the mat with Teta at his side.

Chapter

Sunshine streamed through the window to signal another beautiful day. Ari felt the warmth on her face as she stretched. What a wonderful feeling to wake up in one's own bed—absolutely glorious, she thought. It seemed like years since she had been in her own room in her own bed. Ari, too exhausted to appreciate it last night after she returned from the med-plex, savored the feeling.

The birth was rather easy considering Ena delivered twins—a boy and a girl. Ari had never seen Martin and Ena happier than when the babies were placed in their arms; she was thrilled for them. After such a horrible ordeal, they deserved the double blessing and all the happiness and joy they would experience raising the babies. Ari was more determined than ever to see the Emigee's plan fail. The safety of her family depended on it; plans had to be made to ensure that the Lovell's were secure.

Ari jumped out of bed, hurried to get dressed to search out her parents. She needed advice on how to keep Martin and Ena safe; how could she do that and continue with the trials at the same time? She was only one person, she would need help. Ari didn't have to go far to find her parents. Waiting for her to come for breakfast, they were still at the dining table. Relieved to see them, Ari greeted them with a kiss.

"Good morning," Ari said cheerfully, "I was just coming to look for you."

"Good morning…did you sleep well?" Ashi'nat asked her as she sat down across from Ayotal.

"Yes, I did…it was wonderful to be back in my own bed," she said truly relieved and happy to be back in the city with her parents.

"Are you hungry? Can I get you something to eat?" Ayotal asked as she started to get up to fix Ari breakfast.

"No…I'm fine. I need to talk to you about Martin and Ena," Ari said urgently. Becoming serious, she started fidgeting with one of the ties on her shirt.

"Alright…is there a problem?" Ashi'nat asked noticing the change in Ari's demeanor.

"No…everything is fine for the moment. Ena had a boy and a girl by the way. They are absolutely beautiful," Ari paused for a long time then continued. "I wanted to ask you, do you think the Emigee will try to take my family again…are they in danger?"

Ashi'nat glanced at Ayotal prompting her to reply, "Your father and I have been discussing that very possibility. After the abilities you displayed to immobilize their soldiers, we believe they will use whatever means they feel will lure you into a trap. The Lovell's are very much a target for the Emigee."

"Is there anything we can do to keep them safe?" Ari asked. She could not allow anything to happen to them again, even if it came down to surrendering to the Emigee. Any option would be better than that one.

"The consul will meet in a few days. I have an idea that should benefit everyone concerned. In the meantime, the Lovell's can stay here in the city until plans are finalized. Your mother will be acquiring a place for them to live until they recover from their ordeal," Ashi'nat explained. "I will speak with Martin today to explain the danger that his family is in and propose my solution."

"Ari, I would love to have your opinion on the Lovell's living accommodations. Will you assist me?" Ayotal asked hoping to spend time with her to catch up and discuss future plans.

"Yes…of course…father what is your plan?" Ari asked curious as to why the consul would be involved.

"I would rather not say until I talk to Martin and the consul," Ashi'nat said. Ari was disappointed with that response, but she knew Ashi'nat must have a very good reason for keeping silent.

"When will you be able to tell me about the plan?" Ari asked eager to know all the details.

"After I meet with the consul, I will give you the details. In the meantime, I think we all have plenty to do and for now the Lovell's are safe," Ashi'nat chuckled as he left the table to start his day.

Ayotal turned her attention to Ari and asked, "Are you ready to go?" Ari nodded with a smile.

Ari was in her favorite meditation room reflecting on the day's activities. The soothing sound of water trickling down the rocks of the focus center always calmed and relaxed her quickly. Meditation had become a habit for her now, almost second nature. She took a deep breath and let her mind float freely, touching on the success she and Ayotal had acquiring suitable accommodations for Martin and Ena, visiting Ena and the babies at the med-plex, watching the babies as they slept. She liked the names Martin and Ena chose— Zoe and Vian. Very appropriate names for two miracle babies having survived such traumatic beginnings—both names meaning life. Life such a special gift yet the Emigee treat it with contempt.

Tomorrow she would start training for the second trial after she helps Ena get settled in her new home. She knew Ena would rather be home on the ranch, but it wasn't safe there at the moment. Hopefully, the plan Ashi'nat has in mind will keep her family safe. Genocide of the humans must be stopped. There must be a way to reach the Emigee, to convince them to end the war. To become Legate in the fullest sense after the completion of the trials is the key—but why? Lark alluded to it but wasn't specific. Her cryptic comments still lingered in her mind—'all will be revealed.' What will be revealed? Ari tried not to dwell on those remarks but focused on 'you must complete the trials, the future depends on it.' Lark was helpful in some ways teaching her to master her new skills, but most of the time she caused more uncertainty by her words.

Ari had so many things to be thankful for, two sets of loving parents who would support her in whatever endeavors she pursued, reuniting with her people to reclaim her heritage, incredibly loyal friends who would move heaven and earth for her, and Jace. Jace flowed through Ari's mind continually. Calling to him, her heart was bursting with love; it was if she drew him to her as he appeared in the doorway.

Moving to sit next to her on the mat, Jace took her hand in his, gently caressing it, "I'm sorry about the other day at the med-plex. I was completely out of line."

"I know this is difficult for you, I'm sorry you are having such a hard time with my role as Legate. I love you Jace, from the first moment I met you, I knew that you were my soul mate, my partner, my heart. We have a connection beyond words, I feel it every time you're near and I don't want to hurt you. What can I do to make this easier for you?" she confessed.

"I want you to know what is behind my feelings. My mother was killed by the Emigee when I was very young. I was devastated. I took every precaution to bury my feelings so I would never feel that kind of horrific pain again. I never let anyone get close enough to me to have any feelings for them. Consumed by work, I didn't have time for anything else. It worked until I met you. You were supposed to be just another job, teach you, deliver you, and leave. You're not, as hard as I tried to keep it professional; I had lost before I began. From the moment I saw you galloping out of the forest on a white steed with your glorious red hair billowing on the wind and that angelic face, I was yours. It terrified me, the last thing I wanted was to have feelings for someone, but I do. I'm just not dealing with it very well. I'm hoping that with your help we can overcome my fears together," he admitted.

"We are partners and I want to be partners in every sense Jace. Starting with our work is the best way. We can walk the path together, the path to protect our people, help the humans, and reconcile with the Emigee. As long as we have each other, we can accomplish miracles."

Her love for him was apparent, but she could not give up becoming Legate or the trials even for him. With all her heart, she prayed that he resolved the issues he had about her and what had to be accomplished, she would help him. He was her love; she knew it in her heart, there would never be anyone to take his place. She would wait for him as long as it took—life, love, and happiness are worth struggling for no matter how long it takes to attain!